DELICATE GEOMETRY

By the same author

BLACKBIRD DAYS

Delicate Geometry

KEN CHOWDER

1817 HARPER & ROW, PUBLISHERS, New York
Cambridge, Philadelphia, San Francisco
London, Mexico City
São Paulo, Sydney

All the characters in this novel are fictitious, and any resemblance to actual persons, living or dead, is purely coincidental.

Grateful acknowledgment is made for permission to reprint:

Quote from *At Swim Two Birds* by Flann O'Brian. Copyright 1951 by Brian O'Nolan. Copyright renewed 1979 by Brian O'Nolan. Reprinted by permission of Walker & Company and Brandt & Brandt Literary Agents, Inc.

Quote from *Utopia or Oblivion* by R. Buckminster Fuller. Copyright © 1970 by R. Buckminster Fuller. Reprinted by permission of the author.

DELICATE GEOMETRY. Copyright © 1982 by Ken Chowder. All rights reserved. Printed in the United States of America. No part of this book may be used or reproduced in any manner whatsoever without written permission except in the case of brief quotations embodied in critical articles and reviews. For information address Harper & Row, Publishers, Inc., 10 East 53rd Street, New York, N.Y. 10022. Published simultaneously in Canada by Fitzhenry & Whiteside Limited, Toronto.

FIRST EDITION
Designer: Sidney Feinberg

Library of Congress Cataloging in Publication Data
Chowder, Ken.
  Delicate geometry.
  I. Title.
PS3553.H64D4 1982   813'.54   81-48052
ISBN 0-06-014973-6   AACR2

82 83 84 85 86 10 9 8 7 6 5 4 3 2 1

For Arnie, and for Ruth

Contents

PART I CAROLYN BY EVAN   1

PART II RICE BY CAROLYN   77

PART III EVAN BY RICE   201

The author wishes to thank the Ingram Merrill Foundation and the Mary Roberts Rinehart Foundation for providing financial support necessary for the writing of this book, and Yaddo and Ossabaw for time and setting.

Evil is even,
truth is an odd number....
    —Flann O'Brien

Nothing odd lasts.
    —Samuel Johnson

There is divinity in odd numbers,
either in nativity, chance, or death.
    —William Shakespeare

In the row below where there are seven experiences there are twenty-one relationships. Count the circles in the symmetrical triangle and you will find there are just twenty-one.

$$\frac{n^2 - n}{2} = 7^2, \quad 49 - 7 = 42 \div 2 = 21.$$

Now it is very interesting that the *picture of the relationship is always a triangle.*
    —Buckminster Fuller

PART I

CAROLYN

BY EVAN

Chapter 1   Twenty After Six

Surprisingly enough, our Carolyn Kingston was not born at twenty after six. But her first memory of a clock shows its blunt hour hand propped up on the V of an ornate Roman six, while the minute hand neatly cleaves a four. Time forms the half-finished outline of a lopsided mountain, and for Carolyn it has always stayed so, as motionless and permanent as that frozen mountain on the horizon.

George, Carolyn's father, thought he'd taught her to tell time at a spectacularly early age. In the first throes of this education, she would occasionally ask, with a peculiar urgency: What time is it right *now*, Daddy?

I never called him "Daddy," Evan. Always Pop.

It was twenty after six; it was always twenty after six. It was so uniformly twenty after six that George Kingston became convinced tiny Carrie already understood time perfectly well, and was playing precocious jokes on her pop. But it was no joke; it was out of her hands, and it still is. Now, during those weeks when I sleep with Carolyn, I'm awakened first by her interior alarm, which buzzes before my real one. I notice a rustle in the bed as Carolyn rolls, wearily consults the glowing plastic face of her square clock, nods, rolls over, and dozes. Rice confirms it: Carolyn still performs this involuntary rite every morning, come nightmare, reverie, or sleeping pill. In the evening, too, no matter where she is, she feels the implacable desire to find a clock. She waits one minute, and the yearning passes. "Probably twenty after," Carolyn comments, with a sigh. Carolyn's complex about twenty after six has long made her uneasy; it is as if something great, or grave, is fated to happen to her at twenty after six. And twice every day, from her earliest days, Carolyn has felt compelled to consider her own death.

But that event is beyond the time-frame of this work.

Thank God.

Chapter 2   One Kind of Courtship

Carolyn's mother—Saskia—was Indonesian Dutch, born and raised in Java. For some the line of destiny seems clear very early on. There was no mistaking Fate's intention for Saskia: she was to be a ballerina. At sixteen she signed on with the Ballet Batavia, Djakarta's best if only company. That, unfortunately, was in 1942. Nineteen forty-two was not a good year for ballerinas in the South Pacific. The Japanese invaded; most of the Europeans fled. The Ballet Batavia, however, was an apolitical organization, so the dancers knew no harm would come to them. They remained in the city, outfitted themselves for war in leotards and toe shoes; and the twelve Japanese soldiers who burst into their studio one midmorning, machine guns at the ready, found the company preparing for the fray with strenuous repetitions of pliés at the barre—before a wide-eyed, admiring mirror.

The entire troupe was taken prisoner of war. They were incarcerated in a circus-big tent with hundreds of other Dutch civilians. This arrangement was considered by everybody to be inhumane and therefore temporary; even the Japanese thought it was temporary, according to Saskia; but that didn't change the housing situation. Nothing changed the housing situation, in fact—not for three very long years. But at that point things changed rapidly. The Allies liberated the city.

Carolyn's father—George—was a young, handsome, mustachioed RAF pilot.

Liberation Day in Djakarta found the ballerinas of the Ballet Batavia performing a spirited, impromptu can-can for the victors. They danced in the tent where they had just waited out the worst years of their lives.

Because liberation called for certain excesses; because one handsome, mustachioed RAF pilot particularly liked the way one stocking fell down a young ballerina's leg; and because Saskia knew only three phrases in English—yes, no, and thank you—the weight of numbers was too great, two out of three falls decides the match, and after the fall Carolyn was conceived on the spot.

The ardent spot was the hard ground. On the leeward side of the tent, beside the oozing latrine, there was a cozy, less muddy undulation all but hidden from prying eyes. Here Saskia and George rolled, at first just joyously hugging each other

The expression is: holding on for dear life.

and then fumbling wildly underneath each other's sloppy and sopping garments, muttering endearments in two urgent, needless languages. They were dead drunk, and so inexperienced as to be almost incompetent, but consummation was finally achieved in the fading darkness that introduces dawn.

Saskia was barely nineteen then, and her arrest had halted her social and mental development at sixteen; she was an utter virgin. It was not only her gratitude, a determination to be generous to her hated keepers' overthrowers, that kept her from pushing George away as he pushed in. The truth is that Saskia was never quite sure exactly what it was they were doing, she and George. Had she known, she would have grabbed George by his handsome mustache and literally thrown him over.

Or so she said.

George wasn't without virtue of his own—though in George's case this quality was close to a comic romanticism. Coincidentally, George too was largely ignorant of the enterprise they were vigorously pursuing there beside the latrine. When he deduced the true nature of the act—for he was not unobservant, at least—George quickly proposed matrimony, and he was serious.

George had his reasons. They weren't sound, but they were understandable. He liked the lay of the land: Saskia was of a breakable, doll-like beauty, with small features and perfect teeth; her body, her dancer's body, was breathtaking.

But best of all, for my Pop, Saskia couldn't speak to him. She couldn't interfere with the image he constructed of her.

No one ever found out how George transmitted his intentions to Saskia, but these intentions were good. Apparently Saskia understood; she accepted, nodding gravely. According to them, they were engaged to be married.

The sun poked up. George and Saskia made madly passionate

goodbyes—"for now," George probably said, though Saskia wouldn't know. And then she wandered out into the jubilant chaos of the city to find her parents.

By the simplest miracle she found them. She trotted blithely to what had been their house before the war, too full of the flush of freedom and first love (which she would always confuse in her mind) to be truly anxious. The house was still standing. Saskia pushed the door open; her parents, released the night before, sat quietly at the wooden table eating an enormous, unbelievable breakfast. Dutch, her father was about to slander Edam cheese with red currant jam.

The word you wanted was probably "slather"?

This was more than one miracle, this was a whole cornucopia. Time had stopped; the war had never happened; Saskia had been dreaming, or was dreaming now.

They exchanged huge hugs, exultant exclamations of their great fortune. Saskia told her parents the wonderful news: George. She was going to marry George. He had a most handsome mustache. Can I, Ma?

They were appalled. There was to be no question of such nonsense, no mention of this thing ever again.

I've heard that my Opa was a man of short stature, but given to fierce fisticuffs. My Oma was over six feet tall; her hair fell past her waist; she had ramrod posture and iron morals. My mother didn't argue with my Oma and Opa.

The case was closed. Saskia was forbidden her dashing, unintelligible lover, and George his silent dreamboat. Weepy, haggard (as she tells the story. Personally, I cannot imagine Saskia as haggard, or even uncoifed), Saskia retired to her room at the back of the house, among the soughing bamboo. She found her old stuffed animals still resting cozily in their miniature sailor's chest. She took them out, arranged them in a circle on the floor, sat down among them. Then she engaged in the kind of conversation she used to have before she spent a war in prison.

"Would you like a cup of tea, Mister Elephant?"

"Yes."

"Would you like a cake, too?"

"Yes."

"Yes *please*, Mister Elephant!"
"Yes, please. Yes. Please."

It was a good thing for Saskia that George was a more persistent romantic than she. Saskia's family, like much of the Dutch ruling class in Indonesia, was sent "back" to Holland—a place where none of them had ever been. They landed in Rotterdam in a state of unbearable tension. This anxiety was probably induced partly by a flight halfway around the world in an unpressurized troop transport; partly by the abrupt loss of their true homeland, and their home; most of all, perhaps, by the residue of horror from the long war just ended.

The Ruisdaels had no sound idea of what they might reasonably expect as they stepped, sea-legged, onto Dutch soil.

Pavement, Evan. It was an airport.

But none of the various mental constructions they made of Holland included George Kingston—who, with uniform snug and snappy, and mustache gleaming with wax, waited at the bottom of the ramp, tenderly saluting his beloved and her beloved.

Carefully George pronounced: "Wilkommen."

Saskia's parents were not impressed with George's Dutch. They were polite but adamant: such a match was unthinkable, impossible. And it remained unthinkable, impossible, for several weeks—until the doctor told Saskia what she already knew: the unthinkable, impossible match had already borne fruit.

The newlyweds lived with the Kingston family on their Wiltshire pig farm until the child was born. But Saskia was no more popular with George's parents than he had been with hers. Out of earshot, their pet name for her was "The Whore." To say that Saskia was alienated and estranged is an understatement: she was a stranger, an alien. George's parents found it hard to believe that Saskia actually did not understand English, no matter how plainly it was spoken, how clearly it was pronounced, or how small the words were. At first Saskia cocked her head and tried to allow the words to penetrate, as if by bathing her brains in English she would eventually absorb it like a sponge, and then be able to squeeze the words out again on command. In the damp gray Wiltshire farmhouse smelling of coal, Saskia adopted the manner that later became the mother Carrie knew. Not a minute went by without Saskia failing to understand one thing or another: *not understanding* was her mode of existence. Saskia was wrong one moment, stupid the next, hard of hearing the next. Eventually she just gave up. When she wanted the bread, she smiled and pointed at the bread; when she was finished, she left the table. Saskia lay back on the bed and began the retreat to the fastness of her own version of the world, a mix of wistful memory and pure invention.

England was a prison. The baby was born, in good health and apparently convivial spirits, in Westbury, Wiltshire; she celebrated the onset of her second month in Hempstead, Long Island, New York. George got a job with, and later helped run, a small charter airline, whose wild fluctuations of fortune affected his cheerful disposition not at all. George whistled tunelessly between his teeth, shaved off his handsome mustache, was made an honorary member of the local chapter of the American Legion, and enjoyed being alive, all more or less simultaneously. He took great delight in barbecuing bright red meat outside their little Cape Cod–style house: he wore an apron and a chef's hat and swung his shining utensils with abandon; he waved to neighbors, kissed his wife constantly, flipped the meat too late. If he didn't often speak to Saskia, that didn't mean he didn't *love* her, did it? Since, after all, he made perpetual goo-goo eyes at her, kissed her elbows fondly and often, and jumped her nightly in bed?

Saskia must have carried some singular notion of America across the ocean with her. One day not long after her arrival, she carefully tucked the covers around tiny Carrie and went out to play in the streets with the other girls. She had seen them jumping rope. Saskia knew how to jump rope. This was America, the land of the free. This meant she could jump rope with the others, no matter how old she was.

I don't think she was even aware of how old she was. She had this idea of "Saskia"—not quite "I" for my poor mom—who was a nice, pretty, proper girl. Who danced, who jumped rope, who played with her stuffed animals. I'm not sure how thoroughly my mom realized she had a child.

The kids on the block stared at this long-haired woman who wanted to play too. What was that language she was speaking, anyway? German? "Go away, you old Nazi!" "Germy germy German! You smell like a fish," one said—inaccurately, I'm sure.

Saskia ran back to her house. Inside, she began to cry. She picked up her dollie and caressed it desperately. But her dollie, Carrie, began to cry too.

When she went back into her house Saskia went back into her quietude and her distance. Like a snail, whose image is dominated by something it wears, one could not say for certain that Saskia's protective armor was not, finally, a part of Saskia herself. With the help of an enormous, constantly crackling Zenith, Saskia learned to speak English at last; but she tended not to, as if frequent use would wear out this dearly bought possession. And so Carolyn remembers her mother as a gorgeous, eerily calm woman, posed like a mannequin on the edge of Carolyn's life.

On the edge of her own life, too. Which is pretty sad.

Saskia suffered George's friendly, good-humored onslaughts on her sex with sighing and silence, secretly conversed with stuffed animals all her life, and spent every evening "reading" books in English—which she did not really read at all, but merely stared at, drifting off. Drifting off, on, off.

I always thought my mother was "odd." Later I decided that for a long while she had not been there at all.

Chapter 3   Suburban Sherbet

Carolyn grew up on suburban Long Island. Home was white, had honeysuckle around it. There were two flavors of honeysuckle, white and yellow. They did not taste the same. Around buzzed bees, and right in their midst sat tiny Carrie—not only unafraid, but pleased, tickled: because the breeze blew the honeysuckle vines, while she could just sit there. She sat for what seemed a wonderfully long time, and that is why she laughed. Because the leaves blew, and she just sat. That was funny.

First intimation of power. Is that what you're trying to say, Vandypie?

On another day Carrie sat in her pool. This was a little inflatable plastic job that her father filled with a hose while Carrie jumped up and down beside him in expectation. The pool possessed a mysterious attraction for grass clippings, which accumulated at the surface, then sank, and unfailingly got stuck among Carrie's toes. She demanded the removal of all grass from her pool. George half-obliged; he scooped out a handful, kissed Carrie's brow, and sat back to his beer. The water grew warm. Carrie, reminded of something, squatted and peed. Then she was sorry she'd done it. Then she wanted new water. "That *is* new water, Carrie," George said absently, without looking up. Then Carrie began to cry, and even wail; but before she did, it occurred to Carrie that life is never the goddamn *party* you think it's going to be—that, given the choice, she'd rather be jumping up and down in expectant joy, while George lays the business end of the hose in the pool, than be sitting, with nothing to wish for, in hot, stinky, grassy water, nowhere to go but Out. Or that's how Carolyn tells the story now, at least, as she relentlessly shreds matches and lays them, cross-hatched, atop each other. Building.

It was hot on Long Island in summertime, all right. Almost as if the heat fixed the images in Carolyn's memory: memories of other seasons blur at the slightest touch, but summer pictures can be repeatedly held up to the sun, fingered no matter how carelessly, and still retain their bright clarity. The Good Humor truck ambles down someone else's street after dinner; Carrie, on baby-fat legs, chases its tinkle. She has toasted almond. The vendor, awesome in his white suit, smartly whacks a lever on his polished change-dispensing belt, then firmly presses into her palm a small coin. It is over now, she knows that; but she lingers to watch, dazzled, as the Good Humor man—who resembles a photographic negative of a policeman—flips the latch, swings the door open with exaggerated efficiency, nabs the right ice cream without looking, and then slams the door with a loud, satisfying crunch. In her memory ice cream is always dropping off its wooden stick; her whole bar lies in the street, agonizingly irretrievable. But perhaps it was someone else's bar that took the dive, Carolyn? You remembered that because it stirred your powerful sympathy, maybe, and not because your ice cream was the fall guy, always?

You're an apologist for Life, Vandy.

One of those summer nights, Carrie lay and listened to the whirr of the fan forever. Too hot to sleep. Today the noise of the fan seems to her some kind of secret, spoken in a soft roar. She closed her eyes and counted sheep, as she'd been told to do. No matter that she'd never actually seen a sheep, an endless stream of them were supposed to blithely jump a great white wall. But Carrie's sheep shied away at the last second, afraid. Out of filial piety she continued to run them at the wall, here we go, up and over . . . no. Her sheep were too smart for that. They refused, wandered away, bent their bearded heads

They all wore beards; I didn't distinguish between sheep and goats. They were all white, goateed, and sheepish.

and gnawed at the plentiful grass. She couldn't really blame them; she let them be. Carrie removed her blue pin-striped pajamas, as she had been told not to do, and her pale fat legs searched for cool pockets in the sheets. Her restlessly shifting limbs made the sheets hot and sticky; at last she gave up. She pulled her pajama bottoms back on and grimly padded downstairs.

Her parents were sitting on the patio, fanning themselves—in silence, in darkness. The moist whites of their eyes glistened as they turned and regarded Carrie, and she had the sudden thought that she had succeeded: was asleep: was dreaming.

There must have been clemency in the air. George gave Carrie a bowl of orange sherbet, and Saskia tenderly held ice cubes behind

Carrie's hot ears. They all sat on the patio, and Carrie meticulously, thoughtfully eradicated her sherbet. The still, warm evening; the sharp repetitions by a single suburban cricket; the sticky plastic cushions of the lawn chair beneath and behind her; the oddly relaxed feel of the moment, as if she had been allowed into the intimate life of her parents, the only place in the world where they were truly comfortable: in Carrie's mind these coagulated into orange sherbet, and even today orange sherbet smells not of diglycerides or guar gum, but reeks of summer, of intimacy, of the vanished past.

Chapter 4 Strangers

George, honorary member of the American Legion, became a Lion. He then threw in the Elks Club in the bargain, and faithfully attended the meetings of all three. He tried to become the postwar Long Island equivalent of a Good Old Boy. He drank too much beer, or acted as if he had; he was the voluble, back-slapping, insincere life of the party.

It wasn't my pop's fault. He just never knew how to act.

He loved Saskia—or he loved her person, at least. He loved to bring her to the Lions' dinner-dances, where they swooped around the hardwood floor to continual applause: "Such a lovely couple." "Such good dancers."

I'm sure George thought Saskia loved it too. She bought stacks of expensive coffee-table books about the ballet, after all, and spent hours dreamily leafing through them, admiring the dancers, admiring the dance. She was a marvel on the dance floor. How was George to know how she felt, when all the other Elks applauded their waltz that way?

The Elks. The Lions. The American Legion. These were all one to Saskia. Saskia could be very anxious. She had eyes in her head, as she was fond of saying—which is saying something, since she didn't say much—and she could see when she was playing the fool. She contrived to mislay George's appointments calendar when a dance was in the offing; George, remembering, told her that it was nearly time for the dance, she should be getting ready. Oh, was it tonight? I forgot—Oh, I didn't even get a babysitter! George would take care of that, don't you worry; he'd get his boss's daughter, Berta Durer, who loved little Carrie. I have a little cold, though, George. I'd better stay home. There's a scratch in my throat. See how red? she asked, opening. George was solicitous. After the dance, he promised, we tuck you into bed. We'll see you get some soup for dinner. That's the ticket, soup. Bundle up well, dear.

The dinner was always tired chicken. The Elks were always drunk. Saskia didn't always understand the jokes, but she knew they were jokes; she wore her heaviest smile. Look how beautiful she is, with even that kind of smile; imagine what a winsome queen she'd be with a real one. Periodically, though, Saskia would have to put down her smile. Saskia got the heaves. She'd find the spotless bathroom, around the corner from the stinking kitchen, reeking of chicken; she'd lock the door, go down on her knees, on her nylons, before the toilet; she'd empty out the chicken, which she'd neglected to chew— she swallowed before her teeth were finished with it, because she was anxious, and because it is hard to smile and chew at the same time. Saskia brought her toothbrush to the dinner-dances, just in case she had to give them back their chicken.

After soggy pie and weak coffee the band began to blare. Here was the worst: the Lions looked at George and Saskia, grinning; Saskia said no, no, my throat is scratching tonight; the American Legion wouldn't take no for the answer, they urged and pleaded, and Saskia's smile grew heavier and heavier; until finally the Elks, all grins, literally pulled her out of her chair, and shoved her into George's waiting arms. For they were certain that there was nothing in the world that Saskia wanted to do more than dance for them—unless it was to pretend not to want to, and be talked into it.

The music swelled. George swung her about, his smile brilliant, his happiness as apparent as a stripper's bosom; and the horned, frocked, or leonine brothers stood and applauded happy George, miserable Saskia.

Saskia held it in until they reached home.

"No," she said, as soon as they stepped inside. "This was the maximum. This was the limits."

"What do you mean, dear?" George asked, still smiling. He shut the door noiselessly.

"This was the last dance tonight."

He was helping her out of her seal coat. One arm was in and one out. He stopped. "What are you talking about?" George said.

"I'm sorry to be disappointing you"—she struggled with the coat alone—"but I am sorry."

I think Saskia thought she'd explained herself. "Sorry about what?" George asked. "Is something wrong, dear? Your throat bothering you?"

"I am saying," Saskia said slowly, exasperated, "I don't want to be going to these meetings." She paused, as if to judge whether she'd said what she intended to. Then she added, "Any more."

George yanked her coat off. "For heaven's sake why not? Where will we dance?" George folded her coat over his arm absently, like a waiter with a seal towel. "Besides," he added, "it's only very seldom that you have to come."

"I don't have to be coming at all," Saskia announced.

George regarded her, finally, with astonishment. "Don't you like these dances?" he asked. She shook her head vigorously. "Why not?" George asked.

"I don't like when they make fun of us. Why do you, Jairge?" Saskia spoke George's name infrequently, and only when she was excited; she didn't do it very well.

"They don't make fun of us. They cheer for us. They always applaud our dancing. They love our dancing. We're quite well-liked, dear."

"Well-liked!" Saskia snorted. "They are laughing at us!"

George seemed to stop and consider what Saskia was saying. "Why should they laugh at us?" he asked at last, halfway between curious and disbelieving.

"Because we're not the normal," Saskia explained. "We're not the red-blood Americans couple."

"We will be, someday," George said, and smoothed her coat with his hand, fondly petting it. "Don't you think?" he asked.

"I don't want to be it!" Saskia cried. "We are strangers. I only want to be not pretending."

George gave her a strange look. "All right, dear," he said, and he finally hung up her coat.

Saskia didn't wear that coat for some time; the wool one would do. But the look that appeared on George's face for the first time that night began to appear with some regularity. On some occasions it replaced the self-satisfied smile he'd sported while watching Saskia quietly remove her clothing at bedtime; sometimes it replaced the look of vast contentment he'd assumed evenings, after dinner, in his favorite armchair, with his slippers on; and sometimes it replaced the final tender glance he had given her before heading off to the airport, mornings, between door and screendoor, when she bent for the traditional kiss goodbye—as if he'd noticed, finally, that they were strangers, and never stopped being surprised.

George's attendance at the weekly gatherings of presumed brothers began to drop off—first a slight slope, then a dizzying descent. He seemed to prefer to sit at home, at first.

He began to lose the crest of his splendid waves of auburn hair. He grew gradually fat.

He started to take long walks in the evening. The walks grew longer and longer, and Saskia grew upset. One evening she urged him to take Carrie on his walk—since Carrie's bedtime was only an hour distant, George would be forced to return quickly. The two went out in good spirits, George acting peculiarly like a papa, Carrie skipping beside him, early but high summer, dappled sunlight, lovely evening, prosperous America.

They were back within five minutes. And George never took Carrie out with him again.

Because the bar four blocks away wouldn't let my pop in. "Not wid da kid, Jawch." The bartender was an immense man, the biggest creature I'd ever seen, and his cigar was a part of his face. "It's da law, Jawch. Sorry." We went right home.

Chapter 5   Lovers

Saskia was "reading," and George was out drinking; Carrie was on her own. Or would have been, had Saskia not felt the chill of solitude herself, admittedly in the form of paranoia. She asked for a guard dog. George's compliance was largely theoretical, for the dog he brought home

At twenty after six

one memorable evening was half German shepherd in breeding but totally Labrador retriever in spirit: amiable, tail-wagging, drooling, ear-scratching spirit. George had barely enough time to open the door, and not enough to announce his purchase, when in wagged Peaches. She raced into the den, where Carrie was perched on the couch, and she urinated excitedly on the floor; then she began to run around and around the couch, barking in puppy yips, her overlarge feet knocking down every unsteady object in the room—while Carrie stood on the sofa, shrieking with happiness.

It was love at first sight. Though intended for Saskia, Peaches was Carrie's boon companion. Like lovers, the two developed small, secret rituals. Carrie had always spurned the sandbox; now she virtually took up residence there. She would choose the day's assignment, and begin work. Peaches would sit discreetly in another section, legs sprawled, head lolling, tongue dangling, spittle occasionally dropping from the monstrous chops. Carrie first smoothed the sand flat, using her entire forearm; then she began to work it more carefully, adding a few drops of water from a purple plastic bucket festooned with a brace of cartoon ducks. Carrie packed the dirt till hard. Then she would actually polish it, using the palms of her hands. The dirt acquired a dull sheen and her hands became layered with thick flakes of dirt—flakes she picked off easily, unmasking, to her own high-pitched delight, her bright, pink, miraculously clean hand.

"Peaches," was all Carrie would have to say, and Peaches would struggle to her feet, wag over, and plop down on the newly hard, polished part of the sandbox with an overblown sigh. Carrie would rest her head on Peaches' heaving ribs, staring at the puddles of greenery splattered on the vast blue backdrop. She'd listen to the dog's breathing, to the tasteless gurgle of the digestive mechanisms, and even to the hollow, distant thumping of the dog's great heart. Carrie had an undisguised interest in the workings of Peaches' body, which included curiosity about the dog's ample bowel movements and glee in watching the contorted look of shame Peaches adopted when depositing those movements on the lawn. Everything about Peaches' physical existence amazed and entranced Carrie; it was her first love affair, and a simple one. Carrie loved Peaches more thoroughly, and certainly more consciously, than she ever loved her mom or pop.

That's not true. And neither is the part about the bowel movements.

Carrie's second love came much later, when she was twelve—oh yes, I forgot to mention that Carrie played with dolls, learned to read, was an excellent student, grew tller and thinner, her dog was run over by creless psserby... I am no biographer. And today I seem to have this irritating habit of omitting the letter a when I type.

One morning, brushing angrily away at her pale, frizzy tangles before the bedroom mirror, Carrie became aware that someone was watching her. She stopped; she stared; she fell directly in love. Carrie found her lover just this side of the quicksilver. Moist, startled eyes stared back at her, eyes like those of a deer at the edge of the deep forest. This backwards Carrie was a piercingly lovely one, a queen—a woman. Puberty had happened; and in Carrie's case it had done well.

The discovery was almost too much for her. She sat down, placing herself carefully on the bed; she smoothed her blouse, tidied her tucks; and then, for no reason, she wept into her hairbrush—wept the way a soldier will when he hears that at last he is to go home. A long struggle was over for Carrie too. Or so she thought.

She dabbed her eyes dry. She rose, resolute, from her bed, again drew strength from her image, and marched downstairs. Her parents sat silently over poached eggs and toast, George reading the paper and Saskia "reading" the paper.

"I have an announcement to make," Carrie said. The papers dropped respectfully. "From now on," Carrie said, "my name is Carolyn. Carolyn Kingston. No one is going to call me Carrie any more," Carolyn said. She hesitated. "Is that okay with you guys?"

"That's okay," Saskia echoed, sounding as if she didn't understand. But Saskia never called her Carrie again.

"Whatever you say, darling. Absolutely," George agreed, but somewhere in his mind he must have dissented, for he never managed to remember the name his only child wanted to be called.

It's clear enough, and you know it. He didn't want to lose his baby girl.

Chapter 6 Camelot on Long Island

Carolyn found her first male lover when she was fourteen. The affair began quietly enough, one April afternoon that seemed, in its heat and stillness, to be imitating a dead day in August—think of a possum. Carolyn walked toward home carrying an armful of books, carrying them in the way schoolgirls are born to, clutched protectively across the breasts rather than crooked in the nook of the elbow, where boys carry footballs and books alike.

That's only because boys carry fewer books.

At the entranceway to North Hempstead Junior High, the Kennedy-for-President Committee had luringly anchored its blue, white, and lurid red Kennedy bandwagon. It was no wagon; it had once been a trailer for a big boat. Now it contained a couple of plywood stands decorated with bunting and crepe paper, staffed by red-faced Democrats in Styrofoam boaters who flogged leaflets and buttons. None of this caught Carolyn's apolitical eye. She started to walk unconcernedly past the flimsy piece of Americana, thinking how much the loudmouthed show reminded her of late-night television pitchsters who rapidly hawk handy-dandy gadgets that can peel, chop, dice, slice, julienne, knead, or mutilate all the known world . . . when she stopped, suddenly transfixed. Behind the local Democrats there was Another, Greater Democrat. It was only a poster. Its colors did not quite mesh, so that out of every curve of the man's head and shoulders slipped a matching pink shadow, and every detail of his face was edged with a pink replica, as if he were about to reproduce himself by the simplest method known to nature—and in another minute, beside this beautiful Democrat, there'd be another Democrat: his red double, with a similarly perfect set of teeth and an equally boyish quiff of thick, fair hair flipped across the forehead, and an only slightly more mauve pair of clear, penetrating, intelligent, dazzling, dazzling eyes, and Carolyn would have to be in love, in love, with this red Democrat too.

The poster said that it WAS A TIME FOR GREATNESS.

Carolyn put her books down. She reached out her hand, and a soft

Democratic hand helped her board the bandwagon.

"You for Kennedy, honey?"

Carolyn didn't reply. She stared at John Kennedy; it seemed to her that John Kennedy stared at her too.

"You want a button, honey?"

"Yes please."

The Democrat handed her a small plastic disk, and Carolyn's heart began to thump loudly and irregularly, a syncopating conga drum. She turned the button over in her palm. It read: ALL THE WAY WITH JFK.

She looked at the thing. Her button was small, where the poster was giant; her button was lettered in a pale, dull blue, against an off-white background, while the poster blazed with voluptuous color; her button, in short, was a few meaningless words, and the poster a picture of lavish life itself. Or even something greater, more glittering, than the whole of her own dull life. Carolyn felt that she was perfectly capable of shedding tears over this one small, exemplary indignity.

"Do you have one with a picture on it?"

The Kennedy worker eyed Carolyn strangely, then shrugged. "We got a couple," he said. "You for JFK, honey?" Carolyn nodded gravely. He rummaged in a cardboard box. "Here you go, honey. Show it to Mommy and Daddy, now."

This button was three times the size of the first. It was red above, blue below, and in its white midriff was a gray circle: a photograph of the candidate. This was a grainy, grim, unsmiling JFK, without the jaunty humor and bronzed good looks of the image on the poster. His face was composed of readily apparent dots of gray ink, all slightly blurred. Nevertheless, something about the face managed to remind Carolyn of her lovely Democrat, and she regarded it fondly, smiling, the way an aunt will dote and note that niece Nancy's nose is an *exact* copy of her mother's at that age.

Carolyn, still smiling, slipped the button into the pocket of her blouse.

"Oh no, honey. If we give you the big button, we want you to wear it for us, okay? Especially around Mommy and Daddy."

Carolyn now smiled at the man, too, as if the pleasurable warmth of her loving could extend to anyone associated with Her Democrat.

"I want to work with you," Carolyn said. "I want to work for Kennedy."

After school, and then through the summer, Carolyn worked for her man. She became a fixture on the Nassau County Kennedy bandwagon, its most popular inhabitant. She sweated less than her fellow Democrats, and she smiled more, and more beautifully. She smiled with feeling—a feeling that was nothing short of piety. "You're going to vote for Jack, aren't you?" she would ask, already nodding to her own question, as she pressed JFK buttons into palms as if passing out wondrous secrets, magic elixirs. Of course they would vote for Jack; who in this sunny universe wouldn't vote for Jack, some madman or fool? Look at that hair. Look at those *teeth*.

Carolyn's picture appeared in the local paper. Under a caption reading, "She's Climbed onto the Kennedy Bandwagon," Carolyn leans down toward a shirt-sleeved man, smiling gloriously; she's in the act of slipping a Kennedy pin into the man's thin collar. She wears a Styrofoam boater with striped band, and a long striped dress. The larger-than-life image of John Kennedy's head appears behind Carolyn's, out of focus but easily identifiable. By accident, one might guess, the photographer clicked his shutter just before Carolyn's curiously puckered lips passed in front of Kennedy's enlarged cheek: Carolyn appears to be stretching forth to kiss her candidate.

Carolyn cut that photo out. She kept it in the top drawer of her dresser, under underwear.

That is a scurrilous touch, and an unimaginative lie.

From time to time she would casually approach the chest, just happen to dreamily open the drawer—oh, it could have been any drawer, of course, she wasn't opening it just to—and there to her shocked surprise they'd be: Jack and Carolyn, the two smiling lovers, united perhaps by photographic sleight of hand and perhaps by destiny. Carolyn would kiss the weary scrap of newsprint, or dance it around the room, holding it aloft—or sit next to it on her narrow bed and try to squeeze out a painless tear. The photo fell apart in short order, disintegrating from a surfeit of tenderness.

One June evening, after a quiet family dinner of frozen fishsticks and canned succotash, after George had retired to his local establishment, Carolyn noticed a curious phenomenon. As usual, Saskia sat upright alone on the far edge of the plush living-room sofa, as if making room for two ghosts to sit with her; as usual, Saskia "smoked" by lighting a cigarette and letting it smolder, solus, on the pudgy lip of a glass ashtray; Saskia held her book in front of her, at a distance, as usual. But then normalcy dropped away, for Carolyn noticed her mother's eyes darting back and forth, always steadily dropping; then Saskia's head pivoted to the opposite page; then she flipped that page, and her gaze rose. Saskia wasn't "reading." She was reading. The book was *Profiles in Courage* by John F. Kennedy.

Two weeks later Carolyn came home early from campaigning, doused by a sudden bout with corpulent, wind-blown raindrops in Great Neck. She found her mother sitting in her room—*her* room!—blatantly mooning over a poster she had tacked up, the sleek head and manly shoulders of her candidate in full color. Saskia did not notice Carolyn's tread on the stairs; she remained perched on Carolyn's bed, staring and smiling, here and there touching her hair lightly with the tips of her fingers, as if regarding a mirror rather than a political poster.

"Mom!"

Saskia started. And then Carolyn heard her giggle—not a sign of complicity or shame, but the free, unfeigned giggle of a rapturous little girl, perhaps the very girl who danced and played with stuffed animals before the war.

Carolyn was deeply ashamed; she adopted a severe frown. She stood there ramrod straight, demonstrating displeasure. No more words were spoken. Saskia rose, smoothed down her skirt, and went out, her humorless half-smile again stationed on her face. Left to herself, Carolyn grew more and more furious, and most infuriating of all was the realization that she did not know the reason for her fury.

Certainly Saskia's nonsense gave Carolyn some sobering thoughts about her own. Saskia had held up a caricaturing funhouse mirror to Carolyn's face; but Carolyn was not laughing.

The shock waves from that day launched some curious tides. Carolyn decided that politics were her life, that she would become a Kennedy pro. She read voraciously: several daily newspapers, *The New Republic, Commentary,* even the leaflets she gave out daily. She grew expert in defending her candidate against verbal blows. She memorized Kennedy stances on crucial issues, if there were such stances.

And if there were such issues.

Even in her wearying dreams, where thousands of outstretched hands reached for buttons, Carolyn kept on espousing Kennedy gospel. All summer she followed delegate counts; her moods varied according to opinion polls. Like any fan, Carolyn wanted to win. There was nothing she wanted more, except perhaps love.

On election day, Carolyn took an afternoon train to Manhattan to watch the televised proceedings from Kennedy-for-President headquarters. Late that night, as the pattern of voting seemed to become clear, a chant erupted spontaneously among the packed house of Kennedy workers. "He's *gon*-na *win*, he's *gon*-na *win*, he's *gon*-na *win*," they sang jubilantly; the anchorman on television sternly, unemotionally affirmed that, yes, he probably would. Standing, swaying, the campaign workers kept singing their iambs—"He's *gon*-na *win*, he's *gon*-na *win*"—all but one, who still sat tensely on the edge of her hard plastic chair, fist clenched around a Kennedy button, pleading, "He's *got* to win, he's *got* to win," unheard.

Chapter 7 The Old Kazoo

It's hard for me to imagine Carolyn faithful to any sort of celibacy. Today, as a special Sunday treat, I made coffee and French toast and carried it upstairs to Rice and Carolyn—who still lay, those lazy layabouts, in Carolyn's big bed. I think they were laying. It's Rice's week, we change on Fridays. French toast was an inappropriate choice, perhaps; the tray bounced as Rice tried to sit up in bed, and syrup climbed overboard.

No one wants syrup in bed. "Jesus Christ, Vandy," Carolyn said, disgusted. I started back downstairs to fetch a sponge.

"It dudden matter," Rice called after me. "Don't trouble." I troubled, of course, for troubling is my big trick, but Rice was right. It was a matter of either stripping the bed, or else nothing; there was no moderate course. I offered to strip the bed, wash whatever was syrup-sodden—here, drink the coffee anyway, it'll do you good—and I grabbed a corner of the sheet. But Carolyn stopped me.

"We'll take care of it," she said. "You've done enough," and then her clear, beautiful laugh came out. "Damage," she added.

I wanted some blame. "It's my fault," I claimed, "and I think I should be responsible for cleaning up the mess." I started to yank the covers apart.

"It's *not* your fault," she said. "Nothing in recorded history has ever been your fault. You have the world's best intentions. I can take care of my own sheets. You should get back to your painting."

"I don't mi—" I began. Then I realized that Carolyn's hand, under there, was on Rice's big, bulky knee. I'd broken the rules. It's Rice's week, as I think I said. It was my fault, really.

I looked apologetically at Rice, who shrugged.

When I looked back at Carolyn, she was nodding before she started to speak—the way she must have done when passing out buttons for Kennedy. "You're going to vote for Jack, aren't you?" she had asked, nodding.

"Why don't you get back to your painting?" she asked sweetly, nodding.

Sure. I would vote for Jack, sure. I went back to the bathroom, sat down, and had hardly squeezed out a worm of cadmium red before I heard the sounds of them in there. Sometimes they sound like one animal. I think of a wolf who's been tracked to his lair (if wolves have lairs. That's how much *I* know about the world).

It doesn't bother me, you know. It's just hard for me, I repeat, to imagine Carolyn celibate. But at fourteen, fifteen, sixteen, she was faithful to Jack Kennedy.

On weekend evenings, instead of going out on dates, she tended to read *The Making of the President 1960*. She read it seven times. She had a lot of dates to not go out on.

She grew increasingly (heartbreakingly) beautiful. According to reliable observers, these yellowed, dog-eared, report cards, she worked well, if not hard, in school: A A A A A A A A A A A. Here and there the symmetry of this vowel's march up and down the crossed rows is marred by a jarring + appended to the usual letter. If the detective, seeking the cause of this disturbance, tracks the source horizontally, the end of his pointing finger comes quickly to the subject: French. For Carolyn's other high school passion was the language of love and romance—and snide waiters, "movements" in art, cookbooks that read like sacred texts. An avid Carolyn followed Kennedy's trip to Paris with the mania for detail of a would-be assassin. The President described himself as "the man who accompanied Jacqueline Kennedy to France." But Carolyn was not jealous of Jackie; she simply imagined that it was her. John F. Kennedy was the man who accompanied Carolyn Kingston to France; Carolyn wore her pillbox hat, spoke breathy French, the dumplings of her cheeks bulged charmingly; she was *étonnante, élégante, ravissante.*

It was Carolyn's tendency during her high school years to answer the question, What career are you interested in? with an unhesitating, "Eventually, I'd like to be our Ambassador to France."

I suppose anything foreign looked good to Carolyn, who in her long adolescence lived her life, as her mother did, primarily in the mind, rather than the world. In her mind, bohemian Paris—with its well-known surplus of dwarf painters left over from the last century, and cafés where nothingness occupied the table against the window— Paris was sublimely antithetical to her life. Antithetical to the silence that had grown up inside her parents' house, to that house itself, to all the houses, to Hempstead, to Nassau County, Long Island, New York, USA.

The entire senior English class stopped talking at once when the principal came in, which he never did. He was a completely bald, warty man whose features were so sharp that Carolyn imagined them to be brittle. He opened the door without knocking and walked slowly to the teacher's desk, averting his eyes from Miss Cassatt. He looked out at the class; his face was soaking wet. Carolyn, sitting in the second row, imagined that some incomparably brave and foolhardy class clown had doused him with a Dixie cup, and he was about to take revenge on the world as a whole.

The principal said, "I have bad news for you." And then without warning he gave a loud, undisguised sob, and a pack of tears raced out onto his face. "For all of us," he added. "The President has been shot."

The principal shook his head ruefully, then started to leave, his hands in his pockets. The principal's trousers suddenly seemed baggy, their pockets endlessly deep; he shuffled toward the door on old, scuffed shoes, his back slumped. At the door he turned. "There is no more school," he said, and went out without putting a term to school's demise; as if his grief were so strong that school might be out forever, ended along with everything else.

Carolyn's first impulse was to laugh—not at the principal, and certainly not at the President. She didn't ordinarily laugh at shootings; she wasn't sure why she laughed now. In any event, she wasn't alone. A burst of snickering followed close on the heels of the principal's departure. But Miss Cassatt did not chastise; Miss Cassatt said nothing. Instead she slowly put her books one on top of another; when all nearby books were stacked, she began to neaten up her desk; then she sharpened a good half-dozen pencils—till the points were sharp as needles.

Carolyn filed out with the rest, walked with measured step toward home. It was a pleasant early afternoon, not so cold as it can be in late November, clear skies, a slight freshet blowing. Lawns were still green in Hempstead, though recent mornings found them shining under a touch of frost: it was, in short, nearly Thanksgiving.

The time for Thanksgiving. Carolyn trudged toward home, walking more and more slowly, until she just stopped. Then she ran up to the first person she saw, an old man with very sparse white hair. He wore suspenders, a string tie, and clown-size shoes. When she came close, Carolyn saw his age: the maze of creases, the softness of his skin, the unfocused look to his blue, blue eyes, one of which was blinded by cataract.

"Excuse me," Carolyn said. "Have you heard about the President?"

He regarded her without curiosity. "Yup," he said, and spat out: tobacco, Carolyn thought, looking at the brown spot on the sidewalk. The old man seemed to think the conversation terminated; he fixed his gaze on a spot in the distance, and his wide, flat feet began to carry him slowly toward it.

"Wait," Carolyn said. "Could you tell me something, please? Do you know where he got shot and all? I didn't hear."

The old man's eyebrows pulled up. "In Dallas," he said. "That's in Texas. Dallas, Texas."

Carolyn shook her head impatiently. "I mean, where on his—" But for some reason she wasn't able to say the word *body*.

"Head," the old man said. He reached up and slapped himself on the back of the skull. He held on to his skull, his hatless, old man's skull, white wisps of hair fluttering in soft breeze, and he said: "Right in the head. Right in the old kazoo."

"Oh," Carolyn said, and now she breathed out. "Thanks," she added softly, lamely. "Thanks very much."

The old man slapped himself in the head again. "The old noggin," he said. Carolyn turned away. "Right inna bean," he said, and suddenly Carolyn began to run.

She ran home. Her mother was sitting outside, on the front stoop, a place where Saskia never sat. Saskia stood up, her face distorted; she put her arms out for her daughter. To the surprise of both of them, Carolyn ran into those arms, which wrapped around her, books and all. They both started to sob. Books began dropping between them, landed unnoticed on their feet. Saskia patted Carolyn. Carolyn patted Saskia.

The tears didn't last long. In the midst of a spasm of sob Carolyn caught a glimpse of her mother's face, furrowed like a field, irrigated by a mad river of tears—with no hope of a harvest. Carolyn stopped crying then. Saskia stopped too. Saskia dropped her arms heavily to her sides. The two of them stood, panting; they stared at each other with unfathomable disbelief, like two prizefighters who had fought long and hard, to a standoff.

Perhaps I didn't tell you. My mother and I hadn't touched each other in years. I can't recall ever having hugged at all.

Chapter 8   *All She Wanted Was Out*

The human mind reacts to a dose of depression in any number of ways. So I withheld my surprise when Carolyn, sounding guilty, told me that she spent the days following Kennedy's death playing pool.

George had purchased a miniature pool table at a Lions' auction, years before. He had tried to center a basement "family room" around the toy, but Saskia and Carolyn steadfastly refused his wheedling invitations. George spent a few solitary evenings striding awkwardly around the table, bumping his head on the heating ducts, jabbing at the white ball with stabbing strokes of the cue; the table, folded up (for it was little more than a felted card table), had gathered cobwebs in a corner ever since. Now Carolyn pulled it out in response to an obscure yen: a pickle for our pregnant lady, a pool table for our shattered high school princess. She set it up in the living room, turned on the television set, and began to play pool. The verdant felt of the table had turned an appropriately autumnal shade of dead brown; its playing surface was warped, making one pocket inaccessible and one unavoidable. Newsmen droned in the background, intoning grisly details. Apparently a fatal bullet had entered here, exited here—pointing at a huge chart, a cross section of that dear skull invaded by arrows and dotted lines. Here is a photo of the precise moment. If we look closely we can note the President's brains leaving the President's head. The billiard balls clicked comfortingly. One of them dropped, with a noise more like silence than sound, into the side pocket. Here's a First Lady in a pink, bloodstained dress; a new, elephant-eared President, drawling official solace; calling the six ball in the corner pocket. The unavoidable corner pocket.

For several days Carolyn lived on tunafish sandwiches, orange sherbet, pool, and sorrow.

Now they were bringing out the prisoner, the suspect, flanked by policemen in white cowboy hats. And look there: now they were shooting him.

The news reporter became confused, and then hysterical; Carolyn, cue in hand, stared, silent. They dragged a dark-suited man away;

Carolyn turned away to line up a bank shot. The next time she passed the television set she turned it off with a decisive snap of the wrists.

This turned out to be my last political act.

Tempting to compare that wrist's twist to the turning of a key, locking away Carolyn's heart. Something was shut, certainly, but was it her heart? Carolyn, whose heart has been accused of structural curiosities (extra ventricles, guest rooms) but never of short visiting hours? No, it wasn't her heart. For a week Carolyn ceased to eat.

She made no pronouncements. She just wasn't hungry. Pecan pie, orange sherbet, fat fillets, and crackly roast chicken were all paraded temptingly in front of her uninterested nose. "Looks good," she said, trying to avoid trouble. "But no thanks." When she came up against threats of reprisal, she reluctantly forked a chicken's wing, or slipped a dainty, quivering slice of pie onto her plate. But they sat there untouched.

Obviously it wasn't the food. The doctor didn't know that. "Ask her what she wants to eat," he advised sagely, leaning back in his huge leather chair, his chin folded over the phone. "She's probably dieting," he added. "I have a teenager of my own, you know. All she cares about is boys. Girls are pretty damn stubborn, you know." The doctor thought of his own daughter, whose every request was eagerly, gratefully granted. "You know," he said, "I think a little force may be in order, Mr.—aah—Kingston. If she doesn't want to eat, just shove that food right down her throat." When he hung up, Dr. Reynolds felt much better. You have to know how to treat these teenagers, he told himself.

George knocked on Carolyn's door, then timidly let himself in. She wasn't sulking. She was sitting. She had mentally presented herself with every possible activity; but none of the alternatives would do; so for now she just sat.

"All right if I siddown, Carrie?"

Carolyn nodded. George walked across the room as if treading on eggs. He pinched his trouser legs above the knees and tugged on them, revealing his pink ankles when he sat. The bed sighed deeply.

"We've spoken to Dr. Reynolds," he admitted, spreading his hands.

"What did he say?"

"He said to ask you what it is you want," George said. But he neglected to add, To eat.

Carolyn said, "I really don't know." She looked blank; then an unexpected look of ferocity passed over her features. "No, that's wrong," she amended, teeth clenched together. "I want out."

"Out?"

"That's all I want," Carrie said, and shivered.

What's made the girl so angry? George thought. "I'm talking about food, Carrie," George said soothingly. "I'm talking about what you want to *eat*."

The ferocious look left Carolyn's face. "Food," she repeated; but she said it so slowly and deliberately that the word sounded foreign, or meaningless, as it came out of her mouth. Her face was calm, and completely blank.

Chapter 9 Wider Than a Mile

After a week, Carolyn's sorrow found the crack under the door and slipped away, tired of such close quarters. The fast finally passed. Carolyn's body made her eat.

In Carolyn's mind her return to food is linked with the end of abstinence from another desired thing—traffic with the contrasting sex. The choices, however, are not always ours to make; Carolyn learned this now.

She was a lovely girl, cool and remote; just the kind you'd think the whole high school would dream about. Perhaps they did dream about her, but they didn't talk to her. She wasn't involved in a set: didn't lead cheers, debate, work on the blurry newspaper, or belong to the Future Teachers' Association. She was kissed exactly twice that year—both times by Alfie Sisley, who was neither kind nor bright.

Carolyn enjoyed those two kissing sessions, especially the one with the tongue in it, but the pleasure was a mixed one. Half-sitting, half-lying, with Alfie's serious face pushed up hard against hers, Alfie's long tongue wagging wildly in her mouth, and Alfie's arms squeezing too hard: all this made kissing Alf much like being at the circus, for there too, Carolyn had been virtually encircled by sensation, surrounded by a nimbus of sight and sound—everything came and went so quickly. But a second visit to Madison Square Garden dulled rather than rekindled Carolyn's bright memory; she suspected the same thing would happen with constant repetitions of kisses with Alfie.

She didn't, however, get the chance to find out.

You probably remember your Senior Prom.

That's because you're supposed to.

In the spring of the final high school year, an overwhelming sense of the imminent future makes jittery eighteen-year-olds impossibly sentimental about their past. The world you are about to lose seems sweet, charmed, irreplaceable. At the same time, certain among us will be conscious that the magic is an illusion, that on Monday morning the sagging crepe paper and papier-mâché backdrop illustrating the prom's theme will be stowed in the garbage, the tuxes will go back to the rental companies, the taffeta gowns to the back of the closet, and the gym again be owned by ninth-graders in shorts, playing aimless, shrill volleyball.

The theme of Carolyn's prom was "Moon River." Rivers of pale yellow crepe paper drifted around the gym, under the all-seeing eye of an off-white cardboard moon. The dance floor, striped by foul lines and baselines, was ringed by card tables, which were draped with tablecloths of white paper and surrounded by metal folding chairs.

Carolyn wore a flowered, orange, backless, fluffy, ruffled chiffon gown, made of virgin polyester—serious prom-going attire, if something of a fire hazard. Her gloves were tight, white, long; her shoes tight, white, too short. Alfie Sisley was short too, and too nervous. Alfie was always nervous. The good opinion of his peers was of tragic importance to Alfie, and was as a result almost impossible for him to obtain. He liked Carolyn because she didn't seem to care if he could play football, drive a stickshift, or drink a can of beer in one swig. But Carolyn seemed distant to Alf. He was convinced that she disliked something about him, though he wasn't sure what.

Carolyn liked Alfie. She liked him because he was nervous and defensive; because he assumed that everything was his fault; because he knew that people have problems, even if he didn't know how to express it.

At the door an eager freshman took Carolyn's wrap. A draft of air slid quickly down the length of her exposed back. She shivered; and as if she'd shivered with dread she suddenly thought: Something's wrong. She examined the room, trying to figure it out. It hasn't been trans*formed,* she thought petulantly; it's just the gym, with some stuff in it.

Alfie fidgeted, pulling his shoulders back to make it appear as if his tuxedo fit. Well, it was the closest they had. It looked as if his shoulders were undergoing a rapid series of spasmodic contractions.

"Are you okay, Alf?"

"Oh yeah, sure. You wanna dance?"

No one was dancing yet; few people had arrived. Alfie now seemed to notice this. "Want some punch? I'll getcha some punch."

The music was slow and dreamy. It seemed to float out from the loudspeakers, wander randomly around the room, and fall in silence.

It was quiet music, romantic music, because it was unheard—or so it seemed to Carolyn.

Alfie came back with the punch. Carolyn accepted it with two hands and watched Alfie shift his weight back and forth from one foot to the other. The punch was watery, punchless. Carolyn inspected it, disappointed; you could see clear to the bottom of the glass. She inspected it a bit too carefully.

"You got a bug in there?" Alfie asked.

"Unh-unh. It's just that it's kind of bad."

"Lemme have a taste," Alfie said, and drank from his own glass. "Jeeze," he assessed. "Yuck."

"It's kind of like Kool-Aid or something."

"It's kind of like yuck, is what it is. It needs like a little shot of something. Hey, you want a shot, Carolyn?"

"In the punch?"

"Yeah, in the *punch*," Alfie said. "What did you think I meant, in your axilla?"

Axilla was Alfie's favorite word. It meant armpit, but he assumed no one knew that. He used it to make veiled reference to some unnamed, vulgar portion of the anatomy. Carolyn had heard that one a few times now, but she laughed politely for a second.

She stopped laughing. "What have you got?" she asked.

"Tekwilla."

"What's that?"

"Tekwilla? It's Mexican. They make it out of worms or something. It's good." Alf patted a pocket of his tux jacket. "You have to kind of acquire a taste for it," he added. "I mean, you might not like it right off and stuff. You want some?"

"Maybe later," Carolyn said. "I want to be in my right mind for a little while. You go ahead."

Alf looked around. "I'll go have a drink with some of the guys, I guess," he said without conviction. He took two short steps in the direction of a cluster of boys, who preened and twitched in their exotic get-ups. "I'll be right back," Alfie said. "Okay?"

Carolyn didn't say anything. "Right back," Alfie repeated. "Okay?"

Carolyn told herself to stop looking at the damn papier-mâché, for heaven's sake; it's not the way it looks, it's the way it feels. But oh God it looks so shabby.

Three of her classmates, two fat and one blind, sat by themselves at a table. "Can I sit with you kids?" Carolyn asked, trying to sound gay.

Carolyn heard talk of many things: teachers, teachers with dandruff, teachers who were cute, teachers who were quick to hand out detentions; a pretty girl's possible pregnancy; upcoming vacations to Cape Cod and Miami Beach; and, most of all, couples. Who had come with whom, and what she saw in him, and what he saw in her; whether it was true love, whether it would last. Carolyn tried hard to think of some incisive comment, but her mind wandered. True love, Carolyn repeated to herself—and the only images that appeared in her mind were an old political poster and, somehow, a rowboat on a shining lake.

At last Carolyn managed: "Isn't it hot in Miami during the summer?"

"You don't go for the heat. You go for the beach."

"I see," Carolyn said, without assurance.

"And the people, of course. God, there's tons of people from the Island. I met my friend Jackie from Roslyn. And Aaron from Forest Hills. Aaron really looked really great. He tans so easy you wouldn't believe it. And here I am, with tons of goop on, out there all day, and I'm like a *sheet*. I'm serious. A *sheet*. Aaron comes up to me and he says, very matter-of-fact, 'Just get into town?' I could have died. I'm serious. God he looked great. I could have died, practically."

A batch of boys hee-hawed behind the backdrop, drinking hard liquor from flasks. Southern Comfort was popular. Alfie tried to swill tequila, retched. Gerry Dou tasted it. "Hey, Alfie," Gerry complained, "where'd you get this stuff, the toilet?" The laughter was general.

"Well, I like it," Alfie said stoutly. He took another gulp, and kept it down. "Southern Comfort's too sweet for me," Alfie added.

Gerry nudged a buddy. "At least it don't come from the toilet, hah?" he said. Everybody cracked right up again.

Alfie loitered around behind the backdrop for quite some time, assiduously avoiding the reprehension he imagined in Carolyn's eyes. Finally he'd had enough to drink, and emerged. He marched bravely over to where she was sitting. "Let's dance," he said confidently, and pulled her to her feet. But he put his arm around her, and his fingers promptly discovered the naked curve of her spine. His confidence washed away in a wave of uncontrollable, uncomfortable fantasy. He saw Carolyn's eyes wide with excitement, her lovely body, *without clothes,* an absurdly lustful look fixed on her face. With a body like that, she would be tough to satisfy, Alfie reckoned. He touched her back again, as if testing it, and when he felt her skin, smooth and supple, his mouth became grim.

Alfie held her stiffly, formally, and they swayed through hours of listless dancing.

"Are you okay?" Carolyn tried.

"Unh-hunh."

"You have a lot of tekwilla?"

"Unh-hunh."

"You feel okay?"

"I *told* you," Alfie said. "How many times do I hafta tell you, anyway? I'm *fine.* Jeeze."

Carolyn gazed slowly around the gym. Other couples were dancing close, leaning; it appeared as if they were keeping each other from falling. Their faces were dull, and close to sleep. Some of the crepe paper had fallen off; a portion of the Moon River trailed on the floor unheeded.

I'm one of those people who goes all sad in the middle of the party, Carolyn told herself. I'm one of the ones you see sitting by herself in the hall.

I was cursed with a vivid imagination. With an excessive capacity for hope.

Carolyn stopped dancing. "Get me out of here, wouldja?" she said quietly to Alfie.

"They haven't picked the queen yet," Alfie said.

"I have to go now," Carolyn insisted, whispering.

"But they haven't picked the queen. Don'tcha want to see the queen?"

Carolyn felt sorry for everybody. "I have to go now," she said.

"All right already."

The gym doors boomed behind them. The parking lot was lit by lurid violet streetlights. Alfie and Carolyn sat in the parking lot, sat in an opulent rented limo with nowhere to go. They passed the tequila wordlessly back and forth, both of them nursing themselves.

After a while Alfie turned in the seat. "You wanta kiss?" he asked, and then he held his breath.

"Not just now, Alfie. I'm sorry." Carolyn looked out the window:

endless rows of cars, no people, violet light. "Not tonight," she said. "Is that all right?" She looked at him hopefully. "You mad, Alfie?"

Alfie shrugged. "I gotta have some coffee, is all," he said. "If I'm gonna drive you home and everything." They cruised to an all-night diner—and this is the way the evening ended for Carolyn: sitting silently at the diner counter beside Alf, watching him slurp coffee and conscientiously avoid splashing his white tux; above their heads a television set was on, without sound, and two professional wrestlers made snarling mouths at the imagined event; the jukebox played endless, scratchy repetitions of "Georgia on My Mind" for the other customer, a bleary-eyed ancient who spoke fondly to the false teeth he cradled in his hand. Carolyn intermittently pawed at a lukewarm bowl of alphabet soup. The letters swirled around and around under her spoon but never spelled anything at all.

A week later Carolyn and Alfie "broke up." It was Alfie's decision. Carolyn was puzzled but not, as she reluctantly admitted, very upset. Alfie spread the rumor that Carolyn was frigid; perhaps he believed it. I find it difficult to believe that anyone could think Carolyn lustless. I don't guess that her high school classmates, who sound perfectly normal to me, held that bizarre opinion. Alfie's classmates kept their distance with Carolyn that spring, but not because they guessed her cold. Not cold: odd. In Hempstead at the time this was the most damning quality you could be the sad possessor of.

Carolyn still knew roughly nothing about sex at the end of her high school career. But a sympathetic observer, regarding her as she heads up the gangplank, can make out the crackling of static electricity in her aura of frizzy hair, note the high-intensity buzzing in the features of her face, feel the heat emanating from her. Carolyn was a light bulb that had been left on too long—a bulb that burns the bumbling wings of the cloddish moth happening too closely by, that sputters and pops in metallic indignation at the end of its illumination, and then flashes once, shedding brighter light than it's ever kindled before. It was no coincidence that Carolyn made love for the first time not one full day out of New York Harbor.

Chapter 10 Everyone's at Sea

Yes, gangplank; yes, harbor. This was George's great plan: his graduation gift. By 1964, luxury liners were of course an anachronism, and an expensive one. But for George perfection was located in the past. He made up his mind to send Carolyn to Paris for the summer via the S.S. *France*. Airplanes, those most astounding twentieth-century commonplaces, were his business, and so to George both extremely boring and a little uncouth. "Now a lovely boat ride," as he explained it, "is something else again. You relax. The salt air is invigorating. The fish jump beside the boat. Dolphins, I think. And you dine on board," he added, as if this were the most startling facet of sea travel. "You're served tea in your deck chair," he finished, and smiled broadly, displaying the pleasant humor of every person who had ever been served tea in a deck chair.

Saskia worried about George's plan, but didn't speak out. Once George managed to coax an idea into his brain he was loath to let it go . . . probably why Carolyn today is so intent on getting her way. I remember when we first moved to Oregon from New York, and Carolyn insisted she could drive a stickshift, she'd seen people do it *hun*dreds of times, for Christ's sake. Then you had to let her do it, closing your eyes in anticipation of the crash. But that's the beautiful thing about Carolyn, or one of the beautiful things: she *could* do it, she just treated that car as if it were a machine, built to be mastered by people. She is so immensely strong in her mind.

I just wish that were true, Vandy. The car hopped, skipped, stuttered across the parking lot.

"You may not be the U.S. Ambassador yet, Carrie, but you'll be the Kingston Family Ambassador, at least," George pronounced impressively, and he laughed the way he'd learned to at the American Legion—loudly, from the chest, bellowing two individual *ha*'s. He seldom laughed that way any more; only when he was both relatively sober and extremely uncomfortable. And when he was extremely uncomfortable he did not tend to be relatively sober for very long.

The Kingston Family Ambassador, Carolyn repeated silently. She detested the fiction. There was no Kingston *family*. There was her morose, heartbroken father, growing daily in girth and shrinking in spirit; there was her placid, arctic mother, interior and harmless; and there was Carolyn—*me,* she amended. She didn't know what she was, or who. She had great, nameless hopes for herself, for she saw the brightness of life as it might be lived; but usually these hopes, after drifting about looking for a resting place, changed to anger and bitter resentment—like a wasp in a windowless room.

Carolyn has a talent for anger. To me this capacity is marvelous and foreign; I admire her the way I admire the bull in the *corrida,* for doggedness and for curious passion about what are to me inconsequential things.

Sometimes I feel that this is the strongest bond between Carolyn and Rice. I have no such power. Oh, I like to paint. I can do it for days and weeks at a time—because there is nothing better to do. That is no passion. And I wonder, too, about my attachment for Carolyn. I see no reason for ever leaving her. I know I never will. I admire her without fail, without end; there is nothing I would not do for her. At the same time, there is nothing I would ask of her. What she chooses to do is a matter of indifference to me.

This is an idea that Rice says he fails to understand.

He doesn't believe you. But I know better, and I do.

Three hours out to sea, and sure enough, Carolyn was offered tea—just as her pop had foreseen. She half-sat, half-lay in the canvas deck chair; its green and cream stripes sagged like an oriole's nest. Carolyn looked shyly up at the white-coated steward standing by his linen-draped cart. His hand caressed the silver samovar; he smiled lavishly. To Carolyn he seemed like a refugee from another, a better, age.

He *wasn't the refugee. It was the samovar.*

She refused the tea. "Would you like something else?" he asked. The question gave Carolyn a sharp spasm of pleasure—possibly because it was asked in French. A shiver shot down her spine, and her bare shoulders arched convulsively. The steward noted her reaction with apparent, complacent satisfaction.

He was perhaps twenty-three. He had tawny skin, wiry black hair brushed back. He flared his nostrils on purpose from time to time. His bright eyes too were mostly black, but that evening, as he clambered noiselessly into Carolyn's bed, his short, lean body taut with several types of tension, Carolyn lit a match: under its yellow flare she noted that his irises were a dark, burnished brown, a color that reflected back the excited image of her face but said nothing about him. There were three small scars on his face: one curled away from the edge of his eye like an exaggerated smile line, though he had no other such lines; one rough patch at the point of his chin seemed a misplaced vaccination mark; the third scar quietly echoed the line of his upper lip. He seemed young for such ornament. Carolyn compared her own life, which already seemed a secure distance behind her, with the fictional contraption she rigged up for her lover. She assumed knives; imagined a short, fierce scuffle on the Rue St. Denis, fought over some particularly pretty whore. When she pictured the whore, she saw her own face. But that body, got up as it was in black stockings, a slit skirt, and a tight, skintight, blowzily open blouse, could never be hers. She didn't even *own* a skirt like that, she told herself, as if lecturing.

Perhaps the scars came from an automobile accident instead. Perhaps he'd lost his mother and father; it would probably be too painful for him to talk about. But that wouldn't be necessary, Carolyn imagined it all with perfect clarity, right down to the twin spiderwebs smashed into the shattered windshield, the accordion folds of the crushed front end, smoke, screams, blood. Actually, they were *little* scars, she remembered, and the screams ceased abruptly.

Even his name was a mystery. He wouldn't say it, or rather, he wouldn't repeat it, since he'd mumbled it once in bed. His name sounded like someone spitting. She asked him to repeat it, but he refused. She asked again; he spoke very fast, after all. He wouldn't do that. But she kept asking, and he kept refusing, and the question became a game: their first idiosyncrasy, and thus their first intimacy. Occasionally, when it seemed least appropriate, Carolyn would ask him again, as, for example, when he threw his clothes beneath her bunk and slid in. The sight of his sleek body gave her such pleasure that she tried to hide her delight: "What did you say your name was?" she teased, touching his buttock the way you touch a soap bubble on a windy day.

He was plainly, inexplicably irked. He told her to call him Jean, or François, or Frère Jacques, for all he cared. So Carolyn, who was doggedly happy, called him Frère Jacques, and continued to call him Frère Jacques, Frère Jacques (sometimes singing it), despite his obvious annoyance. His annoyance seemed the keynote of his disposition. It didn't matter to Carolyn how *he* acted, but every motion of hers, and certainly every awkward turn of phrase, called for criticism and correction. "Do you come from Paris?" she asked, translating it directly from English, and Frère Jacques snapped, "Am I of Paris, you mean? Of course." He laughed mirthlessly. "Everyone is of Paris. All the world is of Paris."

I think a biographer in these liberated days has the freedom to talk about sex. Actually, I think that a biographer in these singularly one-tract, hedonistic days has the obligation to talk about sex. Carolyn is of normal sexuality; but of course there is no such thing as normal sexuality. Carolyn fell in love with her dog, then her own image, and then her president—to the exclusion of pimply, obnoxious, unfeeling, leering, nasty, brutish, and short, but normal, high school boys. But Peaches was tender, faithful, selfless; Carolyn's own face was bright, sensitive, sensual; JFK was witty, urbane, powerful, and had his college degree. Only the most strict heterosexual, cocksure that consummation is the only higher good, could fail to understand Carolyn's first love affairs.

Frère Jacques was another kind of lover. The attraction was surely something other than his cute little body, since Carolyn had never evinced real interest in even the cutest or littlest of bodies before. Frère Jacques was curt, sardonic, unkind. Carolyn, I understand why you would be romantically inclined—they say French is the language of love—but why did you suddenly have to lie all the way down?

Think for a second, Vandy. There are so many reasons. My dreams have always been in color; I wanted someone extraordinary. I wanted someone out of the realm of my experience. I was influenced by the romance, and the boredom, of the sea. You've probably never made love on the sly, Evan: stolen kisses the sweetest, there was that too. But I don't want to divorce reasons from moments, because the most important reason of all was the moment: on a tilting boat in the sunny, lilting sea, a man with perfect teeth and burning eyes smiled gracefully at me, and I couldn't see any reason why not. I wanted it to happen while it was still forbidden, still mysterious. I wanted the sex to be with someone who knew how; I didn't want to be poked and prodded by blundering, apologetic fingers, I wanted to be punctured. I wanted it to be in the dark, so I could be by myself while he was making love to me. I wanted to be by myself.

I left the light out, and lit just one match, for one look. His eyes were cold, even if they burned. That pleased me. Because in the end I knew I'd want to walk away from it. There are so many kinds of romance, Vandy.

They spent three days together—ten minutes he could steal from work, an hour while her cabinmate was playing bingo. They sat beside the pool; Carolyn in bathing suit dabbled her toes, Frère Jacques in steward's uniform scowled, and Carolyn laughed. Even on those placid, sunny days he was always about to storm. From here I can't see him clearly enough to know why, but my guess is that Carolyn's laughter infuriated him. For she felt eternal delight, and laughed whether he rained or shined. She was out of his control.

Look at it this way: he'd managed what might have been the greatest seduction of his sexual career, and I was having all the fun.

Or perhaps it was on account of some other kinds of contrasts Frère Jacques saw between them—gaps he'd never be able to bridge, luck he'd never have.

On the third day out Frère Jacques had the last half of the afternoon off. Carolyn had convinced her roommate, a stout fortyish woman, already a widow, to take exercise class. That gave Carolyn and Frère Jacques a full, safe hour. The first half of that hour was one of those times when you actually *feel* the luxuriousness of time itself, and it's as if you can bathe in the minutes, or examine the fingerprints of the seconds—you're in the pleasant element of time, not air. There was time, for example, for ample teasing, and then for hot kisses while still fully dressed, and for a little foreplay, an institution that Carolyn didn't even know existed. Next was sex itself, and then there was even time for small talk.

You forgot to mention that I had my first orgasm, Evan. Jesus, you forgot to mention that I had an orgasm.

"What's Paris like?" Carolyn said, snuggling.

He shrugged like a Parisian. "It's big," he said.

"Tell me marvelous things about Paris," she said. "Astonishing, marvelous things. But only the truth, please."

"It's not marvelous. The restaurants are crowded, and expensive. The women are snobs. Everybody is a snob."

"That's marvelous. Is the snobbism the best aspect of Paris?"

He shrugged again. "The coffee is good, at least," he said. "French cigarettes are strong." He reached down to his trousers, which lay in a pool on the floor, and dug into a pocket. His hand came out with a pack of Gitanes; with them came his passport. It seemed to leap out of its own accord, like a small deus ex machina late for its appearance on stage.

Carolyn put her arm down, groped for the passport, got it. "I want to see your picture," she said, and flipped to the front of the book.

Suddenly Frère Jacques became animated. A stream of French poured out of him, much too rapid for Carolyn to understand. He grabbed her arm. "Hey," Carolyn said, in English. "Hey. You're *hurting.*" Perhaps it was the English that made him give her arm a painful twist. "Willya quit it?" she cried, shrill and angry. But Carolyn didn't let go of the passport; it was the *princ*iple of the thing, and anyway what was he so—

He slapped her face; she heard the sound of his palm before she felt the sting. He took hold of her wrist and wrenched her fingers apart. "It's *my* passport!" Frère Jacques shouted.

Carolyn's eyes filled with tears, but only one went down her cheek. "My life isn't open to you," Frère Jacques said, more quietly. He got out of bed and pulled on his pants.

No, Carolyn decided; no tears for him. "I only wanted to look at your picture," she explained. He stuck his arms into his shirt-sleeves and began to fumble with the buttons. His hands were shaking. He was trying to button the shirt while still holding the passport and the Gitanes. Carolyn watched, curiously calm. She thought about asking if he wanted her to hold the cigarettes for him. But she was curious, after all. "What's the problem?" she asked him.

His face was suddenly directly in front of hers, and he was shouting again. "You desire to know the problem?" he yelled, staring furiously. "Look at this, bitch!" He gestured at the passport; he was holding it open to the page where his picture was. That was him, all right; grim mouth, eyes blazing. His fine teeth were hidden behind his pout. Carolyn looked dumbly back to the live face, which registered her beautiful blue eyes, and snarled. "Yes, that's correct," he said ironically, smiling. "Place of birth, *Algérie.*"

Why is he angry? Carolyn asked herself; her eyebrows knit; she frowned.

Frère Jacques spoke sardonically again. "You've never heard of it, perhaps? It's in Africa. They forgot to put that on the passport: Arab." He cocked his fist and held it under her chin; Carolyn cowered, and he laughed. "Dumb," he commented. "Rich bitch. I hope you have an Arab baby." He shook his passport at her once more and went out, stylishly slamming the door behind him.

Carolyn stared at the door, uncomprehending. Minutes ticked by; the hands read twenty after six. Slowly she began to understand what had happened, and what Frère Jacques had meant. Poor Frère Jacques, she thought, and now she did try to cry for him; but now no tears would come. She was surprised, but really she was not too sorry.

Of course I was sorry. I just couldn't cry on command. Even my own command. Feelings don't take orders. They give them.

Chapter 11 *The Absinthe Drinker*

  I don't paint abstracts. I don't know how. I begin with the world, with a particular portion of the physical world at a given time: afternoon light falling on Carolyn's white, textured bedspread, the long shadow cast by her bed, the way the mind is led by looking. I don't pretend that invention is absent from my painting. I'm aware that you have to make the transition from the reality of the scene to the reality of the paint. But I repeat: the world is my basis; I shall not want.
  Carolyn didn't work that way. She invented the world in its entirety, invented several full-blown worlds. Think of a child who watches, amazed, as her first balloon bursts, and then patiently blows up another—while somewhere the dart is already poised. Carolyn kept blowing up balloons.
  Carolyn went to Paris. She did everything she'd told herself she would. Her bones vibrated with the bass notes of the gargantuan organ in Notre-Dame; she took her café and croissant beurre with decided indolence of a lengthy midmorning at Le Sélect; she threw herself into the sea of humanity massed around the best green beans, the best, not expensive, not expensive, at Les Halles; she strolled, bathing in lemon sunshine, late afternoons in the sandy Tuileries. She did what she came to do. And then she wondered, as tourists do, exactly what she was doing there. Who was she trying to please? Was it herself? How did one please oneself?
  She asked herself these questions one perfect, listless afternoon as she found herself by the pond in the Jardin du Luxembourg. She was immune to the delights of sun-gilded flowers and shady plane trees; indifferent to bright toy boats on the glistening pond; bored by the gaiety of all children. Carolyn hovered over the pond, leaning. Just this side of the relentlessly monochromatic blue background, she saw the head and shoulders of a young woman, watching herself watch herself in a watery looking glass. And Carolyn was prey to the sudden, unnerving fear that she hadn't come to Paris at all, but had sent this person, her alien proxy, and was watching that twin through a powerful telescope, peeking like a rooftop voyeur at someone else's distress.

Carolyn straightened up, as if she'd caught herself shamelessly engaged in mortal sin. She marched herself out of the gardens, down the Rue de Odéon, down the Rue Dauphine, keeping her eyes fixed on the pavement before her; she crossed the Pont Neuf, not admiring the Louvre or Institut.

Bet you had to look up the Institut.

Carolyn was in a state of interior tumult when she reached her hotel—the Henri IV, which was small, cheap, and packed with Americans. Carolyn went quickly up the narrow stairs to her little room. She threw herself onto her lumpy bed, grabbed fervent hold of her musty pillow, and contemplated violent acts to her person. Then she spent the rest of the summer reading eighteenth-century novels, in English, in bed. She emerged on occasion to buy a novel from one of the English bookstores on the Rue de Rivoli, or a box of pear tarts from the bakery right on the Place Dauphine. If she'd been too ill to eat after Kennedy was killed, she was now too ill not to. She regarded her burgeoning appetite with curiosity; she knew it was some kind of comment on her life, and she knew it didn't speak well for her. But she *wasn't* well, she told herself; her life had never yet been what she'd hoped for; and now, in Paris, the city of her old dreams, she didn't know how to go about hoping for another one. She read *Pamela,* and ate another pear tart.

She wrote in her journal: "But there are wholes with holes in them, too, like doughnuts or wheels of Swiss cheese. And I'm still hungry when I finish eating."

Carolyn was not destined to be a fat woman. Perhaps she didn't hate herself enough; perhaps she didn't really like pear tarts enough. Carolyn, despite herself, had something of the survivor in her. Ten days before she was due to leave Paris, she spent several minutes in careful examination of her body. It dripped and rolled down from her neck. It hung over itself. Portions of it, like chin and belly, seemed to have duplicates nearby—understudies, perhaps. Carolyn decided that what was absent in her life was clearly not another pear tart. She threw out the half-eaten pastry that she happened to have, not so coincidentally, in her hand. She threw out the rest of the box. She didn't eat again until she was back in the United States.

This was the summer Carolyn had before entering college. It was in Paris, reading eighteenth-century novels, that Carolyn first decided to be a writer. But it would be some years before she went from being a writer to actually writing.

Things might have worked out differently. I was in Paris that same summer. I had been there before, but never by myself; and this time I went as a painter. The picture always comes to me, when I think of that gentle summer, of the scene that might have been: how I might have bumped into Carolyn while admiring Cezanne's fruit or Monet's lily pads, might have admired the dazzling light in her eyes, the delicacy of her features, the painterly sweep of her fine sturdy calves; how we might have become a young, fresh painting ourselves. Instead of Carolyn as Degas' melancholy Absinthe Drinker slipping away into a trance, we might have seen Carolyn as Manet's Olympia, reclining on a couch, naked rather than nude. We might have sipped tall heady tropical drinks at the Rhumerie through a single straw, might have gazed down fondly at our Paris through the wide spotless windows of the Tour d'Argent as we shared pressed duck; might, in short, have been the romance that Carolyn had been building in her mind, and which, that summer, she watched fall limply to the ground—no longer a bright, plump balloon, but a shred of torn rubber with a compressed cartoon duck emblazoned on the side.

As it was, by the time Carolyn and I met, I'd lost the freshness I'd have needed to make her my Olympia, if I'd ever had it. Instead we lived together as a sort of youthful version of American Gothic. And Carolyn had to wait until Rice came along....

You're mistaking modesty for frankness, Vandypie. You, we, had that ability. We still have it. Don't you think?

Chapter 12 *Not So Sad*

I met Carolyn in her sophomore year at Barnard—I was a junior at Columbia—and what concerns me here is the discrepancy between the tormented girl we have just seen, tucked away in her little hotel in Paris with a tart in one hand and an epistolary novel in the other, and the woman I met: sociable, gay, much at home and apparently at ease. Carolyn could be wrong, of course, and so could I; but I think not. The objective reader (I guess that's you, Rice) will have to take that on faith. This is a straightforward biography. It may be incomplete; it may put its stress in the wrong places. But you'll have to believe me, or we'll never get anywhere. By a similar token, I believe Carolyn; so that leaves us with this small change to account for....

Recently Rice told me a story he liked, which he thought I'd like too. It was about a Portland friend named Otto Veen, a homosexual whose sexual inclinations instilled a powerful guilt. Otto wanted to be "cured," as he put it, and he began weekly visits with a psychiatrist. The doctor asked Otto when he had first become aware of homosexual tendencies. "When I was thirteen," Otto answered with confident certainty, a certainty the doctor seized upon: "What happened when you were thirteen?" "Well," Otto said, "that was the year I went away to school for the first time." The doctor nodded, but said nothing. Otto felt compelled to go on. "My sister went away to college that year," he said. The doctor said nothing. Otto thought for a while. "I think it was around then that I realized I would never be any good in sports." The doctor merely gazed. "Oh, yeah," Otto realized. "My face broke out that year." The doctor did not speak. "It was the first time," Otto said. "It was really bad." The doctor just looked at him. "It was really bad," Otto repeated. "I got a boil in my nose." No reply. "I didn't get a job I applied for that summer, as a lifeguard." The doctor began to tap his pencil against his pad. "My parents built a garage that summer," Otto tried. The doctor tapped his pencil faster. "And, unh, my father died that year."

"Oh?" asked the doctor, and he raised his eyebrows very slightly.

I laughed when Rice told me that story, but not because I thought it funny. Rice wanted me to laugh. Rice's father died when Rice was seventeen; my own father died in a shaving accident (he was a hemophiliac, and an unlucky man) when I was just five. Rice has lavished a good portion of his life on "working through" that death—a process that Rice, who drops his g's, also calls "acceptin it"—though for me acceptance has always carried with it the implicit possibility of rejection, an option which Rice, unfortunately, does not have open to him. Rice feels that the loss of paternity is something important we have in common; it takes on greater importance because we don't have much else. It would be, too, I grant him that, if we felt the same emotions concerning the loss. We don't. I was hysterical, at five, when my father died; but I was also hysterical when I skinned my knee. My sense of apt proportion was not yet developed, and by the time I realized what had happened and what that meant to me (or should have meant), some years had passed. I regarded my father's death from across the protective moat of time come and gone. Whatever pain I might have felt could not alter the fact. I missed having a father while I was growing up; but I cannot say that I missed *my* father; nor that I miss, or even remember, him now.

It may well be, then, that I'm not perfectly suited to describe Carolyn's transformation. But it can be said to have its beginnings, Carolyn tells me, one afternoon in the fall of her first year at Barnard.

A portly man was seen that afternoon, haunting the halls in one of the apartment buildings that masquerade as Barnard dormitories. He was in obvious search of something. He blundered his way down dead ends, bumped walls like a pinball. When he found a student in the hall, he rushed up to her as if she might be a mirage. "Have you seen Carrie?" he asked, and nearly tipped over. The accosted student seemed taken aback. "It's my daughter," he said, to reassure her. The accosted student, cut off from her room, began edging toward the elevator; she leaned insistently on the "down" button, hoping repetition would induce more speedy action. The elevator arrived with a cheerful ding-dong (as though there was no large, lunatic ghost barging around the halls), and the doors shunted aside with a calm, mechanical hum. The woman jumped in; the elevator simultaneously emitted three replacements. Our intruder staggered up to this new batch. "Anybody seen Carrie?" he asked them, weaving. They laughed nervously, and herded each other into a nearby room. Their door shut with a resonant smack—leaving the local ghost with nothing but his own unanswered question and the echo of a slammed door.

This toper was not jolly, but he was persistent. He bumbled soddenly about the hall for hours. By the time he'd vanished, the inmates of the floor no longer regarded him as a threat, but as a comic institution: their own fool. Carolyn was at the library, and didn't return until dinner. Her roommates eagerly regaled her with the Haunting of Eakins Hall—as they called it, with what Carolyn considered excessively side-split hilarity. Most of us have had moments when parents were an unholy cross to bear in the presence of our peers; this night was one of the last of those times for Carolyn. She mimed belly laughs, and silently cursed the day she was born.

She dreamed her father that night. George wore a gorgeous plush jacket and feathered hat, brandished a flashing rapier, and swilled whole flasks of brandy; his waxed RAF mustache reappeared on his face, and his hair was dark, thick, long—historically inaccurate. He strutted gaily around her dream's center stage, its star, its hero; the other players of her dream, all in drab modern dress, gaped in awed admiration.

I was just trying to make it all better.

George appeared in the dormitory the next day. This time he knocked, however unsteadily, on the right door; and to her regret Carolyn was in. She ushered her father out of the building as quickly as she could, promising him a drink in the West End Bar.

Carolyn was over eighteen, and she was legally entitled to have her drink, although she couldn't hold it. On this occasion she had two, which was double the number of her previous high firewater mark. Her memories of the afternoon remain clouded by the warm, softening glow of alcohol.

They sat at a small table by the wall. Carolyn suggested hamburgers. George agreed, and then cheerfully ordered two gin and tonics instead. "Best thing in the world," he commented. "Cheers."

Cheers, George. Carolyn cannot recall, among other things, the weather that day—so we'll imagine bright, dry autumn, with the smog still at its normal level for the 1960s (that is, somewhat below the conscious) and the temperature at the sweater stage. Carolyn cannot remember the West End Bar very well, since she made it a point never to go there again. She remembers that the air inside the bar was yellowish and thick, smoky and sunny. And she'll never forget that man across the table, his features puffed and sagging.

His rheumy eyes found hers, despite her attempts to elude them. "Tell me, Carrie," he started. "Are you having a good time at your new school?" He looked at her intently; he seemed almost sober.

"It's a university, Pop."

"Yes. Well. University. Barnard. Are you having a good time, darling?"

"It's okay."

"Have you got good friends, Carrie?"

"Sure."

"Best thing in the world, friends."

"Unh-hunh."

"You've never been good at making friends. At making—pals." He looked down at his glass, and then spoke to it. "Neither is your mother." He nodded wistfully. "Neither am I."

Carolyn twisted in her seat. "Oh, you're not so bad," she tried. "You have your pals."

"Pals!" he said scornfully. "Who?"

"Al Durer."

"Al is my boss."

"Speck Snyder," Carolyn said quickly.

George made a pained expression. "For the love of God," he said. "Speck is my bartender."

Carolyn was silent. "Ah, Carrie," George said affectionately—though he caressed his glass, not her—"I'm just trying to tell you something very simple, Carrie."

"Well, what is it, then?" Carolyn challenged, her voice impatient and insistent. Immediately she felt ashamed.

George didn't look sober any more. "Trying to tell you something," he said stubbornly.

"Yes, Pop."

"Simple," he said.

"Unh-hunh. What is it, Pop?"

George looked at his daughter. His eyes were clear. "I don't know, darling," he said. He gave her his bewildered smile.

George picked up a napkin from the table and idly, carelessly folded it; unfolded it; folded it, unfolded it; folded it, unfolded it.

Carolyn got the call from her mother a couple of weeks later.

Her mother had to apologize first. "I'm sorry," she said, instead of hello.

"Hello, Mom."

"I would not wake you up, except for these bad news."

"What bad news?" Carolyn asked, cross, irritated as always by her mother's backward presentation—as if the way she *did* things had also been translated from another language, another mode of being.

Saskia didn't answer. She abruptly wailed into the telephone, and then dropped the receiver in favor of her handkerchief, so the convulsive grieving that Carolyn heard was muffled both by distance and the insulating presence of Saskia's handkerchief, which stabbed at her eyes and rubbed her watery cheeks and stopped the open wound that was Saskia's sobbing mouth—enveloping and comforting her bit by bit, like the zealous, tender relative that Saskia ought to have had with her, but did not.

"Take it easy, Mom," Carolyn said softly, grimly. "Tell me," she said, although of course she knew quite well.

George had fallen down the stairs the night before. He was knocked out when the back of his skull struck the well-glossed parquet. Saskia got him conscious long enough for him to crawl into bed, fully clothed; she slipped in next to him, turned onto her side, and slept without stirring. But when the murky fingers of dawn began to expose the gloomy vista of suburban rooftops, it became clear that George was dead.

For a day Carolyn tried not to believe it. You don't die from falling down stairs, she kept telling herself, a sleeper struggling to surface from the illogical depths of a nightmare: you just *don't*. She was not surprised, then, when the Cause of Death was unceremoniously listed as: Alcoholism.

You have to bury the father to become a man—so goes the old song. It's tempting to guess that George's death caused Carolyn's flowering because Nature abhors a vacuum: as one adult makes his bibulous way offstage, another rushes to take his place. Perhaps George's absence allowed Carolyn to develop. Like putting goldfish in a larger bowl. The darn things grow as housing permits.

My goldfish all died. So did my turtle, Billy. I found him upside down on his pretty spectral pebbles, and I always wondered most of all how he managed to flip himself over. Please ignore me.

But George's absence could not have made such a striking difference in Carolyn's life, because his presence resembled nothing so much as absence in the first place.

We don't need to probe Carolyn's subconscious for the seed of her transformation. The place to look is her conscious mind—which is, after all, where a great deal of revelation takes place.

On the afternoon of the funeral Carolyn wandered out of the house, dazed. She was tired of her tears; she was tired of a great deal more. It was an unseasonably serene and warm day. Carolyn plunked herself down on the short-haired lawn and lay bathing in sunlight. She watched a droplet of sweat form on her forearm and glisten. The shouts of small children echoed down the street, and then died out. Japanese beetles drifted in the air around the honeysuckle; sunlight gleamed on long strands of spiderweb, which swayed in an imperceptible breeze. This was the most placid of seasons, Indian summer. Everything seemed so motionless that Carolyn found it hard to believe that the season would change. But it would, of course: she'd lived long enough to accept that inevitability. That spider there would die of the season's change. The shouts of the children had died out; the children would grow, then grow silent; they too would die out. Carolyn's knowledge, her experience, now extended to human seasons. She'd lived long enough, now, to know that inevitability too.

She shaded her eyes with her damp forearm. It just happens, she thought. It just happens. Humans have seasons; it's that simple. Like a wordless question forming in the back of her mind, or a nameless object she'd accidentally left behind, this had been troubling her for a long time—no, it was not yet twenty after six—and now it had come forward. Well, what do you do then? she asked. How do you act against relentless time? Carolyn dropped her arm back on the grass; she began to rub clipped blades of grass between her fingers. If you're a spider, she began, you simply weave; if you're a droplet of sweat, you glisten; if you're a Japanese beetle, you drift. But all of this was nonsense. It was merely backdrop. These objects, these creatures, have no choice. She was at the center. The question was for her.

It had something to do with the touch of the grass against her fingertips; something to do with the shimmering haze, the thickness of the smoky golden air. What do you do? she asked again. You notice. You don't forget. The magic trick is that we know: about seasons, about Japanese beetles and droplets of sweat, about inevitability. This is our miracle, why pretend it's our curse? Carolyn asked. But she was becoming rhetorical. She was speaking to herself. She did not need to do that.

But when Carolyn sat up she glimpsed, open to the year's last warmth, a white honeysuckle blossom—and for her the future seemed to open up just then, like a small, fragrant flower.

That scene was beyond me, I'm afraid. I'm not writer enough. I'll just say instead: at her father's death, Carolyn became one of the living. She saw something in the front yard of her old house that she'd missed before; she kept her eyes on it, for this thing seemed to mean something to her. That will have to do.

No, leave it in, Evan. Leave it in, please.

Since the light is slipping away—the fickle Portland light—I should retire to the bathroom, where I'm painting a tolerable representation of two small, bald hills, a dun-colored path winding between them, and an interestingly shaped rock. Everything about this picture is adequate (which is the best I can do), except for its subject. For that reason I've worked long and hard on it, lavished the best hours of my day on making perfect its imperfections. I have an abiding affection for this little cripple of a picture—the way parents do for a severely retarded child, whose virtues can only be guessed at, or invented, but never denied.

But my picture is not so sad as this.

Chapter 13   I Come In

Here's where I come in. That should make it easy. I met Carolyn in her sophomore year at Barnard. Sophomore comes from the Greek: *sophos*, wise, and *moros*, foolish, or fool: the wise fool.

I know no Greek, incidentally. The foregoing information comes to you courtesy of my erratic spelling. Curious as to whether the second o in *sophomore* was the invention of addled sportscasters in obscure need of extra syllables (see *athelete*), I consulted my chubbiest reference book. Mr. Webster knows Greek, fortunately. In my defense I can claim prep school Latin—which is pretty close to Greek, no?—although these days the only Latin I remember is how to decline *amo, amas, amat*, etc.

You conjugate those, Vandypie. Declining to love is something else.

A wise fool: Carolyn's Western Civ teacher, his invisible antennae purring after a conference with Carolyn, put his feet up on his office desk, made a steeple with his two hands, like so, and said: "Having you as my pupil, Carolyn, has made me understand how Haydn must have felt teaching Mozart." He meant well, but Carolyn knew he was no Haydn. She knew, too, that she was no Mozart: a wise fool.

She was a willowy sophomore and wore sweaters and skirts, mostly. The latter were called "miniskirts"; this was an archaic form of titillation which impressed upon the viewer the muscular promise of Carolyn's calves, knees, and (the next year those skirts rose again!) thighs, much in contrast—here we proceed up that beautifully proud, erect carriage—with the delicacy of her face, haloed as it was by an airy, kinky, massless mass of angel's hair. If you say that eyes are "pools of blue," you mean a cold, clear depth and sandy bottom, yes? They were deep, all right, but warm, those tropical pools of hers; they were cerulean, but cerulean as it is squeezed from the tube, not the pale sky color that looks pastily back from the upper portion of the canvas. Bright.

You're talking about my contacts, Vandy. And I know that you know.

She was bright. She wrote well. She wrote poetry, for one thing, and though she claims now that all collegiate poetry is bad, hers was pretty good. She led what is called "an active social life," which at that time meant that she slept with various boys and took various drugs. She "dated"; this detailed the difference between sleeping with boys and living with one. Her drug-taking was somewhere between seldom and average. Smoking dope made her drowsy, which she liked, but it was regarded as a social activity, and as a social dope smoker Carolyn was a failure. She tended to curl up in a corner about midway through a party, just when the dancing, she heard later, was getting hot. On the occasions she stayed alert, she became anxious. She would start out worrying about the police and being busted; then about how much schoolwork she had; about whether she was being *fulfilled* by her present relationship(s); making a leap of doubt, she fretted about her mother, her father, about death itself; then back again to the police and being busted. She was never busted.

But you were right to be anxious, Carolyn. The smooth flow of the collegiate years, demarcated here and there by due dates and terms' ends, first dates and clattering breakups (think of a china saucer and red-tiled floor), was an illusion, and you knew it. You gave it thought, always; several voices spoke to you, and you listened to them all. Perhaps this is what separated you from the rest, as you strode purposefully around the campus (long strides, heavy strides, you were half Dutch and the first to wear clogs). Perhaps this is what separates you from the rest, for me, today.

She was a tall girl. I'd watched her go up the steps of the library every day for a year. I'd been to the same parties on occasion. By now I blindly recognized her loud, delighted laugh. Lounging in one of the soft chairs at the Lions' Den, I looked up from my solitary cup of coffee (black, no sugar, occasionally flanked by a brittle Danish), and there among a group of admirers, her generous smile shone. To me it seemed that this was a ubiquitously cheerful, a happy person.

I rose unsteadily from my chair, abandoning my coffee, my Danish, and walked over to where she sat. More precisely, I walked right by where she sat, carried by the powerful current of my awkwardness. I turned myself around, headed toward her again—and she burst into laughter (someone's joke, I don't get it), startling me so much that I canoed back to my Danish, beaten. But destiny is a creature of habit, and immediately tried again. Carolyn's cronies abruptly rose in a body, all ordered away by sympathetic stage directions, and Carolyn was left, crossing and recrossing her very white legs, playing with a matchbook, quite alone.

This time I stopped by her table. I asked her—I bent over, spoke softly—if she'd like to go out for a beer. Carolyn didn't like beer, but she didn't mention that. She just said no, thank you. But she said it so beautifully that a few days later I asked her again. She still didn't like beer, and refused again. In the innocence of her heart Carolyn thought I was interested in the beer. I, for my part, took her refusal for a NO TRESPASSING sign, and I kept my distance after that. It still irks me to think that I missed seasons with Carolyn on account of her distaste for beer.

That's what I told you, but it wasn't the beer. For a long time I was looking for the man of my dreams—which involved an ideal bodily architecture, a certain bravura, an overstated bravery. You were quiet, and very skinny. You wore thick glasses and stood with a stoop. You were nobody's dreamboat, Vandypie.

I was not particularly hopeful, then, when among the bespectacled worms enrolled in my Senior Seminar ("The Bloomsbury Group") I spied this startling underclasswoman. Despite the prior demise of my hopes, my heart jolted my chest—because the heart is the slowest organ to learn the sad truth, much as oak leaves, bound by loyalty other deciduous foliage will never understand, are the last to drop from stout limbs to frozen ground. But I swear I did not hope.

She came up to me, that first day of class, as if I were her oldest, dearest friend. "I'm not surprised to find *you* in here," she said. She touched my wrist; I remember that she touched my wrist—just a small touch, admittedly, but it counted, and I noticed. And I remember.

I asked her why she wasn't surprised.

Evidently she didn't have an answer ready, though I still can't think of any other response I might have made. She shrugged. "You're just the *type*," she said.

I think she must have noticed I regarded that remark as a species of insult. You don't want to be the *type* that does anything, after all. You're supposed to have your own, fantastically original reasons for doing everything. For example, I sleep every night, not because I'm tired but because I think it's only fair to give my unconscious equal time.

But Carolyn noticed my pique, and was quite willing to help me out. "Of course I'm that type too. Or I wouldn't be here."

I asked her what kind of type that *was*.

"A Virginia Woolf type," she said simply, and gave me a quick wink that was intended, I think, to be conspiratorial. I realized that it would be helpful for relations if I joined the conspiracy, though I didn't know much about Mrs. Woolf, who wasn't yet the cottage industry that she is at the moment. I smiled mock-ruefully, as if she'd caught me—got me dead to rights, with all my affinities showing.

"Which is your favorite?" she asked me.

I named the one novel I'd read by Woolf.

"Unh-hunh," she said, and nodded reflectively, thinking about it. "I'm sort of a *The Waves* person myself. Pretty far gone. But I see what you mean. *Mrs. Dalloway*'s a clean one." She laughed at herself. "What a ridiculous way to talk," she said. "I guess I just meant that it doesn't have many imperfections. *The Waves* does, but God, it tries for everything."

I replied that I had liked *Mrs. Dalloway* fine; then I felt that I had to look down at my hands. Particularly my fingernails. Carolyn was that pretty, that bright. Well, the class will start soon, I thought; I can stop making a fool of myself any minute now.

"Where do you live?" she asked; I noticed the brightness of her transversely striped skirt, wrapped around the long column of her legs, and at the same time the little train finally made its way around the bend, chugging manfully, and I understood that this paragon was trying vainly to engage me—*me*—in conversation.

I told her that I lived on West 109th, just off Riverside, in a breezy, all-white apartment overlooking the river.

She pulled the curtains to the side and gazed out. Sharp shafts of sunset fell on the bones of her face, and in various places inside my hollow chest similarly sharp little cupidities were telling me that I was in love. "I like your place, Vandy," she said happily to me, and I nearly bowed.

How nice. But is "cupidities" right word?

I adored her. I was conscientious in my adoration: flowers (I'm a relic), dinners out, typewritten letters, tenderness. But I think that our affair—as she pointedly characterized it—would have died quietly, of an acute case of imbalance, if I hadn't discovered her one day among the deserted stacks in the basement of the library. I was "working": slowly and aimlessly wheeling a cart of recently returned books around the quieter corners of the library.

I heard someone sob. I wheeled my curious cart that way. I found her slumped over a desk, her head placed firmly on her arms, soaking them.

She looked up. "What're *you* doing here?" she accused.

"Working," I said. I held out my handkerchief. She took it, but that didn't temper her wrath. "You carry a handkerchief?" she said scornfully, as if the whole world despised handkerchiefs.

I told her that, personally, I hated handkerchiefs. I said I just happened to have this one because I was on my way to an anti-handkerchief rally, and was using it as an example. Actually, that very handkerchief she was blowing her nose into—she trumpeted miserably—would probably be hung in effigy that afternoon. I said that my middle name was Tissue, and that my maternal grandfather had been the original Mr. Tissue of the Tissue Company.

"Oh, Christ," she said, drying her eyes. Immediately they brimmed again.

I told her I was proud of my Tissue loyalties, damn proud. I tried to put my arm around her. She shook her head.

She stopped, sort of. "In your totally inoffensive way, you're kind of a nervy guy," she said, and held my handkerchief out to me.

"What am I supposed to do with it *now?*" I asked. "You keep it. It's yours, de facto."

"Thanks a heap," she said.

The way she said "Thanks a heap" seemed indisputably lovable to me; it was a faultless expression. I had the definite sensation that I could dispense total adoration to anyone who used that fine turn of phrase.

She blew again. "How are you feeling?" I asked, feigning nonchalance.

"Would you please go away?"

"Anything wrong?" I asked pleasantly.

"Please, Evan," she said, wearily.

I grabbed her shoulders and started to give her a massage. It sounds like a ridiculous thing to do, but at the time it felt perfectly natural. Or almost perfectly natural. I'm not altogether comfortable with emotional circumstances. But Carolyn didn't stop me, and I must have rubbed her neck and shoulders for a good five minutes. Finally my fingers got tired, and I stopped.

She looked up at me again. "You wouldn't understand," she said.

I shrugged.

"A lot of it is my father," she said.

"I thought your father was dead."

"I knew you wouldn't understand," she said.

I thought she was about to start crying again. "What is it about your father?" I suggested.

She put my handkerchief against her forehead, staunching the unseen wound. "My father," she said, speaking slowly, "was really crazy. He was really ... really crazy." She stopped.

"And—?"

"And I didn't help," she said grimly. She put the handkerchief down. She began to open and close the book nearest her on the desk.

"But how could you have helped that?" I tried.

"Well," she said, making slow circles with her index finger on the book's plastic library cover, "it was as if he wasn't himself. It was like, here he is, in a glass prison sort of, and he can *see* outside and everything, but he can't get there. He can't touch anything. He can't change anything. Not one thing." She opened the book again, and for a second I thought she had started to read.

"Unh-hunh," I said, trying to be generally comforting. But I didn't understand what she meant at all.

Carolyn turned around in her chair, and then she calmly began to whack me on the arm with the book. Not hard, but over and over. I stood there, embarrassed, and let her do it. I kept thinking, I wonder what you're supposed to do when someone starts whacking you with a book?

She stopped as suddenly as she had started. She faced forward again and put the book down neatly, almost daintily. She appeared to be completely composed. "You don't see, do you, Evan?" she said drily. "That one of the things he had to just sit there and watch, and not be able to do anything about, was himself?"

I was thinking maybe I should start joking again. "I'm sorry," I said.

"I could have helped him," Carolyn stated again. "I didn't do one thing for him. And I kind of knew, you know? I pretended I didn't, but I kind of did." She gave me an unfathomable smile.

"He *is* dead. You can't change that," I pointed out, cruelly and stupidly.

"Yes," Carolyn acknowledged. "But it's not over. There's my mother."

"Your mother—?"

"My fucking mother," Carolyn repeated. She grabbed the book again, and now she threw it as hard as she could. It banged against the half-empty stacks, clanging, and fell to the cement floor. "My fucking mother is the same fucking way," Carolyn said. Tears reappeared, chasing each other down her face. I put my arms around her, trying to hold her, trying to calm her, but she began to struggle against my arms, and she began to wail. "So am I," she wailed. She was sobbing again. "So am I," she sobbed, looking right at me. Her face was bright with tears—bright, even there, even underground. "Hey, tell me something, would you?" she said, licking tears from her lips. "Is everybody that way?" For some reason I put my hand over her mouth to quiet her, though no one else was close. "But that's what I want to *know*," she cried, still struggling with me, as if it were my hand and my arms that were preventing her from knowing. "Is everybody that way?"

"No, kiddo," I said. I tried to kiss her everywhere all at once. Though she tried to stop me, I tried to kiss her all over her head— ears, nose, forehead, chin, mouth, neck, jaws, skull. I tried to kiss her everywhere.

Chapter 14 *Love and the Dishes*

From here, those days—the first ones, fourteen years ago now, when we began to live together for the first time, the only time that would ever be the first time—seem redolent of bliss. I don't know why, but even the smallest details of our lives at West 109th seem almost unbearably touching to me now. I regard with tender amusement the lime-green pair of men's pajamas that my Carolyn sported with such absurd gaiety through that first winter. Despite its age, I can examine without a distracting fingerprint or dog-ear the mental photograph I took of her in the kitchen: she stood before the stove, wearing open-toed terrycloth slippers, and she scrambled eggs; the vigorous scraping movement required by the fast-sticking eggs made her buttocks joggle within those sporty peejays. I stood behind her behind and loved her ridiculousness. But this, for me, is more than low comedy. It's acquired the status of private myth.

I don't think you can be immune to it. Look at us. In the sixties Carolyn loved the color purple, and so one day she bought herself a pair of purple tights. Strolling casually beside my library cart, I spied out of the corner of my theoretically uninterested eye a whistle-short blue skirt trailing a marvelous pair of purple legs. Who *is* that fancy woman in the purple tights? I said to myself, and then I saw enough of the woman to discover that it was my own lover. This sighting gave me profound joy. An objective observer had pronounced Carolyn worthy, desirable, even fancy. I recounted the event to Carolyn, and for a year or so, whenever I felt unaccountably pleased with her—with a look, a manner, an incisive comment or witty aside—I would whisper to her (whether she wore the tights, something else, or nothing at all), "Who is that *fancy* woman in the purple tights?"

Sounds to me, mister, like you recall me as a collection of anatomical parts and their clothing.

Perhaps we were not such a cute couple as I assume; perhaps every couple has its purple tights and its scrambled eggs in steamy kitchens; perhaps I am just talking about the passage of time, time shared. I tend to forget the problems. Living with someone, sharing everything, has its little impossibilities. You do not wash your feet, or for that matter your socks, with the frequency your partner would desire. You forget on occasion to wipe your feet on the mat. You hang your underwear on the bedroom doorknob, and your partner is not pleased.

You've been much better about that lately.

Your partner, for her part, is also surprisingly imperfect. She rises at eight, but is never pleasant until ten. The noise of her long, hard nails scratching her skin (always. Every part of her itches, always) grates against the sensibilities with exaggerated resonance. She is markedly unsympathetic when you slice yourself instead of the onions; she does not seem to care if you are on the verge of a debilitating cold.

You always slice yourself instead of the onions. You're always on the verge of a cold.

Let me now state the rule. The two biggest problems in life are Love and the Dishes.

Actually, I'm not so sure that Love is all that much of a problem; but there is no such thing as a relationship in which the Dishes plays no part. No two people do dishes in the same way, but for every person there is only one Correct way to do dishes. No one in the world does his share of the dishes; at the same time, everyone feels that he does more than his share. It is never *any*one's turn to do the dishes, for in a given household *every*one has just done the dishes. Moreover, no one has ever dirtied a dish: dirty dishes are perhaps the only exception to science's prohibition against spontaneous generation: dirty dishes are, pardon the phrase, immaculately conceived.

In some relationships, however, there comes a time when such small irritations turn themselves around. I'm speaking of love here, and nothing less. It arrives unspoken, unrequested, at its own pace. I remember the day.

Carolyn had developed a distressing habit of biting her lip. Not the inside of her cheek, so as to be harmless. She chewed the corners of her chapped lips till they bled. At first, of course, I was horrified by this self-mutilation, and a little disgusted as well. I told her to stop. But warnings, reprimands, threats, pleas, were to no avail. She bit on. Instead of growing more desperate, I gradually grew used to this oral flagellation of hers. For a short while I stopped caring; I watched her thin blood run down her chin as if all the people I knew went around wearing trickled red stripes on their faces. Then the next phase arrived. The heart is governed by contradiction, and one day I found myself leaning in my chair, eyes peeking out from my book, trying to spot her gnawing. Not in disgust; no, I was entranced. I found imponderable delight in the sight of her reading under a cone of white light, her pale angelic hair glowing, her teeth bright and shiny-wet, her blood crimson and flowing.

This interest smacks of the morbid and macabre, but I swear such sentiments were not its cause. Her gruesome habit had by repetition lost its grisliness; all that was left was the fact that it was hers, hers alone. It became, in fact, her: became an emblem for Carolyn herself. When I watched her absently rip scar tissue off her dry, cracked lips, I was reminded for the millionth time that this was Carolyn. And so for months I craned my neck, glanced slyly to the side, and even tiptoed around our apartment, in the hope of catching Carolyn in the act. The act of being herself. Because it was her that I loved.

When you love, I think, you start with a mental picture of someone, which you believe is your lover. Over the course of time you discover who it is that you love. It's only then that you fall in love with her—or else become used to her, which is a short step away from indifference, and then dislike.

But over the years we have each learned, painfully and painstakingly, to allow the other certain idiosyncrasies, liberties. We have made the amazing discovery that two people can coexist: a man and a woman can be friends, even if they live together. I do not use the word love lightly, I mean an unspoken affection, an unseen connection, an unmoving permanence. An adamant tenderness.

We've now lived together a decade, and nearly half another. For nine years we scratched out a living in New York, where I went from student to teacher, and Carolyn from student to secretary, to secretary, to secretary. In 1975 we moved to mythic Oregon, only to find ourselves in ordinary Portland; then, seemingly stuck, we began to like it. Two years ago, Carolyn published a brief, incandescent novel, a novel of love, *Human Wishes:* good reviews, a decent paperback sale, interviews in the local press—in short, Carolyn became at last what she has always been, a writer. Together, we have survived the years when things start to fall apart in a big way, a physical way—when the body suddenly seems a mere repository for hemorrhoid and hangnail, and on Christmas there will be backache and baldness for me, cellulite and a lump in the breast for her. But for Carolyn and me all small impossibilities vanished. And we lived happily ever after.

You might have mentioned one small impossibility, Evan. I know you don't like to talk about these things; but it's our problem, really, not yours. I think you should have talked about our little sexual peculiarity.

Chapter 15 *State of the Union*

Carolyn has the habit of making houses. She shreds matches, cross-hatches them. She doesn't smoke, but she keeps boxes of matchbooks on her desk, and when her writing gives her problems she's apt to cap her silver fountain pen, push her papers to one side, and build. Her constructions are elaborate but modern: often the match houses are cantilevered, with wings that ascend from stolid squares and march imperturbably into the air like tiny Towers of Babel. Before I left for work this morning I poked my head into her room. Her body was already bent over her match house; her hands shook with the difficulty of fashioning such a fragile thing. I'm not sure what to call this work, but I suspect it's as much art as Carolyn's writing itself.

Before I painted, I pictured the process of making art as dreamy and relaxing, something akin to stroking yourself with a feather. Wrong. It's nerve-racking, enervating. I'm not even sure why I do it. It feels good when you stop, of course; it's a wonderful thing to *have done*, like a sauna or a run. I'm in the habit of doing it; but it's more than habit.

I'm reminded of Carolyn's relations with her toothpaste tube. I try to roll my tube the way she does hers. I'm a little sloppier, leave the cap off from time to time; but what really sets Carolyn apart is her attitude toward the tube: her seriousness, her exacting attention, and the mysterious pleasure she derives. Every morning Carolyn faces herself grimly in the mirror and begins work on the face she sees. She scrubs this, flosses that, brushes there. She applies healthful substances to various sectors of her face. She splashes, shivers, none of this is fun. At last she turns to the teeth, and her satisfaction is evident as she examines this perfectly rolled toothpaste. She measures change with dents on the tube: time marches on, and apparently. Unlike most changes that time inflicts on us, the slow metamorphosis of the toothpaste tube (from something to nothing) can be done well. For Carolyn, it is a way of visualizing time: but it is a chance to enjoy the process as well. For this I have frank admiration.

You could probably find something to admire in my particular fashion of nose-blowing. You must be enchanted by my method of opening tunafish cans.

I am talking, I suppose, more about Carolyn's writing, and not so much about that toothpaste tube. I am this woman's typist, and even, at times, her copy editor: I have watched her work for fourteen years. She began with short pieces, little spangled snatches of imagery. They could all have been titled A Sensitive Girl Looks at the World; they were cloistered *naifs* frocked with adolescent feeling. At Barnard, Carolyn wrote only when blessed by simple inspiration, like a child in a deserted playground. The change was not instantaneous, but during her years as a Manhattan Gal Friday Carolyn became more and more regular in her habits. She would come home, put down her bag, quickly remove all traces of her daily degradation in the office; then sit at her spacious, empty desk for two hours. She might squirm in her chair, or she might let her head drop onto her work (pressing paper to forehead, as if trying to make a more direct communication, without the hindrance of arm or pen), but she sat there. When she rose, she did so unsteadily, waking to a world she did not quite recognize.

Now, of course, she writes every day. She merely works until she's done what she must do.

I remember the first time I considered that Carolyn might be an artist. When we first went to Oregon, we took the train across Canada, Canadian Pacific, and somewhere near where the mountains began—they began proudly, abruptly, in stark black and white in the dim evening—a man in our coach car began to die. He was a distance away from us, and all we saw was a knot of people clustered in the corridor. It was a heart attack, we heard. There was no doctor aboard. He went quickly, we heard. I said, "Sad," and Carolyn said, "Yes. Yes, very sad," but I had no idea that her sympathies were engaged, her imagination fired, as she sat quietly turning the thin pages of a Heinrich Böll novel. A month later, Carolyn wordlessly handed her typist a short story, "Better Off Than You Are." In it two old women are traveling on a train. The old man in the seat across from them has a heart attack; he suffers, he dies; the two old women gallantly and ridiculously carry on with their conversation about cheesecake and canning fruit, about cold weather and young grandchildren. They are old, they are intimate with death; watching the old man die, they conduct an organ recital, discussing the condition of each one they own. All but the heart. At the edge of this absurdly trivial discussion, one hears the overtones of fear, pity, resignation. Meanwhile, the train is rushing toward the station where we must all get out.

It was a good story. The faded, sagging seats, the landscape racing by the window, the casual litter in the corridor, were all real, clearly real. But this was easy; this was sheer memory. There was more: the face of the dying man, the way the women adjusted the plaid blankets on their laps as the dying man emitted a soft rattle, the recipe for cheesecake. These were real too. But where did they come from? Even the elderly ladies were invented, as far as I know cut from whole cloth. Except in the most general sense, the story was not about Carolyn at all. The story sounded lived; but it did not sound like Carolyn—it was the work of some anonymous artist, someone I did not know.

As I typed the story it seemed to me that Carolyn had spent ten years fashioning an airplane in her basement; now she could fly. She had ventured from the safe and sound citadel of self; she had learned how to see with other eyes; she had given her characters her sympathy, her kindness, and then let them go. And they too could fly.

This is a ridiculous way to talk about my writing. I thank you for all your kind effusions, Vandy; but I write quietly, and sometimes I think the only thing I've learned is how to be quiet. Or is this what you mean?

When I came home this afternoon Carolyn's matchhouse was gone. A layer of soft gray matches graced the bottom of her woven wastepaper basket. Her pen was capped again, but underneath its securing weight lay four neatly scripted pages of prose in Carolyn's curious but flowing hand (the tails of her letters run the wrong way). This can be considered a typical day for her.

I teach high school English for a living, at Van Buren High in Southeast Portland, Oregon. This is too bad. Oh, I don't say that no one should teach school. But I find it curious that it should be me. I have never been comfortable speaking in front of groups. When I first started teaching I was extremely anxious; I dreaded each class. I was told, and I believed it, that after a while I would "find my stride" and relax in class. I'm sure this has proven true for a number of teachers, perhaps most, people who somehow manage to become inured to insult, injury, loathing. It has not been the case for me. I have now been teaching for ten years, and I still dread each class.

Students. I dread students. I never liked children. (Can you call people of high school age children? If you watch them long enough, yes.) But recently a new emotion has held sway within me. This is not mere, petty dislike; it is fear. The students haven't changed, unfortunately, but their conduct has. The secret is out. These people realize at last what little power I have over them. I'm not talking about physical power; it's not as if they were ever intimidated by the threat of me. What has suddenly occurred to them is how little I matter to them. If I am speaking at the front of the classroom, talking about "Young Goodman Brown," what reason can I possibly offer them to leave silent their new, handsome, suitcaselike cassette players? I threaten to send them to the dean's office; for a little diversion, they go willingly to the dean's office. They would rather go to the dean's office than listen to their cassette players. It is more interesting at the dean's office; the dean is an amusing man; they like to make small jokes about his bald spot; they enjoy watching the colors of his face become progressively brighter and deeper.

My students have recognized at last the uselessness of school. In the age of pocket calculators and television sitcoms, boys and girls have learned all they need to know for adult life by the time they are eight years old. How do you turn the key in the ignition? How do you adjust the fine tuning on the TV? These are necessary skills, perhaps the only necessary skills. The power I once held over my students was the implication, even the belief, that they had something to learn—and that I, of all people, could teach it to them. This curious fantasy has long since vanished. What is left is social convention: till a certain age, you go to school. What you are to do at school is, of course, an open question.

Last week four students of mine, a pair of female twins and two male clones, wedged themselves into a single booth in the girls' room. When discovered, and I can't imagine how they were caught, two of them were upside down, none of them were clothed, and all of them (somehow. This is truly delicate geometry.) were smoking dope. This activity was their inspired alternative to reading "Young Goodman Brown." How can they be blamed? They have conceived of the unusual; these twins and clones are gifted and talented, unquestionably. I am the one who has something to learn—for I do not understand how such an entanglement can be effected in such a space, and with such ease, such grace. Twins and clones make the improbable look easy. How are such godlike acrobatics accomplished? I wonder. But I am afraid to ask. Instead I stand doggedly at the front of the room, hoping that my students will ignore me, as I ignore them. They are not a bad bunch. Most seem willing to forgive me my trespasses against silence. There is the odd showoff who takes aim at easy prey to enhance her standing with the others. But the others are usually not so easily impressed. Target practice is over soon enough.

Teaching is, somehow, both terrifying and boring. But there is one advantage to teaching. It is this: as I sit beside my painting, dabbing it, sometimes pointlessly I think, with wobbling hand, the thought runs through my head, and it keeps running through my head, endless as a marathoner's daily lapse,

Delete the e.

the thought occurs to me over and over, ever with greater and greater joy: I am not teaching. Painting is a joy to me, because it is not teaching. Doing the dishes is a joy to me, because it is not teaching. Teaching, like Dante's Hell, provides blessed contrast. It gathers together and localizes my *Angst,* a service similar to that provided by my protean credit card. While I teach school, there is really only one bill to pay. Pity it's such a big one.

It is afternoon when I return home, and raining. I am not speaking solely of today, but of always. The bathroom has the only good light in our house. I set up my easel by the generous window. I begin work on a still life: fruit, tub, sink, or toilet—the usual. And I try with all my heart to forget the schoolday. There. Done.

This afternoon I sat very happily at my painting for a long while. The light changed, but I was almost giddy with pleasure. I wanted to somehow share this pleasure with Carolyn.

I knocked on her door. She said "Yup" instead of "Come in," which meant she was working and would rather be left alone. I went in anyway.

"What's today's project?" I asked. "Are you doing Rice Cook or Tillie Olsen?"

"Tillie."

"How's Tillie?"

"Not good. She has a lot of ironing to do."

"Poor Tillie."

"Poor me. I'm trying to find something to write about, and Tillie's busy bringing up the kids. Who wants to read about diapers?"

"Everybody," I said. "All most people want out of a biography are a few disgusting scatological details."

"That may be true," Carolyn said. "But it isn't what I want to write about. Tillie's life has been so *typical* it's painful."

"So why don't you write about Virginia Woolf instead?"

"She's been done," Carolyn said flatly. "Besides, this is exactly why Tillie is important. She's had the kind of life that women have always been forced to live. Most potentially great women writers never had the time or education to write even one line."

"Unh-hunh," I said. I'd heard this particular speech before. I think Carolyn only said it then for her own benefit, to help her get through Tillie's diapers.

I put my arm tentatively on her shoulder. "How's *our* potential diaper-dirtier doing today?" I asked.

"In the afternoons I feel almost human," Carolyn replied. Then she looked at my hand on her shoulder.

Carolyn has this peculiarity: with her the onlooker often senses a clear separation between those bookends, the world in which she acts and the one in her mind. On the one hand, she is having a normal, easy conversation about Tillie Olsen, about diapers, about morning sickness; on the other, she is regarding my hand—regarding it with such open curiosity and puzzlement that you'd think she's never seen such a thing before, and its presence on her shoulder has caused her silent shock. We all have two such worlds. With Carolyn they are both apparent, and apparently unconnected. In conversations with Carolyn there is often this other, unstated level—something we're not quite talking about, perhaps because we're afraid to, since we never do, never.

I don't understand what you're talking about.

She stared icily at my hand on her shoulder. I removed it, and became morose.

Carolyn now looked at, and probably through, my face. "How are *you?*" she asked.

"I—am fine," I replied, having considered a different response, composed it, and rejected it midway.

"How's your toilet coming along, Vandypie?" she asked, speaking about my painting. We never talk about school. This is an unwritten rule, which I have stated plainly, many times over.

"The toilet is awfully white," I said. "There's nothing in the world as white as white paint. The toilet doesn't look as if you could actually sit on it. It is definitely a *painted* toilet." Then, suddenly—and uncharacteristically, I think—I added, "I'm never going to be a great painter, Carolyn." I was still thinking about the look she gave my hand; I've lived with this woman for fourteen years, I was thinking, and she can still look at my hand as if it belonged to a stranger.

"People don't want to sit on paintings," Carolyn said solicitously. "They just want them to be good paintings."

"I'll never be a great painter," I repeated stubbornly, though that was something we'd both known for a long while.

She reached out for the same hand she'd just stared off her shoulder. I think that's probably why I mentioned the business about greatness: to make her take back the look she'd given my hand. I now gave her the hand with some alacrity—although I had the fleeting feeling that it was true: this *wasn't* my hand.

She smiled briefly. "That's all right," she said, and I realized that she'd taken my hand not in reassurance but apology. Now she turned away quickly and looked at the opposite wall. I looked over there too: the clock's hands: twenty after six. Carolyn frowned, and turned back to me. "Give me ten good reasons why you want to be a great painter, Evan," she said.

"I *don't* want to be great, I don't think."

"I know," Carolyn said, and patted my hand like a doctor. "That's why you never will be," she added. Terminal.

I might have been irritated, but she was patting my hand very tenderly; and she was, after all, quite right.

"Why do you want to be a great writer?" I asked. I'd never asked her that before. I'd never been curious about it before.

Now she was staring at the clock. I imagine that she was still thinking about twenty after six, but I can't know. She answered my question, still scrutinizing the clock, as though it had been the clock that had asked.

"Oh, I don't know," she said. "I think I just like it when it comes out."

"It comes out . . . ?" I said, feeling stupid.

"The words," Carolyn said. "The words come out right."

"That's nice," I said, fairly idiotically.

"More than nice. When it happens, it's wonderful. You can live on the feeling for weeks at a time. And sometimes you have to."

I started to leave then, but as I reached the door Carolyn said one thing more. "I'm glad I don't ever have to lie to you, Vandy," she said. "I love you for that."

I did not have to reply; at the best times one never has to speak. I

74 / DELICATE GEOMETRY

smiled at her, and went on downstairs to look for Rice. Rice wasn't hard to find; he never is. He wasn't at his usual table in the kitchen, but he was at his alternate location, in the living room, sitting sideways in an armchair that he drags in front of the fire. His hoppy dog Lancelot lay beneath the chair; a portion of him protruded. Rice was reading a paperback, holding it with one hand, bending the binding back. The fire was a decorative, April fire, quiet and small, a red hole between two logs. A tin pot was perched on the logs, and I heard rustling in the pot.

"What've you got there?" I asked.

"Popcorn. You can't hear it?"

"Popcorn roasting on an open fire?"

"Not roastin," Rice said. "Just cookin." He let the book fall, slapping the floor. "Almost done, too. Your kids have twelve kinds of sex during recess today, buddy?" Rice hunched over, picked up two hotpads, shook the pot. Faint fireworks from within. He dropped hotpads, swept up book again.

"What are you reading?"

"Goddamn book." He wrinkled his nose. "Novel."

"Well, is it good?"

"Nope. Unh-unh."

"What's wrong with it?"

"You don't know who to root for," Rice said. "You'd probably like it, buddy."

Carolyn comes down for the popcorn. Popcorn is a well-known group activity here. Rice makes it. He's an excellent chef; he never burns a kernel, and leaves very few of them unpopped. He eats the unpopped ones anyway. He calls them Old Maids. Rice dusts his portion with a brownish-yellow coat of brewer's yeast. He says he performs this atrocity to improve the taste, a story I find patently unbelievable. Carolyn, meantime, squanders butter and salt all over hers; and I—I have mine plain, thank you.

Plain popcorn, one kernel at a time. I don't know how you could be summarized any better than that.

"Well, Vandy," Carolyn begins, her hands full of popcorn, and greasy, "you should see the hatchet job I'm doing on Rice." She gives Rice's curls a pat. "Yellow journalism," she adds. "How's your writing going?"

"I think I can stop now," I say.
"Finished?"
"Close enough."

We are sitting, then, beside the low fire, all in a row, all eating popcorn, waiting for the film to begin. Or perhaps we are posing, the three of us, for our portrait. Group Portrait with Popcorn. With love.

PART II

RICE

BY CAROLYN

Author's Note

Evan, my long-term lover, sits in the room across the stairwell from me and composes on the typewriter; the noise of his work drifts under my door, more like a distant thumping than a clattering; the words come to him, I hear, rather fluently. It is a dull, wintry day in April, and Evan has begun writing the story of my life.

I too have a story to tell. It is not my own, though it joins onto my own; it is about someone very different—someone close to me, yet impenetrably different. He is downstairs now, sitting at our tiny kitchen table drinking. I can all but feel him there. I can even notice (with amusement, pity, admiration) the small touches on the picture he presents: his cramped knees lift the table up off two of its legs; his thick fingers vainly try to peel the label off his bottle; he pets his poor dog on the head, and Lancelot's leg feverishly scratches at the air. This mountainous man takes a delicate sip, the alcohol burns down him, and I can feel that too. For he and I have entered into that vast confusion of the senses, love. And this is the story of my lover, my second lover, Rice Cook.

Here is where his story ends—in this house, with his enormous body curled around the tiny table. But to begin, we must go to quite another place. We must hear Carolinian voices, slap Carolinian mosquitoes, analyze the smile on the faces of Carolinian alligators.

This, then, is how it must have been for Rice.

SECTION ONE

One

Marge Murry, of Charleston, South Carolina, met Eugene Cook, of Yauhannah, South Carolina, at a potluck dinner in 1947. Eugene's contribution to the dinner was a bottle of Jim Beam bourbon. This mundane prop has been much celebrated in Cook family lore. Eugene mishandled several melon balls, like imps they hopped from spoon to table, from open mouth to floor; Marge's consequent giggle was girlish, charming, endearing; throughout the course of this mythic evening, Eugene seemed possessed of an unlikely sociability, Marge of an uncharacteristic boldness, the melon balls of a spirited independence— and all of this was attributed to the extra guest, the square-cut Mr. Beam.

Destiny thus takes the form of a whisky bottle in the Cook family. Once uncorked, Pandora's spirits fly from it; there is no stopping, no reversing of single-minded Time. The bottle is opened as the human heart opens in love: it can never be properly closed again.

Eventually, three boys were born to Marge and Eugene: Rice; then Boston, called Bo; and later, Anthony. The choice of Rice's name was an act of thanksgiving. The week his first son was born, Eugene placed a large bet on an impossible underdog; when Rice University promptly managed an unlikely football victory over a powerful Texas rival, Eugene's first son was gratefully named Rice U. Cook.

Across the long lawn from the house in Yauhannah the PeeDee River, wide and slow, slid through reedy marshes; you found herons there, and alligators, and sometimes cottonmouths as long and thick as your arm. A chain of loblolly pines trailed down the long driveway, edging the backside field; here and there a live-oak tree, impossibly old and looking even older, extended gnarled limbs—but held on to its leaves, always. At the bottom of the field a swamp simmered, complete with cypress trees dripping Spanish moss, their cypress "knees" like gray bumps on the dark, rank swampwater. There were clouds of droning mosquitoes; red-shouldered hawks crying overhead, like cats mewing; and strange noises, or else silence. You dabbled your foot in warm water; imagined alligators; pulled it out, quick.

Camellias, azaleas, and laurel ringed the screen porch. Forsythia bushes surrounded the other end of the house. Two small boys were on their knees among them; bees hovered above, bathing in the spring sea of flowers. The boys clipped a tunnel through the bushes with garden shears: the secret passage, leading to the secret place. You could stand up in there, if you were lucky enough to be a child. The clusters of forsythia blotted out sunshine and rain both: the secret place was a separate world, with its own weather and its own rules.

When you drove up to the house at night, you approached along a flat tarred road. For a while the car's headlights made twin pools in featureless blackness; the car turned, and its beams swept along an old, fallen stone wall, then captured under their bright, bare gaze the white-painted mailbox, labeled with unstudied black block letters: COOK/MURRY. The car pivoted onto dirt, small stones popped under tires, and then you saw something suddenly blaze back at you: an orange reflector, placed there for who knows what reason who knows when, each plastic facet glowing, looking like the huge, sightless, compound eye of a hideous insect—a creature that had waited long hours for you to fall into its trap. But sometimes you were not the only one who was surprised: the headlights swept on, and the beams fell on the upturned faces of white-tail deer, staring, frozen, with shining moist eyes and quivering black noses. The car pulled to a noisy stop. Its occupants stared at the deer, and the deer at the headlights. Finally the deer turned and bolted on long spindly legs, white flags bouncing behind—or else casually, almost proudly, they melted into the forest.

Later it was the reflector that Rice remembered best, glowing like a cabalistic eye. It marked the entrance to the swamp: to the kingdom of terror: perhaps even to Hell. In the back of the car Rice shivered with a pleasurable dread.

Eventually the reflector fell over in the field. No one bothered to right it. Years later Rice found it again, wrapped in greedy weeds; he freed it, stored it in a corner of the shed. He still has it. Somewhere, Rice still has everything from his childhood.

Life was unspoiled; life was benign, easy, and endless; life was magic. People often think of the world they were born into as the original one, the true and right world. But Rice is right about his. He can point at a pink-ribboned sunset over a statuelike egret; at a wide river full of bright fish and slow as time itself; at secret passages among the bushes, staring deer, smiling alligators.

The house was old, wooden, a pale and peeling white. It was dark inside, but this is what you could see: plump furniture standing stiffly on round legs, and one brocaded rocker made by a Cook great-great-grandmother; sayings in needlepoint framed on the wall; glass cabinets housing thin china rimmed with gold, and chubby little ceramic figures, huge-headed, wide-eyed, and smiling. Mirrors and clocks were everywhere. You could stand in the living room and see yourself in five places, and see yourself seeing yourself in two. You could hear four different rhythms of time, variations on the theme of tick and tock—with no discernible space between one clock's tick and another's tock, no time when there was no time sounding.

Upstairs, under the eaves, there were boxes of old books. Rice liked books. He stacked them up to make forts. Books were solid; old; smelled of must and age; sometimes they had pictures. Marge read the boys a story each night, after wiping behind their ears with a warm washrag. She read them stories about frogs with waistcoats; about boys who were allowed to fight in the Civil War; and once a story where children ate orange sherbet on a train, sherbet that was so hard the children had to whack it with a spoon before they could eat it. Bo and Rice giggled till their stomachs hurt, though they'd never eaten anything on a train. It was something to do with that word: *whack*.

Rice and Bo lived upstairs, in the same room, their beds almost touching, foot to foot. One Christmas Eugene bought them a cheap record player, which sat between the beds; on occasion they were permitted to play one of their two records. One was "Davy Crockett"; the other a Harry Belafonte record, now nameless. The boys talked, sometimes, late; their father would have to come up, scold, feign gruffness. When Rice was finally ready, he would nestle in the overhanging tuck of the bed, beneath the blankets but beside the bed; there he'd rub his feets in circles against the sheets, till both feet and sheets were like toast; and then, hanging warm and cozy, it was his infinite pleasure to drift, and to dream.

Two

Rice was sitting on the floor in his room listening to "Davy Crockett" when his mother called up to him. He was imagining he'd just shot the coonskin tail off of Davy's hat, and now they (Davy and he) were laughing about it, and being pals. Rice took the record off and ran downstairs.

Marge said she'd just seen Donny Duckworth. She told Rice to put some shoes on, it wasn't summer.

"Did he stop?" Rice asked.

Marge put her hands on her hips. "Why would I be asking you to put shoes on?" she said. Rice just shrugged.

"Come on," she said, gently.

She watched him tie his shoes, hunched over them, grim. He does that the way I used to do math: sure it'll come out wrong in the end. She checked the muddle of laces. Well, close enough, she thought. For Rice always had trouble mastering simple acts. "That's just fine!" she said, brightly, gaily.

Donny Duckworth had whipped something in their box, slammed it shut. It couldn't be anything good, of course; Donny only delivered bills. But what else was there? Marge asked herself as she held the screen door for Ricey; what was it she was always waiting for?

"I don't think Lucas is coming today," Rice said.

"Why not, honey?"

"I think he's busy. I think he's chasing moles."

"We'll just have to do without him," Marge said. "You think us two can do without that cat all the way to the mailbox?"

"Unh-hunh," Rice said, seriously.

They started along the corridor of loblolly pines. Rice was counting his steps, avoiding cracks, keeping an eye out for quartz chips, thinking about the fly. Marge walked slowly beside him, trying to talk herself out of her happiness, her hope. What am I always waiting for? she wondered again. She was not an ordinary person. She didn't want an ordinary life; she wanted to be launched; launched into space. Like that Sputnik, she thought—for if they could send that out into space, with its poor dogs, they could accomplish anything. Yes. The human race could accomplish anything.

But that had been the Russians, of course. The Russians weren't about to launch her, Marge Cook of Yauhannah.

They had reached the bend in the driveway. A lacy-winged fly buzzed her. "There he is!" said Rice. "The same guy!"

"It can't always be the same one, Ricey," Marge said irritably. Her hand brushed vaguely at the circling fly.

"It is, though," Rice said. "It is." Rice turned about, following the fly's laps around his mother's head. "He's always right exactly here, right?" Rice said.

"That doesn't mean anything."

"You've never swatted him, right?"

"No. But surely by now—"

"I haven't either. And we've never seen *two* of em here, right, Ma?" said Rice, becoming excited.

"Do you know how long flies live?" Marge asked him.

"How long?"

How long *do* flies live? she thought. "Well, I don't know exactly," she said. "But if that fly is just one fella, then I think he's been around a whole lot longer than I think flies get to be around for."

"He's real big," Rice pointed out.

He's not convinced, Marge thought. Well, let him. What do I know about flies, anyway? Maybe they just live on, on and on until somebody swats them. But I bet not. I bet they die after Christmas, like—what was it that died? Bees?

They turned the corner to the mailbox. Seeing it, Marge felt hopeful again; she burst into song. "Meet me in Saint Looey, Looey," she sang, in her high, erratic voice.

Rice screwed up his face. "What's Saint Looey-Looey?" he asked.

"Saint Looey? That's a city. And Looey is the name of a man."

He looked at her as if she were crazy. "But *who?*" he asked.

Looey, Marge thought. She tried it on for size. Did she actually want to meet Looey in Saint Looey? An unknown, unspeakable Looey? She couldn't imagine one. She tried. Looey wore spats and a big felt hat; he danced, very slick; but his face was in shadow. He disappeared regularly at midnight.

"Looey's nobody, honey," Marge told Rice. "It's just a song. They wrote that because it sounds funny: the Looey and the Saint Looey."

"It sure *does,*" Rice said, and abruptly bent again to his shoelaces. He crossed the laces; looped one behind, under and up; pulled at both ends. So far, so good. Now he made a big loop, pinched it between thumb and first finger—then what do you do, kind of stick it somewhere? Rice sat there, holding the loop with his index finger and his clumsy thumb. He gave it a suspicious look; a solemn look; then he despaired. His shoelaces hated him. They followed him around, like Bo.

Marge stood in front of the mailbox; waiting, delaying her daily defeat.

"Ready, Ricey?"

"Yup. Unh-hunh." Rice directed a bitter glance toward his dangling laces, then stuffed them quietly into his shoes.

She opened the mailbox with a flourish, scanned the mail eagerly, and then fell silent.

"Anything for me?" Rice asked, without hope. He always came down here; you'd think that if you came down here every day, once in a while you'd get something. But no. Unh-unh.

"Looks like the world dudden have much to say to either of us today, punkin." Marge smiled—a thin, wan smile that faded quickly. "Guess it's back to the bright lights of Yauhannah for you and me."

Rice saw the downturn on her small mouth as she moved slowly by him. She was peeved. Was that on account of him—on account of his shoelaces?

"Hey, Ma?"

"What, punkin?"

Rice had started talking just to talk: to clear the air: to make it so she wasn't angry at him any more, on account of his shoelaces. Now he didn't know what to say.

He took a hop; landed on one foot. "You're pregnant again, right?" he said.

"That's right, Ricey." We've had this conversation before, she thought; Ricey likes to repeat conversations.

But Rice said something different this time. "Are you glad?" he asked.

She stopped walking. "Am I *what,* punkin?"

"Are you glad? Being pregnant and all?"

He wants me to say that I am; I should say I am. But something took hold of Marge. She cleared her throat and spoke clearly. "It dudden really matter to me, Ricey," she said, watching him.

"Oh," Rice said. He fell into step beside her.

It dudden matter to him either, she thought, and for a second

Marge was shocked. Then she thought, I guess that's just as well. They started back up the hill.

No, it dudden matter. It dudden matter *what* happens. Marge decided that; and then suddenly she felt very full, as if she were a balloon that someone had puffed up; not with air, with something else. She didn't know exactly what it was, and after a moment the feeling passed. It had been something important—something good, she thought. For just that second she'd been more alive. She'd become more alive, just by saying, It dudden matter, to herself.

Peculiar, Marge thought, the times in your life that can mean something to you. Here, for example: it was a Saturday; it was noon; they'd have tunafish sandwiches; then Bo would refuse to take his nap; later Eugene would come home, have a beer, put his feet up, put his arm around her; they'd have some supper, God knows what; there wouldn't be any bad news slamming into her ear on the telephone; no new world crisis, probably; nothing special—but this was an important day. It was special to Marge; because we live, she thought, by ourselves. We live all by ourselves; because life is lived in the mind. It isn't even what *happens* at all, Marge thought again, as they reached the bend, and Rice yelled, "It's *him,* Ma!" and she put her hand up to ward it away, not even looking at the fly.

Carrie,

    I don't know what all you want me to write down. I told you that already, and you said, "That's fine, Sweets. Whatever you do will be exactly right." Hell it will.

    I was just watching you write. I got home from Angela's Vault about a half hour ago and I've been sitting at my kitchen table watching. It's getting cool, but you're out there lying on that old blanket with your straps down. You're not tanning, Carrie. You're just getting sort of generally pink.

    But it doesn't look bad. I've been thinking about how it looks like your whole body's been rubbed, thinking about all the blood running around under your skin, about the way you're concentrating so hard you don't even brush away the flies. The flies are loving you out there with your back naked and your cut-offs, and so do I. I know it's me you're writing about. Lying there on your old soft blanket writing about me. I just want to tell you how glad I am about that. When I got home Lance wanted to go out real bad, he's been hopping all over the place and ducking his head up and down, but I've just been sitting at my table watching you lie there, with little pieces of grass all stuck to your ass.

    I guess all I mean is that I could watch you lying there for quite the while. I like those cut-offs.

    Sure is weird reading the stuff you write about me. I guess you're allowed to make up the things people are thinking, but if you would've asked me I would've told you what I was actually thinking. I doubt my mother thinks the kind of things you say she thinks, but I don't really know. I guess it makes me uncomfortable when you say what people think, because you don't really know either. So it's like you're talking about yourself instead of them.

    That's all I can think of to say. I'm going to Laurelhurst with Lance and I'll stop at Safeway's on the way home. Snapper okay with you? It's on sale.

                                R.

PS. I don't know where you got the part about shoelaces. I guess I figured out how to tie my shoes same time as everybody else. Then in Cub Scouts I learned about twelve knots. I don't know why you'd want to make up stuff like that.

Three

For Rice, summer smelled like his grandfather.

Even in summer Pup wore an undershirt in bed, the old-fashioned kind without shoulders. His underpants were saggy baggy ones, with little beginnings of legs. His socks were long, dark, and thin—silk, Rice thought. Pup shaved with a shaving brush and a bowl of soap, using an old razor with no electricity in it; he was thin, but had a nice round potbelly that you could watch jiggle while he dressed. Pup, in short, was great entertainment. He wore bow ties. He came out from Charleston for the summers, put on his big straw hat, and sat out beside his easel, painting paintings and placidly waving an impossibly skinny brush at the bluebottle flies.

Rice and Bo had finished lining the driveway with tiny American flags, for Pup's return from England; now they were standing beside the live-oak tree, waiting, their hands in their pockets and their bare toes tracing aimless circles in the dirt.

Here they came now; finally. Their old car, Putsy, turned in at the bottom of the driveway and puttered up the rise through the corridor of loblollies. The flags are all limp, Rice thought. Soon as they get here, the breeze goes. It was always that way.

Putsy pulled up, coughed, fell silent. Bo went running up. Rice walked behind. "You in there, Pup?" Bo shouted at the car.

"I'm not too damn sure, Bo," Pup answered, clambering out.

Pup stretched, pulling his arms as wide as he could; he looked thin. He was always thin, though, if you took a good look. He looked old, too. Well, he *was* old: his skin was soft and loose; he smelled like the boxes stored under the eaves.

Bo stood proudly under Pup's wing; Pup held the other arm out for Rice. Rice broke into a run, and then stopped, just short. "How was your trip?" Rice asked, formal.

Pup shook his head. "Get over here, Ricey. I haven't seen you in an eternity and a half." Rice took the last steps; immediately Pup began to ruffle up his hair. "I missed you damn kids," Pup said. "Haven't had a good tickle in six weeks."

Bo graciously pulled up his shirt, offering his ribs. But Pup said, "Not just now, Boston."

Bo put down his shirt. "Did you see any redcoats?" he asked.

"Redcoats? I guess I saw a few. They're pretty well camouflaged, though."

"How do they do that?" Rice asked.

Pup glanced around, taking the place in; a gust of wind, as if in response, puffed the trees. He seemed to hear Rice's question several seconds after it had been asked. "Do what?" Pup said pleasantly.

"How do they camouflage their red coats?"

"Well, how do you think?"

"They shoot em!" Bo tried, enthusiastically.

"No. They don't shoot em. They like em, in fact. You don't shoot something you like, Bo." Now Pup started to tickle Bo; Bo squealed in delight; but after a moment Pup stopped. "What do *you* think, Ricey?"

Rice had been thinking about it. "They could put em against a red wall," he said.

"That's right, they could. That's logical. But you think they could find a big enough wall for all those redcoats?"

Rice was thinking: how would he do it, if he was the general? Finally he said: "They could make *everybody* wear red coats."

Pup smiled. "That would work, all right. Except that it's a free country. Like ours. You can't tell everybody what to wear."

Bo yanked excitedly on Pup's arm. "Make everybody wear red coats!" he shouted.

"That's not such a damn bad idea," Pup said, nodding solemnly.

I already *said* that, Rice thought. Then he went back to thinking about the question. He said, "If it's a free country, how come they can tell the soldiers to wear red coats?"

Pup started to rub Rice's neck. He said, "The red coats are part of their job. Soldiers have to wear uniforms."

Rice accepted this. He put his hands on his hips. "Maybe," he said, "they should try changing the color of the uniforms."

"Well, that's ex*act*ly what they did!" Pup crowed. Suddenly Rice felt Pup's lean old hands pulling at his waist, lifting him up, swinging him into the air. Rice's legs flew out behind him, and his arms stretched out toward Pup, who wheeled, backpedaling. Rice looked down. He saw isolated elements of his world whirling below him: the smooth stretch of lawn; the dirt driveway speckled with smooth egg-like stones; a patch of soft green, the loblollies; Pup's shiny black shoes, performing, it seemed, a tap dance of circles; the house behind, a low blur of white; and Bo—who jumped up and down, arms held up, shouting, "Me next, Pup! Me next!"

Pup was painting the backside field—the hay had been mowed, and the mowed hay lay flat, like parted hair—when Joe Griswold drove up with the bright red baler behind the tractor. Bo and Rice saw Joe from the porch, and took off. "Don't you kids get in his way," Marge shouted after them, but they were gone, following the baler all the way around the backside field, laughing at every bale as it popped up and dropped off, so neat and square and all tied up. They climbed up on this bale; they turned this one on its end. Later they made a hay fort and crawled around inside, the sweet smell of hay close in the darkness. The next day Joe came back, loaded the bales onto the flatbed truck, then drove away, leaving the field a bare expanse of rough stubble that punctured Rice's feet.

But the painting doesn't have the stubble; it has hay like flat yellow hair lying in the foreground, and a black man seated on a tractor, leaving a trail of bales behind him. Two boys are off to the left: one has his arms up, waving wildly; the other is climbing a bale. In the distance, beside the house, three oak trees, with thick snakes for limbs, provide a straw-hatted man sitting beside his easel with shade from the white sun blazing above.

The painting hangs, slightly skewed, over Rice's dresser in our Portland house.

Four

It sounded like rain. Storm clouds had been gathering all day, coming from the south; they were ominously dark, fat, and full. The clouds massed in the south, and together they came across the sky, filling it like black smoke from a bonfire.

You can practically smell thunder, Rice thought.

He sat on the porch with Eugene and Bo and the baby, waiting for dinner. It took a long while. Finally Marge brought out chicken pot pies, frozen ones. Rice liked pot pies. He flipped his pie over with knife and fork—it was hot—and tapped around the circle of foil with the knife; the pie flopped out, whole. Good. That was what he wanted. Then he noticed the bottom of the pie crust: burned. Burned again. She burns everything, Rice thought. And she doesn't even care.

He looked at his mother critically. She wore an apron, and her hands anxiously kneaded its corner. She wasn't thinking about the pies. She was occupied, as she often was, in staring out toward the river; at the lawn; at the sky.

The baby, Anthony, began to fuss in his highchair. "I just saw one," Marge said. "The first drop." She was excited about the *rain,* Rice thought.

"Hey," said Bo. "My pie is all black on the bottom again."

"Oh, is it?" Marge answered, her voice soft and high. "I'm sorry, honey."

"You can't taste the black, kid," Eugene told Bo. "Just go ahead and eat your supper."

You could taste the black, of course. You always could. Bo made a drastic face; began to push the pie's shattered remnants from side to side with his fork, damning them with attention.

Marge finally took the baby in her arms; she jiggled it up and down; she cooed at it. "Is it gonna thunder up there, honey? Is it gonna light up the sky, An-tho-ny?"

She's always looking out there, Rice said to himself. She's always looking up in the sky.

"Is there more supper?" Bo asked.

Eugene glanced at Marge too. "Maybe a vegetable?" he asked. "Can a corn?"

"I think I got sumpin," Marge said. She jiggled the baby again and put him back in the highchair. But *he's still fussing,* Rice thought. Anthony burst into wild tears, waved his stubby arms.

"You wanna pick him up, Ricey?" his mother called out as she disappeared into the house.

"I'm *eating,*" Rice said to the spot where his mother had just been. He noticed that he was listening to the distant growl of thunder as he spoke; he, too, was listening to the thunder.

"*Every*body's eating, kid," Eugene said, disgusted; he rose. "Or trying to, anyway." He lifted the baby out of the chair; Anthony's little head wavered on his shoulders like a bobble-head doll's.

Marge came back from the kitchen with a big white bowl and a cellophane bag. She ripped open the bag and emptied its contents into the bowl.

"*Cheetos?*" Eugene said, as though he'd just been told that Cheetos were the cure for cancer.

Bo got over his surprise the quickest. "Yay! Cheetos for supper!" he cried, and scooped orange puffs with both palms.

Eugene, still holding Anthony, put his free hand toward the Cheetos and gingerly secured one, as if expecting to be bitten. A stroke of lightning noiselessly split the sky to the south.

"When's all that rain gonna come down, you think?" Marge said, to no one in particular.

"Anybody seen Lucas?" Rice asked.

"You don't have to worry about Lucas," Eugene said. "That cat can take better care of himself than you can."

"Still," Rice started; he didn't finish.

Lucas was seven now, Rice eleven: Rice hadn't been much more than a baby when he found the cat. It was one of those cats that appear at the front door as if they already know whose they are. The kitty circled Rice's feet; rubbed against his legs; purred; seemed to like it when Rice held him up by the tail. That was how Rice had held it when he showed his mother. Lucas dangled uncomplainingly, his paws drifting in the air.

"Put it back outside," Marge had said, calmly. "Let it go on home."

"It dudden have a home," Rice said.

"Put it outside," his mother replied. "It'll go home when it gets hungry."

Lucas never got hungry. He hung around and practiced joyful, expert genocide on the local field mouse and mole populations. He purred whenever Rice came within three feet. Lucas never graced a lap other than Rice's small one. He wasn't a lap cat; he was just Rice's cat.

A few drops splattered on the flagstone steps. "Those are real big drops," Marge said. "It's really gonna rain."

"Can I go out in it?" Bo asked.

"No, you may not," his father said, enunciating clearly, his way of trying to sound stern.

"Can I unplug the TV?"

Eugene nodded, and Bo was gone. Lightning flashed over the swamp, leaving its image imprinted in Rice's mind; thunder crashed; Anthony wailed on his father's shoulder. Eugene looked anxiously from baby to wife. Anthony sounded like a fire siren. "Hey, honey?" Eugene said.

Marge turned to him. Her face was bright. "It's pretty close now," she said. She had to shout to be heard over the sudden drumming of the drops, the wild wind blowing, Anthony crying. It was like *Captains Courageous* outside, Rice thought; and his father was like Spencer Tracy.

"You think we should put the baby inside?" Eugene said, cupping his mouth with one hand.

"Okay," Marge said. She didn't move.

"Should I do it, Margie?" The thunder boomed again.

"Would you, honey? I think it's about to start coming down real hard. I kind of want to watch, okay?"

"Sure. Sure." But he carried the baby, Rice thought, like it was a slippery thing.

So it was just Rice and his mother out on the porch. "It's beautiful, don't you think, Ricey?" she said. Rain thudded on the roof. "I love it to rain hard," Marge went on. "I love it when you feel like the storm is after somebody. You just don't know who." She had to shout, practically; but Rice had a feeling that she wasn't really even talking to him.

Wind blasted through the screen, blew a newspaper off a chair, and held it up against the screen. Streaks of lightning struck the sky to the south.

"You ever get that feeling, Ricey? Like the weather is searching out somebody? And sometimes it thinks maybe it has him, and shoots down a lightning bolt after him?"

A stroke brought on a crackle of thunder. It sounds like somebody laughing, Rice thought. "Where's Lucas?" he asked.

Marge didn't answer him. "Sometimes I think it's me they're after," she said. "Those clouds are rolling toward me, and spitting out lightning, and sometimes I think, This was meant for me, and for me alone. You ever get that way, Ricey?"

"Unh-unh."

"Well, I do. I get that way. But what makes me nervous is that I like it."

The features of Rice's face crowded together. "*What* do you like?" he asked.

"When the storm comes after me."

He shifted uncomfortably. That rain was really coming down. "Why?" he asked Marge.

She was smiling. He couldn't understand why she was smiling. "Because it makes me feel important. It makes me feel like somebody knows I'm here."

Rice was silent. About him the wind whirled rain right onto the porch; the lightning bolts seemed to move cautiously, obliquely, toward the place where they were sitting. At last Rice shouted: "Ma, how come you always burn the pot pies?"

His question seemed to wake her. "Do I?" she shouted back.

"Mostly."

"I don't know, Ricey," she said. "Maybe it's because I know you like burnt pie."

"But I don't—" Rice had started, when Eugene came out again.

"I'm sorry, Margie," Eugene said, "but I can't get Anthony to hush up. He wants his mama."

Marge followed Eugene back into the house. Rice was alone with the ripping wind and growling thunder.

It was just then that Rice heard the scratching at the porch door.

It's the storm, he thought: it's after me. His first impulse was to run inside; but he was frozen. He heard the noise again. Because he couldn't move, he listened. To his relief, he recognized the sound. It was just Lucas scratching at the door.

Rice pushed the door open against the wind. A sopping-wet Lucas was standing there slowly blinking his eyes. In the darkness you could see the yellow glow of his cat's eyes.

Relieved, Rice reached down to pet him. Lucas was all sticky. When Rice touched him, Lucas let out a jagged howl of pain. Out of his mouth spewed thick, black blood.

Rice jumped back. The wind held the door open, and Lucas walked stiffly in. He fell. His blood coursed out in waves over the stone floor, as if he were a thrown stone spreading ripples on a still lake.

Eugene said he didn't know what had cut up Lucas that way. If it wasn't people—it was probably people, people were behind most of the misery in this world—but if it wasn't people, Eugene said, it was probably that long-tail weasel, the one you saw by the fallen oak at the bottom of the field. Maybe Lucas chased that weasel down into his burrow; the weasel would turn on him if he did.

Lucas was sure cut up, Eugene said.

Rice waited a couple of days. The weather cleared. His father was off at work; his mother busy with Anthony; Bo riding his bike. Rice went into his father's gun cabinet. He'd been told not to do that. He took out the littlest gun, a Savage .22-caliber rifle. He found a box of ammo and pocketed it.

The weather was still; hot; fearsomely hot; cloudlessly hot. The summer green of the field had a sulphur tint, as if a little of the sun had been mixed in with it. The field was speckled by buttercups and daisies. Rice lay down in the tall grass, hiding behind a clump of dog fennel. Indian strawberry bushes prickled his arms and legs; gnats floated around his face, flew at eyes, mouth, nostrils. Rice loaded. He propped his elbows up on the ground, sighted his rifle at the vague distance, and waited, scratching himself where the grass stuck to him, and sweating.

After an hour the weasel showed its head. Rice saw it snaking along the fallen oak; then it stood on hind legs, and the long slinky body weaved back and forth, its little paws hanging beside it and its nose high in the air, sniffing. You could almost see the nostrils wiggle and flare, trying to catch the scent of something.

Rice began to breathe harder. He took the safety off; he brought the rifle around slowly; he sighted.

I'm gonna shoot this guy, Rice kept telling himself. Gonna blow his brains out. But Rice's arms started to waver, and the rifle started to shake, wobbling with hatred. Jump around all you want, Rice said. I'm tellin you. I'm gonna get you.

Blood came pouring into Rice's head; his face seemed to expand. His rage—which had been lying, waiting for him ever since he had looked into Lucas' mouth—now burst out. Rice squeezed the rifle as hard as he could; he shook it, choking the thing. Hold *still*, dammit! He wedged the stock up against his chin; the weasel appeared in the notch of the sight. Now you just stay, he told it, like a dog. But the barrel dropped, as if from a weakness of its own.

Rice just gave up. His rage gave way. He did not act, he just watched his actions. He was just doing this: he just picked up the rifle and laid it on the prop of his arms; he just moved the barrel a little, till he saw the weasel before him, much larger than life. He just squeezed the shot off; he just squeezed.

Rice saw stuff pop out of the weasel's thin head. The creature did a sudden back flip, but missed its landing; tumbled; lay still.

Got him. The rage came back to Rice. Gotcha, bastard! he exulted—silently, as if he could scare off the corpse of his prey. Gotcha! Gotcha! Gotcha!

Rice made a mistake then. He went to have a look. He found the weasel, all right. It was lying on its back; its blood was bright and fresh, and still running. Flies took a sudden interest.

Rice stood over it and leaned on his rifle. Something was still wrong. It wasn't the fact that the weasel was dead. It lay there with its evil rat's face, its stringy little body; Rice still hated that weasel. Sumpin about the blood? he wondered; sumpin about the look on that face, its brains all lying there beside it, all goopy with blood?

Then Rice realized what it was. The weasel with its mouth full of blood looked like Lucas—Lucas as his mouth spit blood, with the same glaze over his eyes and the same pose arrested on his stiff limbs.

No! Rice thought. It's like it should be. He killed Lucas; I killed him.

Rice turned quickly on his heel and started home, holding the rifle in one hand, out away from his body. Something was wrong with him. First his mouth was dry, bone-dry; then it began to fill up with stuff; thick, bitter, salty stuff.

Rice knew what it was. It was blood: the weasel's blood, and Lucas' blood, and his blood too. That's what it was.

Rice got sick then. Among the daisies and buttercups, one cloudless afternoon when the air draped itself around him, Rice scratched first here, then there, where the grass made his elbows itch; Rice shot the weasel, killed it; then Rice was sick, sick with himself and sick with the world, all over the buttercups and daisies.

Carrie,

I think you're a real good writer. I just wanted to tell you that. I could never be that good of a writer. I wouldn't even *want* to.

I like your weird handwriting also.

There's some stuff I forgot to tell you, about when I was a kid. It's probably too late for you to get it in the story now, but I might as well tell you.

I used to like to put together plastic models, ships and planes. I'd glue them together real carefully, then go out to the driveway and blow them up with firecrackers. M-80s. The plastic caught on fire and burned this dark black smoke. Little tiny orange flames licked all over the superstructure, it was like the model was getting wet with flame, because it got shiny before it melted. Bo and me used to like to do that.

Sometimes I set fires in the woods. I don't actually think I wanted to burn the woods down. They were just little fires. I don't know why I was so interested in fires. I remember I liked the way they would suddenly start leaping around in all directions at once, jumping out like frogs jumping out of a bushel basket.

Eugene caught me setting fires one day. I was just setting there watching it go, hugging my knees and giggling. Eugene beat me. I didn't do it any more after that. He beat crap out of me.

Just now I was trying to remember if he used his fist or his palm, and I couldn't remember which it was. But Eugene didn't beat me too often, so you probably shouldn't mention that part.

I probably forgot to talk about something I should have talked about, but I don't know what it was.

R.

Five

The macrocosm might have been more sympathetic toward Rice and Manda if they had been a little older.

The two families went to the Pawley's Island beach on a May Saturday. When the station wagon plowed into the sand at the parking lot's edge, Rice popped his door open and raced down the beach with the unpolluted joy of someone younger. He reached the wet sand; he dabbled one bare foot in the tongue of a sliding wave. Water sucked softly at the sand under Rice's toes, then drew off, hissing, rolling bits of shell out to sea. Rice turned back and watched the two families straggling onto the beach, hands on his hips. He was thirteen; he was big; he wanted Manda to see him there—standing with hands on hips and the ocean at his feet.

The adults dropped their baskets and beach towels. Rice's mother tugged the corners of the towels to get them nice and flat; Mrs. Ramsey waved a plastic bottle of Sea and Ski. The four adults lay down. Bo dropped his rolled-up towel beside his mother and paced slowly toward the sea, staring intently at the sand itself; several times he tested the sand with his toe; then he dropped abruptly to his knees and dug. In an hour there'd be a sandcastle, complete with round towers and those little notches in the top of the walls. The tide would lay liquid siege, melting the walls; Bo would rebuild his fortress over and over; his mother would make him take a dip to wash the mud off. These things happened every time.

But the Ramseys didn't happen every time. Manda. It was all right to stare, at this distance. The adults passed the suntan lotion around, then lay back on their bright striped towels; Anthony began to pour sand carefully down his little bathing trunks; Manda stood behind them, arms folded, and serenely gazed out over the sea. Then an amazing event occurred. Manda slipped her bathrobe off. She stood in the sun, one arm akimbo. Her one-piece bathing suit was divided into transverse halves, sensational red below and its spectacular converse in green; the dividing line ran a breathtaking course from her right hip, traveled between her breasts, then ended at the strap hugging her left shoulder. Mrs. Ramsey handed the Sea and Ski to

Manda, and she calmly rubbed cream into her skin—white, extremely white—while Rice, gazing, slowly evaporated, melted away like suntan lotion disappearing into skin. The sight of her, of her bathing suit erupting with these beautifully rounded protuberances, of her ice-white, measured motions, made Rice completely uncomfortable. He felt grim. He felt nervous. He felt slightly sick to his stomach. Girls, Rice thought. What they do to you. And how easy they do it.

When Rice didn't know what to do he tended to fall down. He picked up pieces of shell and stone, tried to skip them in the sea. None skipped. Hot-faced, Rice found a driftwood stick and prodded a jellyfish, turned it over; but the way it flopped made him queasy, which made him think of Manda rubbing smooth ice-white shoulders with cream, which made him stop. Rice ran purposefully up the beach to the deep sand. Then what? So he dove feet-first into the sand, as if sliding into a base. He lay in the sand, miserable. He glanced back, hoping that Manda would be looking in another direction; but she stared idly at him, and moved the flat of her hand carelessly along the smooth back of her leg.

It was no good trying to get out of it. He wanted Manda. He did not know exactly what about her he wanted. He had kissed—once with Marcy Jennings on the cheek, and once with Marcy Jennings on the lips, and the two were not much different—but kissing did not seem central to his desire. Her protuberances seemed important. But what did you do with a breast, except put your hand onto it? That was copping a feel; but did a feel feel real good? In his fingers, or where?

Rice was by far the largest boy in his class; he was in the process of becoming a hulking, massive man, a mountain; he felt powerless, and even helpless.

Manda dropped the tube of suntan lotion beside her mother and walked over to Rice. "I'm walkin down the beach," she said. "You want to walk down with me?"

They started down. Wisps of cloud were reflected only figuratively by whitecaps in a bright, heaving sea. The long flat stretch of sand looked like glass, glass that shimmered as the heat rose, quivering. They walked in silence toward the slender island's point. But they didn't seem to be getting any closer: they had passed the same broken crab claw three times; the houses they kept passing were the same ones, over and over; and look here, this is the same flock of little beach birds skittering away on stick legs, jumping into the air and swooping all together as if wired to each other. The same little damn birds, Rice thought, and then he thought: This not talking is getting to me.

"You goin to Winyah Bay High this fall?" he tried.

"Guess so."

"Gonna try out for cheerleader?"

"Guess not."

Manda shaded her eyes to look out over the water. "Ever seen a whale?" she asked.

"A whale? You mean a real whale?"

"You can see em sometimes. You can see their spouts."

"You sure about that?"

"Positive," Manda said.

"You ever seen one?"

"Nope. Unh-unh."

"There you go," Rice said, with some satisfaction. "Who tole you that, anyways?" he asked.

Manda squinted at the sea again. "Ever seen a shark?" she asked.

"I'm tellin ya," Rice said, shaking his head.

They reached the point of the island, a rounded pate of sand with a sawgrass hairpiece. Around the other side, three gawky white birds stood stock-still in the shallow water. Manda pointed. "You know what those are?"

"Nope."

"Egrets," she said.

"I'm tellin ya," Rice said again.

She squinted at Rice. "You don't play football, do you?"

Rice reddened. He'd been thinking about putting his hand on her, somewhere, he wasn't sure where; now he couldn't do that. He thought about lying. "Not exactly," he said. "Sometimes I play touch."

She was looking at him, her eyes moving in their sockets. Rice felt like her eyes were moving around on his face; like there were little eyeballs rolling around on the skin of his face.

"I don't like football," she said.

Rice shrugged.

"I can't ever tell which *down* it is," she said, making a wry face to indicate distaste for downs. "Or *why*," she added.

Rice shrugged again. It seemed that Manda was trying to make some point, talking about whales and sharks and football, but Rice couldn't figure what it was. She just didn't tend to make any sense.

"You like pelicans?" she asked him now.

"Pelicans? I guess."

"Let's go back," she said, and they started walking again. They went for a while without saying anything, Rice kicking occasionally at something on the sand, or at blank sand itself; then Manda said, "Why do you like em?"

"Why do I like what?"

"Pelicans. I ast you if you liked pelicans. You said yes. How come?"

"*I* don't know," Rice said. "Everybody likes pelicans. They're sorta funny. They got big mouths. They look like old men chewing tobacco. Don't you like em?"

Manda peered off into the distance, then turned to face Rice. She didn't answer him. "We're gettin close to the folks again," she said. "You better kiss me now, Mr. Pelican."

Rice didn't even think. He took a deep breath, two steps, and leaned at her; he planted his face squarely against hers. For a minute they didn't move much.

Manda put her hand tentatively on Rice's arm. "You don't have to be shy," she told him. "I like it when you're shy, but you don't have to be."

Rice didn't know what to say. He walked alongside Manda again, and occasionally stole furtive glances at her, gauging. He wondered what he had done to deserve all this—staring now at various luxurious parts of her anatomy, the opulence of her, the abundance—and then he wondered what it was, exactly, that he had got. Were all girls like this? But Rice's confusion eased bit by bit. He went swimming, and found himself in a pool of dreamy thoughts of Manda, as sea currents pleasantly manipulated his genitals within his trunks; then he body-surfed, and as he rode a particularly tall, smooth wave an ineffable pleasure grew within him, and then crested with the wave. His wave threw him over, landed him on his head, and Rice staggered crazy-legged up the beach. He was bleeding, he was dizzy, but his exhilaration rolled on unchecked, rumbling, cresting and breaking, rising again and cresting and breaking, and soon Rice found his slightly cut head resting comfortably, blissfully, in Manda's lap, as she capably staunched that wound and many other old ones that we do not have time to enumerate here.

Rice and Manda were in love for a year. Their breakup was vague: Manda's parents just took her away for the summer. The seasons lasted longer then than they do now, and when Manda returned she had changed, or Rice had changed—or something else, some third party, perhaps time itself, came between them like a shadow. So, without the standard device of either heart-to-heart talk or letter of dismissal, Rice and Manda fell apart.

They had never made definitive love, though Rice would long think of their tender marathon kisses as a paradigm for heightened love, even after he had accomplished what is considered the ultimate sexual act.

Which happened when Rice was fifteen. Rice's first lover was a direct if impoverished descendant of a President of the United States. She lisped charmingly; she had one dazzling black and white dress; she had mastered early the art of swinging her hips as she walked; she was a wonderful swimmer. One of her breasts was considerably smaller than the other, which astounded Rice. They made love in a motel room in honky-tonk Myrtle Beach. This arrangement would have been normal, even stock, had it not been for the presence of Rice's friend Ben. Ben was a good friend, and nothing if not discreet. He retired early to the bathroom, where he seated himself in the arid bathtub, made more comfortable by an adjoining case of beer. Ben began to sing as loudly as he could, trying both to distract himself and assure Rice and mate of an unusual sort of privacy. Ben's singing went on for several hours—much more time than Rice knew how to use. Eventually Rice's paramour, who will remain nameless (it was not love), irritably requested silence. It was Rice's task to relay the request to Ben. "Did you get it?" Ben asked him in an eager whisper. Though it was not for many months that Rice perfectly understood what "it" was, he assured Ben that he had. He thought he had. He had.

Six

Rice wasn't a good driver yet, and maybe he was never going to be a good driver, but Eugene let him have the car.

Eugene slapped Rice's back as he handed over the keys. "I'm passing the old torch on to you," Eugene said, trying to sound hearty. But Eugene was a little dubious about it; he didn't know what the hell he *was* passing along, and why he should let Rice smash up the car just because Rice had had another birthday. So when Rice got home that night Eugene was waiting for him. Eugene was in the living room, holding a book in front of his face. He'd been holding it for several hours, looking at it, thinking.

Rice sauntered in, and his face was completely covered with a silly grin. "Hi, Eugene," he said.

Looking at his son, Eugene felt a great discrepancy between them. Eugene felt that he knew a great deal; that Rice did not; that somehow he should communicate what he knew to his son. "You have a pleasant night?" Eugene asked.

"Yup. Unh-hunh."

"Car run okay for you?"

"Yup. Thanks for lettin me use it and everything."

"No problem, kid," Eugene said.

Rice stood for a second, loitering. He was still grinning; Eugene still looked serious. "I guess you can go to bed now, Eugene," Rice said, and he laughed. Like he's played a joke on his father, Eugene thought; he doesn't know anything.

He doesn't know a goddamn thing, Eugene kept thinking, as he watched his son smirk. The light from the standing lamp shone through Rice's hair. It was getting long, flipped up in back. Like all the kids, Eugene thought. They wear their shirttails out and they just don't know anything.

"You got a sec, kid?"

"Sure," Rice said. He was supposed to sit down, he thought; he sat.

"How old are you?" Eugene started, closing his book.

It killed Rice that Eugene never knew that. Rice had just gotten his license; that made him sixteen. You'd think Eugene would remember that, at least. "Sixteen."

"Sixteen. Going out on dates. In a car. Well, I've got sumpin I'd like to ask you, son."

Rice's eyes narrowed. Eugene never called him "Son."

"Tell me," Eugene said, "have you been a man with a woman yet?"

Rice tried to discern the shade of Eugene's meaning. "I don't think so," Rice said. "I guess I don't know."

"Jesus Christ. What do they teach you kids down to that high school?"

"The usual, I guess," Rice said.

"Jesus. Well, let me put it this way. Have you ever slept with a woman?"

"Oh," Rice said, relieved. "*That.* Well, yeah."

"I mean gone all the way, kid. Have you gone all the way?"

"Well. Yeah."

Eugene shook his head. "You kids," he said. "You poor kids."

"It's not so bad, Eugene," Rice said softly.

"Bad? Hell, kid. It's great. It's the best." But Eugene was still making a face. "Tell me sumpin, kid," he said. "Do you know how to take care of yourself?"

Rice knew he didn't know that. "Unh-unh," he said.

"Good," Eugene said, and he smiled expansively. "I'm glad I talked to you. Now tomorrow we'll stop down to Litton's. I'll go with you, kid. We'll fix you up with some condoms."

"Condoms?"

"You know. Rubbers." Eugene paused. "You know what rubbers are, don't you?"

For a second Rice didn't respond, though his mouth was open, and it was moving. Finally he said, "Unh, the girls all take the pill these days, Eugene."

"Jesus Christ! You goddamn kids!"

Eugene regarded the distance with rueful awe. "Look," he said. "I got one thing to tell you, kid. I *know* you don't know about this part. And you won't listen to me, either. But that's only normal."

Rice started to say something, but his father cut him off. "Just listen up for a second, kid. There's sumpin I gotta tell you about women. Now with women you're gonna win some and you're gonna lose some. Sooner or later you find out you lose em all. Everybody does. You probably think you're in love right now, and you probably think it'll last forever, so you won't listen to me. But listen anyway. There's only one thing you gotta know about women, kid. One thing."

Eugene waited. He's waiting for me to ask what the thing you have to know about women is, Rice thought. Rice hated Eugene's generalizations, particularly the ones about women.

"What's the one thing?" Rice asked.

Eugene nodded at him. "This is it," he said. "No matter what happens with a woman—no matter how wonderful or terrible it is— you gotta keep your sense of humor. That's all that matters, kid. You gotta keep your sense of humor. I tell you. You remember that, and you'll be better off than about a hunnerd percent of everybody else."

He nodded triumphantly, agreeing with himself, and leaned back on the sofa. He put both hands behind his head and waited.

Rice felt a little dazed. It's late, he thought. "Well," he said, "thanks, I guess."

"Don't mention it, kid," Eugene said. Then he leaned over toward Rice, and whispered. "Really," he said. "Don't mention it to anyone."

Carrie,

It's interesting enough to read this stuff, but it doesn't much remind me of my life. It sounds like the kind of thing somebody would write about their life if they'd been wearing eyepatches on both eyes the whole time, and had to guess the way things were out there.

When I read the stuff you wrote about me, I thought about you, not me. I thought about the day before yesterday, how we went out for matches and ended up parked in the cemetery by Central Catholic School. I was remembering about how my head kept hitting the back-seat window, and the way you put your hand on top of my head to protect it. I guess that's what I get for having a lover who drives a VW. We should have taken my truck, right? But I'm glad that didn't stop us.

I know it was Evan's week, but I don't feel bad about it. I feel real real good, and I want you to too.

I'm still sitting here thinking about making love in your VW. I can't stop. I'm wondering why it was such a powerful fuck. The leverage wasn't real good, and it wasn't a big enough space, and my head kept beating against that window, and I kept getting worried that somebody would see us, in the cemetery. It didn't go on too long, it was practically a quickie, but it was the best. When you took me into your mouth in the back seat of the VW, I came like the Milky Way or something.

Speaking of sex. I don't think it's too funny, the way you talk in this story about me trying to get Manda. I actually don't. It could be, but it isn't. You had to not be there to think it was funny. If somebody looked at you and me in the VW, two people giving head in a cemetery by a Catholic school, you might think *that* was funny. But it wasn't. It was the best.

Next time you show me some writing I'll stick to the subject better.

I told you I put the shot in high school. How come you didn't talk about that?

I wasn't as uncoordinated as you make it sound. I was just a little unlucky. Like Eugene.

              R.

Seven

The doctor, stepping back from the patient, said that maybe the boys should leave the room.

He spoke slowly; but that was just the way doctors spoke, Rice thought.

Rice was seventeen; he was sitting in an armchair; his hands lay quietly on the arms of the chair, miming calm. Anthony sat on the floor clinking a cat's eye and a steelie together, and Bo leaned uncomfortably against the bed, jiggling the change in his pockets.

"Rice can stay," Eugene said. "You others scoot." Bo trudged reluctantly out into the hall, and Anthony followed, leaving the steelie on the brown braided rug.

Dr. Partridge said that the news wasn't good, then scowled. Rice remembered the doctor's face from years before: "Roll up your own sleeve, dammit," the doctor had said, hobbling toward Rice, the hypodermic in his hand pointed toward the ceiling. Dr. Partridge was already old, even back then; he had only one arm. The other jacket arm dangled against his side; Rice had tried to stare at the jacket, not at the flash of the needle. "I just don't care how you feel about getting a shot, dammit. You want polio, boy?" Rice was only six; he cried; Dr. Partridge scowled. "I delivered you, boy. I deserve a little gratitude. Roll up that sleeve, dammit."

Out in the hall Anthony dropped the cat's eye, picked it up, dropped it again. Twilight lingered outside the half-drawn shades; crepuscular half-light crept through, and rain fell fitfully in the east. The wind of dusk breathed in the loblolly pines; a spiny cone thumped the lawn, bounced, rolled over, played dead. Dr. Partridge breathed through his nose, frowning; a woodpecker attacked a dead bough; Rice gripped the arms of his chair and thought, They always exaggerate: so they can feel important: that's all.

Rice said loudly to his father: "You look fine to me."

"I feel fine."

The doctor patted Eugene's knee. "The biopsy indicates malignancy."

"Malignancy?" Marge said. No one responded.

Parts of Rice's body began to stage a revolution. His hands shook like religious ecstatics before the convulsing Word; his lips went numb; his tongue darted wildly around his mouth like a snake's, feeling; his heart made distant thunder.

"Well, I feel fine," Eugene said again, arguing the point. *He should know*, Rice thought. Then Rice noticed the doctor still patting Eugene's knee, and Eugene said, "Y'all are probably wantin to take it out, I bet."

"We've got to," the doctor said.

Rice had never seen tears on his father's face before. Seeing them, everyone began to cry, each in his own way. Everyone but the doctor, who frowned and breathed heavily through his nose; his damn hairy nose, Rice thought, and a fierce resentment rose in him for this one-armed, hairy-nosed gimp of a man. Damn him; he had caused it all.

Eugene cried the least. "Hell," he commented, and wiped his face. The doctor nodded, as if he agreed with this assessment. Eugene stared moodily at the bedpost, his lower lip curled petulantly over the upper one. "Probably hurt a little, hunh?" Eugene said; Dr. Partridge shrugged.

Eugene bit the corner of his thumbnail. "Why don't you just leave it in?" he said.

"You *can't* just leave it in, Eugene."

"Why the hell not?"

"Well, the cancer'll spread."

Eugene grunted. Rice heard marbles rolling and clinking out in the hall. "I think you should do that," Eugene said softly, almost to himself. "I think you should just leave it."

Another loblolly came down, thunking; another scarlet sunset blazed away over the river; a heron stalked awkwardly at the muddy water's edge, stiff as a cripple, then stood motionless on one leg, neck folded into undertaker's hunched shoulders; and the doctor was back, touching Eugene's knee again. *Like he's a fucking kid,* Rice thought; *will you quit patting him, dammit?* Rice raged along the riverbank; he swore up and down at the smiles frozen on alligators' crusty snouts, and tears kept tracing the skeleton of his face.

Anthony was going up to his attic, he announced. That was the one place in the house where he'd been allowed to hold sway, among his stacks of comic books and walls covered with pasted-on superheroes. At the top of the stairs, at the entrance to his one-man clubhouse, a Halloween paper skeleton swung—denoting terror and children within. Anthony was tall for his age, a gawky heron of a boy, silent, self-contained; a reluctant boy, for the most part. In general, he just wanted to be left alone. It was hard being the last one.

"You can go," Marge said, "when you clean your plate." Reluctantly Anthony mouthed his crusts. "The chips too." He crunched the last of them. His mother nodded. Lately Marge seemed to care about what they ate; or how much, at any rate. She had gotten older.

Anthony backed his chair off; it shrieked against the Congoleum.

Rice dawdled over his coffee. He didn't like it yet; he'd been trying to like it for several years. He drank it regularly, with a great show of appreciation. "You might try it with milk," Marge would say on occasion, and Rice would reply, "I like it fine black." To himself Rice added: I'm *gonna* like it fine. He raised the pale blue cup to his lips. He opened them slightly, tilted the cup, and coffee seeped into his mouth—like sewage, he thought.

Marge cracked the newspaper to turn the page. She read it folded in quarters, and she was always folding and refolding the pages; licking her fingers, and folding, making noise: so it would seem like she was busy. She spent a lot of time reading the newspaper. She didn't used to do that. She always wore her plastic apron, clear with red piping, now; she didn't always used to. Her face had become red and rough, and somehow longer; skin hung down from cheekbones like soft wax. Her nose dripped constantly. At the end of it even now a clear droplet hung. She wiped with the back of her hand. She snapped the newspaper flat; gave it a shake; creased it the opposite way, now.

It was like river mud, Rice thought: silt: sewage. He stared into his cup, discouraged. He drank it down to the grounds.

When he looked up he noticed Anthony hovering behind his mother, standing stiffly, keeping still.

What was wrong with *him,* anyway? Anthony's arms hung at his side; no, they weren't hanging exactly; it was as if Anthony were holding his arms down. As if, left alone, they'd fly right off his shoulders.

"What's up, buddy?" Rice said. Anthony was shaking; standing there shivering. It wasn't cold.

"Hafta tell you something, Rice," Anthony whispered, over

Marge's shoulder. Marge crossed her legs; she turned her newspaper over. Rice stood up and followed Anthony into the hall. Anthony motioned for him to bend down. Anthony's teeth were chattering.

He's done something bad, Rice thought. He's broken something. Something old.

Rice bent down till his head was at Anthony's level. "What is it, buddy?" he asked, trying to sound both stern and kindly, like his father.

Anthony whispered into Rice's ear. "Daddy's hung up," he whispered, and bit his lip.

"What are you talking—" Rice started.

"In the attic," Anthony added—and to Rice's surprise Anthony burst into wild tears, and his fists rubbed at his eyes.

The attic? Rice repeated to himself; but even as he did, a bubble of warning rose in his chest—a bubble that was about to burst and reveal its contents: reveal what Rice already knew, and did not want to know, ever.

Rice left Anthony standing there rubbing his eyes. Rice took the steps two at a time, furious: furious, because he *knew,* dammit.

He heard the sound of his own footsteps come up the stairs behind him, and reach the top, and stop; a snatch of song flickered in his head, and Rice stood listening; his hand rested on the doorknob, fingers feeling the coolness of brass. He twisted it, pulled the door open. Before him, in place of Anthony's Halloween paper skeleton, Rice's father dangled from the rafter, a rope around his neck, and an expression of terrible pain fixed on the face that would drift into Rice's dreams for a thousand nights, and more.

Eight

On the last day of the year they talked Rice into playing basketball. This didn't happen very often, because he was bad. He was big and slow, and the ball always seemed to be hitting him in the back of the neck.

Later Rice would say it had been the basketball itself that struck him—as if the game of basketball, capsulated into one orange sphere, was after him. But Hal Nicholson insisted that the offending implement was his own middle finger. Hal described the vile jelly of Rice's eye under his finger with such disgusting vividness that the listener was obliged to rub his own in sympathy. But the sympathy was more for Hal than for Rice: as if Hal had stepped in dog mess, and Rice was the mess.

Rice was a mess. The finger, probably, went in, Rice went black; he immediately headed for the sidelines with an entirely gratuitous limp. For a few moments he tried to look out of the hurt eye, to see if he could see: he saw a cubist universe, in which everything had been changed from curves into fractured lines, so that circles were octagons, and light hopped madly from broken plane to broken plane, and everything was colored a light, bright blue. Then the palette changed. and Rice's eye saw rosy. A pink wash came down, as if falling from buckets above; its hue deepened, became crimson, then black—a black curtain—and Rice put his hand over his eye, so as not to see that he was not seeing.

"You okay now?" Hal shouted over, still playing.

"Sure," Rice called back. "It's just my eye."

It was Rice's idea that the brow had swollen over the eye, shutting it like a banged-up boxer's. Rice decided to go home, where he could apply an icebag or raw beefsteak, then lie in state on the fat green corduroy couch in the living room; he would be given sympathy, aspirin, ice cream. He would be given whatever he wanted by whoever was nearest. Bo, for example, would do nicely.

He did not lie in state on the green couch. He loitered a little, waiting for his mother to notice and then comment on his stoicism. But she was reading a newspaper, and her eyes darted only as far as the page's edge. Finally Rice took the direct approach. "Look," he said.

Marge looked up. "My eye," Rice said.

A lot of the time Marge didn't quite *focus;* now she turned her gaze, not exactly on Rice, but on the world at large, waking in slow stages from the newspaper. Rice looked around, trying to see what might be more important than his red, raging eye. The good eye noticed a pale green curtain rustling in response to no obvious breeze; a quartered newspaper lay on the coffee table beside a squat stack of *National Geographics*; a record spun soundlessly on the turntable. The bad eye noticed only its own black curtain.

At least, Rice thought, it doesn't hurt. He was amazed that it didn't hurt.

"It hurts," Rice said. "My eye."

"Sumpin in it, Ricey?" Marge said dreamily, and licked her index finger in preparation for flipping the page.

Rice bent down to show her. "Should I put some ice onto it?"

Marge began to wriggle her feet into shoes. "We're going to the hospital," she said.

"It's just a shiner," Rice said. "I don't have to go to the hospital for a shiner. It's just a shiner, right?"

The Georgetown doctor gave a low whistle. "Wow-ee. Look at that hemorrhaging. Haven't seen hemorrhaging like that in a while." He smiled. "Don't even know what they do about that nowadays. Think they stick a needle in there. Try to drain off the blood. It's not my field, but I think that's what they do."

"What all is wrong with it, exactly?" Rice asked.

"Well, we don't know, do we, son? We don't know what kind of damage you got going back there, do we?" The doctor smiled again; he straightened up. He was very fat; his body puffed his white coat out like a sail before wind; his chins were legion. "Besides," he said, with some satisfaction, "this just isn't my field, son."

By ten o'clock that New Year's Eve Rice was already sitting in a Georgetown hospital bed, outfitted in the hospital's white smock, with the hospital's band of clear plastic encircling and identifying his wrist. Marge sat beside the bed, speaking to herself of the weather; of snow. Of course it hardly ever snowed.

Rice didn't recognize his doctor. Someone small and dark paused at the door, checked the room number, and then walked briskly in, heels making distinct, crisp taps on the floor. "My name is Dr. Hassan," he said, and one of his hairless hands shook Rice's. "Pakistani," he added.

Dr. Hassan had not bothered with a doctor's coat; he wore a three-piece suit of gray-blue herringbone, closely tailored and sleekly new. His hand touched his vest. "I shall be going to a party," he said. "To be celebrating the New Year."

"Happy New Year, Doctor," Marge said.

"Happy New Year," Dr. Hassan replied evenly, and he made a little bow.

"You look very fine," Marge approved.

Dr. Hassan did look fine. On his small and extremely round head an emphatic part made a decisive, even unquestionable, division, and it is true that not one of his short black hairs was out of place. He smiled, and laid both his hands on Rice's skull, turning it this way and that.

"Hurt?"

"No."

"Hurt now?"

"No."

"Mmm." Dr. Hassan placed his slender briefcase on the cart beside the bed and clicked it open. He took hold of a silver implement with a black rubber cone at its tip. Dr. Hassan held Rice's injured eye open while he peered at it through the cone. A light flashed. Somehow Rice saw an elaborate tracery of veins, like vermiculate rivers squirming on a curving map. This must be the view, Rice thought, of the back of my eye from inside my brain. I'm seeing without my eyes.

The doctor clicked the light off, clicked the briefcase shut; when he moved, his heels clicked together.

"Sorry to say, but these"—he suddenly held up two black circles of coarse cloth—"must go over the eyes."

"Over *both* eyes?"

"Yes please. So as not to be moving the injured eye along with the good." Dr. Hassan turned Rice's head. "And now, perhaps, you should be looking."

"At what?"

"At around and all about." The doctor made a cheerful circular motion in the air, indicating the vista of the hospital room. "Because, you see, you shall be being blind. For the while, perhaps."

Rice looked. There were five other beds in the ward, all but one occupied; all four men dozed; the light that came in from the hall did so quietly, discreetly. Through the frame of the door and down that bright hall occasional white nurses cast long black shadows. Rice's mother sat in the bedside chair, still wearing her gray coat, though it was hot. Being blind here could not be so bad, because there was nothing Rice wanted to look at anyway. He looked at his mother: she stared out the small square window, into the blue-black night. But there's nothing out there, Rice thought. There's nothing out there at all.

"And so," the doctor said. A nurse started to tape the eyepatches to Rice's temple.

"How long these things gonna be on for?" Rice asked.

"A week. Ten days, perhaps. Please try very much, however, to be not moving your head. Always be lying down very still. This is the most important."

"Well, am I gonna be all right in the end?" Rice asked, annoyed with the stupidity of his own question.

Perhaps Dr. Hassan smiled. "We shall see," he said, and Rice wondered, Does he mean me?

That night someone shook Rice's shoulder. "It's midnight," they told him.

"That right?" Rice said gamely, and he tried smiling. "Happy New Year," Rice said.

"Turn over for your rectal thermometer."

Rice's hearing did its best to make up for the sudden absence of sight. Rice began to listen. It didn't take long for him to be able to place the room's four breathers. There were no similarities in the four breaths; they came from separate species. One was a stuttering half-snore: its breather seemed to hesitate on every syllable of air, tick it off, and proceed cautiously to the next, measuring the intake; the exhalation was all but soundless, a faint sigh of relief—*I have lived again,* its author was saying, *I have lived through that breath too.* Another sleeper used his mouth, and sucked hard. The air he pulled in whistled through his teeth, a cold tuneless whistle. There's a problem there, Rice said to himself; but he hadn't been blind long enough to see what it was. A third sleeper drew in breath through his nose, in short disdainful sniffs—as if, Rice thought, he's always trying to do without air, then all of a sudden finds he can't make it. The last breather was the closest, the quietest. He drew in breath easily and regularly, and Rice could almost see into his dreams: the man walked along a long winding path through loblolly pines, and his breathing was the sound of a small cool breeze through the needles. He was dreaming that he was somewhere else, not surrounded by problems, his own and everyone else's; he was merely walking along. Along pines, to a secret place, where sun-warmed needles made the forest floor soft and dry. He might lie down there and rest. Rice, exhausted, joined him there at last.

They shook him awake. "Time for your wash," they said. Or perhaps it was only one, one with several voices. They cranked up the bed. They held his body this way and that, swabbed him with warm washcloths. They went after his secret places. They liked the crannies and nooks of him where hair grew. They got behind his ears, but they couldn't get behind his eyes: they couldn't get him. They dried him, dropped him back against the bed. "There. That wasn't too bad, was it?"

When they were gone the nearest breather spoke to Rice: "Hit's difficult ven they vash you, don't you sink? For me hit's fery hard."

"What's hard?" Rice asked.

"Hard not to *get* hard," the man said. "Because hit's fery arousing, don't you sink, ven they handle with you?"

This whole place is full of foreigners, Rice thought. The whole place is . . . sick. "Where are you from, anyway?" he said to the voice, and the voice said, "Sawannah. Sawannah, Chorcha." The voice laughed; that had been a joke, some kind of joke. "But of course before that I am turty-vun years in Hamburg. Western Germany. And you?"

"Yauhannah," Rice said. "And I've only been in Hell for about one day."

"How fery lucky you are," the voice replied, and Rice thought, Is he kidding?

They shook him awake again. "Time for your breakfast," they said, cranking him up. Rice heard rubber wheels rolling, then felt the bedside tray being shoved into place above his lap; it did not quite touch him, but Rice knew it was there. He could sense it, no, he could *feel* it, feel it above him, just beyond touch, the way a believer might feel his God. "Your breakfast is in front of you now," they said, and then Rice heard the soft squeak of rubber soles trailing away down the hall.

"Where?" Rice asked no one, to no response. He put out his hand, like a paw. Something warm and moist... in a bowl. Hot cereal. Must be a spoon around somewhere. No. This is... soft-boiled egg. Rice sucked his fingertips. He could picture a trail of yolk connecting tray to mouth, yellow dots flecking the white sheets, but he was distracted from his image by the taste of the egg. It was surprisingly good, incredibly good. It was like something other, something rich and sweet; something rare. And this too was his secret—the taste of a soft-boiled egg.

"Vould chew like me to call zuh nurse? To make less zuh mess?"

Rice put his hand into the cereal now, and sucked the finger again. "That's all right. I'm doin fine."

They shook him awake. "Time for your sleeping pill."

The Germanic voice in the bed next to Rice's was visited daily by a small, quavering, female voice, also Germanic. Every evening she brought two items and took away one. The two items were always the same, a bottle of Jim Beam and a box of Sen-Sen; and the one item was also always the same, an empty bottle. After Rice dabbled his fingers in dinner and sucked dinner off his fingers, he felt a bottle press against his ribs. Rice opened the bottle and sucked on it. Then he held the bottle out, it left, and in its place came the box of Sen-Sen, the contents of which Rice also sucked.

The alcohol went directly and pleasantly to Rice's head; he lay securely on the bed while images spun on the inside of his eyelids. The images moved rapidly; Rice saw dots, lines, shapes, in all colors, swarming on a black, and sometimes on a red, and occasionally even on a shining white field. He saw places that he knew, and places that he did not know. He saw fragments of his life acted out, both the way they had happened and a way they had not happened. He saw fragments of no one's life, or at least of someone else's life, acted out. The cast of characters included his dead grandfather, Pup, whom Rice now saw for perhaps hours at a time, painting a subdued representation of a pond and hillside that Rice suspected did not exist. Rice's father, Eugene, came around even more often, remarkably like himself. Rice spoke to Eugene, but his father did not reply—did not seem able to reply, perhaps because he was in fact dead. But Eugene was capable of other activities, there on Rice's eyelid. He could throw a baseball to Rice, who was also present inside his own eyes, and Rice could catch it with no problem; no one ever missed in these long wordless games of catch, but as they went on Rice began to miss his father. Eugene seemed to be possessed of an extraordinary ease there; now that he was dead he had been freed from awkwardness, from unhappiness, from all constraint; he had acquired a grace. Eugene was a blessed man now, and with a small smile fixed on his face he caught and threw, caught and threw, as the blossoms came out on the peach tree he caught and threw, as the mosquitoes and gnats showed up and swarmed around he caught and threw, as the oak leaves lost color and finally fell he caught and threw, as the sun arched above and then dropped toward the west bank of the PeeDee, Eugene caught and threw.

Rice wanted to talk to Eugene; wanted to repeat small rituals. Rice wanted whatever had happened to happen again. The time he had spent with his father took on a sheen of wonder. Eugene had liked beer; the beer, the Budweiser can, even the ink on the can, gained the status of hallowed objects; this image, of Eugene gripping the can, was an icon. As the figure of his father drank from a bottomless can of Budweiser, Rice realized that he had lost everything he had ever cared for. That the crucial matter of his life had been broken, and the important parts thrown away; that he had lost—

"Time for your sleeping pill," they said, shaking him. But he was already asleep, or so he thought. He slept a lot, for a lot made him sleepy. Sleeping pills made him sleepy; alcohol made him sleepy; having his eyes shut all the time made him sleepy; sleep itself made him sleepy. Rice was always tired. His head was never clear. It was never clear what was real. He dreamed that he was lying in a hospital bed, could not see, could not move, could not feel.

After a week Dr. Hassan pulled the tape from Rice's eyes. The clear morning light was blinding, and for a second Rice panicked: he saw nothing but a wall of white, and was convinced that now both eyes were blind, or that it was snowing. But it seldom snows in South

Carolina. Dr. Hassan said nothing. He put the tape back over Rice's eyes, patted him gently on the head, and said: "Three days more. Try very much to not be moving the eyes. Be lying down always very still."

The three days passed in a bright haze of alcohol, pills, and dream. Only the bedpans were real. Rice began to to be able to hear the cries from the floor below, the maternity ward. The nurses called a woman having a first child a "canary." Rice heard the canaries sing by day, the nightingales by night. He heard many births accomplished. He found out all about the pain and trouble of birth. He grew to hate birth. No one else in his ward heard—until one evening, when Rice was clumsily pawing mashed potatoes, a canary sang a loud, clear song. Rice heard his ward's chewing stop. The Germanic voice said, "Viz such a bic pain, it kut only be childburz."

Dr. Hassan pulled the tape away gently, letting in the white wall of light. He studied Rice's eye with his conical instrument, and then stepped back from his patient "No," he said. "I am sorry. It is not being of help."

"What do you mean?" Rice cried.

Dr. Hassan shook his head. "I am sorry. You are not to be seeing with this eye."

Nine

On the once-white concrete-block walls of the restaurant, Marion's Oyster Roast in Murrell's Inlet, maritime paintings hung in rows. In one painting sailors, their feet not quite touching deck, battled high and luridly green waves under a sky apparently on fire; in the foreground, fish seemed content to loiter on the sea's orangey surface, as if buoyed by the peculiar pigment. In another painting an orderly, hard-edged rainbow arched over a flat white beach, while in the distance several remarkably tiny boats sailed on collision courses. These paintings were for sale, and had been so for as long as Rice could remember.

Rice ducked his head and pulled it through the doorframe. He was managing. He was going to make it. He steered himself toward a corner, picking his way between chairs as if displaying miraculous balance. For Rice was drunk, and walking the line.

Go easy. One foot at a time. Focus on where you're going. Forget everything else. Don't look down. Made it.

The waitresses were white and wore aprons over their bluejeans. Manda took a look, saw Rice, and came over. She said, "Are you okay?"

He said he was. He thought he was, or would be, eventually.

"If you say so, sweetie. Well, what do you want?"

"Six cans of Bud."

Manda tapped her pad with her pen, glared at him. "You want anything to drink with that?"

Rice wasn't listening. He looked into the kitchen, where the tall black guys stood watch over oval metal pots: gas burners bathed the pots' bottoms in blue; you could see the white steam collected at the old gray ceiling, rolling like thunderheads, and you could see it, white against the mahogany-brown arms of the kitchen help; you could see it rolling this way.

"A single roast. No, make it a double."

"One peck. Got friends coming, Rice?"

"I'm a hungry man, Manda. I'm a big man and I'm real hungry."

Manda nodded. "You're a big man, all right. You're big, and

you're hungry." She dropped her hands onto her knees, and her voice dropped too: "And, you drink too much."

"Would you just bring the beer, Manda?"

"Don't have to. Don't have to do anything, sweetie. Delia says if somebody is drunk don't give em more."

"I'm not drunk. Not actually." The steam was rolling out of the kitchen, rolling this way. It rolled over the Richardson family in their baseball caps at the next table. The Richardsons were watching. "Why do you want to give me such a hard time?" Rice asked, straining his whisper. "Why don't you just act like a regular waitress?"

"Because I hate it when those big beautiful blue eyes of yours look all bloodshot like that, sweetie." Manda's whisper became softer: "This is too small a place to drink in, Rice. Everybody knows when you drink."

"I don't care," Rice said, too loud. "You know what that does, Manda? That makes me the only free one in this whole place."

Manda shook her head. "I tell you," she said. "You're big, and you're hungry, and you're dumb. Lucky for you you're half cute." She went away still shaking her head.

Rice put his palms on the plywood, feeling. He liked feeling when he was drunk. He liked the flat. He liked the way his fingers and palms felt flat. He began to bounce his hand lightly against the plywood, patting it, till he could feel the plywood even when his hand was in the air. He liked that. What was it, Rice began thinking, that was so good about being drunk? He liked the way it made him hungry; he was hungry now. He could eat a horse. No, not a horse. Well, he could eat oysters. Lots of oysters. What else did he like about it? He liked the way it made him tired; the way things moved slowly, and sometimes not at all.

He wasn't as bad as Manda made out. She was just mothering. Ever since Eugene had died the whole town tried to mother him. It didn't make sense; but there you go. Even the goddamn *Rich*ardsons, for Christ's sake: sitting there pitying him. It was enough to make you sick. Rice was sick of it. Sick to his stomach. He swallowed hard.

A giant black man carried an oval pot out of the kitchen. "Peck a oysters," he said, smiling, and banged the pot down in front of Rice

"Here's your hush puppies," Manda said, and put them down. "Butter. Cocktail sauce." She placed two small paper cups to one side, then slapped newspaper down on the table in front of Rice. "Got a shucker? Okay. Good luck, Rice Cook."

"Hey, you wanna hear sumpin funny, Manda? Listen." Rice's eyebrows pinched together, and he recited:

> "An oyster met an oyster,
> And they were oysters two.
> Two oysters met two oysters,
> And they were oysters, too.
> Four oysters met a pint of milk,
> And they were oyster stew."

Manda didn't smile. "An oyster met an oyster?" she repeated dubiously.

"You must of heard that one a million times. That right? A million times?"

"Nope. Unh-unh."

"Like it?"

"Not a lot, sweetie."

He knew he would do it badly, but he wanted to do it. "Hey, Manda. You want to go out again sometime?"

"Go out?" she said. "You mean with you?"

"Unh-hunh."

"Oh no," Manda said. "You're too big and too much trouble. Bring your beer in a sec." She never brought the beer.

The plywood table, painted white, was missing its center; you dropped your oyster shells there and they clanged into the garbage can below. From time to time the tall black guys, always smiling, came to take the cans out and empty them out the side door. The shells had mounted up for some time: there were several dumptrucks' worth piled up down below the door.

Rice ate his oysters slowly, alternating between butter and cocktail sauce. He rolled the oysters around in his mouth and thought about them. His mother always said they were just little blobs of glup. They were squiggly and tasted like the pier, where the smell of rotten fish lingered no matter the season. Rice remembered cleaning fish; they were full of weird things. Flat disc eyes that stared everywhere at once; rigid gray scales his scraping knife sprayed in an arc; long trains of pale opalescent innards, like translucent worms, like glup.

That was just his mother. Most people loved oysters. Most men, anyways. Women didn't like them much. Probably that was because oysters were like sex. And most women didn't like sex much. Wasn't that right?

Rice found two pink crabs among his oysters—tiny ones, smaller than dimes. Their shells were soft, but had a nice crunch to them; their juices were sweet. Rice liked those little crabs. They were neat, complete organisms, with heads and feet, sort of. They had little eyes; they could see, and move around, and meet other crabs. They had their own wills; they were not like oysters. Not just blobs of glup.

The Marions' small retarded child wandered up to Mr. Richardson and began to pat him softly on his baseball cap. Mr. Richardson cursed. He called to Delia to get Goody out of there. Delia, who was round and pleasant, just called out: "Goody!" Goody moved off as if floating; a dreamy, implacable smile sat on her full face, curling around her tiny features.

The place was full. Outside it the summer sun went down, and the gibbous moon rolled up to the east, over the inlet. You could see flickers of moonlight in the water stirring in the inlet; the water shimmered here and there with ripples of light.

Rice found a pearl. It was just bigger than a silver cake-sprinkle and the color of lead; it swam in the oyster shell, shining a little, reflecting light from the bare bulb above. Rice turned it with his finger, then put it in his mouth and meditatively sucked on it. Rice was thinking about it, about how people were like pearls somehow, but when he came to think that Life must be the Oyster, he stopped. Because an oyster was just a blob of glup. And because he was too drunk to let stuff like that into his head. If he did he would lose something. Like his oysters, probably.

Steam was everywhere. The room was intolerably hot. Sweat soaked Rice; his shirt stuck to him along the length of his back, holding on to him. Rice had to get out of there. Life was a blob of glup. He had to get out of Yauhannah; had to leave home. He would never come back. At the same time, he wasn't sure he could successfully rise from his seat.

He waved Manda over. "Couldn't finish, sweetie?" she asked archly. When she added up the bill she moved her lips.

"Could of," Rice said. "Just got tired."

She circled something on her pad. "Five ninety-five," she said. "Beer's on the house." She handed Rice the slip. "You gonna be all right?" she asked, as she patted his shoulder.

He didn't look right at her. "Want to go out with me?" he asked the table.

"I guess you're all right. Don't forget to tip."

Goody Marion came up after Manda left. She took her curiously large hand off her forehead, where it usually rested on a lumpy temple, and ripped a blank piece of paper from a pad. She held the paper out to Rice, talking; her voice was low and moaning, and had no words in it. Rice took the paper and thanked her. Goody talked again, growling; then she lifted her skirt right over her head.

"Goody!" Delia called. Goody dropped her skirt and sat down at the next table. She put her damn head down on her arms. She had the littlest ears. She was making noises, and Rice thought maybe she was crying. Sometimes Goody did, and you couldn't figure out why.

Rice bounced the flat of his hand against plywood again. He was concentrating on another equation that suggested itself to him: that being drunk was like being retarded. That he was like Goody, and Goody knew it. Retards are smart, Rice thought. They know a lot; they just can't tell you about it. Like me, right now.

So what did he know? He knew he was drunk. He didn't want to be any more. Steam still billowed from the big pots on the burners. Being retarded, being drunk, was like being in a room full of steam at night. These were true things: he was drunk, Life was glup, he had to get out of Yauhannah, and he couldn't move.

But he had that little pearl. Rice held it tightly; he could feel it giving him wishes. He had three. You always got three. Rice leaned forward, and his shirt peeled right off from the chair with a soft ripping sound. He wasn't stuck; that was one wish. Hold on to that pearl. He was up. He was moving. Hold on to that pearl.

Across the wobbly room. Stand up there by the cash register. Fish out the wallet. Don't forget the tip. Go back to the table? No. Give Delia a bill for Manda. Push the wallet back in, that's still yours. Bye, Delia, Manda. Get to that door. Out that door you're free.

Rice remembers the door. He lingered there for a second, watching the fish-eye moon stare down on the waves of the inlet. It was the wrong door—the one leading out to the graveyard of shucked shells. No one actually saw Rice fall. Manda saw him standing in the doorway, but she thought he was just looking; she didn't suspect that in another second he'd be falling—like a ton of bricks, and with about the same level of consciousness. Manda had to go fetch a Dr Pepper for Davey Naughton right then, and she missed Rice's first sauntering, sloppy step out onto nothing and into nothingness—not to mention his midair spin, which though graceless was marked by a certain placid resignation, and then his crashing landing among the oyster shells, which sounded like someone dragging chains along a stone floor.

"Jesus God!" Delia cried from behind the cash register. "Only one guy's ever done that before!"—as if she was more surprised by the statistical oddity of Rice's fall than worried about its possible consequences. Rice may have heard her, but he doesn't remember that. He remembers the feel of the oyster shells beneath him, sharp-edged and loose like gravel, clammy (despite the contradiction); he remembers the fetid smell down there, the seaside stink of ancient shellfish juices aged in Carolina heat.

Manda remembers rushing to the doorway, still holding Davey Naughton's Dr Pepper. A crowd gathered quickly behind her, and hung, wordless, over the edge. They all watched Rice as he rolled among the oyster shells. Manda remembers that Rice held an oyster aloft in each hand, as if he'd won them; that he was laughing at a joke no one else understood; and that he kept saying something—kept repeating a syllable that sounded like "Glup. Glup. Glup. Glup."

Carrie,

You're like a newspaper. You only talk about the bad things that happen.

I had a happy childhood, Carrie. I always knew how to tie my shoes. I didn't fall on my face every time I drank a beer. I still don't. I wasn't such a damn fool with girls. I wasn't such a damn fool about anything. I had friends you never talk about and some real good girlfriends and some real good times. I didn't usually go out eating oysters by myself. I did that time, but I didn't usually.

You make it sound like I was somebody I wasn't. I think I know why you're doing it. But I'm not so sure *you* do.

I've got two questions I have to ask.

Carrie, why didn't you come down and get that teakettle?

Carrie, what were you doing in the damn bathtub?

Ten

Rice left Yauhannah.

He traveled a long time.

A modern Frédéric Moreau, he experienced the melancholy associated with fleas and crabs; the chill feeling of waking up on bare mattresses on the floor; and the dizzy effect of mountains and marijuana.

He worked, but only for a living.

First he was a house painter; he was stung by wasps with remarkable frequency, and by the fear that he'd fall and somehow fail to land, anywhere, ever. He became an offset printer, and despised printing. The whole idea was to end up with what you'd started with: producing and performing repetitions. Next he apprenticed as a carpenter, only to spend most days breathing in the pink dust from insulation; he imagined his lungs tangled and choking in an immense, hairy, pink ball, a creature from inner space.

Rice never felt content with a job. He was sure he never would.

He moved first to Columbia, South Carolina. Slowly, Columbia began to seem too close to home—as if Yauhannah were creeping toward the center of the state, impelled by the batty longings of his mother, who mailed Rice packages of store-bought cookies and telephoned him at meaningless length every other night.

He then tried Washington, D.C. He stayed there for years; but it was all wrong. It was hot and crowded, and in the winter it was cold and crowded. He was expected to come home for each paltry holiday (President's Day), and when he did his mother tended to call him Eugene. The deglazing solution he was obliged to use on the rollers of the offset press gave him fierce headaches that lasted through morose evenings. In D.C., Rice lived with a woman he did not love, for reasons he did not understand; when he finally left her, he didn't understand why he was doing that, either. D.C. was wrong for Rice; it kept getting more and more wrong; but when he left, Rice was not at all sure he was doing the right thing.

He formed attachments to many women. Years went by; and he endured the idleness of his mind and the inertia of his heart. He dreamed restlessly and hard, as if looking for a solution, a secret passageway; he believed in his dreams the way people once believed in demons. In a dream Rice walked over a golden bridge spanning azure waters; he was linked to sea and sky, happy as breeze. In this way Rice fell easy prey to a disease endemic to Americans: he piled his belongings in a truck and moved to San Francisco.

In 1975 San Francisco was shorn of most of its hair—or at least of the novelty of hair, and of drugs, of revolution, of free love, of faded bluejeans, of dreams of change, and even of the phrase Far Out. Rice managed to move into an apartment on Clayton Street, just a few blocks from the corner of Haight and Ashbury, without much feeling for the way things had been in the summer of 1967, the Summer of Love. For Rice the Haight was just a low-rent district, a place where he could afford to live while making two-fifty an hour as an apprentice locksmith.

Rice's dream quickly developed a few kinks. Somehow the Haight did not seem like California, at least not like the California that Rice had dreamed. It was cold. It was always foggy; they could hardly be said to have a summer at all. Rice missed the endless Carolina summer, the thunder and lightning, the murky, humid air in the swamp, where stillness was almost palpable; he even missed the bugs. "Where are all the damn mosquitoes around here?" he asked someone who was almost a native Californian.

"Isn't it great? There aren't any."

"I'm *tell*ing you," Rice said, shaking his head.

There were bugs: cockroaches. But there was no golden bridge at all; it was red.

Instead of dreams, in San Francisco Rice found the sediment of the sixties: people who had been left behind, stuck in time—the shed skin of the era. Rice only noticed them bit by bit, but gradually came to think himself surrounded. There was, for example, Emma, who rode Rice's bus in the morning. "Don't you look at me that way!" Emma would suddenly shout at a fellow passenger—any fellow passenger, usually women, though one week she singled out a man in hospital whites for daily treatment. The accused often tried to defend themselves: "I *wasn't* looking at you." Emma would sneer, "Oh no?" and then abruptly begin to bang the offending party about the head with her black plastic handbag. "This'll teach *you!*" she shouted. "You can't go around staring at people, you rotten bitch. You scumbag."

Emma went on, curse after curse. Sometimes Emma's victims tried to enlist the driver on their side of the dispute. To every protest the driver, a thick-necked black man with a silver star inlaid in a front tooth, replied in the same calm way. "That's just Emma," he would say.

"But she hit me with her handbag!"

"Don't worry," the driver always said. "She's crazy. She does that every day."

Rice repeated this to himself, trying it out: Don't worry; she's crazy. There were many regular oddities in Rice's life—the man with the bananas on Haight Street, the skinny kid in whiteface and navy captain's uniform, the beautiful woman who did cartwheels up and down the Panhandle, the guy in the three-piece suit who played dead at noon on Market Street. The bus driver's advice seemed to make sense. Don't worry, they're all crazy.

Rice applied this principle now to the spiritual people who abounded in the Bay Area. Some worshipped a sixteen-year-old perfect master from India who had a Rolls-Royce and a suitcase full of money; some shaved their heads, donned peach-colored robes, and congregated in the streets to sway to tambourines and chant nonsense syllables; some excoriated each other and themselves in group talk sessions; some managed to become unborn babies again, and screamed real loud, the louder the better, as they got birthed in their doctors' offices; some joined together to repeat several Japanese words over and over again, for you could have whatever in the world you wanted if you said these Japanese words enough times.

Rice had been raised in rural South Carolina, where you were either a Baptist or nothing, or a little of each. He was a true disbeliever, and he had trouble making sense of all this erratic behavior in the name of God. But now he merely repeated his bus driver's panacea, felt better, and went on about his life in San Francisco, for a time.

Rice was slow to make friends, but he did do it. His best one was his boss, a thirty-year-old Jewish locksmith named Marv. Rice had known lots of Jewish people before, but he had never known just one. "Don't worry about that," Marv told him. "You're in luck. I don't believe that Jewish stuff. Except for blintzes."

One day the two of them were strolling in Golden Gate Park, heading vaguely toward the aquarium, because Rice loved all dolphins. It was a cheerful, vacant Saturday afternoon in the years before roller skaters made the park dangerous on such afternoons. Rice's eyes were half closed in squint and dream, but eventually he noticed a woman walking beside him. Her hair was shoulder-length and absolutely straight, her teeth perfectly even, her blue cotton blouse flawlessly ironed, her severe gray A-line skirt smooth. She was not exactly pretty, but a certain amiable directness was transmitted by a quick and steady smile. "Hi," she said to Rice, and fell into step alongside him. "Could you tell me the time, please?"

Rice examined his watchless wrist. "I don't exactly know," he said, with some regret. "Getting toward four, I think."

"Thank you," she said. "Thanks a lot." Rice nodded, but she didn't stop thanking him. "You know, most people won't even give you the time of day any more."

"I did the best I could," Rice said. "Sorry."

"No, you were really nice," she said earnestly. "Thanks a lot. What's your name, anyway?"

"Rice."

"Rice. That's a very unusual name. You must be a very unusual person, Rice."

Rice didn't think he was especially unusual, especially in San Francisco. He didn't especially want to be unusual. "Well, thanks," Rice said, uncertainly.

"Thank *you*," she said, her smile placid, fixed.

Thank *you*? Rice repeated to himself, testing the emphasis.

Marv leaned across Rice. "You're a Moonie, aren't you?" Marv said.

"Thank you," she said. "I'm a member of the Unification Church."

Rice thought he knew the Unifications; they were somewhere below Congregational.

"The Moonies," Marv stated.

"Hey, Marv. Take it easy. She just wants to know what time it is."

"Marv. That's my favorite name, Marv."

"You and my fucking mother."

"Hey. Hey, Marv. Cut it out."

"My name's Oz."

"Now that's a *real* unusual name," Rice said.

"I happen to think you Moonies are full of shit," Marv said.

"Thank you. How did you make that decision? Has someone talked to you about our group before?"

"You don't know how many times," Marv said.

"I'd like to talk more about it, Marv. I think you've probably heard the wrong information. Can you spare a minute?"

"Not even one second."

The woman turned on Rice, and he noticed the flash of a bright object in her hand; she took several purposeful steps toward him, brandishing it. Rice flinched, stepped back. The woman caught hold of his shirt; Rice put up his hand to ward off the blow.

"Have a good day, Rice," she said, and stabbed Rice's collar.

Rice looked down. A small yellow pin, fashioned in the shape of a cartoon duck, danced between her fingers. "Would you care to make a donation to our church?" she asked, her hands still fumbling with Rice's shirt. Rice felt a tiny prick from the pin, and with a grunt of imagined pain he leaped away. The duck dangled half-hooked in his collar.

Marv jumped between them. "Leave us *alone*," he bellowed, and raised his fist menacingly—as if the woman really had stabbed Rice, and might stab him too.

"Okay, Marv," she said calmly. She turned away. She looked back once and waved. She was still smiling.

Rice turned to his friend, marveling. "Hey, buddy. How did you know what she wanted?"

"I'm from New York," Marv said. "I know life." He freed Donald Duck from Rice's collar. "Besides," he said, "in Berkeley I used to live across the street from those assholes."

As if they had been rescued from violent danger, Rice and Marv now saw all the beauties of the day. The afternoon seemed even sunnier than before, the park even lovelier. Everything gave Rice pleasure. They walked on, then stopped by some tennis courts. The players on this court seemed extraordinarily, impossibly good; the game was an endless succession of miraculous retrieves. Rice and Marv watched for a long time. Finally Rice became aware of a presence close to him; someone else was watching these amazing players. Rice looked down. A tiny man with short red hair and shiny white face smiled pleasantly up at Rice. "You like tennis?" he asked.

I've seen that smile before, Rice thought. "Little bit," he said.

Marv leaned over. "Moonie?" he asked casually.

The little man grinned. "No," he said. "Not at all. No." He chuckled. "No, I'm a Scientologist. Would you like to know about Scientology?"

Marv was a short wiry man with short hair and a long nose, which he regretted. Rice liked it, because he was tall and heavy and had a short nose. Marv was a fast talker, an adept locksmith, and a wonderful cook. He tried to teach Rice the skills of his trade, but Rice's hands fumbled forever. Rice became Marv's permanent apprentice, tagging along like a huge dog as Marv drove from locked car to locked apartment, doors springing open under his fast fingers. "You'll get it," Marv kept saying. "Your problem is your ridiculous background. What we're doing here is bringing the technology of the age, of New York, to the backwoods of South Carolina. It's going to take some time to transport a whole century into your swamp."

Rice never learned locks. He had better success with cooking, probably because he was already interested in eating. "I'm giving you a whole world here," Marv said, as he showed Rice how to make basic spaghetti sauce. "I'm your Auntie Mame, fella. If you can do a red sauce, a white sauce, and pie crust, and never overcook your vegetables, then I can personally promise you a spot in Heaven. Angels gotta eat, you know."

Rice admired Marv, because Marv hated sports (which he called "the opiate of the people"), liked every form of alcohol, and smoked large quantities of good dope. Marv's North Beach apartment was immaculate—blond wood floors, voluptuous tropical plants, Georgia O'Keeffe posters, and a steadily absent roommate. In San Francisco Marv was Rice's one pillar of wisdom. But not forever.

Later Rice would decide that it had been coming on for some time; in retrospect he noticed a whole crew of quirks—bland quirks. A shift in the tempo of speech, toward slow; a dullness of gaze; long pauses before locked doors, though the right tool was already in hand. But Rice did not notice anything different about Marv until Marv went to Santa Cruz for three weeks. Marv went away making vague jokes about how everybody else was retreating but he was going to attack; he came back just like himself, and to Rice's mind it was the essential Marv who sat that morning in an overstuffed armchair, North Beach sunlight haloing his head, as he ate with green salsa a steaming burrito of his own making.

"You interested in coming to Santa Cruz with me on Thursday?" Marv asked casually. He dipped a spoon into the salsa, then emptied it on his burrito; it was a tablespoon.

"What's in Santa Cruz on Thursday?"

"The Bunyatta," Marv said.

"What's that?"

"The Bunyatta? You haven't heard about the Bunyatta?"

"Nope. Unh-unh."

"Well, Rice, I'll tell you. He's an amazing man. He's pure. That's all he is. When he gathers his disciples around him, he puts on the Crown of the Ages, which is this ring made from the hair of a hundred pure women. He puts it on and his aura begins to glow. The whole room takes on this weird light. His face starts to grow and grow, till finally he's like this big, fat, beaming baby, with white light shooting out of his head. It is amazing. Finally he becomes the perfect incarnation of compassion."

"What's an aura?" Rice said.

"An aura," Marv began, his voice slow, clear, and sonorous, "is that part of the soul that closely surrounds the body. It is the energy that emanates from every living being."

"No shit," Rice said. "What does a—what'd you call it?—a carnation of compassion do?"

"He doesn't do anything. He doesn't have to. He just puts out this aura, and you slowly understand the true nature of life. He doesn't do it for himself; he does it for you."

"How many shows does he do a night?" Rice asked.

"Just the one," Marv said, and Rice thought: Uh-oh.

He tried not to believe it. "When the aura turns yellow, do you stop, or just slow down?" he tried.

"You just look at it," Marv explained, and then stared off into the distance, though the wall was only about five feet away.

"What color aura does he have to start with, before he puts on the crown?" Rice asked.

"You can't see it then. You just know it's there."

Rice gave up. "Hey, buddy. You kidding me?"

Marv turned his quiet gaze to Rice. "No," he said, as if he were saying something profound.

"You're talkin about auras as if they're printed on train schedules or sumpin. If an aura was as clear as all that, what would be the point in it being an aura?"

"The point is," Marv said, "that it is well defined. But you have to believe it before you see it. And you have to see it without looking for it."

"There you go," Rice said unhappily, and tossed the last bit of burrito into his mouth. He chewed quickly, swallowed a lump. Another appeared in his throat. "Well, I guess I gotta go," he said. "Have a terrific time in Santa Cruz. Thanks for the burrito and all."

"Thank *you,*" Marv said, and he gave Rice a faintly familiar smile.

A few months later Rice moved again. He took with him a painfully clear memory of Marv's blissful smile. That well-pleased face came to Rice often and without warning, the way Eugene's contorted one, supported by rope, still did. Rice imagined that things kept happening to him because of his own frustrations—as if his life kept cutting the same pattern out for his overcoat, and it was always ten sizes too small; he was bound, he was choked, and in his haste to pull off the tiny garment he always ripped his life to shreds. He felt that he was always compelled to be someone other than himself; and he was never good at it at all.

This is Rice's way of looking at it; someone else might read the events quite differently. Someone else might regard all Rice's disasters as a series of crude spurs, blows to the mule's rear, applied by a heartless rider; someone else might choose to believe that Rice was being maneuvered all the while; someone else might see that Kismet, the kitten's mother, had him by the neck's nape, and was slowly, laboriously dragging him across time and space. To Portland. To us

Carrie,

In this one you didn't mention Bethany. We lived together in San Francisco for two years, we were real happy, we almost got married. You know that. But all you talk about is Marv. Goddamn Marv.

I know you're trying to make it look like my life was one long disaster before you came along. I mean, you're practically inventing my life.

Meantime, we got our own problems, the mountain is going off, everything is nuts. We've got more important things to talk about than this stuff.

Love,
Me

SECTION TWO

One

Evan and I took the train across Canada in the false spring of 1975 and when we arrived in Portland neither of us had ever seen the place before. I don't know what we were expecting, I truly don't; it was raining a little, we expected that. Most of Portland seemed to be one-family houses, as if the city contained its own suburbs; most of the houses reminded me of boats, and the sidewalks were full of water, and so were our shoes, soon enough. We lugged our things into Scott's house, and stood dripping in his hallway. Scott was a Columbia friend of ours who had moved out West and gotten into computers. He was ridiculously omniscient about sports and that day he was watching, I think, basketball on his minuscule color TV. He pointed us to the room where we were to crash, then hurried back to his game; there we were, the room was redolent with the smell of Scott's used socks, and you could hear the rain blithe on the roof and the cars splashing on the street, and at that moment I did not think that Portland was the place for me. I was ready to go back and Gal Friday in New York for the rest of my born days, no matter how many Oregonian check-out cashiers said Hello and smiled at me. But for the next few days Scott took us around the state, hiking out to the windy tip of Cape Falcon on the coast, walking behind waterfalls in the Columbia River Gorge, strolling under umbrellas in the Rose Gardens—and when we looked down on the city of Portland from Pittock Mansion that Sunday afternoon, the sun promptly scuttled into view, throwing snatches of rainbow in every direction, till it seemed that all the clouds in the world had an opalescent lining. Snowy mountains thronged the horizon, and it was clear that we must move to this blessed spot.

That summer we did. Evan got his job at Van Buren High; we found our white house on 31st Street; I began to write *Human Wishes,* and when I reached page 100 I quit my job at Northwest Natural Gas. It was a terrible, terrible job: the company name sounded like a Mel Brooks joke, and in the office everyone felt constrained to assume a deathly formality toward everyone else, as if making money were a serious, important thing to do. I had never been happier than the day I quit. It snowed that day in Portland—fat, wet, lazy flakes that perched in your hair like white flowers—and I walked all the long way home, drifting home the way the snow drifted down. As I walked home, more and more of my novel became clear to me, I could actually see the words printed on a page in my mind, and at the same time I could see Evan and the fire I knew he would have going in the living room. I remember that I began to salivate, because suddenly everything in my life took on a savor, a richness, as if I knew that living with Evan in our house, with the whole day to write my novel, would be like eating a subtle and marvelous dessert, a crème brûlée or oeufs à la neige. When I got home, it was as I had guessed and hoped. Evan rocked in front of the fire; he wore his overlarge white fisherman's sweater, so familiar that it was suddenly precious; he gave me his small, exact, benign smile. I walked in and I had quit forever and I was free: I took off my coat, my scarf, my boots, my sweater, my blouse, my skirt, my tights, my bra and my panties, then helped Evan out of his clothes, and we made love on the braided rug in the soft firelight, crackling like the fire. And at the time it felt as if forever would come and go; we would stay just as we were, quite happily.

All the same, it was less than three years later that Evan and I had our little talk. It was not that I was unhappy with Evan; I wanted Evan's love, Evan loves with all his generous heart. But a seed of dissatisfaction had sprouted within me; I felt restless roots churning, grabbing hold; something started to make its sinuous way toward the surface. It would be a long time before I had a good look at the full flower; in the meantime I could feel something, but not understand what. This thing took curious forms in me; the heart moves in mysterious ways. I had, for example, weeks when I craved sweets as I had not done since I was eighteen, in Paris. Twice I bought gigantic bags of Snickers bars, kept them hidden in my study—as if Evan would even *want* a Snickers—and I ate them in secret, downing the chocolate in three bites, my pleasure acute, even as I asked myself, What *are* you doing? I began to stay up later and later, watching movies on television; any movie would do. I watched, for pitiful example, the Three Stooges; I *identified* with Moe. Perhaps that's stretching it, but I did feel an ineffable kinship to that stooge when he adopted one particular expression of perplexity. He adopted it regularly. So did I. I stayed up later and later, became groggier and groggier by day. I began to read books about gardening, lots of books, though I do not garden. I had the idea that I would enjoy gardening, that it would suit me.

Perhaps it would have, but is that any excuse for finding yourself parked in front of the TV, chowing down on Snickers, reading about how they twist and warp dwarf plum trees in Japan—at two oh five A.M., while Curly hits his own head with a hammer?

I did not understand myself, and I can see why. I had no idea what I wanted; if someone had come along and told me, I doubt that I would have believed it. I loved Evan, and I knew it, and I wanted to stay with him forever. Yet here I was, talking to him about opening up the relationship. I think I used the word fun. I think I talked about static states and broadening horizons; I don't think I mentioned Moe, or warped dwarf trees, or all those Snickers bars. Perhaps I could have said: Evan, everything in our life is so settled, so obvious and inevitable, that we could just stop where we are and it would be the same thing. I could have said: I am a writer, and for a writer a little security is a good thing, and a lot is poison. But these are arguments, not reasons; the reasons were deep within me, which is to say they were beyond me. The reasons weren't reasonable; they were merely feelings. Of course I would never have accepted that kind of talk. So it's not surprising that I didn't mention that. There were peculiar crocodiles crawling around down there, but it's not surprising I didn't mention that. Because I thought they were just mossy logs floating on the water.

The discussion was the kind that married people have in the living room, over coffee and cognac, after the kids have gone to bed; they come out with a plan, a program which they try to carry out as if it were a task. With Evan and me there were no kids to put to bed first, no wedding rings to slip discreetly into pockets, no cognac, and not even a living room; there was coffee at the tiny kitchen table, amid a minefield of empty wine bottles, and that familiar conversation that wound like a picturesque path toward other people's beds.

For a long time I thought that Evan said Okay only because he was indifferent about me. I was wrong. I think he understood my need more than I did. Evan knows where I keep rubber bands; he knows when I bought my burgundy swim suit, and how much I paid at Nordstrom's for the lemon yellow sweater, and he knows the words to my high school alma mater; it's not surprising that he knows about the important stuff too, we've been together since we were kids. I'll never know anyone as well as I know Evan. When the waitress leans over the counter I want to say, He'll have two eggs over medium, hash browns, coffee, toast. Whole wheat. But I never do. Both that knowing and that not-speaking are involved in the way I love Evan.

Evan was perfectly happy with me. Logically, he could not become more perfectly happy. He had not come on to a woman for almost twelve years; the idea that he should now begin nightly invasions of singles bars, his shirt unbuttoned halfway to the waist and his buttocks wedged into designer jeans, both annoyed and exhausted him. Evan was not, is not, adventuresome. We can leave it at that.

But I was delighted. I felt that I was suddenly not so much living as watching a movie, a romantic comedy where anything could happen. That dreamboat in the brown sweater, back toward me, is about to trip over my feet, bump into me; he'll turn around and be Cary Grant, and I'll be Katharine Hepburn, and at first, of course, we'll hate each other, and it's only in the last reel that— I left off the ending; we hadn't even seen the credits, who wants to know the ending now? But in the meantime I felt ecstatic, the air had been infused with possibility, on Portland streets I regarded passers-by as if browsing, window-shopping. Just the notion that I could buy this one or that one gave me a feeling of luxuriant wealth. The mere looking provided a palpable sexual tingle, the way a rapturous description of Dungeness crab dripping drawn butter can make you salivate, hours away from your own slightly overcooked scrambled eggs.

It pains me to admit that I did not even once manage the thing— the taking on of a lover—the way I meant to. There must be a correct way to do it: with grace and humor and a modicum of detachment. No one cares, no one is hurt, all are amused: a proper affair is an afternoon in an amusement park. This roller coaster is quite a thrill, you bet, but when your time is up you merely hop out, go on to the next ride. Well, my heart turned out to be on the ride. I never learned how to store it in a little gilded box for those occasions when its presence was a burden. I modeled that little knot of a heart on my sleeve, and that was all the trouble.

I still ask myself why I didn't know the trouble I'd bring on my own house; why, in this century of free will, I couldn't help it— couldn't help myself.

I was given a sign that afternoon, which began so happily, so blithely. I sat on the number 14 bus headed for downtown Portland, where I would meet Rice for the first time. In a nearly empty bus I was seated toward the back, directly opposite a young and very black woman who was eating a bright red apple. I gazed straight at her, in the way mass transit encourages you to do—that dull, anonymous stare that is meant to communicate nothing at all, as your head bobs on its neck with each shake and rattle of the bus. The woman's apple had the quality of apparent perfection that a piece of fruit, or an egg, or rows of waves on a windless day can have. The woman took a bite, and juice arched into the air from her snapping incisors. I could feel her enjoyment of the apple's sweetness and tang; I knew that the apple alone was sufficient to make her happy. Suddenly her head bobbed down violently, as if she were ducking a blow, and a piece of half-eaten apple shot out of her mouth. She jerked her head up; her face was bloated, contorted with pain. I thought she was choking, and I was about to jump up and slap her back, when the woman let her head drop, her chin sink onto her chest. And then it was clear that she was sobbing, uncontrollably and unashamedly.

The next stop was mine. I stepped onto the street, and the bus pulled away, puffing exhaust. I caught one more image of the woman through the smoke—her head leaning back, her legs stretched out randomly into the empty aisle, her two hands still clutching the half-eaten apple.

I started to walk, and found my legs shaking beneath me. Perhaps my unsteadiness had to do with the abruptness of the woman's woe, or perhaps just the apple itself. It was round and smooth-skinned, shiny with highlights, a perfect object; but, as an object, unable to contribute even a drop of happiness against the dust storm of her despair, because people's lives (I began thinking, as I walked toward the library, slowly putting one foot just in front of the other one, just making it), because people's lives don't have much to do with the objects in the world, because people's lives are imagined—yes, perhaps it had to do with the distance between that poor apple and that poor woman: I let loose my own flood. I blubbered. Blubbered all the long way to the Multnomah County Library, shocking my own innocent passers-by, whose O-shaped mouths and huge eyes of surprise made them resemble grotesque creatures in a Munch painting. I cried on and on. There was one part of me that was slowly and meticulously turning over in my mind (like some bright, unnameable thing picked up in the street) why it is that some days you walk around and everyone you see seems a metaphor for yourself, and for the whole pathetic race of men and women; and I was thinking about using the woman's trouble in my writing; and I was crying, drenching my face. My tears were only halted by a debilitating attack of hiccups.

At times, you see, I am horribly unhappy, and don't know why.

The appearance of the sorrowing woman with the apple was a portent. For there were difficulties—more, there were storms—to come.

I went to the library that afternoon, but I couldn't get settled there; I tried to "shop." To me this meant browsing crookedly over glass cases—staring at, but not seeing, agates whose gently undulating tan strata mimicked desert landscapes, pale pearls in a heap on black velvet, rings starring diamonds, plain bands of yellow gold. I was not in the market for these items; I waved away a toothy salesman whose clasped hands rubbed each other reassuringly. It was no good trying to lose myself in the nature of shining objects: pretty things gave me back only a warped image of myself—a tiny, lithe, and nacreous me executing miraculous back bends over the slippery curvature of this rounded pendant, that pearl. I left my image on the pearl and went out into the street again.

I was still suffering from a curious dis-ease, aftershock from someone else's tears; I decided to find a friend. I don't have many, and people aren't supposed to live in cities any more, but I do know one person who lives downtown: Louisa, a gentle, pallid tropical fish. Louisa's apartment is below ground, in a windowless basement. Rooms are separated by hundreds of wooden fruit crates stacked to the ceiling, containing everything Louisa owns. When Louisa wants to change her shoes, she drags her stepladder beneath a battered cardboard square calligraphed with the letter B; seven feet up, Louisa fishes in a crate, humming with pleasure, and when she finally pulls out two boots (a right and a left but not necessarily the correct right or the right left), an expression of mild triumph flickers on her wan face. Louisa is calm as an aunt, and when I visit her she reads me her sing-song poetry, about which I am polite, and makes me green tea, about which I am lukewarm.

Louisa was not alone that Saturday afternoon. I said I would go away, but she insisted I come in, come in. Obediently I followed her down the dark hall. I'm not that guilty, you see. I'm not responsible for all that happens: events occur, propelled by the secret workings of some infernal machine, devised by committees of bald men bent over blueprints in small rooms with trap doors.

In Louisa's living room fluorescent bulbs cast a purplish, underwater glow. Two people lounged on a brown sofa, whose floral pattern (irises) one could feel with fingers but not quite make out with astute pupils. One of these people was a woman, black-braided, wearing a faded red scarf on her head and pin-striped overalls everywhere else. Her hand covered like a cap the knee nearest hers.

The knee belonged to a mountainous man. The features of this man's face included a pale forelock, a curl that drooped into the picture; one burly eyebrow running nonstop over both eyes; mild, dazzling, saucer-big, innocent, apologetic blue eyes—one, I would find, wildly bloodshot; a small bowed nose; an arching mustache; and a wolflike, slightly insane grin that was apparently difficult for him to eradicate from his face, though he often made an effort. Later I would find a free-spirited tangle of curly strawcolored hair, a liberal quantity of freckles, a mole on his right buttock, a semicircular patch of blond pubic hair, a long uncircumcised penis, a set of ticklish ribs, an oddly high-pitched giggle.

Louisa smiled at each of us in turn, nodding, which was her way of introducing us, since she is terrible with names (she calls many people, including me, Jenny). She announced that she'd make tea, then went away and left the three of us in the dark.

"Louisa's abandoned us," the braided woman said, and there was a silence. "Let's guess names," she suggested playfully, and gave the man's knee a squeeze. He didn't seem to respond. She began on her own: "You ask us one," she said to me," and then we'll ask you one."

I was about to say that I couldn't begin to guess (though she looked to me like a Jenny), when I peeked into the man's wide eyes, and I saw in front of my own eyes the blurred form of a letter; the shadowy landscape of an old, half-remembered dream; the titles of a film flickering, and then fading out.

"Yours begins with an R," I said.

"There you go," he said, in a drawl, with a grin.

"You knew," the woman said quickly. "How do you know her?" she asked the man.

"I don't," he said, pleased. "Nope. Unh-unh."

"Louisa told you," the woman tried.

"Louisa would never remember," I said, defending myself. "It was just a guess."

"What's the rest of it?" she challenged.

I looked at this man again, and I knew. I said his first name.

"How'd you guess *that?*" the woman accused.

I made an exotic little movement of the hand, curling my fingers around space; I raised and lowered my eyebrows mock-mysteriously, trying to make a joke out of it.

But I must admit that pictures came into my brain. As a child I won spelling bees without trouble; but I was convinced I did not actually know how to spell at all. The teacher would intone the word, I would repeat it aloud, then close my eyes. The word would run, right to left, across a silver screen in my mind; I would merely read off the letters as they entered the frame, the way you count boxcars at a railroad crossing. When I came to nothingness the barrier slowly rose, the lights turned to green; I stopped talking, opened my eyes.

I told Rice what I saw. I saw a black mountain. I saw swamps. I saw alligators. I saw three tow-headed little boys, arranged according to height. I saw a yellow and a red machine, rolling on black circles, dropping yellow squares behind them, and two boys chasing after. I saw an old man painting a picture beneath a gnarled oak. I saw lightning split the sky like a crooked grin. I saw a black and white cat bleeding on a gray stone floor. When I came to a man whose head was held up by a rope, I stopped talking, and opened my eyes.

All that I had seen was beyond me; I felt startled and strangely annoyed by my sudden prescience—as if it were a bumbling intruder, knocking over chairs, bumping objects from shelves, announcing its presence, when all I wanted was for someone to steal something from me, swiftly and soundlessly, in the dead of night.

Rice held his silence. When he finally spoke he said, "I'm tellin ya," to no one. A while later he chose to add, "Well, there you go."

The braided woman was more direct. "Who have *you* been talking to?" she asked, a little piercingly.

"No one," I said. "I don't even know where my little outburst originated."

"I see," she said, more calmly. "You make these things up."

"I write fiction," I admitted.

"That's not fiction," Rice said. "I wish to hell it was."

I wondered if he knew I'd seen the hanged man. I wondered who that man was. More than wondered: I think I knew that somehow I'd have to find out.

The woman said, "You do tricks like that for a living?"

"Listen. I've never seen pictures like that before. I'm not the type. I don't even believe in that kind of thing."

Louisa re-entered, carrying a tray: a glass teapot, four glasses with handles, four pieces of Chinese pound cake. "Sorry it took me so long," Louisa said as she put the tray down. "I imagine you know the story of each other's lives by now."

Louisa probably noticed, at the corners of her vision, three sudden, synchronized movements. A quiet immediately roared in, then faded awkwardly out.

"I guess *some* of us do," the woman in overalls said peevishly—a little cat, claws still dug in at her man's knee.

Louisa said, "Pardon?"

"We've been having a regular little séance here."

"That's nice," Louisa said, ignoring the woman's tone. She handed tea first to me, and said, "I love séances. For some reason they do very well in this room. I used to speak with my dead aunts quite regularly. Then I came out of the closet, and they never spoke to me again. It was a shame, really. My aunt Vivienne has the best recipe for rhubarb custard pie. I wish I had written it down."

There was a long silence after that. For me it was a miserable one. I was sorry for what I had seen, for the hostility I had provoked, and for this ridiculous instant intimacy. I swear I did not want such a nexus; not with that someone, not with anyone but Evan.

The man whose life had passed before my eyes looked down. Eyes down, he began to pick invisible pieces of foreign matter off of his brown corduroy trousers with fanatical deliberateness. He studied the texture of each wale under the microscope of his embarrassment. I felt pity for huge, handsome him.

"We still don't know *your* name," the woman in overalls said.

"Carolyn Kingston. And yours?"

"Vanessa Jordan," she said bitterly.

"And I still don't know *your* last name," I said.

When Rice looked up at me, I saw his freckles for the first time, a touch of boyishness that disarmed me almost as much as the innocence and sweetness of the smile he gave me now. "I'll have to write it down for you," he said.

He dumped wooden matches out of their box and into a pocket of his red chamois shirt. He wrote with black felt-tipped pen on the inside of the box, then slid the box shut and passed it to me.

I opened it, like a secret. It said:

> RICE U. COOK
> Yauhannah, South Carolina
> Born Nov. 7, 1951
> At Your Service
> 281-6204

"Rice U. Cook," I said.
"No jokes," he said.
"No jokes."

When I left Louisa's I found myself staring at sidewalk, at store windows, at unimportant things, startled at the power of what had happened. But it did not compare to the power that was to come.

Carrie,

There you go with that destiny stuff again. You know it wasn't that way. You bring in all this extra stuff, and you leave out basic stuff. Like who that woman Vanessa was.

But mostly I just want to apologize about the chicken hearts. I'm sorry about that and I want to apologize.

Talk to me, Carrie. You have to talk to me.

Love
Me

Two

It didn't take long for Rice's voice to jump onto the other end of my telephone. He coaxed, but didn't push. He wanted to know whether I could still see events from his life; I couldn't. He wanted me to tell him everything I had seen: What did the old man look like, what was he painting, where was he sitting, what kind of day was it, what was that old man wearing? For the most part I didn't remember. I remembered a mustache, I thought. That was wrong, there was no mustache. I remembered a spot of red on the old man's painting. Was that all? I must have disappointed Rice terribly.

Rice said he wanted to see me, that was all. I knew what he wanted, even if he didn't. I just thought of his saucer eyes, bewildered but not dull, like a fawn's, and I said that I would. When I heard myself say that, a peculiar melancholy overtook me. After all this time, I thought. Why, after all this time, should it be this man?

There isn't much men can do in the way of courtship that you haven't seen before, and nothing that can distract you from seeing through them. The central object never changes—the word object is used to elicit a cameo appearance from its other meaning. In the end, what you regard as an acceptable approach depends on how much you like the man. There's no getting around that.

Apparently Rice was a romantic, or wanted to be one. Just before I pushed open the library doors, five-thirty on the dot, I saw him framed in one of the door's twelve panes. He shifted his weight uncomfortably and jammed one hand into his pocket; but the other one, dangling beside him, held a long-stemmed white rose by the throat. When I came close he held it out to me with a stiff arm, the way you might thrust a cross at a vampire.

"Bought you a goddamn flower," he said, and grimaced. "Cost a buck."

I took it between thumb and index finger. "Nice," I said. "Why damn the poor baby?" I stroked the rose. I didn't know what to say any more than he did. "Poor maligned baby," I said.

Rice scratched his chin and frowned. "Real dumb thing to do," he said. "Corny. You bring a woman a rose, you look like you're playing puppydog or sumpin."

"Nothing wrong with puppies," I said.

Half his puppy face bent into a twisted smile; somehow the other half was still frowning. "Puppydogs are only good for one thing," he said. "Shittin and pissin."

"I don't mind puppy poop. It's innocent and smelly at the same time. I like puppies. And white roses, and white Christmas, and breakfast in bed. And New England in the fall, and Paris in the spring. All that stuff."

Neither of us laughed. The words were dead. Rice has a straight stare, and when he doesn't know what to say he puts it on without disguise. I stood there in front of the library, awkwardly conscious that I was standing with a staring stranger and a rose. I looked around at the lives that went by us. Below us a silver-bristled black man, saxophone dangling from his neck, slowly rolled his belongings, piled high in a supermarket shopping cart, along the sidewalk. People walked briskly down the street, sat dumbly on benches, marched blithely in and out of shops. All these little lives by the library. Including us.

It was time to look at Rice again. I did, and he tried out a smile. Then he banished it from his face. For a second he showed no expression at all; he looked . . . inscrutable.

"You know who you look like?" I asked, brave and ridiculous. "You look like Toshiro Mifune."

"Hunh?"

"Toshiro Mifune. The guy in the samurai movies. Didn't anybody ever tell you you look like Toshiro Mifune?"

"Nope. Unh-unh."

"Well, you do." I looked again, and he didn't. He reminded me of Toshiro Mifune, but he didn't look like him. "At least for a second you did," I said.

Rice looked away. The muscles in his jaws started working; it looked like he was trying to work up the courage to say something.

"Well, there you go," he said.

He scratched his chin. "I like Toshiro Mifune," he said. "You can always tell which one he is and everything." Rice looked at the people walking on the sidewalk below us, as if looking for someone he knew. "You know, all these people going in and out right here all the time doesn't make it too terrific to talk. I feel like I'm broadcasting." He lowered his voice a notch. "You want to go someplace where we can talk?"

I am not the type to be put off by a hackneyed line or two. And I liked him, after all. "Sure," I said. "Where?"

"Well, I'm kind of hungry," Rice noted, with a certain chagrin.

Why that chagrin? I wondered, until I accompanied him to a wretched, crowded little restaurant nearby, where I watched Rice eat and tried to avert my eyes from the noxiously cute paraphernalia glutting the walls. I sipped gingerly at a sour cup of coffee; Rice put down a bowl of chili, a plate of hash browns, then ordered a burger. He ate quietly and quickly: his fork took on a preposterous load, jumped into his mouth, and came back to rest, poised at the edge of the food. He hardly chewed. He swallowed, and then after a moment's enterprise his swift fork was diving between his lips again. Short repose, quick gulp. All the while he watched me watch him, wearing a look of vast apology for his nature.

The cheeseburger came. Rice lifted its top off, and started meticulously picking alfalfa sprouts off the meat. "You can't get a sandwich in this town without these damn things on it," he said. "Even a cheesebug."

"You don't like them, Sweets?"

He didn't even notice the Sweets. He said, "Mostly I don't like that they put them there without asking. I didn't ast for them. They only put them there so you don't know you don't have anything to eat." He looked up from his plate. "You a vegetarian?" he asked.

"No."

"You use to be?"

"For a little while."

"There you go," Rice said, and bit into his cheeseburger.

"Why do you ask?"

"The way you keep looking at my cheesebug."

"I *eat* cheeseburgers," I said stoutly. But he was right. I eat burgers, but I look at them while I do. I watch them carefully; I have certain suspicions; I do not turn my back on burgers.

"Sorry about saying that," Rice said. "You want a bite?"

"That's all right."

"Everybody in Portland is still a sort of vegetarian," Rice said. "But they eat fish, of course. And they eat a piece of chicken now and then—but they do it real grudgingly, you know, like somebody is forcing it on them. I'm tellin ya. So I'll be eating a bug, and the person across from me will be giving it this disdainful look, like it's the bug's fault. Then they'll go home and jam down a drumstick. They're closet meat-eaters, I'm tellin ya." Rice took a vigorous bite and chewed energetically.

I watched his jaws working away, his Adam's apple jump and then slowly descend. And I realized, just then, that nothing was happening. What I had assumed was the object of this adventure, the oasis toward which we were plodding, awkward as camels, was my own mirage. We were going to sit and talk about vegetarians and Toshiro Mifune, and then simply go home to our separate houses. I could see Evan, painting pears in a porcelain bowl as he sat on the toilet. I was immediately dry and depressed, a desert traveler with four more days to go before she experiences even one earthly pleasure. My gloom persisted, and thickened. I put down my coffee. I watched Rice finish off his burger. We paid. We left.

We faced each other on the corner of the street, and Rice began goodbye. "You gonna go home now?" he asked.

I didn't know why this man mattered to me. I just knew that there was some kind of connection. The heart of a conversation is usually in things unsaid; but on this occasion I wanted its beat heard clearly.

"Why'd you bring me that rose?" I asked Rice.

He stared, then nodded. "It was dumb," he said. "Stupid."

"That's not what I mean," I persisted. "What did you mean by bringing me a rose? Did I get that wrong, or did that indicate romantic interest?"

Rice started to mumble something about a sign of admiration, that was all, when I interrupted him. It's curious how hard it is to speak straight to a point—even when you most want to do that and only that. "I'm sorry," I said. "I'm really very sorry, Sweets. I just wanted to know if you wanted to sleep with me. Forgive me for being blunt, okay? I'm tactless. And I don't have lots of patience."

Rice stared again. "Louisa told me you lived with a guy."

"His name is Evan," I said.

"She said you were real tight with him. She said you'd been living with him for about eight years."

"Ten," I said. "No. Twelve."

"So I thought— Well, I come from South Carolina, you know. I'm not the type that goes around trying to break up happy homes." He smiled with embarrassment; the smile seemed to bring out his freckles. "I'm trying to be a good guy," he said. "White hat and stuff."

I liked his freckles again. I liked them so much it alarmed me. Is that something you're supposed to like about a man? He was twenty-six, you see; I was thirty-two; there were distressing implications to my interest in those freckles. It occurred to me that I might be falling in love with the shadow of a little kid spotting the face of that great big man. I shut those asinine thoughts out of my mind. I had never wanted a child then.

"I didn't ask you if you wanted to break up a happy home," I explained. "I asked if you wanted to sleep with me." Short silence followed. "I want to, incidentally," I said, with a casual certainty that I certainly did not feel.

"Sounds good," Rice said, but he was shaking his head. "I think I should give myself a little time to digest the idea, though."

I laughed loudly and unhappily, causing his forehead to develop a series of deep, wavy furrows. "This is a hell of a time we're living in," I said. "A woman who wants to sleep with a man has to make a formal proposal, complete with outline. Then he has to bring it before an ad hoc committee of board members. Stockholders have to be polled, and proxy ballots sent off. These days it's kind of amazing that any sex gets accomplished at all."

"I know," Rice said. He put his hand on my arm, and held it; I thought he was going to pull me toward him, and we'd have a movie kiss, but he didn't: he just left his hand hooking my arm. "Sometimes people manage it," he said.

"Bozos," I said. "Dated simpletons. Simian romantics."

I think he wanted to put a stop to my caustic talk. "Well, is this an okay place to make a pass at you?" he asked.

"Good as any," I said.

We kissed. We kissed at the corner. We walked a few steps and kissed in the parking lot of the International House of Pancakes. We walked three blocks and kissed at a bus stop, under the sign of the Brown Beaver. My bus came and we quickly kissed again, holding it as long as we could.

I staggered onto the bus feeling drunk. It had been years since I'd kissed anyone but Evan; I think I was practically slobbering over Rice. It's easy to find that pristine character, romance, in the clear sunlit eyes of your lover as you gaze at each other over white wine; but not in the hot, humid, cavelike environs of a thirsty kiss, where bacteria breeds and teeth decay. Those kisses were hot, and a crew of gamy ganglia quickly spread the news to my various areas, making my liquids bubble and flow. I was on the bus, Rice was not; but my body, on its own, my renegade self, kept reacting to his kisses. But that was all right, wasn't it? This was all open and aboveboard; this was the affair I'd figured on, planned for, discussed with Evan over red wine; there was to be no passion, no pain. Just fooling around. That's right. That's right, Carolyn. Everything was fine; but I kept seeing the image of a man horribly strangled by a rope, and I kept feeling an unearthly warmth rising inside me, and I kept thinking: Carolyn is about to experience pleasure: no stopping it now: no stopping.

I didn't want to fool around. I went right up to the bathroom. The canvas stood on its easel, but against all odds Evan wasn't with it. As if it might give some sort of clue to Evan's whereabouts, I looked over his painting. The pears (1978 was the year of the pears) huddled together in their bowl, green and yellow—one of them was rimmed, flushed an embarrassed red—in a cool, olive-tinged bowl. Those pears might have been cowed into a herd by my presence, or one of them might have been blushing for me, but they remained silent. They did not insult or berate me; neither did they give me away. They were Evan's pears, and like Evan they said nothing, but merely gave me back my gaze.

I found him in the kitchen, cleaning his brushes. That is about all he cleans. I saw with familiar regret the muddy traces of his thoughtless footsteps. At home he always wears his boots, and leaves Vibram-sole smudges wherever he goes; his shoes are walking biographers. After fourteen years of this, I feel that the image of a bucket frothing with ammonic suds is constantly before my eyes.

"Hello," he said cheerfully. "What's new?"

"I've just come," I announced, "from being kissed in a parking lot."

"Unh-hunh," Evan said, and surrounded a tiny brush with an oily rag.

"Please don't put that rag down on the table," I said mechanically.

"I won't." Then, for a minute, no more words were spoken. The only sounds were the small ones of rag against brush and a drip in a distant sink.

"Well, do you want to hear about it?"

"Not that much," Evan said. "If you don't mind," he added. He poured something strong-smelling onto the rag from a rectangular tin can, then screwed the cap back on. He gave his favorite brush a loving wipe and looked at me. "It's your business," he said. "Not mine."

I don't know what I wanted him to say, what I wanted him to want. "Don't you care?" I asked, but not so tragically as that sounds.

He was done cleaning. He held the rag in one hand and all his brushes in the other fist, like a torch. "About what?" he said. "About you? Yes. About the person you were kissing in the parking lot? I don't think so. No."

He wanted the conversation to be over. But I had another question. "Vandy, if you were jealous, would you tell me?"

"Probably," he said, "not." He tossed the wet rag randomly onto the table, and bounded back upstairs to his painting.

Three

Even the memory provides a tingle, a faint stirring in far reaches of the anatomy. You know the feeling when you first step into a greenhouse—a sudden entry into a wholly new world, whose rich reek seems exotic yet troublingly familiar, as if recalling a forgotten childhood in the jungle. Well, we came into Rice's house through the kitchen door one afternoon: the first time I'd set foot there, everything was new, but what stopped me was a smell—a mix, maybe, of that morning's burnt toast, spaghetti sauce from the night before, garlic, banana peel. It did not smell like my house, and that is what hit me in Rice's kitchen: this was a different house and a different man. I was immediately upset; I did not know what to do next. How does one go about having an affair, after all; what is the first thing you say, do you exchange polite talk for ten minutes and then retire to bed at a prearranged sign? Any behavior seemed unnatural; it was ridiculous to put ourselves through this; why should we bother?

Rice turned to me; I think I vaguely expected him to ask if I wanted a cup of tea. But Rice was not interested in a cup of tea. Rice had no questions about how to act. He faced me; his face was serious, almost somber. Gravely, solemnly, he bent and kissed me.

Bit by bit, my questions went away. Everything underwent a gradual metabolic change. We kissed long and slow, and the longer we kissed the slower we kissed, and I'm quite sure that time slowed down to join us, and our kiss was at the center of our selves, and our kiss was at the center of the world, for I know that objects slowly revolved around our kiss, the stove and the refrigerator and the kitchen sink and everything else drifted by like languid planets.

I began to feel things that people can't feel. Rice touched my breast, and through my blouse I could feel his hand; I could feel it more than I could believe I could feel it. I felt its heat, its bones, the curve of its palm. His lifeline. His heartline. No, that was not possible. But there it was. His heartline.

We stopped the kiss and stood, leaning. How remarkably still everything was. Rice was very warm. It seemed that I began to draw heat from him, for I was terribly hot. I was too close to the fire, but there was no fire. I felt exposed to my own desire, as if that desire obeyed someone else's commands and would do me harm, like a fierce dog who recognizes only its master. I had the sensation, as I leaned against Rice, that my clothes were already lying beside Rice's bed, melted, Sambo's tigers, and that I was already naked, extremely naked, naked and vulnerable, and a hot dry desert wind blew through Rice's house, spattering my face with sand.

My body gave a single short, sharp convulsion. That shudder was the forerunner of the endless series of spasms that shook me later as I straddled Rice in his bed, my hands pushing and pushing on his ribs. The shaking seemed to transport me; suddenly I was not quite there, like a rickety train my consciousness went from station to station, barely staying on track. I began to think with my body and feel with my mind. My body thought that Rice's cock in and out of me seemed somehow different from Evan's—even the cells of my sex were aware that this was someone other. But I was not aware. My mind felt consciousness fade in and out, the white wall developed a pulsing grid pattern, the cracks in the paint seemed to be moving like rivers, and then the movement turned into waves; there was a momentary disconnection, I was no longer exactly myself, not exactly human and not exactly there; control was gone, I was a wild animal racing through a sunless jungle, on top of Rice I suddenly felt like howling; and I did, I did howl.

Rice lived with three others in an old Victorian house in Northeast Portland. They did not share food, or much else. Each shelf of the refrigerator bore a masking-tape label identifying the owner of this carton of milk and that bottle of mayonnaise. Rice's bedroom had gleaming hardwood floors, a crippled dog asleep in the corner, fleas in the summer, a 1930s London Underground poster, an R.E.I. calendar, a set of squeaking bedsprings, and no mirror at all. On the bedside table were two books (*Alive!* and Salinger's *Nine Stories*), a half-coiled hooded desk lamp, a roll of one-ply toilet paper, a Little Ben wind-up clock, and the skull of a goldfinch; on the bed, among a tangle of sheets, was naked Carolyn Kingston. Stand up and be counted: me.

The door opened. Rice, naked, silhouetted by the bright beyond, appeared in the frame. He swung the door shut behind him, regaining human colors. He clambered into bed beside me, and looked at me with his perfect and his bloodshot eyes.

"What's goin on?" Rice asked, and touched my cheek, already incidental with his tenderness. We had slept together six or seven times by then.

I looked over at the bedside table, quite sure what I would see. "It's twenty after six," I said. "That's what I'm thinking."

"Time to go home?"

"Not exactly. I'll tell you about it sometime."

"When'd you tell him you'd be back?"

"It's not like that, Sweets. *Evan's* not like that. Evan doesn't mind. Don't make him out to be some kind of villain, okay? It's really very simple," I added, slowly and clearly, so it *would* sound very simple. But Evan did not seem simple to Rice, and he did not seem simple to me, either.

"You know what surprised me about you?" Rice asked, stroking me. "I didn't think you'd be affectionate. I thought you'd draw the old line—it's okay to fuck, but not be all kissy-face afterwards."

I too had thought I would draw such a line; I had intended to. "I like to kiss," I said, with easy, moronic lucidity.

"So do I." He stroked me again, waiting.

"Well. Let's see," I started, and then didn't see how to go on. "I'm very sweet on you," I said.

"Funny expression for you to use," he said. "Sweet on somebody. That's the way they talk in Yauhannah."

I remembered the swamps I had seen when I first met Rice. I pictured myself walking a winding trail beside Rice, through cypress swamps, on an Edenic blue day. Sunlight would pour in like translucent syrup; Rice and I would entwine like Spanish moss and cypress branch; forever would occur all at once.

"I want to go to South Carolina with you. I want you to take me there," I told him, childish, determined.

Rice was not pleased by the thought. "Sometimes you say the stupidest fucking things. You know that? For a happily married woman just having an affair, you say the fucking stupidest dumb things. I'm tellin ya. How come you talk like that?"

I didn't know why I had said that; it had just been part of the dream. "I'm a bozo," I said. "I wasn't thinking."

Rice said simply, "We'll never go to Yauhannah together." But that was quite enough. I looked at Rice and I saw sadness in his bloodshot eye; the sadness came from that word, *never*.

I told myself that we had not done so much to each other: we had inserted a small section of Rice's body, a vestigial limb, into a disappearing slit in my body; we had rubbed against each other, sweating; viscous fluids made an appearance, then dispersed. Small motions, fed by biological urgency; but it didn't take much. For someone like Rice, affable, open, tender at his center, it didn't take much. And for me. For me too I was astonished to find that it didn't take much.

Rice was already projecting loss. I could see that by the way he held me, as if I were a brimming glass ready to spill, and by the grim set of the features on his gigantic face. If I had thought of it at all, I had done so only to resolve not to think about it; but now I too let the future creep into my consciousness, and I knew that Rice was thinking of forbidden happiness, of inevitable endings, of little deaths. He turned over in bed, latched on to the only pillow, and hugged it, a bandage for internal bleeding. Poor baby; he was hurting for me, and all at once it didn't matter that we labeled it a simple affair, that we made it a point not to kiss hello or goodbye, that the limits we'd set for ourselves were clear, and close; all that mattered was that Rice was hurting. I wasn't his "date"; I was his problem; I was his wound. I buried my head swiftly in the hollow at the base of his neck and began kissing him, adding little licks and nibbles. His pain was quickly banished. He rolled over and I rolled on top of him. His tongue came into my mouth and seemed to metamorphose there. It thickened like a member being aroused; I could feel all its deep pocks and bumps, its swollen geography. When I closed my eyes I could visualize the pink and purple lunar surface of his tongue: immense craters and dusty seas, ridges and rocks, hard to keep one's balance, I took only tiny steps, stumbling here and there, my space suit bulky and cumbersome but brilliant silver—though this seemed the dark side. But there was always that danger: if I forgot myself for a second, if I took even the smallest leap, I would soar into the darkness, I would float weightlessly away, I would never come back; I would float and float and never come back.

Where was I? I was in the middle of Rice. There was the puddle of primeval slime, as though Rice and I were creatures just emerging from the sea, or being born. There was the rhythm of the bedsprings, the hoarse pulse of the two of us together; but the sound seemed to come more from the air surrounding us, which took our gasps and our panting and the iron creaking of the bed and made of it a soft sound, a lush score for love, which Rice and I did not compose but only joined in on for the chorus. There was the maze of soaked sheets, and the pale afternoon light, and us: us two.

Rice did not say much, but he wore a perpetual, charmed smile to tell me about bliss. We just stared at each other, sharing it. His pleasure was my pleasure. My pleasure in his pleasure was his pleasure. His pleasure in my pleasure in his pleasure was... Oh, it went on and on, as endless as images in facing mirrors.

We did not so much make love over and over but do it once and for all. It was hot in his room, and our bodies slick with sweat; both of us dripped with our mutual outpourings, barrels of lubrication; we trembled with excitement and exhaustion; but we did not stop. It was not possible to stop. Love was a pulse, a timepiece. Love was breathing in and out, there was no choice. This was a strange and an intricate toy, and like teenagers we tinkered with it, tried it this way and then that, how was this, oh this was fine, do you like it this way, of course, do you want to try this, with pleasure. With warm pleasure.

I didn't know what it was about Rice, but that afternoon I came steadily, in sturdy waves; row upon row of waves, and a windless day.

I didn't know what it was about Rice; all I knew was that suddenly I didn't want to let it go. I wanted to lay permanent claim to that moment—to the fast-fading sunshine and the shadow the bed cast crazily on the warm brown floor, to the docility of late summer late afternoon, to our sweaty, silent intimacy, to Rice's blocky body, to my tender storm of feeling. At thirty-two, I was still young enough to have it all, thank God.

Rice was capable of dalliance; he could let go of me. But I saw that he was capable of a lot more; I saw that I could look at him while we were in the throes of lovemaking and give it to him with my eyes, and he would give it right back to me. I couldn't stop doing that with sweet Rice.

That summer and fall I worked on a series of stories that would eventually win me a grant from the National Endowment for the Arts. They were scenes from the life of a black woman in Charleston, South Carolina. I named her Elda Miles, and I made her scrub floors and weave wicker; in recompense for such a hard life, I gave her a great big brain and let her tell her own story. It was not altogether convenient to ask Elda to live in Charleston, since I'd never been there. But I did know someone who came from South Carolina, and whenever I needed facts, historical data, or local color, I could go find that someone. Eventually I began to find him every time I had trouble getting in the mood to write. I often had that trouble late in the evening. I did quite a bit of research for those stories.

My Carolina research inevitably ended up in a love-brawl with my source, my passionate reference work. Eventually the association became too close; I couldn't write my Carolina stories without thinking of Rice. There was no Elda without Rice. I even allowed him to creep into Elda's stories, forced her to take on a broad, handsome, grinning white lover with a mangle of curly hair, a pile of freckles, a blond mustache, and a bloodshot eye. It was wrong, it was absurd, and I did it just so I could be allowed to write about him, to keep him in my mind's eye always. If Franz Kafka was bothered because insects kept stepping from shadow to crawl across the page where he was inscribing his fictions, I too had a ubiquitous bug in my ear. The image of Rice was so powerful in my mind that poor Elda finally withered away because of a disparity between realities. I sat at my desk in what is now Rice's room, dreaming him, remembering him, wishing that the cloud of steam that ascended from my cup of tea would contain an adept genie who could whisk away all earthly limits—deny time, repudiate space, go fetch him, snatch him up, bring him here, and leave us, leave us just like that.

> It was easy to be with Rice. It was strangely easy. It was too easy.
> One evening, like others, I abandoned Elda and drove to Rice's house. I hurried, and tried not to notice that I was hurrying. I drove fast, and then I hopped out of the car, stubbed my toe on the curb, and still limped quickly to the front steps. I pictured myself in Rice's room, flicking off a shoe with one already bare foot, my face charmingly registering a certain insouciance, the bed and Rice both beckoning with twin smirks; at almost the same time, my vision's nightmare double appeared in my mind, where I imagined Rice's bedroom door swinging open to reveal naked Rice plunging between the legs of some anonymous but very blond floozie, whose mouth is open and eyes closed, and who does not notice me as I stand holding the doorknob, with *my* mouth open but my eyes, unfortunately, tragically open.
> These two fantasies assaulted me as I raced to Rice's front door;

strange to say, the first image plopped a dreamy smile on my unthinking face, and the second stuck a knife in my stomach and rotated it slowly, several painful times. I stopped on the top step. I stood there a second—I could see into the living room, where a bright light illuminated the bald spot crowning the head of Bart, a roommate of Rice's, as he sat spooning cold cereal into his sizable mouth, hunched over what I knew could only be the sports section—I say I stood there, halted by a series of thoughts. These were not very deep thoughts, and they had taken so long to reach me that an observer, a biographer, would have to speculate on why they should reach me at all. Bart stood up, and his bald spot and cereal bowl and sports section stood up with him. These were the thoughts: my reaction to my two fantasies just now was exaggerated beyond sense, the fantasies themselves were horribly banal, I can't understand what prompted them, and why they should affect me so, it's almost as if, but no, but yes, this lovemaking has its own inertia, it no longer stops when I apply the brake, and if that is so then that means that everything is in danger, if I can't write without ending up here then everything is in danger, if I can't control my damn fantasies or even my reaction to my damn fantasies then everything is in danger, this lovemaking has its own inertia, and to be safe I should turn around and go back home right now, because I am risking something here, I should go home, there is inertia and there is danger, I must go home.

And with that I knocked on Rice's door. Bart opened it with his free hand, and his bowl of cereal pointed me toward Rice's room, which Rice was already coming out of, grinning.

After that evening I allowed my obsession the run of the place. I wasn't capable of leaving Rice in the role I'd cast him in, this spring's divertissement; I was not a candidate for a trifling affair with Rice. It is a disgusting, stupid stereotype that men can have affairs and always remain distant, while women (those gentle, pitiable innocents) will ineluctably become involved. But sometimes even stereotypes are true, and in such cases the only course of action open to a woman is trusting acceptance of her own tenderness. With my sweet Rice, it was true of me: I couldn't not fall in love. Pardon my execrable double negatives. I couldn't not.

Four

Agreed: a writer's daily life is an easy one. Except, of course, for the writing itself. You can't beat the hours: I seldom write for more than five or six a day. There is no office where I must report, no boss—my editor is my alter ego, my other voice, not my boss—no dress code, no bout with a time card. I could take a day off whenever I chose; I could, at least theoretically, work even while on vacation. Bring me my briefcase in the Caribbean, and you have a writer at work. The life of a novelist is an idyll.

But regard, if only for one second, the pitiless stare of the blank page. Every morning the empty page itself, my whip-cracking tamer, holds hoop after hoop for me to jump through. No matter the state of my sinuses, the dull periodic throb from my ovaries, the nag of business that must be attended—bank, grocery store, post office, all must wait. The particulars of my life must step aside. We must clear a space for the leap of the imagination; snarling, she springs from the stool, performs the unnatural act, bounds through the suspended circle. Out of all the hundreds of thousands of words in the lovely English language, my mind has unaccountably come up with the right one; but now it must do it again and again. Come cold toes or hangover, come dirty dishes or bounced check, every day the imagination must ignore its setting and make some quiet transformation. I must set my self aside. The writer must open the doors of perception, but she must not peek through those doors and notice that her own house needs cleaning. She must imagine all the minutiae surrounding her characters' lives, see with their eyes, inhale deeply the faint odors that come unbidden to their noses—and ignore the reek of garbage that cries to be taken out of her own kitchen.

Some days I am able to do this, and some days I am not.

As every day, Evan arrived home from school at 3:45. He deposited his umbrella, still wet and not properly folded, in the ceramic jar stationed beside the door; he cautiously freed himself from his tan trenchcoat, then—with a Labrador retriever's careless aplomb—he gave the coat a vigorous shake, liberally spraying the area, before slinging it onto the nearest peg of the coatrack nailed to the wall. (I don't know how he manages to get *both* umbrella and trenchcoat as wet as he does.) Having rid himself of these storm-gathering portions of his apparel, Evan now felt free to wipe his shoes. He moved both feet onto the synthetic throw rug by the door; but a noise on the street caught his attention, and he gazed through the door's glass. Two children, one white and one black, were playing basketball; at that moment the white child flung the basketball at the head of the black child. Evan avoided the sight. He tramped through the living room to the foot of the stairs.

(He had not wiped his feet.)

At the stairs he called up: "Welcome ho-ome." As always. He thinks, I think, it funny. His jokes, which he makes whenever no one is likely to laugh, are strictly for his own benefit.

"Welcome home," I answered. I was standing in the kitchen, that is to say about five feet away, and I had been watching him go through the process of arrival—watching him with fond wonder, the way you watch your dog chase its tail.

He saw me. He was happy to see me. He always is. "Hello, miss. You okay?"

"Okay."

"Get much work done today?"

"The downstairs floors. A load of wash. I stripped the polish from the dining-room table. Now I have to put more polish back on."

"That's good," Evan said dubiously.

"All in a day's work."

"Don't forget to write," he said, and a smile flickered on his face.

"I didn't forget. I just couldn't look at those floors any more."

"I'm sorry, Carolyn," Evan said. "It's my fault. I never remember to wipe my damn shoes."

"Agreed," I commented, although I appreciated his apology. Not that he is loath to apologize. Evan is one mass of apology. In any given situation he regards the blame as belonging uniquely to him. Blame is probably the only thing he's territorial about.

Evan took off his jacket, and then tie. It's no longer necessary for teachers to mimic businessmen with such formal gear—at least not at Southeast Portland's Van Buren High. But Evan, who must be considered something of an eccentric by his students, always wears a tie and jacket. He often carries an umbrella. He thinks a watch and fob sporty. Somehow he manages to be both tweedy and raggedy at once.

It was a Wednesday. On Wednesdays Evan forsook his usual scurry upstairs to the easel. Instead we sat down with the hebdomadal newspaper, the *Willamette Week*. First Evan made a fire. He constructed the stage for the coming blaze with the tireless energy and interest which he otherwise reserved for his painting; he almost chuckled as he struck the match, and then watched with admiration the restless, hungry tongues of flame as they fed. Evan loves fire; quiet people often do.

We sat at each side of the fireplace in symmetrical, slightly battered rocking chairs. Evan opened the newspaper with a great sigh of worldly comfort. He turned toward the back, and his eyes searched the close columns of small print. "Here's one," he said, and then read aloud:

> "White male, 54, 5 feet 8, 200 lbs., brown hair (thinning on top), blue eyes, retired and divorced, no dependents, with back problem (two ruptured discs), considering surgery for them, arthritic knuckles, and minor heart problem (shortness of breath on exertion). Would like to meet nonsmoking woman who is not fat, who likes to dance, but can forego fast ones, who likes to play cards and Scrabble, who is affectionate and not looking for the performance of a 20-year-old male in a 54-year-old one. Exchange photos. Box 903, *Willamette Week*."

Evan shook his head. "Arthritic *knuckles?* Who ever heard of arthritic knuckles?"

"I'm sure lots of people have arthritic knuckles," I said.

"But why mention them in an ad for yourself? Couldn't you let some things just discover themselves?"

"It's the law," I said. "Truth in advertising."

Evan smiled at the newspaper. "It's as if this guy feels he has to list all his problems. Then someone can go ahead and fall in love with him. Because he's bald, five-eight, and two hundred pounds, with a bad heart, bad back, and arthritic knuckles. Because he's so pathetic."

"Or because he's so honest?"

"Why bother with honesty," Evan said, "when you have a good pair of arthritic knuckles?"

"People like people who are blunt about their own problems. Look at Woody Allen. Self-deprecation can be cute."

"That's very true," Evan said, "but I notice that Woody Allen has been very quiet about his arthritic knuckles lately."

I laughed; he beamed; he read another one aloud.

> "State pen inmate seeks adventurous real female lady to take care of business. Must be free to visit weekends. Salary commensurate with ability."

"What kind of ability do you think he means?" Evan said.

"The ability to take care of business," I said.

"It's not as if prisoners are allowed to make love to visitors. I think there's usually a screen separating them."

"So his problem," I said, "is to find a real female lady who can do it through a screen."

"That's probably why salary is commensurate with ability," Evan said. His eyes returned to the newspaper. "God," he said, and then read:

> "I'm compassionate, fun-loving, domestic and more. I'm not a hiker, biker, jogger, or skier. If you're interested in meeting a petite, attractive, nonsmoking lady with a Christian background, and you're willing to accept a physical handicap—which doesn't prevent enjoyment of life & etc.—then please write. I'm seeking a mature male who appreciates inner beauty. Box 1128."

"I guess we know why she's not a hiker, biker, or dancer," I said.

"Skier," Evan corrected. "Hiker, biker, jogger, or *skier*. She's probably a very *good* dancer."

"Maybe we should get her together with the guy with the arthritic knuckles and bad heart. They can forgo the fast ones together."

"No," said Evan. "Not compatible. The crippled lady would look for the performance of a twenty-year-old from the fifty-four-year-old."

There is an unspoken pact between us. At some point we have silently agreed: Evan will read these pathetic messages aloud, we will make jokes at the expense of other people and their problems, we will ignore our own problems, we will laugh at each other's jokes. And I must admit that I enjoy it.

Evan folded the newspaper several times, bunched it into a small whole. "It's good to know there's still lots of lonely, odd people out there," he said, and he laid the newspaper on the floor. Immediately the paper sprang apart, as if the last fold had been a species of insult. Evan lifted a pair of fire tongs off a hook and jabbed twice at the end of a log, sending up a shower of sparks. He busied himself with the odds and ends of the fire: rounding up unburned kindling that had migrated from the center of the flames, pushing the three major logs into tighter formation, and rotating one a half-turn to expose different bark. Evan regards each fire as having an ideal order. He pokes and prods it into shape, rigorous drillmaster for adamant, inanimate things. Tidy nowhere else, Evan is a tender fanatic with fire.

He did well. A waving corona of flame circled the principal logs; beneath that, the coals complacently shimmered a bright, even orange. Yes, I thought, *bed* is the right word for that soft layer of coals. The room warmed; I rocked happily, extending toes. Evan was quiet, as he tended to be. For a while he read, fat novel lying in his lap. It was *Moby Dick;* Evan read some books over and over.

"How's the book?" I asked, rocking.

"Tremendous," Evan said cheerfully.

"Every time?"

"Why not?" Evan replied.

"Why do you do that? Why do you read things over and over?"

"It isn't just things. I don't read the newspaper over and over. I reread great books, works that have meaning on several levels. You can't get everything out of *Moby Dick* no matter how often you go through it. You should read it."

"I've read it."

"You should read it again. It gets better and better." He moved his look to the fire, where it became a stare, and then back to me; he smiled. "I always enjoy Moby. I read it because I know I'll always like it."

"There are lots of great books waiting out there for you, spurned, unread," I said. "Don't you think there's a way in which the first time is always the best? First trip to Europe. First bite of the apple. First love."

"For some people I'm sure that's true. For others the opposite is. I see the world as being composed of repetition people and first-timers. First-timers are escape artists; they're afraid of routine, of boredom, and they're particularly afraid to look back. Repetition people like to examine their lives, even the trivial parts of their lives. *Especially* the trivial parts. With repetition, trivial things take on a private meaning; they become ritual. Flossing your teeth can be a small celebration."

"So why don't you floss your teeth more often?" I said.

Evan ignored me. "Wittgenstein said, 'I don't care what I eat, as long as it's always the same thing.' I think that's because repetition gives you the space, and the means, for reflection."

"Besides, it's—" I started, and I was about to say, "easy," when I realized that we'd had the same conversation, all but word for word, years before. We'd probably had it more than once before, for that matter. A spasm of unpleasantness emanated from the bottom of my spine; the shiver went past my ears and into my skull. I put my hands out to the fire. I do not like repeating myself. I do not like my life repeating itself.

Perhaps Evan too realized the circle we were about to complete; but he just stirred the fire, arranging it, unabashed. It was perfect now, and he sat back with *Moby Dick.*

Later Evan broiled a steak and fried potatoes—a meal he had cooked for me many times, countless times, but one I managed to appreciate with relative constancy. Butcher's luck, this particular steak was the very form of a sirloin, and obediently fell apart under my dull knife. I am an enthusiastic eater, and get carried away by what I eat. As I sat rocking before the fire, stabbing strips of steak from the plate on my lap and champing on them, I noticed happiness welling within, and brimming. I forgave, accepted everything. Perhaps Evan carries repetition to absurdity, I thought, but I may as well enjoy the spectacle. For I had to admit that it pleased me to watch him run himself through his maniac paces. He asked nothing of me. His habits were gentle solipsisms. This is not, I thought, chewing, a bad home life. I was feeling almost gay. I dwelled for a moment on my satisfaction; it lingered in me, glowing faintly, like a cat's eyes in the distant dark. I tried to coax it closer: Not a bad home life, I repeated to myself, and aimed a fond gaze at the nestlike top of Evan's head, which as he bent over his plate was pointed at me. But my pleasure stayed within, burning only quietly. What was this powerful, nameless delight that warmed me, cozied me, made me secretly ecstatic?

Oh yes. It was Rice. Rice again. With that realization he sprang out from behind the curtains and into the brazen spotlight of my imagination. It had been Rice the whole time. While Evan came in without wiping his shoes, and cheerfully read me the newspaper, and cooked me my dinner, and curried the fire for us, Rice had been on my mind. More than the fire, Rice warmed me.

I couldn't stand it. Why couldn't I have my simple dinner with Evan, a few short hours in his company, without this man always beating on the doors of my mind? Why should *he* always be there grinning at me, strong and handsome as an archetype? What was it about Rice and me that constantly claimed my attention? Couldn't I just leave it alone from time to time?

Obviously not. I sat there and I desired Rice, ached for him.

This was ridiculous. And for some reason it was very sad.

I left two pale moons of potato on my plate, and put it down. "Evan," I said, to shift his look from the fire.

"Hmm?"

"I've got to tell you. I'm in love."

He looked up, and his stare was blank; I saw something unfamiliar reflected in his glasses—then it moved slightly, and I saw that it was me.

"I know," Evan said, and he hung the tongs back on the hook. Something in me recoiled with astonishment, but all I thought was: That's peculiar. He usually leaves them on the bricks. I'm the one who hangs them up.

"I've had that feeling tonight," Evan said. "That you've been sitting here thinking about the man you kissed in the parking lot."

I started to answer, but Evan held up both hands. "I wasn't asking," he said. "It's none of my business. I just told you what occurred to me. I wasn't asking," he repeated.

He scurried over to the fire again, and I think it was the way he moved that told me what he was doing. He moved like a small, timid creature, mouse or mole, something that always tries to make itself invisible. But I saw why he was doing it; I knew Evan a little. It took only a gesture or two, a little scrape to shepherd hot coals together, a knock that sent sparks rising into the black chimney. I saw that Evan was making himself meek and mild because he thought he should; because he thought it the right, the loving course. A long time ago Evan told me, "Love is largely tolerance"; now he turned a log so its glowing underside faced us and warmed us, I felt its warmth, and I saw that Evan was trying to protect us, that his meekness was his peculiar expression of love.

A wave of tenderness rose in me, and images of the past floated to the surface with it. I saw myself wearing Evan's shirt, just his shirt, as I paraded breezily around our New York apartment, royalty of a sort; I saw stoop-backed Evan hunch over me in the Columbia library and try to dissuade me from my sorrow with a series of bad jokes; I saw the Vibram-sole smudges from his boots on any number of floors, and his tired underwear hanging limply on myriad doorknobs, and the grimy cap from his toothpaste tube lying in the bathroom sink for all eternity—and memory gilded even these dreary emblems of our time together, gave the paltry images a power and a sweetness. Evan was right: these trivial things had become our ritual; they were mementos of our long shared past. If I lost Evan, I would lose all that time; would lose, in a sense, myself. If I didn't love Evan, who would I be?

I managed to ask, "Are you okay, Vandypie?"

Evan looked straight at me, his face still expressionless. "I think so," he said tenuously, as though he'd tried to gauge his feelings, but wasn't sure he should believe the readings the instruments gave. "I don't *want* it to bother me. We'll see how I do." He shrugged; then reached over and picked up the newspaper again, climbed back into his chair. "I think it'll be okay," he added, and absently opened the newspaper. "I'm sure it'll be fine." Evan began to read the personal ads again, but this time he did not read them aloud.

Five

When I slept with Rice, he existed absolutely. The sum of him—including wild hair and strangely mismatched eyes, thick thighs and crooked smile, fidgeting penis and restless, reptilian tongue—composed a private universe. While I was with Rice, my daily life (my orderly prose, perfect house, kindly lover) seemed a fitful mirage produced by a chance collaboration of sun and sand, hard to see, harder to believe in.

I had the opposite feelings when I left Rice's house. All that passed between us abruptly became a distant dream. It was as if someone had spun me totally around, taken off the blindfold, let me stagger home in a state of confusion; now Rice's house was the dream kingdom, and now the Carolyn who entwined so effortlessly and so often with Rice seemed unlikely, and unlike me.

Of course, she could say the same thing about me.

Something had to be done about this internal diffraction; you can't go around with half your life grotesque and distorted. For everyone's sake, two dream kingdoms had to be reconciled. I talked it over with Evan. He suggested a treaty.

I tried to slip it into the conversation, but I wasn't exactly successful. Rice was talking. "I must have started doing it a little early," he said. His arm was around me; we lay back in bed; he looked at the ceiling as he spoke. "Because nothing came out for a while. About a couple years. I came and all, but nothing came out. Then one day my cousin Miller was visiting from Charleston—he was on my mother's side—and staying in my bedroom. On the cot. I wanted to do it, but Miller never went to sleep. He just lay there talking. So finally I ran downstairs and did it next to the piano. And stuff came out for the first time. It was all over the place. It was a terrific mess. I thought I was sick, because the stuff sort of hurt as it came out. I didn't find out what that stuff was until ninth grade."

"What did you think it was before that?"

"I just thought it was stuff that came out."

"They didn't teach you about it in school?"

"You kidding? In Yauhannah they're still debating whether they should tell the kids the bad news about the Civil War." For some reason, or maybe not, Rice began to rub his thumb against my nipple. "The people there are mostly all good people. But they're not real good at remembering which century we're at."

"That's peculiar," I said. "Evan once told me that he didn't masturbate until he was in high school because he *knew* what that stuff was. But he had the idea that you don't want semen to come out, just like you don't want blood to. As if it's evidence of some kind of wound, maybe. Or maybe it's just too precious to spill."

"He sounds pretty crazy," Rice observed, and he turned away from me onto his side. The bed registered the change, and so did I.

"Oh, I don't know. I don't think he's very crazy. If anything, I think he's exaggeratedly sane."

"What does that mean, anyway?" Rice asked the wall.

"Why don't you come find out?" I asked.

"What does *that* mean? All of a sudden you stop talking sense."

"Evan says he would like to meet you. I think it would be a good idea. You could come to our house for dinner."

Rice turned onto his back. He stared at me: his glistening blue eyes, showing surprise and hurt.

Rice didn't say what I thought he would. "When?" he asked.

"Whenever you like."

Then he said what I'd thought he would. "Why?" he said. "Why does he want to meet me? I don't want to meet him."

"He is curious about you," I said. "Sweets, we've got to stop acting cloak-and-dagger. If you two get to know each other, then you'll both feel better. I know you will."

"What are we gonna do, sit around and give each other foot massages after supper?" Rice started biting his lip. "I can see it now. First we're gonna hold hands and say grace. Then we're gonna eat. Then we're gonna give each other foot massages. Then we all have to go to bed together. It'll be a real sort of New Age evening. It'll be Marin County as hell."

I was about to say something back, some kind of quip that showed I didn't care about it, about any of it. But when I opened my mouth it emitted only desolate silence. It had taken me a long time, an unpardonably long time, but as I lay there in Rice's bed I realized what I had done, and where that was taking us. I told myself that I had the simple ability to take pleasure in a man; now I saw exactly how simple that was, how stupid, how that ignored everything I should have been most careful about. I began to tell myself things that I already knew, that everyone knows, as if I were a child writing repetitions on a blackboard. Loving has consequences; I knew that, I had forgotten that. Lovemaking makes love; I knew that, I had forgotten that. You don't fool around with people, you don't play pretend with people's lives. Had I actually forgotten that too? Was it really possible that I had loused up our lives for good? How did I do that? Who was I, anyway, when I made love with Rice? Was that me? I guessed it was, in a way. But it was a Carolyn I hardly recognized, who lived only for herself, who squeezed everything but the moment out of her head. I went to the moon, I went to the jungle, I let it all slide—because I was hungry for feeling, for love. Well, it had come to this. I sent us down a blind street; I had accomplished a sadness. I had stumbled across the power to hurt people—the two people I least wanted to hurt. I didn't want that power, but there was no way to relinquish it; and someday, like it or not, I'd have to use it. Because I'd let my feelings take me out for a joyride, I'd gone out of control, ended up in a head-on collision with love; bits of myself and the two lucky men I cared for were about to be splattered all over the pavement, and despite all my forgetting and pretending the pain would be real, and it would belong to all of us.

A few tears went public. They skirted my mouth, met at my chin; jumped off from there, plopping onto the sheets.

Rice stroked my chin, and as he did his fingers wiped away the trembling drop at the point of my chin.

"All right," he said. "All right. I'll come to dinner. Dammit."

"No," I said fiercely, protesting. "That isn't what I *meant*. I was thinking about something else."

"It dudden matter," Rice said. "I'll come."

I asked Evan not to cook steak. I have my reasons, I said, but I didn't know what those reasons were. Chicken, I said confidently, nodding as I said it. Evan gave me a You're-peculiar look, but he didn't say anything, and he cooked chicken for Rice.

Right away you could tell that Rice was trying as hard as he could. On arrival he gave Evan a big hearty handshake, complete with toothy grin. Rice can be so warm. When he smiled it seemed that he was smiling at the human race as a whole.

We all sat in the living room. "How's the painting going?" Rice asked Evan, employing one of the few facts he knew about Evan.

Evan wrinkled his nose. "Bad," he said.

"Why, what's the problem?" Rice was one of those people who expect things to flow smoothly—he had his own difficulties, yes, but surely these must be an aberration, a tiny wart on the smooth face of life.

"I guess the problem is I'm not a particularly good painter," Evan stated. He wasn't expecting me to contradict him, and I didn't.

Rice remained moodily quiet a moment. It almost seemed that Evan's remark had caused him pain. Evan began, predictably, to apologize. "It doesn't matter," Evan said. "Don't misunderstand. I only paint just to paint, if you see what I mean. I try to get better, but I'm not certain I will. That isn't the point. I don't mind being a bad painter."

Rice brightened; a mischievous grin spread across his face. "You're kiddin, right?"

Evan shook his head.

Rice only smiled harder, a demonstration of the good will behind his disbelief. "What if... lemme see. What if you knew you'd never get better. You wouldn't just keep at it, right?"

"I'm not certain," Evan said—to provide an acceptable margin for error. Then he said, "But I think I would. Yes."

"But how come? Let's say you're not gonna make even one good painting. Why bother?"

"Good is a peculiar word," Evan said, with a properly peculiar smile. "I might make something that's good for me—good by my standards, that is. Did you ever hear what Dr. Johnson said about women preachers? He said that a woman preaching is analogous to a dog walking upright on its hind legs—it's not so much that the thing is done well, but that it's done at all. Well, I feel the same way about my painting."

Rice looked at Evan the way you might look at a dog walking upright on its hind legs.

Evan asked him, "Do you paint?"

"Oh no. Unh-unh. I can't even draw a straight line."

"You could make paintings with no straight lines in them."

"Guess so," Rice said. "But what would I do if I wanted a straight line?" he added, perhaps not rhetorically, and made a suppliant gesture with his hands—palms upward, littlest fingers just touching one another. "That would really get to me," Rice said. He paused, then summed up. "You can't do a thing if you can't do it."

And then there was nothing more for either of them to say about painting, or even trying to paint; they had established that their views were diametrically opposed. Strange to say, I found their divergence of opinion soothing, even cheering. Socially it made me nervous, for I *was* a hostess, and my dinner-party guests seemed born to disagree; but that confirmed something I wanted badly to believe: I was not repeating the same tried, true, and tired cycle. I had not fallen in love with the same man twice over. Just, in fact, his opposite.

I asked Evan if there was something I could do to help with dinner. This was a pure gambit, since I had no interest in helping with dinner. Evan would know I was not speaking literally. The conversation took a well-marked fork, toward dinner.

But it was twenty after six just then, and for a second I faded away, wondering what time had in store for me, and when my check-out time would be—and why I found myself caring about all this, or anything at all, since life was a tiny dream.

"So what's for supper?" Rice asked, so uncomplicatedly interested that I felt a kind of gratitude.

"Chicken," Evan said.

"Chicken and Rice," I put in.

"No," Evan corrected. "Applesauce. Green salad. Orange sherbet."

We ate those things. The applesauce came out of a jar, but I don't mind it; the chicken was very plain, but it was fine. We talked, or rather they talked, cautiously; the weather was much celebrated, since before rainy today it had been a bright October, with only odd traces of gauzy cloud, after a long, lean September. As if stirred to speak by the food he was devouring, Rice waxed enthusiastic over what was then a new restaurant—a Chinese one called Uncle Chen's. It was so good, Rice said, that they have problems with the Department of Immigration over the kitchen help. Rice seemed to forget that he'd gone there with me; I had taken him there. Evan listened with good-natured indifference to Rice's account of the lunch at Uncle Chen's, just as he'd listened to mine; and later he claimed not to have noticed that Rice was raving about the same four-story-high skylight, the same spicy scallops, the same tea-smoked duck, the same black bean sauce and the same bottle of Kirin beer.

I sat at the head of our smallish Duncan Phyfe table with Rice, huge, curly, and mustached, on my left hand; Evan, thin, sharp-featured, and eyeglassed, on my right. Across the narrow width they talked, and though they talked about trifles, I felt an intimation of happiness—the foreglow from a warming bath, the moment when the pointed toe descends, the steam rises to meet it, the rubber duck bobs its greetings, and mentally you are already in the bath, all the way in and soaking in bliss and bubbles.

I think I knew what I hoped for then.

"What do you do?" Rice asked Evan.

"I teach," Evan said quickly, and dropped it. This was sheer reflex. Then he heard what he'd just said. "Didn't you know that?" he asked.

"Nope. Unh-unh."

"Huh. That's curious. It's such a permanent, central fact in my life. Pitiable, but central. What else don't you know about me?"

I think Rice must have thought he'd made an egregious gaffe, for he leveled an earnest, solemn glance at Evan. "I don't know a whole hell of a lot about you, to tell you the truth," Rice said. "I didn't ask Carrie much."

Evan smiled. "You didn't want to know?"

"I guess not."

"How neat," Evan said. "How—parallel." He looked delightedly at me. "Rice didn't want to know about me. I didn't want to know about him. Carolyn," Evan said, giving his plate two short raps with a chicken wing, as if the wing were a baton and orchestras awaited, "were there conversations that you had with each of us? Was there ever a kind of symmetry?"

He seemed to enjoy the idea. They *both* seemed to. "Not exactly," I said. "The tone was always different."

This made them both erupt in laughter. I hadn't wanted to be funny. I stood up, picked up my plate and Evan's plate. "I'll just leave you two here to get acquainted," I said caustically. I looked back in from the kitchen; they smiled admiringly at each other.

I cleared the wine glasses. Evan was saying, "So. Who *are* you, anyway?"—and both of them, I don't know why, boomed common laughter again.

In the kitchen I pretended to busy myself with the dishes and the coffee; but I did everything very slowly, like a waitress on her first day at work. I was not exactly afraid that I would drop the plates; but I was afraid. It had started, I think, with twenty after six, with that daily sighting of the dark, absurd side of the moon, as if the evening that is falling will finally fall once and for all. But it was no longer twenty after six, it was eight-oh-five, and it was not merely simple death that afflicted me just then. I peeked into the dining room, glimpsed again the faces of the two men I loved; they were both laughing and, in their own ways, both lovable. This should have pleased me doubly, but I saw beyond them—in time, not space. For the first time I had an intimation of the power of the three of us together—the sparks that would fly, the warmth that would be generated—and of the danger in that power like any other. Rice and Evan, I knew, saw nothing, were unaware of the power and of its shadow. I saw them solitary, vulnerable, in pain; I saw their smiles reversed, as if the mirror of my reflection had produced not a backwards image, but turned everything upside down.

I tried not to consider these images; I turned my thoughts outward. I scrubbed the plates with useless care, then painstakingly dried them, then put them away so slowly that they did not clatter against each other. I stationed the coffeepot—the kind Rice calls Italian drip, it drips up—on a back burner, and turned that burner to Low. The water had to boil in the bottom of the pot before it would rise to the occasion, and I knew that Low was not hot enough to boil it. I had hoped that my oddly timed burst of sorrow would simply go away; but like the pattern in the wallpaper, which once discerned can never be unseen again, my vision refused to vanish. Instead, like some strong contaminant, it rendered distasteful everything it touched; everything I saw was tinged with despair, with mortality. I stood and stared about our bright, barren kitchen. A too-bright light glared from the center of the ceiling, casting aspersions at the dull objects gathered in the room: a weeping spider plant, a shrinking violet, a thick-stemmed bromeliad turning a burnt brown; a pyramidal series of clanking chain-link baskets that contained various examples of rotting fruits and vegetables, to the delight of a cloud of fruit flies (they would all die soon); a dusty blender with clouded bottom and no top; a lopsided, tilting wooden salad bowl, which we permitted to limp around the kitchen, free from detention in the cupboards, because we somehow thought it beautiful; a tarnished toaster encircled by an aura of crumbs, frequently visited by other, larger flies, who would also die soon; two dented, demented ceramic vases; and over here a plant I'd long forgotten, it was dead, quite dead, and some days ago Evan had failed to empty his tea strainer, here it was, rank and (it seemed to me) sad. I threw the stinking tea leaves into the plastic compost bucket beneath the sink and chucked the nameless, skeletal plant into the garbage, pot and all. The plant had died so swiftly and with such ease, and Evan had left the tea leaves in the tea strainer for the millionth recorded time, and—but then the coffee came up, volcanically bubbling and spitting in the top of the pot. It had never done that on Low before. Are you trying to distract me? I asked the coffeepot. The pot hissed back at me. I poured coffee into demitasses and left the kitchen, first flicking the light switch in order to silence the accusations all those dead and ugly things made.

Evan and Rice had shifted to the living room; Evan had lit a little fire, and was just now done arranging it. He sat back down; Rice and he were arrayed in the rocking chairs, flanking the hearth, rocking in time with each other. Firelight darted out and flowed around the room. I had put puffy scarlet roses on the mantel and windowsills, but I don't suppose either of those two noticed; I did, and for a moment I admired them: roses by firelight, softness on softness. Then I handed the two men coffee and curled up on the braided rug between them, like a little pet.

Rice gestured energetically: "I spend most of the working day underground," he was saying. "Three floors underground. It's called Angela's Sub-Basement Vault. Angela is this tiny little woman who works on the third floor. Every once in a while she calls me up. When the phone rings, it's always Angela. She says, 'Well, Rice, what are you doing?' I tell her, and she says, 'Well, stop. I want you to do something else.' I ask her what I should do. 'Something else. I told you,' she says. 'Look, I'm very busy, Rice. Don't bother me any more.' Then she hangs up, and I do something else. I pay real strict attention to Angela. She's the boss, and she knows best."

"So what is it that you do down there?" Evan asked.

Rice spilled a little coffee on his once-white sweater, looked at the stain, and went on. "Lots of different stuff. I build filing cabinets, and then I fill them full of files. We're going micro now, so sometimes I empty files out, and take the stuff up to the micro department. When they're finished up there, I take the papers back down to Angela's Vault and shred them. Every day more papers arrive for filing. I don't know where they come from, or what they are. The stuff comes in great big huge boxes with strapping wire around them, and I file everything, even the wire. Sometimes after I file everything Angela tells me to shred the whole file. 'You haven't shredded much lately,' she says. That's never true, but I don't argue with her. She's the boss. She knows best. 'Shred something,' she says, 'but don't tell me what. I'm very busy, Rice.' So I shred something."

Evan put his index finger on his lips, the way I imagine he does when he teaches school. It's his way of showing that he has an illuminating question to bring forth. "Why do you think Angela likes to give you a hard time?"

"Angela? She dudden. She likes me. It's because I take short breaks. You're allowed fifteen minutes. Most people take about forty-five. But I go up to the cafeteria, drink down my coffee, and come right back to the Vault. Angela thinks it's because I'm conscientious. But I'm not."

"Why is it?"

"I just don't like it up there," Rice said. "You get used to being three floors underground, and the sixth floor feels kinda high up. I even get a little dizzy on the ground floor when I first come up. I feel better down in the Vault," Rice concluded.

"So you really like it down there, hunh?" Evan asked.

"No," Rice said quickly. "Not really. It's dirty. It's hot. The air feels like it's already been breathed about three times. It's like Hell down there." He drank out of his little cup, drained it, set it down almost on my foot, without seeing the foot. "Tell you what I think," he said. "I think Hell is hours to get rid of, useless tasks, and nobody to talk to but Angela."

"And she's busy," Evan put in.

"There you go. She's busy."

"Don't bother her any more, Rice."

"There you go, buddy," Rice said. "She's real busy."

Both men leaned back, rocking and beaming—as if Angela was boss of both, and this was a story they'd told together, many times.

"Do you think you'll stay?" Evan asked Rice.

Immediately Rice turned to me with an anxious look. Then something passed through his mind, and his features eased again. "You mean, at my job?"

"Yes. Your job," Evan repeated, sounding a little unfamiliar with the words.

"Guess not. I never do. Longest I ever stayed on a job was twenty months."

"Lucky for you," Evan said—speaking, it seemed to me, with a slight drawl.

"How about you, Carrie?" Rice asked, looking down at me. He seemed to be talking to my foot. "What's the longest you've ever held a job?"

I understood that Rice was making an effort to include me in the conversation. The talk had been easy, unforced; now they were trying to include me. They had to try.

But I could make an effort too. "I haven't ever held a job," I said. "They've held me. I worked as a Gal Friday for seven years in New York. It was for different Guy Saturdays, though. All men. And all but one wanted me to sit on their laps."

"What did the other one want?" Rice teased.

"He wanted to sit on *my* lap," I teased back.

"Did you let him?"

"For a while," I said. "But he couldn't take dictation. And he made the worst coffee in Manhattan."

"Why'd you two ever leave New York?" Rice said. "You seem like New York types, you know what I mean?"

"Lousy coffee," I said.

I was making that effort: I was taking part, becoming part. It was hard, conscious work, but I was acting gay. I had thought that an alliance between Rice and Evan was all that I could wish for, but my wishes had always incorporated me: I wanted to be at the center of the merger, the middle panel in a brightly lacquered triptych with a lapis lazuli sky filling the background.

Instead, I was immediately jealous. A woman must always feel that friendship between her two lovers has a creepy, powerful aspect about it. On the spot I could imagine the things they'd have to say to each other when I was away, intimate notes they could compare. There could be accurate discussions of my anatomy, general laughter at my quirks, airing of my dirty laundry. My brain would be laid upon the board, and with their sharp tools my two good-hearted surgeons could have all my little aberrations out in no time; the white-coated boys would hold the gnarled tumors up to the light with their gleaming forceps, and they would grin and in comradely fashion slap each other's back.

When it came time for Rice to go home, I walked him out to his truck. I was a mix, a mess, of emotions; a spasmodic rain fell too, into pools of streetlight and Portland gloom. We walked down the six wooden steps from the porch, and a solitary gust of wind hit us with raindrops, then fell quiet. Rice jammed his hands into the pockets of his down vest, and braced himself against the cold. I fought off a shiver, slid my hand through the loop of Rice's arm, and clutched the crook of his elbow. But for the dull scrape of soles against cement, we walked in silence to Rice's truck. A white pick-up, it sat and gleamed in a puddle of blue streetlight; the grass beside it was colored an unlikely gold. Running rivulets at the edge of the street seemed bent on finding the mouth of the sewer, and bent to do so. We stood beside the truck and I listened to the noise of the water's small fall, the distant but obligatory urban siren, and my heart, thumping loud and clear for Rice.

I turned to Rice to match faces, but he wasn't there. I found him crouching in the darkest of three shadows cast by a well-forked chestnut tree. Rice bent toward me, and his hand waved over and over, with a motion you might use to splash water on your head.

I walked slowly toward him. He continued waving me on until I was quite close; then he wrapped me up in his tree-trunk arms and gave me the kiss I had expected beside the truck. Only a little more violent; a little more needy. There was a moment when I thought he was going to say, I've been waiting for that kiss for *hours,* like a hard-hat gulping down the first beer after work on a summer day.

He didn't. He said, "Evan's a nice guy." Then he grabbed me and kissed me again. When that kiss was over Rice said, "A *real* nice guy"—as if we hadn't been kissing, but talking about Evan.

"Yes. He is," I said. In the course of the evening I'd been surprised and relieved when it seemed they'd struck up a friendship, and then surprised again, and worried, when I imagined they'd accomplished an intimacy. But I was still not ready for what Rice told me next.

A leaf drifted down from blackness above and tumbled against the back of Rice's neck; he peered up into the tree's dark arms, and now I could make out his troubled, uncomfortable expression. "Real nice,"

Rice said again, still looking up at the branches. He added, "And I'd just as soon not see him again."

I started to say something, but Rice cut me off. "I'd just as soon not talk about it, either," he said.

"No, I'm sorry," I said. "I can't let you get away with that. You have to talk to me. You *have* to."

There must have been a fierce note in my pleading. "It's not *you* I don't want to see, Carrie," Rice said, soothing me.

"Look," I said. "This is a problem we can deal with. You liked Evan; you just felt uncomfortable here. That's normal, Sweets. Next time will be better."

"I don't think so," Rice said. "Every time I look at that guy, I keep thinking the same old thing."

I think that Rice expected me to know what that thing was. Perhaps I did know.

"What's that?" I asked.

"Well, I'll tell you," he said. He looked thoroughly unhappy. "I keep thinking, *Some*body's being a crumb-bun."

I nearly laughed. A crumb-bun, for Christ's sake. And he was serious. A crumb-bun.

"That guy," Rice added, and jerked his head in the direction of the house, not looking at it, "isn't. Now you"—his index finger jabbed the air between us—"you can't even help it. At all. So I think it's me. I'd just as soon not be reminded of that. I'd just as soon not think about that guy in there."

I was still standing there in the shadow of the chestnut tree, an occasional raindrop plunking onto my skull, as Rice drove away. Too fast: the gears sounded progressively angrier. I listened to his machine express his state, and I began to wonder whether I *could* help it: what I could change, and whether the future might not be as inviolable and adamant as the past.

Six

Since I left that disease, New York—I lived there for my first twenty-nine years, so I have the right to talk—I've tried to get back to visit my mother every year, usually at Christmas. I say "usually at Christmas," but the fact is that for the last five years I have visited every Christmas, and only at Christmas. I don't know whom I'm trying to kid.

I began seeing Rice in the late spring of 1978; by Christmas we were stuck in stalemate. Rice didn't want to see Evan, and I didn't mention Evan to him, unless I felt like risking his grimace and sulk. I saw Rice in the evenings during the week, but never intentionally spent the entire night at his house. I thought I'd be hurting Evan if I did, even though he kept insisting that he was fine; as much as I could, I took Evan at his word.

One weekend Rice and I went away together, to the coast. It was November, it rained constantly, we set foot on the beach only once and only briefly, but Cannon Beach had never been so memorable. I have the image of that pine-paneled motel room by candlelight and then by fuzzy dawn; a constant wind boomed all around, the bottle of tart red wine sat neglected on the night table all weekend; the lumpy bed rose and fell in familiar waves; and the two of us bobbed like buoys, mariners beautifully at sea. Briefly, we suspended time there. But we had to be back Sunday night.

The Cannon Beach weekend spawned a plan. I spent every Christmas in New York, and Evan never went—sometimes he visited *his* mother in Philadelphia or Massachusetts, but this usually disheartened him. Evan sees his mother as a particularly ridiculous example of ornate nineteenth-century Salon sculpture, and she regards him the way she does the incoherence and generally bad breeding of that frightful mistake, modern art. Most Christmases Evan seizes the chance to stay in Portland and paint. So I called my mother and told her I would be coming with a friend. Perhaps I should have told Saskia what kind of friend; but I had the feeling, always, that Saskia didn't want to know.

She met us at Kennedy airport. She saw me first, and made her way toward me—but in tiny and uncertain steps, as if the massive, foreign presence of Rice made me somehow unapproachable. For a second I couldn't focus on her face; I registered only a heavy gray woolen coat, a conservative tan dress, and high, polished leather boots. I couldn't find her face. I had the sensation that we were still separated, and I was trying vainly to recollect her features. But here she was; she hugged me hard, the room brightened, and I recognized the person before me: my mom. That is of course ridiculous, there's no airport that's not always bright, but I write it just as I saw it: she hugged me, and the lights came up.

I miss my mother quite a bit, and I'm always astonished to remember how absent she was in my childhood, how unimportant a figure she was to me then. She was a name, a shadow, a hallucination—like a grandaunt tucked away in the nursing home in Florida, or some elder brother who died before you arrived (his photo is on the piano). But these days my mother's on my mind a lot, even if I don't know why. I find her walking there, with her arms folded tightly over her chest, and the configurations of her forehead constantly telling of puzzlement.

It must be the same for her. In the airport her hug was long and unrelenting, and a pair of tears fell. She made no sound. I said, "Hi, Mom!" too brightly; I said that two or three times. We stood there, two cripples supporting each other. Finally I noticed Rice standing nearby with hands shoved into jacket pockets, a grin of embarrassment lurking on his face. I broke away from my mother's hold, and turned her by the shoulder, pointing her at Rice. "Mom. Mom, this is Rice. Rice, this is my mom," I prattled, but I could see that this simple business was not proceeding correctly. My mother, confused by the size of the mountain, stared straight in front of her. She was peering directly at his chest.

I thought she was about to say hello to his lungs, when Rice reached down for her hand. He got it, and shook it slowly and carefully, a breakable thing. "Real glad to meet you," he said.

Saskia didn't reply for a moment. She regarded the hand that shook hers. I think she knew right away that this was my lover; that I had a second lover, and this was it.

"Yes. Me too," she said to Rice. She adopted a tentative smile. "How's Evan?" she asked me, loudly and cheerfully.

"He's fine. He's doing a lot of painting."

"That's good," Saskia said. Good that he was painting? No. My mother wants Evan and me to stay together forever.

Saskia reached out and put both her hands on my elbows, examining me up and down. "You look okay," she said, dubiously.

"*You* look great," I gushed, noticing. I meant it; my mother just laughed. It was a schoolgirlish laugh, with its artificial carelessness, and something about it let me know that she didn't believe me. But all her life people had been telling her that, and I don't think she'd ever believed them.

My mother was fifty-two then. She had been a widow for thirteen years. She wasn't a merry one, but she was calm about it at last. While growing up I'd always thought of her as supremely lovely. She was, after all, the princess in that fairy story about the ballet dancer and the RAF colonel. I was actively pushed toward a belief in her beauty by the RAF colonel himself. My father called attention to my mother's looks whenever he could; he asked me to pay Saskia compliments when he thought they were her due—for my poor father needed reinforcement to believe anything. But she *had* been beautiful; she was still astonishingly so. Her hair was helped in staying that blond, of course. It was arrayed around her head in a succession of curls and waves, each one all but stapled in its place: the elaborate coif of a country-and-western queen on a fifty-plus Dutch lady. On most people that would look ridiculous, but not my mom. She still had fine features and soft unwrinkled skin. She sported a new potbelly that year, but it was small, you seldom noticed; when she sat down the rusty joints in her knees creaked in complaint, but those were just dancer's knees. For the most part she looked wonderful. I was enormously pleased to find her beauty intact—and not for her sake alone. I've always been terrified of the direct consequences of time. First as a child afraid to grow up, and then as an adult afraid to grow old, I've feared the riderless future as it stampedes in my direction.

My mother drove us home. It was already evening on the East Coast, and the darkness was mercilessly cold.

"I turned on all the lights for your coming home, Carolyn," my mother said as we neared my old house.

"Bet it looks just the same, hunh, Mom?" I said, affecting an affection for the place itself that I thought I didn't feel.

"You'll see," she said in a sing-song voice.

We rounded a corner and I did see: the house, the yard, the garage all blazed with light. My mother stopped the car short of the garage, and we clambered out into the cold.

"The trees are all gone," I said.

"They were elms," my mother said.

"The honeysuckle's gone too."

"I had them take it down. Honeysuckle is a parasite. Did you know that? All the years it was at the front yard, and it was a parasite," Saskia marveled. She led us to the front door, and knocked; not on the door but on the house. Her hand clanged hollowly against thin metal. "I took down all that old wood. This is aluminum."

"It isn't a wooden house any more?"

"Oh, it looks just the same. You can't tell the difference, see?"

I looked; the house seemed to glow under the streetlights.

"You don't have to paint aluminum. Never," my mom added breezily.

"I see."

"It keeps in the heat, too."

"Unh-hunh."

She banged merrily on the house. Then we went in.

Saskia had drastically redecorated. The new kitchen was in red and hot orange; the kitchen table was a bright plastic one, round with rounded orange plastic chairs. A little black four-footed sausage came bounding toward us; Saskia swept it up in her arms, where it unsuccessfully wriggled for emancipation. Dog in arms, my mom showed us her kitchen. She twirled around the room, showing us how you opened these wonderful knobless cupboards—bang them lightly, and they spring open with a hearty boing—and how easily these nice new drawers glided on their quiet rollers. The range was built into the counter. So was the dishwasher. The floor stayed shiny, always. The toaster accommodated four slices, though my mother lived alone. The tiny color TV perched on the kitchen table, the blue parakeet in the pink cage. The refrigerator was vast and empty; the dachshund's name was Sammy; the tissue dispenser was red, blood red. I would not cry, I would not. Of all the square pastel containers ranging along the glitter-speckled formica counter, only the one bearing the word "Sugar" contained anything at all. I would not cry.

Saskia excused herself to go to the toilet. "Sit down, Carolyn. Make yourself at home. Have some Sanka. Do you drink Sanka? Down, Sammy. I'll show you the bathroom next. I've gone Oriental in the bathroom. Down." She left us, but her voice came around the corner: "It's in the cupboard above the sink."

Rice and I stood in Saskia's kitchen, surrounded by silence. "Kiss me quick," I said to Rice.

Out of consideration for my mother, I let her show us separate rooms for the night. I told myself: It doesn't matter, it's of no consequence, in a sense you always sleep alone. But it wasn't easy to sleep at all. I had come from a different time zone, and more than that. I lay amongst the furry inhabitants of this jarringly blue room—white bedspread sprouting blue pompoms, navy-dark shaggy rug, a chest of drawers with a blue-carpeted top, and a matching, fringed shade for my dim bedside lamp. This was dubbed "my" room by my mother. I lay sleepless, dazzled and depressed by my surroundings. It was quite quiet; the only roar came from a distant expressway. I put my hand over my uneasy heart and listened to it by feeling. My heart beat. I felt. Minutes slowly acquired a longevity commonly attained only by hours. I held my breath and waited the night out; at long last half-light seeped in through the window. From the next room I heard Saskia's clock radio click, then blast the air with semi-classical; it clicked again, and I heard the sweep of blankets being thrown aside, the rustle of a robe, nearby drawers opening and closing on little wheels. Saskia went to the toilet, she flushed; she washed, she brushed. She shut several drawers, entered a closet; a wire hanger bounced and jangled, naked. She made the bed, she made frozen orange juice (a wooden spoon bounced rhythmically around the inside of a plastic jug). She poured. Grape-Nuts rattled into a bowl. The refrigerator crunched closed. Her steel spoon scraped endlessly in a bowl, little pings and an occasional louder, more musical one. It did not stop scraping; she would never leave. Time would stop. Sick at heart, I would listen to my mother's preparations for the day all day, forever. I was home; I could never leave again.

As soon as I heard the initial eruption of her car's motor I sprang up and shed my flannel nightgown. I lurched across the hall to Rice's room. He lay stone-still on his side, facing away from me. I came close to him, smelled his sleep, inhaled it. Then I crawled into his single bed, and cupped his body with mine. As he slowly awoke, I clung to him. And only then did I drift off to unquiet sleep.

Rice woke me at noon. He sat on the bed holding coffee.

"That Sanka, Sweets?"

"I been to the store. It's real."

I sat up in bed and took the mug. "You want breakfast?" Rice asked.

"I want to die."

"Cheese omelette?"

I shook my head.

"Well, you feel like being okay?" he said.

"I don't know. Look, come back to bed, would you? I have to be protected."

"Protected?" he repeated doubtfully. But I didn't answer, and Rice bent down to untie his shoelaces.

We made love. We made a considerable amount of love that day, that week. We made love on Saskia's wall-to-wall shag, and we made love in her bathtub; we made love with Rice sitting on the toilet, while I slowly lowered myself up and down, leaning on his shoulders. I had a serious need for Rice; stuck on Long Island in the paltry world my mother had created for herself, I was dying of melancholy, of pity for the peculiar creature who had given birth to me. I needed an alternative; I tried to make Rice my world. We made love on the orange plastic chairs in the kitchen. We made love on the bedspread with blue pom-poms. We made love all afternoon. I don't know what Rice needed to escape, or why he needed me at all, but he matched my longing. When we made love we stared at each other with huge eyes. I came often, endlessly, and so did he; but even these moments of love had a desperation at their center. We were trying with all our power to hold on to something we both knew was out of our hands.

We used the word. Rice used it first, grudgingly. "Charades," he said. He held up three fingers.

"Three words," I said.

One finger.

"First word."

He pointed toward his eye.

"Eye."

He pressed his nose.

"Nose," I said.

"No," Rice cut in. "That means you just got it right exactly on the nose."

"Okay. Eye. Nose."

Two fingers.

"Second word."

He tugged his ear.

"Sounds like."

He made a motion with both hands, pushing something away.

"Push."

Rice's hand made encouraging circles.

"Shove," I said.

He pressed his nose, then held up three fingers.

"Third word."

His index finger pointed at me.

"Me. Carolyn."

He shook his head.

"You," I said.

He pressed his nose again, and held up his hands.

"Eye nose shove nose you nose," I said; Rice shook his head.

"I guess Eye shove you too, nose," I said, and Rice pressed his nose again.

My mother came home from work just after five-thirty, and at twenty to six she was holding a highball; she held it tight. She was sitting, crossing and recrossing her sleek legs, on one of the two matching sofas in her living room, patting it. "It's a Mexican design," she said. "The man who sold it to me told me it was a Mexican." Saskia took a sip, then abruptly sat up straight. This was the second time these actions had been consecutive; as if the taste of the drink made her remember to correct her posture. She said, "*I* think we should go to Mexico for Christmas next year. I've had enough of snow and ice to last me of . . ." She stopped. "Hekh," she said; I think it was Dutch. "My English," she added, shaking her head. "After all these years, I still forget these idiots."

"To last me a lifetime," I said.

"Your English is real good," Rice said. "You talk just like people from New York."

"It's not true. I talk like me, and only me. But I don't care, the hell with them. We *should* all go to Mexico for Christmas," she finished, defiant.

"I went to Mexico a couple of winters ago," Rice mused. "To Baja. My San Francisco girlfriend used to go down every winter to watch the gray whales come in. Come to think of it, she probably still does." He probably *was* thinking of it; of his old girlfriend running naked on a beach somewhere in Mexico.

My mom stared at Rice. Agreed, a daughter's perceptions of relations between her lover and her pretty mother are bound to be suspect; but it seemed to me that my mom was *always* staring at Rice.

"It was real beautiful down there," Rice remembered. "It was sunny and...calm. Everything was real calm. Even the air. We drank a ton of Margaritas. When it got too hot, we just went back to bed."

"You notice any whales down there?" I asked. "I mean, since you were always coming back to bed and all."

"Oh yeah. There's a ton of them down there. There's two little bays that fill up with gray whales. Lagoons. Scammon's and San Ignacio. They go there every winter." He shook his head, marveling. "That was really something," he said.

"The whales?"

"The whales? Yeah, I guess so. Bethany used to get real excited about those whales."

My mother was still staring at Rice. "You've *been* to Mexico?" she asked him now.

It was Rice's turn to stare at Saskia; but as soon as he realized what he was doing, he cut it off. "That's right," he said. "Baja California."

My mother nodded to herself. "How wonderful," she said, her voice high and soft. That astounded her: he'd actually been to Mexico. My mother grew up in Indonesia, was taken prisoner of war, lived in England and America; but she found the idea that someone had taken a trip to Baja with some woman almost breathtaking. Anything outside the realm of her experience enchants my mom.

"You should take *us* to Mexico," she said to Rice.

He shrugged. "Sure," he said.

"Next Christmas. Okay?" She crossed her legs and tugged her skirt down.

"Sure."

"What about *this* Christmas?" I said. "We've gotta get a tree, hunh, Mom?"

I think I should mention that I revert to the age of eleven when I talk to my mother. I don't know why I do that. Perhaps so I can seem a little younger than she.

"Why?" she said. "What is the reason for a tree, always? What is so Christmas about a tree? They cost eighteen dollars now. You can have a lot of highballs for that."

Highball was her word for it; it was always a rye whiskey sour, an unpalatable drink. The only other liquor in the house was cheap sherry, and I don't even like good sherry. My mother, consequently, thought I didn't drink. She was gratified when Rice joined her in a highball, and when he rose to make her a second.

"We've got to have a tree," I said. "We've got to have a tree, and presents, and turkey for Christmas dinner."

"There you go," Rice affirmed. And before he left for the kitchen, he put in, "If you don't have a tree, you spend all Christmas looking at each other and feeling lousy."

"It's a lot of work, though," my mother said. "It's like mowing the lawn in the summer."

"In what way?" Rice asked.

"It's a lot of work," Saskia explained. "Hey. Weren't you going to make me another highball, Rise?"

"*Rice*, Mom," I said, hissing his name.

"Rice," she said. "That's what I said, isn't it?"

Rice began banging about in the kitchen; my mother got up from her sofa and sat down on mine, right next to me. She began to whisper.

"It's amazing," she said.

I waited for her to continue, but apparently she expected me to now ask her *what* was amazing. What's amazing, I thought, is that after all these years my mom still imagines that English conversations will follow the patterns in textbooks.

"What's amazing?" I said.

"The way Rise looks. Don't you think?"

"I think he's beautiful."

"So did I," my mother said.

"So *do* I," I corrected mechanically.

"I was talking about your father," she said. "At that age. When I met him. Don't you think this is an amazing coincidence? How much Rise looks like your father?"

"He does *not*."

In the kitchen Rice turned on the blender; ice clattered and roared in the plastic jar, breaking up. "Yes," my mom said, serenely sure of herself. "He does exactly. Even the mustache is the same."

"Dad didn't have a mustache when I knew him," I said.

"That's true," Saskia said, nodding reasonably. "But when he did, it was exactly the one. One and the same."

"No!" I cried, as Rice returned with my mother's drink; I heard the way I sounded, and it sounded like a howl. Rice came closer, shy, uncomprehending, even fearful.

Rice was my Christmas hero. My mother had to work until noon on Christmas Eve; Rice rose early, drove my mother to work, then came back to pick me up. We went out and bought Christmas: tree, turkey, trimmings, presents, liquor.

We lugged the tree in—it promptly shed needles all over the shag—and arrayed it in state in a living-room corner. I had hoped that its presence would transform my mother's house, but I wasn't in luck. This was a waif of a tree, one of the last ones left on Long Island; its halting growth was stunted here, its crippled limbs almost nude there. We did our best. We looped a string of almond-sized lights, red green blue white, red green blue white, around the tree's midsection; we hung brittle, faceted balls in all shades of the synthetic rainbow at the tree's extremities; we garnished it with a waterfall of glaring silver tinsel; we crowned it with a hollow star. The poor baby, I thought. Maybe it needs popcorn balls. With a burst of energy, prompted perhaps by dread, I made a trip to the store for popcorn; heated oil in a battered pot; and then burned the popcorn, burned it thoroughly and irrevocably, irretrievably burned it. The house stank with the smell. This is all part of a pathetic master plan, I thought, beating back with disgust an impulse toward tears. That ridiculous tree fit perfectly in my mother's house. Poor baby; poor popcorn. I looked around the room, and everything seemed a suitable object for my pity. I had difficulty holding back from draping myself all over Rice. What an idiot, I kept saying, as I hung on to him; he let me do that, and all he said was: There you go.

We made it through Christmas. Rice was kind to my mother and sweet to me; his spirits were high; every night over highballs and then over dinner he told rambling stories about his childhood in South Carolina, and long-winded, unfunny jokes. My blessed mother laughed throughout the length of his shaggy dog stories; everything about them was funny to my mom, except perhaps the inexplicable punch lines. "You have to listen carefully to Rise's jokes," she told me, "because you never know when—poof!—they'll be over." She repeated one of his punch lines—"I'm gonna make you a refuse [garbage: ref'-uz] you can't offer," with the reverent air of one revealing a talisman. There was no explaining a joke like that, according to Saskia. When I tried to elucidate that particular pun, she brushed me aside. "This is like," Saskia said, "the man who falls on the banana peel. What's so funny about that?"

"Nothing," I said. "But this is different."

"That's right," she said. *"This* one is funny."

Rice and I stayed through New Year's. I didn't want to leave my mother alone to wallow in self-pity on New Year's Eve. "We'll have our own little party," I claimed.

Rice went out to get champagne. My mom and I put on our party dresses, wriggling in front of the full-length mirror in her bedroom. We were both vamps. A little sooty snow fell.

"Is it serious?" I asked.

"With Frank?" My mother giggled. "He's my boss, you know."

"Well?"

"He wants to marry me. Can you zip me, Carolyn?"

I zipped her, with one hand on her shoulder; we gazed at our similar faces in the mirror before us.

"Are you gonna do it, Mom?" I asked, eleven years old.

"Frank's nice," she said enigmatically. Then she added: "The only reason he wants to marry me is because I won't let him sleep with me. But he doesn't know it. He thinks he loves me."

We were still talking to each other's image in the mirror. "So will you marry him, Mom?"

"He's already married," she said flatly. "His wife doesn't even know about me. How could I marry a man like this?" She sat down on the edge of the bed and twisted her feet into high-heels; she bent over, but not one hair moved on her head.

"Can't you find somebody single to go out with?" I asked, and then I felt a twinge.

"It's not easy. If you're a widow they always think you're interested. They think you're so . . . What's that word, when you are always wanting to have sex?"

"Horny."

"Horny. They think you're so horny they're doing you a great big favor sleeping with you. Ha," she commented. She must have seen a movie where people say "Ha" that way. She went on: "Then they want to leave that same night. They don't want to see you in the morning, when they have a hungover and feel bad about everything. At my age when you do one of those you feel like it is really hell."

"You do those?"

"No," she said, with a definite shake of her head. "Not at my age."

"That's awful," I said, eleven.

"Carolyn. If you marry Evan, or this Rise now, be a smart girl. Die before they do." She laughed, then stood up. "Well, how do I look?"

"Beautiful, Mom." She laughed again. "I'm not kidding," I said. "You're really beautiful."

"That's nice," she said, with a little smile. Then she added, "I *have* to be beautiful. Frank only has forty-five minutes."

Rice came back with champagne. Two bottles of Piper-Heidseck. "Christ," I said, no longer eleven. "How much did these cost you?"

"Forty-two bucks."

"For a clerk in Angela's Vault, that's a fairly ridiculous sum."

"Money is love. Mine is yours. I'm tellin ya."

"All right," I said. "It's once a year and all."

"There you go. Now you're talkin sense."

The three of us sat on the two couches. First we watched a televised version of the *Nutcracker*. My mother was immediately held in thrall. She perched very straight in her seat, occasionally clapped her hands together, and made comments in Dutch. She almost never speaks Dutch any more, but the sight of the dancers brought it out. During commercials she leafed slowly through a book of photographs I gave her that Christmas: a portfolio of soft-focus shots of dancers. All the girls were very young.

Frank arrived just at eleven. The ballet's music swelled and then stopped, the audience applauded with lunatic madness, and Saskia turned to us: "Wasn't it beautiful?" she breathed, and the doorbell cheerfully rang. Frank was broad, nearly as broad as Rice; he was handsome, if bald; but he was old. He was much older than my mother. He shook Rice's hard hand, and gave me an unexpected hug. "I've sure been eager to meet you," he said to me, displaying a very white set of teeth, or dentures. "I'm a good friend of your mama's."

"You're her boss, aren't you?"

"That too," Frank said.

"Let's have some champagne!" my Mom said; she was gay; she was indefatigable; she was eternal.

"I gotta get home by midnight," Frank said. "I gotta watch the ball go down with my grandchildren."

"One itsy-bitsy glass," Saskia said. "A little champagne, and who knows? We might get on that gondola tonight."

Frank gave her a private smile; his lips reached out and pinched her cheek. Then he squared his shoulders and turned to us. "So. You're not a basketball player, are you, Rice? You said it was Rice, right?"

"That's right. But I'm not."

"I didn't think so. It looks more like football. You've got the build of a tackle if I ever saw one. Let's just hope you don't have the brains of one, hunh?" He nudged Saskia, who promptly began to laugh.

"I don't," Rice said.

"I coached a little football. Jay Vee. But it's not my sport. I'm not really... into it, you know what I mean?" He looked at me earnestly; I knew what he meant; I nodded, and he went on. "I'm a basketball man," he said. "Coached for twenty-eight years. Won three state titles in our class. Had a great time." He stopped, remembering. "A great bunch of kids," he said. "A great bunch of guys."

"Frank coached basketball," Saskia said; then the cork went off, and Rice spilled champagne into my glass. "Drink it quick!" my mom cried, laughing. "Drink it before we lose all our little bubbles!"

I slurped champagne from my full glass. It tasted all right. It tasted fine. There was nothing special about it. Champagne is always associated with wonderful occasions, and people always make a big fuss over it. I always expect something extraordinary to happen to me, something magical and lovely. But it is, after all, just a drink.

"It's wonderful!" my mother exclaimed, holding the drink high. "Isn't it?" But she got the tone wrong when she said that, and it came out as an expression of doubt.

"Those are great little bubbles we got here," Frank said, smacking lips loudly. "That'll do you just a world of good."

"A world?" Saskia repeated uncertainly.

"You know that expression, don't you, honey? A world of good?"

"Yes. I think so. Hey, you're out of champagne already, Frank. You're really fast."

Frank made eyes at my mom. She is a saint, and she laughed.

Rice didn't say anything; he was looking at me, waiting for me to say something about the champagne. I tried to give him what he wanted. "It's fine, Sweets," I said. "It's really very delicious." But then I was rude. "And just think, it only cost you half a day's work for this bottle."

Rice didn't take it to heart. "That's what money is for," he said. "To buy things." He hooked my little finger with his rather larger little finger. "My ambition is to spend all my money on champagne, and drink it with you." Then he shook his head. "I'm gettin to be a good romantic, but I sure as hell am a lousy nutritionist."

"You sure are, Sweets," I said, feeling grateful, even as I took another sip, and was disappointed again.

Shortly after that Frank opened the second bottle; its cork left a dark gray parallelogram on the white ceiling. Frank poured out a glass for each of us, then strode to the window. "I hope it's not getting bad out there," he said, peering out. The snow fell slowly in thick, wet clumps; they hit the sidewalk and melted on the spot.

"Maybe you'll be stranded," my mother tried.

"I sure hope so," Frank said, but he opened the closet for his coat. He put it on the way a child would: the second arm scrunched into his side before struggling into the sleeve. Frank extended his big hand to Rice first. "Sure was nice to meet you," he said. "Sorry I gotta drink and run." He gave me another hug, unexpected again. "I'll take care of your mother," he told me.

"Unh-hunh."

Saskia walked him to the door. I got a glimpse of them kissing, a full kiss; Frank's hand reached out and grabbed my mom's ass, pressing her against him. The sight enraged me. I swear I could have cut off the man's hand.

Saskia came back from the hall with forehead furrowed and mouth in a frown. Rice, in response, picked up the bottle of champagne. "How about another little sip?" he asked her.

"I think I will," my mother said bravely. "I don't mind when I do." Rice poured her a glass, but she didn't drink. None of us did; it was as if Frank's departure let us drop the pretense of a party. We sat and watched the throngs in Times Square on TV. I felt strangely tired, and not at all drunk.

The ball came down. We stood up and kissed one another. We wished each other a Happy New Year. We stayed there, standing, as though there might be some reason not to sit back down again.

My mother never did sit back down. She went into the bathroom, and came out with two bottles of pills. "You should both take these," she said. "So you won't have a hungover tomorrow," she explained. The evening was over; the New Year upon us; she was going to bed. She gulped down two, and did.

Rice and I loitered a little in the living room. Rice twirled the knobs on the color television set, amusing himself at the expense of a Polish band playing polkas; he made them lurid green and yellow, then flashing blue and pink. He left the band blue and pink, then came over and sat next to me.

"Happy New Year," he said.

"I'm tired. I'm exhausted."

"That's okay. You gonna take some of your mother's pills?"

"Unh-unh."

"Me neither."

We sat on my mom's sofa, Mexican design. In front of us were her two bottles of pills, one empty bottle and one half-empty bottle of champagne, one hot-pink Polish band playing polkas. In the corner the Christmas tree soundlessly dropped needles onto her white shag carpet. Outside, the snow fell only slightly less slowly. In a few minutes I'd drag myself to bed; the next day we would fly back to Oregon; but now I was just sitting, holding on to Rice's hand, full of pain and pity for my mother's luck, and indignation toward her unjust stars.

On the plane back, Rice took a bite of something claiming to be chicken and answered my question: All right, I'll move in with you and Evan. And on March first Rice's pick-up truck came down our street, it was full of Rice's things, Rice's dog Lancelot was in the front seat, and Rice was driving.

Hello, RICE U. COOK. I love you, RICE U. COOK. I still love you. Goodbye.

PART III

EVAN

BY RICE

Chapter

It's taken me a hell of a long time to start writing this and for a while I thought I never would. But tonight Evan and I drank off about a bottle of Jim Beam. Got good and loose, so here goes. Some things are hard to begin with, but if you get a little lubricated they get a whole lot easier. Of course some things are hard to begin with, but if you get a little lubricated they get real impossible. We'll see which category this heads for.

I never did get too much research done about Evan but that doesn't matter any more. Evan told me his parents were rich, they had one house in Massachusetts and another one in Philadelphia, on the Main Line. Why would anybody have one house in Massachusetts and another one in Philadelphia? I didn't ask him that.

Evan told me he had an ancestor named Dickens, who wrote books. Fred Dickens. Evan never met Fred, but he said Fred wrote a whole bunch of books, mystery stories. Evan only has one of them, which is a little brown book called *The Albatross' Tale*, by Fred Dickens. Evan never even finished reading it. I asked him why not, and Evan said, "The novel begins on page three. On page four we find a greedy Jewish tailor with a long nose, and we are expected to laugh. This illiberal humor is immediately topped by the appearance of a grinning Negro butler, bowing and scraping on page five. It is clear that my maternal grandfather thinks this person would make, after all, a pretty fair slave."

I told Evan he should remember the time when the book was written, the era and stuff. Evan said *he* wasn't the one who should make allowances, the *book* should make allowances for people who aren't alive yet. That's what a good book does, Evan said. Shakespeare, he said. Melville.

Well, I read *The Albatross' Tale*, and I thought it was a real good book. When I was about halfway through it, I even had a dream that revealed the murderer. Augusta, the real beautiful girl. But I was wrong. It was that Negro butler.

Evan told me a couple of things about his father. When Evan asked for more of something, his father used to raise his eyebrows way up and thunder away, "Oliver Twist wants some more. Oliver Twist wants some more." His father would laugh a big mocking laugh, the kind that says the words Ha Ha Ha, and then he'd give Evan some more. Evan didn't used to think it was real funny.

Evan also remembers his father putting talcum powder on him as he got out of the tub. His father used to slap it all over the place, there were clouds in the bathroom. But that's about all Evan remembers, because Evan was only five when his father died. Evan says his father was a hemophiliac, and died in a shaving accident, but I think the man cut his throat, and Evan just doesn't want to talk about it.

Evan's father did anthropology. He wrote articles for scholarly journals. Most of the articles were about people who eat other people. He was real fascinated by that, you can tell. You'll be reading along in this straight anthropology article, dull and full of words that don't exist, and then he'll get to the part about cannibalism, and suddenly it gets real exciting. You can practically see the gleam in his eye when he starts talking about cannibals.

The last thing Evan's father wrote was an article called "Why Do We Marry?" It was on his desk when he died. There was a rejection note with it, from this scholarly journal. The editor who rejected it said he'd never even heard of the tribe Evan's father had written about, where the men and the women live in separate villages and only have sex once a month, all together. The tribe lived in Tana Toraja, in the Celebes, according to Evan's father. Evan said his father never went to the Celebes. They went to Bali once, and lay on the beach, mostly. Evan doesn't have a copy of that article. He says it wasn't very good.

I don't exactly know why Evan didn't like it. I don't know why he loves some books and doesn't like others. But one thing I know he likes is whiskey. Whenever we have a bottle, even rotgut, you can hear Evan late at night, or I can, at least, because my room is downstairs. You can hear him sneaking into the kitchen. He opens the dumbwaiter, where the liquor lives, real quietly. You can't hear him unscrewing the cap off the bottle, but you hear this tiny little noise, a noise like tip-tip-tiptiptip, or if the bottle is more empty it's glug-

glug-gluggluggglug. He can't help it, his lips make a little smack when he pulls them off the bottle. The dumbwaiter door closes, but you don't hear that, and Evan goes sneaking back upstairs. *I'm* the one you'd expect to pull that kind of crap, because I'm the alcoholic, if anybody is. Evan drinks, but he doesn't usually get drunk. He doesn't smoke dope hardly at all these days, though he used to do it a lot in the sixties, when he was sort of radical. He doesn't talk much about that any more. I don't think he even *votes,* any more. I can't understand that guy.

But I think he's always been that way. On his tenth birthday he got glasses for the first time. He still wears these big thick rimless glasses, and lots of times when you look at him you just see yourself, looking. The day he got his first glasses he went to his friend Linky Bruce's house for a surprise party that wasn't a surprise. Evan remembers that he and Linky ran around to the side of the house during this game of hide-and-seek, and then he and Linky heard a knock from a window on the upper floor. They looked up, and there was Linky's big sister, Alyson, who was almost fifteen. She was standing in the window without a shirt. There were her big boobs popping a bra, and Alyson smiling and waving at them, and her friend Denise smiling and giggling away beside her.

Evan isn't like a lot of people. When he saw Alyson in her bra he didn't grin or make dirty jokes, or even feel proud of himself. He ran away. Linky ran along after him. "It's okay," Linky told him. "That means she likes you. She knows it's your birthday. It's sort of a present." But Evan didn't think it was any present. He thought Alyson was standing there in her bra, her boobs out, because she wanted to humiliate him. And according to Evan it worked.

That was Evan for you. The first time he sees a girl with her shirt off, and all he feels is humiliated.

But Evan was born in 1944. He's over six years older than me. He's from a real different generation. He went to summer camp in the 1950s. You couldn't do anything back then. Evan didn't know anything, anyway. The first night in camp he woke up in the middle of the night and saw a light below. He leaned down over the edge of his bunk, a top bunk, to see what was going on, and there's his counselor shining a flashlight on his crotch. His own crotch, I mean. The counselor's crotch. He was shining his flashlight on his crotch and looking around in the hairs there. Then he shook a bunch of talcum powder on his privates. And all the time the counselor had a real serious expression on his face, like he was involved in some kind of ritual, and Evan was completely terrified. Evan was dead sure the whole process had something to do with physical pain, and it was going to happen to him when he was sixteen, too.

There's talcum powder all over Evan's memories. Even today you can tell when he's taken a bath, talcum powder is everywhere, everywhere his feet haven't been. You can always see the outline of his toes in the mess he makes.

His fifth-grade teacher later wrote a book about what it was like teaching in a country town in Massachusetts, and she mentioned Evan. This is what she said. "Without knowing it, Evan frightened the teachers with his intellectual superiority, but they could neutralize the threat by noting to each other how sloppy, ill-kempt and dirty he always was."

That first week in camp all the kids had an afternoon off. You were supposed to hang out, make friends. Evan didn't exactly make friends, but he tagged along with a kid named Josh, who was a leader-type, the kind who always wants to sit in the back of the canoe so he can steer. Josh got a bunch of kids together and took them into the woods. First they built a little fire, it was a dry day and the flames took off pretty good. Josh told all the kids to stand in a circle around the fire, and they did. Then Josh told them to take their things out. "Why?" Evan said. "It's fun," Josh said. "Ask any of the guys. They've all had boners before." All the other kids took theirs out, real calm, and started whapping the little things around, real professional. Josh put his thing between his hands and started rubbing it the way you rub sticks together to start a fire, except that it never works. "See?" Josh said to Evan. "It's fun." It didn't look like fun to Evan. Their little sticks got all red, like they were sore. The guys were trying to look casual, but they had strained expressions on their faces, like there was too much gravity all of a sudden. It didn't look like it could possibly be fun. Evan already knew about peer pressure. He wasn't the kind of kid that gives in. He just walked away, left them there rubbing themselves up, and when he looked back he saw a big black cloud of smoke hanging over the woods. As it turned out they nearly burnt the forest down, all of them except Evan got into trouble, and now Evan was sure he didn't want to get a boner. Not him. Not ever.

At that time Evan wasn't used to eating breakfast. A fried egg would sit in his stomach like lead, and his insides would creep all around it, like they were afraid of waking the egg up. At home Evan never ate breakfast.

The first day at camp was all right, because breakfast was pancakes. But the second one was oatmeal. Evan said he wouldn't eat it, his counselor said he would, and his counselor was this tremendous huge guy. But even his counselor felt a little sick, looking down at what Evan did then. He made Evan clean it up, and that made Evan do it again. Evan was fine the rest of the day, but the next morning the same thing happened, and it was exactly the same, pretty much. The oatmeal looked the same. It probably was the same. The conversation Evan had with his counselor was the same, only his counselor began to shout earlier on. The counselor felt that Evan hadn't learned his lesson yet, and Evan felt that the counselor hadn't learned *his* lesson yet. Evan had to clean it up again. Only this time he wasn't fine for the rest of the day. After spitting up breakfast, he spit up lunch. His counselor sent him to the infirmary with a note that said, "This kid isn't sick. He throws up because he's homesick." They didn't even take his temperature at the infirmary. They gave him oatmeal for breakfast. Evan didn't have to eat it, because he got dry heaves as soon as they put it in front of him. But now he was getting less picky, and that day he threw up everything he ate. The day after that he did want to go home. They asked him why he wanted to go home, and he said, "Because I throw up everything I eat." They asked him if he missed his mom and dad. His dad was dead, but Evan was too scared to mention that. Next afternoon his mother drove up to take him home. She kissed his cheek, and she could feel that his face was hot. "What's his temperature?" she asked the gray lady dressed up like a nurse. "I don't know," the gray lady said. Evan's temperature was 104° when he got home. He spit up everything he ate for the next two days.

That's how Evan tells the story. As for me, I think his counselor was right—Evan did throw up because he wanted to go home. Evan wanted to go home because he saw his counselor shining a flashlight on his crotch and rubbing talcum powder on his balls. Evan wanted to go home because he was afraid he would have to stand in a circle around the fire and jerk himself off. He wanted to go home because he couldn't stand other people, and because he was afraid that someday he might grow up and have to make love to a woman.

Today Evan says, "My childhood was one long lobotomy." But I don't think he's been cut off from some part of himself, I think he's detached himself. Because there are parts he doesn't want to mention, doesn't want to remember, doesn't want to believe in.

Chapter

Evan told me all this stuff. It would take a long time to write it down. When he was fourteen he had to go away to school, some prep school, Saint Something, I think the Saint started with a P. It was the kind where there are unbelievably rich, fat guys with pins in their hips and their heads down each other's pants, and they have one big drum that they beat when somebody makes a touchdown and everybody jumps up and yells "All right!" They don't say Terrific or Fantastic or even Good. They say All right. After that Evan went to Columbia, right in the city. Evan loved the city, he was real different then, he smoked dope starting about 1965 and he used to go down to the Village and listen to the folksingers. He was against the War and all. He got out of the draft because he knew a doctor. After Columbia he and Carrie stayed in the city, and he started teaching school. The school was this progressive type. He taught hippie-dippie kids English. That was when he started getting less radical, when he taught those hippie kids. After a while he got to be sort of the way he is now.

Every day after school he would go to the Museum of Metropolitan Art, then come home and paint, just like now. Some things never change.

He told me a lot of stuff, but it doesn't matter much now. I don't think there's any reason to write about that now. Besides, I live with the guy, and I guess I'm stuck with him the way he is.

I moved in with Carrie and Evan on March first, 1979. I spent the fall and winter before that just being miserable about Carrie, and I got pretty good at it. I knew she'd never leave Evan, and I didn't even want to ask her to. But I did ask her to. I asked her once or twice a day. Sometimes I'd call her up just to ask her. She never said no. Sometimes she joked it away when I asked, and sometimes she took it to heart, and she cried. She told me that I should watch myself around her, because there was something a little hard about her, and then she would go ahead and cry. Without making any noise, usually. You couldn't tell she was upset, except there was water running all over the place. Other times she would wail away, and hit things. But not hard.

All the same, she might have been right. Maybe there is something a little hard about Carrie. One part, anyways.

Poor Carrie. All of us felt sorry for Carrie. All three of us.

In January I told Carrie that I would move in with them. January first. On the plane back from New York. I was eating airplane chicken and thinking, just then, that Evan wouldn't be a hard person to live with. I was thinking that he would like airplane chicken. Not just say he liked it. He would actually like it. Just then Carrie turned to me, and her eyes were all heavy. She'd been knocking down a number of those little airplane cocktails, not eating the foil packets of peanuts, and she hadn't even touched her chicken, as a matter of fact I was already eating her chicken, since I'd finished mine, they give you tiny little portions. And just then Carrie asked me if I would come live with her and be her love. She didn't mention Evan. "Sure," I said, real grandiose, and thought about kissing her, except that I was all chickeny just then.

So that was that. It was real easy. Too easy. Then I had another couple of months to think about it and be as miserable as I liked. I don't know when she talked to Evan about my moving in, or what she said. He probably didn't make much of a stink about it. He probably didn't make any stink about it at all, as a matter of fact. Carrie probably just dropped it into a conversation, and he probably shrugged. Evan would say that it wasn't up to him. It was her business, he would say. I think he would, anyway. I never found out if she even asked him.

I appreciate that quality of Evan's, though. It's this detachment he has. I think it's his way of trying to be a nice guy. He is a nice guy, too. You know that old saying, about not harming fleas? Well, Evan is that way. He isn't too tough on the fleas. I don't understand the guy, but he's nice as hell.

Then I spent January and February worrying about what was going to happen. I had nightmares about Carrie leaving me, disappearing, sleeping with twelve guys, dying. Lots of times I would wail away. Not exactly cry, but just wail away, and hit things. I had a closet door that was sturdy, real sturdy. I'd bang it with left hooks, knock chips of paint off the other side, hurt my knuckles, they'd swell up, and I'd feel a lot better.

Before Carrie came along I used to treat depression with doses of nothing. I sat by myself and drank until I couldn't move, couldn't talk, couldn't feel anything. But with Carrie, love was my drug. I felt all over the place. I felt bliss, I felt hell. Those days I came out of Angela's Sub-Basement Vault every afternoon and it was like the outside world hit me in the face. It was like my skin was always real sensitive, and my eyes, my nose, my cock. You know when you're in love because you feel more alive than anyone else. And you are.

Just before I moved in with Carrie and Evan there was a total eclipse of the sun in Oregon. It was all cloudy in Portland, like it always is in February, but I definitely didn't want to miss the eclipse. It was this real Oregon kind of thing, but I was into it. I don't know why I was so into it. I got up real early that day, I think it was a Sunday, and started driving east. Past the Cascades it's usually clear, and it was. I started driving before dawn, and the sun came right up, and I started getting excited. I kept driving down the road between Madras and Hood River, looking for the perfect spot to watch, and all along you could see Portland people parked, sitting on top of their cars with their little eclipse-watching boxes all ready. I wanted to be by myself, so I kept driving, and sort of suddenly the eclipse started happening, the first little crescent bite was cut out of the sun. I pulled the truck over onto a knoll. Down the road, on other knolls, you could see groups of people jumping up and down, but you couldn't hear anything at all. This giant shadow came sweeping across the hills. The birds stopped talking, they flew into the trees and bushes, folded their wings and tucked in for night. I looked around the sky and saw the stars come on out. I saw them winking in the night. The sun and the moon seemed close to the earth just then, and the darkness was so close and so complete that I had the feeling all the lights on earth had been put out, and all that was left was the stars, sputtering little bits of light at us from billions of miles away in space and time.

Lance and me moved in the next week, prepared for the worst. Right away Evan acted real normal, which was weird. Carrie acted a little weird, and I acted the weirdest of all. I felt like I was in a movie where the hero—that was me—is in constant danger. People are jumping him left and right. The music is that thumping, scary music that tells you something is going to happen any minute, and it's going to be bad. Except that nothing happened. Carrie showed me the room that was going to be mine, off the living room. It had been Carrie's study before, and it was little. "Terrific," I said.

"I hope it's all right," Carrie said.

"Course it is," I said, way too loud.

I was feeling tremendously nervous. I thought about having a drink to calm me down, then decided not to. But then I did anyway. I really wanted to calm down. I remember thinking, I can't live like *this*.

Evan helped me carry stuff in from the pick-up, still acting real normal. When he came out to the truck he said, "This won't take long," and right away I had some crazy thoughts. Did he mean it wouldn't be long before I was out of there again, or was he going to fight with me, decide everything right then and there, like bull lions staking out territory?

"You're right," I told him. "I don't have too much stuff."

We stood looking at my stuff for a while. Rain began to fall. Evan started scratching Lance behind the ears. Evan wasn't in too much of a hurry. He never is. He looked around at my stuff, at the other houses on the street, at the one-tone, milk-colored sky.

"Well, what should we bring in first?" I said. My voice almost cracked when I said it. It was a real normal thing to say, but there was no normal thing to say.

"I think the bed," Evan said, and I quick looked at him. But he didn't mean anything. So my lover's lover helped me carry my double bed into his house.

Lance and me moved right in, it all fit fine, everything was creepily normal. To me it seemed like something must be working underground, seeping into the pipes, going wrong all the time. You could turn on the faucet, and there it would be in the sink, poisoning the kitchen. It could bubble up any time. But I was the only one who knew about it. Carrie walked around chirping, "How are you, Sweets?" Just the way she said it told me that she was happy, she was ecstatic, and I was supposed to be too.

She looked perfect that day. Not just good: perfect. She even put on a dress, a long black dress with little gray flowers printed all over it. Her beautiful curly hair, almost like blond, fell down over the black shoulders of the dress like a waterfall. It isn't easy to say why a person is attractive, but with Carrie I think a part of it was a feeling you got, that she lived in a different world and time. She came out of a fairy story, she walked around like a princess. A lot of it was in the movements she made, like the slow way she would move both hands back through her hair.

That day it pained me to see her look that beautiful. It actually did.

That first Saturday I sort of didn't know what to do with myself. I wandered around their house trying to convince myself that it was my house too. I felt weird in the room that was supposed to be mine. I wanted to go into Carrie's room and be with her, but I didn't think I was supposed to. So I went into the kitchen. I only went in there so I could be closer to the liquor, which lives in the old dumbwaiter there. But I started cooking, and as soon as I did that I started feeling better. The kitchen is terrific to work in. It's big, there's lots of counters and light, and there's a nook with a tiny little table big enough for about one. That day the kitchen seemed like the only safe place in the house. The rain started coming down hard outside, there was even some wind wailing away, but I was feeling safe and warm. I made dough for bread, then dough for pies. I turned on all the lights, the kitchen turned a warm yellow, and the plants by the windows gained an extra green. It was like a real garden in there or something.

I looked for something else to cook. I started soup, then spaghetti sauce. I cooked away. For hours I didn't have to say a word to anybody.

In triangles a lot of dividing-up has to happen. For example, there was this immediate division of labor, right away I walked in and started cooking. Carrie did the cleaning. Evan painted. That wasn't exactly all Evan did. He helped Carrie out, typing her stuff up, taking it in to be copied, to the post office. For me, Evan was real helpful. Because he didn't mind that I was there. As far as I was concerned, that was how Evan contributed most. By not minding. He was terrific at that.

Another division had to do with territory. The kitchen was my turf. I'm sitting there, I mean here, now. Sitting at the tiny little table in the nook. When I'm home I'm either here or in front of the fire. Mostly here, drinking coffee or whatever. Sometimes Evan even knocks before he comes into the kitchen, though there isn't a door.

The restroom is Evan's territory. He's there right now. He paints in there. He says the light there is the best in the house, because it's on the north side. But I don't think he's in there for the light, actually. I think he's in there because he likes restrooms. I think he's just that way.

Of course Carrie's bedroom was her place. Her desk is in there, her books, her whole life. Her clothes aren't, though.

We had one more dividing-up to do, and that one took longer, because it was complicated.

It was Carrie. We had to divide up Carrie.

That first night we ate the soup. Carrie kept telling me how good it was. She could tell I was nervous. I kept wondering who was going to sleep where, just how we were going to do this thing.

We drank a lot of red wine. Toward the end of supper Evan said, "Well, how does it feel? Are you here yet?"

"I think I'm jet-lagging," I said. "I'm on Northeast Portland time. No, actually I'm fine," I lied. "How's our lucky lady?"

Carrie said, "The lucky lady is tired, and a little drunk. I think she has to go to bed now. Goodnight, lucky men." Then she got up and kissed Evan's cheek. She came toward me and I began shaking. I think I actually began shaking.

"Goodnight, sweet bozo," she said, and wet my cheek. I thought her lips stayed planted on my face a little longer than they had on Evan's. But maybe I was just imagining that.

She went on upstairs. Evan and I sat over the dirty dishes, polishing off the second big bottle of wine. We talked a little, not much. My fingers were like trembling, and my stomach churning away. What happens next? I kept thinking. Does the lady come down in her robe and choose her mate for the night?

Evan yawned. "I'm going to bed," he said. It was like I was in the electric chair, and his words were the juice. Evan was yawning, mumbling. He just didn't care. I can't understand that guy sometimes.

I watched Evan stump up the stairs. I didn't know which room he was going to, but I guessed it was Carrie's. If it was me going up those stairs, I knew which room I'd be going for.

Fair enough, I thought. She has to sort of reassure Evan, show him she's not leaving him. But I didn't know. For all I knew, she might end up sleeping by herself. What a waste, I thought.

I went to bed, but I just lay there listening. I put my head to the wall, trying to hear the sound of them making it. I didn't hear anything. Just hot air coming through the ducts.

I had to wonder about myself. I had to wonder what the hell I was doing. I didn't want to hear them going at it. I was thinking that I should just put my pillow over my head, try to catch some sleep. But I couldn't.

Eventually I figured out why I was trying to hear them. I was trying to hear them not making love. I was trying to tell myself that they weren't having sex, and the only way to be sure was to listen. I listened, I didn't hear anything, and I was glad and gladder.

The next day was Sunday. I felt terrific. I hadn't heard anything. After breakfast I talked to Evan in his restroom for maybe a good hour. I guess I did most of the talking. In the afternoon I baked bread and apple pies. I liked doing that, and being there. But something was still bothering me, and it was Carrie again. I still didn't know how to act around her. Whether to kiss her, to grab hold of her and pull her to me, to make love to her on her bed, the rug, the floor.

I didn't touch her. I was afraid of her. She wasn't afraid of me, she fondled my neck when she went by, talked to me sweetly, called me Sweets. What was I supposed to do back to her? Was I supposed to feel her up in front of her long-time lover?

"So," I said to her, quiet, in the kitchen. "You happy now?"

"Pretty happy."

"It all seems real easy for you," I said.

"Think again," she told me.

I did think again. It still didn't seem too hard for her.

"What am I supposed to do?" I said. "How am I supposed to act?"

"What do you mean?"

"I'm talking hugging and kissing," I said. "Do I do it to you, or not?"

Carrie said, "You wouldn't be you if you weren't kissy-face. I want you to."

"Okay, I will then," I said, but I didn't. I still crept around her as if she was breakable. When she gave me an affectionate touch, I looked around to see whether Evan could see. When I touched her, I was stealing.

The second night she kissed me goodnight again, this time softly on the lips, and she went to bed again. Evan went right up after her, but I thought I heard the door of the little room, his bedroom, open and close. I was pretty damn sure that he had gone to his own room. That meant Carrie was loose. I took off my clothes and sat on the edge of the bed, waiting. I knew she was going to come down and be with me. It was my turn. I sat there with my cock up in the air, and I could hear the rain dropping down. It was cold in my room, my skin stiffened into bumps, but I sat naked on the edge of my bed, waiting, because it was my turn. She was going to open the door without making a noise, come and kiss me without saying anything. She wouldn't have any clothes on. She was going to come down with no clothes on, and first we'd make love with her riding on top, and then I'd eat her out while she still sat on her knees. Then she'd roll her leg over and let me come in her from behind, and then she'd take me into her mouth with her hair falling all over my crotch. Then we'd sleep. The bed would look like a battleground. That's how it would be.

It wasn't. I froze. She didn't come down. I froze, I froze. She didn't come down.

I spent the next day at work thinking about how to get out of the mess I was in. I climbed up on top of a file cabinet I was putting together in the Vault. My head was up near the low ceiling, right by a fluorescent light tube that kept blinking on and off, repeatedly making this tiny sound like a tin can kinking. I stared at the light, not too good for the eyes, and listened to its sound, trying to make out what it was telling me. Because it was going crazy, and so was I.

Finally the light went off for good. I climbed down, seeing spots.

I knew I was going to move out of Carrie's house. I couldn't spend another night waiting for Carrie to come down.

I came home full of courage and resignation. When I walked in, Carrie met me in the living room. She kissed me. With her mouth open and warm, her arms tight around me. She gave me everything again.

When we finally broke apart she whispered, "Are you going to come sleep with me tonight, Sweets?"

"I'll think about it," I said, trying to be coy, but I knew that there was no thinking to do. I wasn't moving out. I would sleep with Carrie whenever she wanted me to.

We made love that night in her bedroom and it was just as I'd imagined it would be. We did everything, we gave each other orgasms right and left. And all the while I was listening, listening to us the way I imagined that Evan might be listening, and wondering which of the noises of love he could hear.

Chapter

After eleven nights, Carrie had slept with me five times, with Evan probably four times, and she had spent, I think, two nights alone.

I didn't count the nights. I didn't have to. They counted themselves. They were right there in my head, and all I had to do was look.

That afternoon Carrie came into the kitchen to talk to me. I was just back from work, sitting at my tiny little table, reading the *Oregonian,* drinking my coffee, or maybe it was a beer, and Lance was hopping around and wagging his tail as hard as he could.

"You're not trying," Carrie said, and you could tell she was angry.

"What do you mean?" I said.

"You're backing off. You shy away when I touch you, then you act hurt when I touch Evan. You're looking for excuses to pout, to sulk. You know you do it, you do it on purpose, you're trying to make me feel guilty."

"That's not true," I said, although it was true. "I can't help what I do," I said. *That* was true. "When the woman I love sleeps with someone else, I feel bad. That's normal. That's the way I was brought up. That's the way everybody was brought up."

"But that doesn't *matter,*" she said, almost crying. "What is the point of being in a relationship like this if you want to stand around and point at the way other people do it?"

"Well, I don't know, to tell you the truth. What *is* the point of being in a relationship like this?" I said. I wasn't saying that for effect. I asked because I didn't even know.

For a while Carrie was quiet, and I thought, She doesn't know either. Then she shook her head about six times. "There isn't any point, I guess. We're not trying to prove anything. This is something that happened to happen to three people. It's not so strange. A lot of people love two other people and don't deal with that fact, but I want to. I *have* to, Sweets. There isn't any other way for me. I can't run away with you and pretend I don't love Evan any more. I can't hide out here and pretend you're not in my life. For me it has to be this way. That's my reason."

"But I don't know what *my* reason is," I said. "I just don't. I don't know what I expected when I walked in here."

"Why don't you just try?" she said. "Sometimes it looks like you want to have everything go wrong, so you can get mad and be righteous at the same time. Why don't you just treat it the way Evan does? He doesn't mind when I sleep with you."

"Evan is amazing," I said, but what I actually meant was, Evan is completely crazy. That's why I don't act like Evan. Because Evan is totally loony tunes.

I said, "So if Evan doesn't mind you sleeping with me, why don't you sleep with me every night?"

Carrie had this way of looking real sad, basset-hound sad, when she was about to say something she knew you weren't going to like. "Sometimes," she told me, "I want to sleep with Evan."

She was right, I didn't like her telling me that. I felt like I'd been punched in the stomach.

I had to think about it a little. Maybe, I thought, she wants to sleep with him sometimes because she likes a rest. Maybe she just feels more secure when she's with him. Maybe she sleeps with him but they don't make love too often. That might be right. Maybe they don't make love.

I guess I was just staring there for a minute. I was looking at the three chain-link baskets with garlic, apples, and onions in them. Only I wasn't focusing on these things too well. Then I heard Carrie's voice. It was real soft.

"Help me, Sweets," she said. "If you leave, I'm in trouble. Please help."

Even then I didn't look right at her, I looked toward the apples. "What can I do?" I asked the apples.

"Try," she said.

I looked at her then. She wasn't crying. She didn't even look sad. Just serious.

"Okay," I said. "But it has to be a trade, all right? We have to change the setup. I'm not kidding, I'm going crazy the way it is right now."

I did feel like I was losing it. I was juggling all these feelings, they were all up in the air and coming down, and I knew I wouldn't be able to catch them, in a minute they'd be on the floor. I felt like crying just then myself. But I wasn't going to do it unless she did it first.

She didn't. Carrie was shaking her head. She was laughing about it. "We're a couple of cases," she said. "Suitable cases for treatment. Don't you think, doctor?"

"Suitable enough," I said. I wasn't laughing about it.

"All right then, doctor. What kind of treatment do you have in mind?"

"I have to know if you're going to sleep with me," I said right away. "Otherwise I spend all day, and sometimes all night too, wondering if I'm gonna be the lucky fella."

She laughed again. "How the hell am I supposed to do that? Call for the envelope over dessert?"

"Just alternate," I said. "Every other day. Simple."

Her face looked like she was tasting something sour. She said, "I'm not sure I could do that. I can't just switch it on and off according to schedule."

"The way it is now, two people are switching it on and off. And they don't even know when they're gonna be on and when they're gonna be off. It's not fair."

She listened, not saying anything.

"It'll have to be equal time," I said. "No winners and no losers.'"

Carrie looked a little trapped. "What about me?" she said. "What if I want to have the night off, just be myself?"

I said, "If you can work it out with whoever's got you for the night, it's okay."

"Jesus. Whoever's *got* me. What a zoo."

"It's your damn zoo," I told her. "You invented the zoo. You're our zookeeper."

Now she was crying. She never did it when you expected her to.

"No," she said. "I'm the damn dancing bear. I'll get up on my hind legs and you can throw a peanut."

She was sniffling. I wasn't going to let her get away with that. "For a dancing bear, y'all have a pretty good life," I said. "You decide the rules. You decide who lives where. You decide how we're supposed to act. When we sleep together, you even decide who sleeps on which side of the bed."

Water was all over her face. She said something I couldn't hear, because of the crying.

"What did you say?"

"That's a mix metaphor," she repeated. That's what I think she said, at least.

"What is?"

"Dancing bears don't sleep in beds," she said.

I figured if she didn't have to make sense, neither did I. "Dancing bears don't usually have two boyfriends, either," I said. "Dancing bears don't usually get to decide about every damn little thing in their life," I said.

"All right," she said, then smiled, wet face and all. "You're right. I make a fairly lousy dancing bear."

Now she was laughing. You could never tell what was going on with Carrie. I'm telling you. She was pretty spectacularly off the wall.

I said, "I don't think you should decide so much. If Evan and I don't get to decide when we sleep with you, why should you?"

She seemed surprised, I guess because I was still talking about deciding. But it was on my mind.

She thought about it, and then she said, "So what you want is for nobody to have a choice."

"That's right. It's only fair."

"I love your logic."

"What's wrong with it?"

"Nothing," she said. "Except that according to you it's better to have three people upset rather than one."

"Two," I said.

"Evan's not upset now."

"Then he won't be when we alternate days, either," I said. "Look, I don't want to add to the misery. I just want to spread it around a little."

I tried to look encouraging. "It'll feel a whole lot better," I promised her.

"It'll feel a whole lot worse," Carrie said. "I feel like I'm being squeezed in an enormous, ineluctable vise."

I ignored that word. "We all do, Carrie," I said.

"Not Evan."

"No. Not Evan."

Evan. Who the hell knew how Evan felt about it?

That is just about the complete history of how the alternation principle started in our triangle, on March 12, 1979. We tried it for

222 / DELICATE GEOMETRY

eight days. Then, over dinner, Carrie told us that it wasn't working for her. She felt like she was being forced into bed with both of us. I mean each of us. I mean both of us, one at a time.

Carrie said she felt like she was on a one-night stand every night.

And she was, actually.

"Well, would you like to go back to the other way?" Evan said to her.

"No," she said, which surprised me. "I just want to spend longer each time before changing. I want to feel a bit more settled with each of you."

She was trying to make it sound like she couldn't bear to leave either of us. But the longer one of us spent with her, the longer the other one went without.

"I think it should be a week at a time," Carrie said. "I think a week would feel a lot less crazy."

A week. Every other week without her. What kind of good did it do me to move in with her? Before I moved in, I'd never gone a week without having sex with Carrie. I wondered what kind of extreme, complete, tremendously total knucklehead I was.

"Who goes first?" I said. Because it was Carrie. Carrie.

So we divided Carrie, and we got equal parts. Separate but equal, like they used to say in South Carolina. But I wasn't sure how equal it was.

I remember that at the time people I knew were always asking me how Carrie could do it, how she could live with two men. "It isn't easy, I tell you," I'd tell them. They'd say, "But why does she want to?" And I'd say, "Wouldn't you? If you knew you could get away with it, wouldn't you like to have a second lover?"

Usually they would just admit they would, and that was the end of the conversation. But Toto Moravia, the only guy at work I ever talked to, asked me something else. "How the hell does she *know* she can get away with it, anyway?" he said.

We were drinking coffee at the canteen upstairs, I drink way too much coffee and someday I'm going to stop. Or get it under control, at least. The way I've done with my drinking, sort of.

"You have to understand about Evan," I said to Toto Moravia. Then I admitted that I did not exactly understand Evan too much myself. "But one thing's for sure," I said. "Evan's never going to leave Carrie."

"Why not?" Toto said. Toto was real normal. He was a nice guy, a sweetheart, but not exactly bright.

"Because it would be too terrific for me," I said. "Things that good aren't supposed to happen." I kept waiting for Toto to laugh. "That's Murphy's Law," I said. I probably could have waited a long time for Toto to laugh. Toto didn't think much was funny, except when somebody on the football team he was for broke somebody's leg. Now that was funny.

"Who's this Murphy all of a sudden?" Toto said.

I was still answering the first question. "Basically," I explained, "Evan just feels that he and Carrie are permanently connected."

"To what?" Toto said.

Toto took a big drag on his cigarette and held the smoke in like it was a joint. "So why don't you say to hell with it?" he said. "Just pack up the meat, Sweets, and head on out."

Funny he said Sweets.

"What do you *think?*" I asked Toto. I said that as if the answer was obvious, but I didn't even know, actually. Why I was with Carrie, I mean. Except because I loved that woman. And because I wanted to give it a chance. You don't love people all that often in your life. You might as well give it a try, when you do.

"You want to know what I *think?*" Toto said. "I think she's crazy. I think her pal Evan is crazy too. And I think if you live with them much longer, you will be too."

The more I thought about what Toto said, the more I believed it. Carrie wasn't living with two men just because she could get away with it. She did it because she had to. And that's what crazy is, having to do something that regular people don't have to do.

She loved us both. But she loved us in different ways. I think she loved us with different parts of herself. Carrie didn't talk in different voices or act like two people exactly, but she had her little habits. When she answered the telephone and somebody asked for her, she wouldn't say, "Speaking," or "That's me." She would say, "Yes, this is she."

One morning Carrie broke a glass in the kitchen, and I yelled in from the living room to find out what happened. Carrie yelled back, "*She* dropped it." It wasn't Carrie's fault, see. It was *her* fault.

Sexually, you know, Carrie and I had a great time together. We got along real well. She was terrific in bed, had all the moves. I mean, Carrie had hot pins. She had something not too many women have. I'm talking about a talent for coming. She was like Miss Orgasm or something.

But mostly it was the way she was emotional when we were doing it. I could tell she was feeling it. Love for me, I mean. We had sex pretty much every night, actually. I'm not bragging about it. I'm just talking about the way Carrie was. She was hot for me. You just can't leave a woman who's that way.

For a while I was thinking that she was that way with Evan too. She said she loved him, after all. But I never heard them making love. Never. Not a peep. Carrie and I did a lot of peeping. We were like a regular marching band.

So for a while I figured they just did it quietly. Different strokes for different people, like Toto Moravia always says. Then one night Evan let something slip out that told me it wasn't that way.

It was like this. Friends of theirs came over for dinner that night. It was Dawn, a woman dietitian, and her husband, Jeff, who was a teacher at Van Buren, same as Evan. It was getting to be spring. The camellia petals blew all over the place, just like South Carolina. Jeff and Dawn brought over a bottle of gin and two bottles of tonic. They called them Gee and Tees. They were real cocktail people. Plus they had some dope, but I think it was male plants. Carrie smoked some, and I smoked a little, but we didn't get real stoned. Mostly we were just all drunk. I had a few Gee and Tees, and then I went in and burned dinner, which was chili rellenos. But nobody noticed. Everybody was pretty loose, and pretty happy, because spring was coming and all, and because we were so damn drunk. Then Dawn started talking about her job. She got off on a tangent, talking about diet, talking about fibers in the diet. She ranted and raved about fibers in the diet, about how she seriously believed that American shit was the worst shit in the world. It didn't have enough fibers. It should all be loose like the kind that cows and African natives do. She said that if we ate more potatoes and less meat we would do cowpies and never have hemorrhoids or hardly any diseases at all.

Jeff came out with, "Maybe, but all the fibers in our diet haven't stopped us from getting that damn yeast infection. Now we can't make love for a month. I feel like we're in prison."

Right away we were talking about sex. That happens with sex. People love to talk about sex.

"At least it wasn't V.D.," Dawn said.

"If *we* got gonorrhea," Carrie said, "we'd be able to provide an answer for the Zen riddle, 'We know the sound of two hands clapping, but what is the sound of three hands clapping?'"

Everybody laughed at that. It wasn't real funny. But I guess everybody was thinking about how ridiculous it would look if three hands tried to get together and clap or something. When you're drunk and stoned you laugh at anything.

"You of all people should be sympathetic to our plight," Jeff said to Carrie. "For you it would be doubly hard to go without sex for a month."

That's when Evan finally said it.

"Oh, it's not so bad," he said. "Several times we've gone months without making love. On at least one occasion we refrained for a year. Chastity is good for you. It replenishes the lymph nodes."

I looked quickly at Carrie to see if she would look back at me. But she just smiled at Evan, and took a long gulp of her Gee and Tee.

I knew it for sure then. Carrie and I would never go a month without sleeping together. Not after living with each other for thirteen years, not after fifty years. There just wasn't any question about it. Carrie and I had a better sex life together than Evan and her.

When you thought about it, it made some kind of sense. It had something to do with Carrie's father.

I still remember how bad I felt when my father died. I used to pretend Eugene wasn't dead. I would pretend I could wake up from his being dead the way you wake up from a bad dream. I had plenty of bad dreams, and Eugene was in them. But every time I woke up he was still gone. It was like a run of bad luck.

Carrie did the same thing. Only she was worse, much worse. Whenever she didn't like something, she blocked it right on out.

When she was completely unhappy, she used to read children's books, sitting with a bowl of orange sherbet in her lap. Sometimes she wanted to pretend her grown-up life never happened. I guess Carrie inherited some ostrich from her mom.

Carrie pretends a lot of things. She pretends she was the first woman I ever had a good time with in bed. She pretends that there isn't anything weird about living with two men. And she pretends that her father isn't dead, that she's still living with him, and that his name is Evan.

So when we divided up Carrie, Evan got to be her father. He did a good job. He took care of her, ran errands for her. He was always there. He was a good father.

But I was the one who got to be her lover. I was the one. I was Carrie's only lover.

Chapter

Today is a real clear summer day, without much breeze. The ash is just laying in the streets. You can see Mount Hood from the roof of the house. You can't see St. Helens, or Adams or Rainier from this part of Portland, but if you went up to the West Hills today you could see them all. In the morning I climbed out the attic window and laid down on the roof, till the black shingles underneath me got too hot. It's still pretty much summer. While I was laying there all those times came back to me real well. I'm talking about the times when the three of us started to get along.

First I remembered the day Evan finally came along to Laurelhurst Park with Lance and me. There was old Lance, chasing ducks into the pond, jumping after them. Lance came up out of the water like a submarine rising, went right to Evan and shook all over him. Usually it was me Lance did that to. And Lance kept giving Evan this real human look while he was splattering him. Evan just laughed, knelt down and started petting Lance, wet and all, and let him lick up his face. You like people who let dogs lick their faces up.

Lance caught wind of a squirrel and went hopping like mad after it. Lance can run almost as good as a regular dog when he gets a head of steam up. The squirrel moved out on a low branch and twitched his tail right over Lance's nose. Lance barked and barked. He kept on leaping up. He got close every time, but he was never going to make it, and the squirrel knew it. If Lance was a regular dog he might have been able to land on his feet, but as it was he always went sprawling in the mud.

Evan laughed his head off. But I didn't mind. You could tell he liked my crazy hoppy dog.

We went home and Evan helped me cook dinner. Evan was always a good listener, and he listened to me talk about home. He liked that, because he's never been to South Carolina and would never go.

Here's a guy who you could tell the same story six times and it would be all right with him. I got a sort of kick out of Evan. I tell you. He was a weird guy but I started getting a kick out of him.

On the roof today it was easy for me to remember the picnic the three of us took out to the lighthouse, on the Columbia River at Sauvie's Island. It was a good summer for picnics, didn't rain all July. Carrie was into picnics. We carried Carrie's huge wicker hamper all the way down the long white sand beach. Cows were standing around on the beach, waving their tall tails and laying cowpies down on the sand and looking out of place. We walked on past the black guys who were fishing for catfish all day and all night long, their poles propped up in the sand. The black guys were sitting in lawn chairs and drinking beer and shooing away the yellow-jacket hornets, who love beer. Then we cut into the woods and walked along the muddy path, Holsteins were standing around there too, and tons of thistles grew up through the cowflops at the edges of the path. At the end we came to the abandoned Victorian house. This year there are dogs yelping on their chains, which means yelping people, but it was empty then. We walked around the lighthouse on the rocky little point, and then we sat on the beach beyond and tried to have our full-scale, go-for-it picnic. But the hot wind coated the chicken drumsticks with sand and there was no point to try tomatoes and mayo, so we just popped grapes and nacho chips and drank the Budweiser. We lay around on the sand, feeling fat and fine, and later went skinny-dipping in the strong current and cold water of the Columbia.

It was an early spring that year. Mosquitoes were out by mid-March, that's a sure sign of spring, and Carrie was tan by mid-April. She sunbathed in the back yard, stretched out on an Indian blanket in her little blue two-piece. I remember her out there, lying on her stomach. She was doing her writing out there, she said. I think she built a lot of match houses and drank a lot of orange juice, but I don't think she did a lot of writing. She developed this complex called writer's block, which meant she got to drink o.j., make match houses, and read old fat novels instead of writing little skinny ones. She said she was doing research. It looked like she was gaining a little weight. But she put it on her hips and boobs, and on her it looked good.

I lost a little weight, myself. Lance and I started jogging around Laurelhurst Park, or up on top of Mount Tabor. Lance kept up with me pretty good, though sometimes he would sit out a lap. I didn't tell a lot of people about it, because the summer of '79 was definitely a little late to take up jogging, and because I never want to be accused of being the kind of person you see coming out of a health-food restaurant with falafel breath and alfalfa sprouts dangling out of the corners of my mouth. I told people I was only jogging so I could get thirsty and drink beer. But the truth is I didn't have to get thirsty to drink beer any more. I was jogging because I was beginning to feel good about myself. About the way I looked, and about what I could do with my big old body. The more I jogged, the better I felt. Except while I was actually jogging.

Carrie seemed to be pretty happy being laid up with the writer's block, and Evan was doing well too. In the summer he did just about nothing but paint, and he started painting pictures of the toilet. Pictures of the toilet didn't exactly do too much for me, but he seemed to like them a little. What was more important was that Carrie liked them too. She didn't usually say much about his pictures, but that summer she loved them. Every time he showed her a new one, she would say, "That's a great idea." Evan was practically bouncing around the house, he was so happy. Every day he wore the same pair of khaki shorts and flip-flop sandals and this huge floppy straw hat. He said he wanted to look like Monet at eighty, but he looked like something else. He smiled his little smile a lot, a smile that didn't show any teeth. He was so pleased he started to be helpful. He stopped hanging his underwear on the doorknobs, something Carrie was always nagging him about, and if he still didn't remember to wipe his feet it hardly mattered now, it was always dry out. He mowed the lawn every week and washed the dishes almost a third of the time. He took my hoppy dog out for walks early in the morning, and on weekends when it was my week he brought Carrie and me strong coffee in bed. He was like some kind of adorable little grandfather. Not that he was little. He just acted little.

On the roof I remembered without trying the first weekend the three of us spent at the beach. We left Friday right after work and got to Cannon Beach early in the evening. Right away we went out on the beach. It's a long, flat beach, and the tide was way out. The wind pumped along the flats. The sun was just about starting down, and the sky was filled with huge clouds, but right down near the horizon it was clear. All the clouds were turning gold, and the clear sky was this lighter color, this pale yellow. Then the sun went below the water, and all of a sudden the whole world turned red. The clouds turned bright red, then so did the ocean, and even the flat wet beach reflected the red. When you looked back at the town of Cannon Beach, all the windows on the houses and motels were shining with the red of the sky and the sea. The houses looked like great big jack-o'-lanterns with red fires burning inside. Then clammers began coming out with their lanterns, the lanterns looking like pinpricks of white in a red sea, and the people like black shadows, silhouettes, against all the red. Way away at the horizon the waves sent up wet black smoke, signaling something. Then the light began to die, the red faded, and behind us the sky turned this deep, brilliant blue. Stars showed up, winking and blinking. All the while the three of us just walked along the beach, not saying anything, but feeling lit up inside.

I was thinking that it would be real nice to be able to paint a picture of that sunset. But for me it was good enough to just see it. It was good enough to just be there with Carrie, and even with Evan, who knew how to be quiet when something was too good to talk about.

We walked back to town, and ate fish and chips at the Lemon Tree restaurant. We drank some chowder first, getting warm, and while we were spooning up soup Carrie told this long story about her high school prom. She and her date ended up in a diner watching wrestling on TV, and Carrie broke crackers into her alphabet soup so she wouldn't try to read the letters any more. The girl in her story didn't sound like Carrie to me. Carrie could do anything she wanted, could charm the eyeballs off anybody, but this girl could hardly even say Take me home. Maybe that's why Carrie liked telling the story so much, because it wasn't her any more. She got real involved telling it, so I thought something big was going to happen in the end, maybe somebody was going to get knifed, since it was New York. I knew she wouldn't get laid, because that was a different story, and I'd heard that one. I was waiting along, but nothing happened, she broke crackers into her soup and the story was over. I guess I just missed the point, but I didn't care. Carrie got worked up over her story, like she does when she tells her dreams. Those don't have a point either.

But I liked just watching her talk. I liked the way she put everything into her story, her whole heart. I liked the way it mattered to her. Everything does, to her. You don't find too many like that. So I just sat there and admired that woman, even though her story didn't have much of an ending. In my mind I was kissing her nose, sucking her big toe, licking her little tiny armpits.

I was thinking I was crazy about her, and wondering just how crazy.

After supper we went to a tavern. Evan and I played a little pool, we were both horrible. Pool is just the kind of thing I exactly can't do, and Evan wasn't much better. But we had a hell of a time knocking it around, accidentally holing the eight-ball, or the cue ball, every ball but the right ball. The most in a row either of us got was about two. Pool is hard, you know. It's not as easy as it looks, anyway. It's hard for me, at least. There are lots of people like me.

We walked to the Wave-Crest Motel and got two rooms, one for me and one for them, it was the beginning of Evan's week. But we all sat up in their room and talked until late. We talked about what it'd been like for us growing up, how we'd gotten along with our parents, that kind of thing. Even Evan talked. He told about what happened to him at camp when he was a kid, and about the birthday party when he was humiliated by Alyson Bruce in her bra, stuff I talked about before, in the beginning. It was like we had finally worked through all that stuff, and had come out the other side. Like we were all okay now.

That was the first night I didn't mind sleeping alone. I wasn't thinking that life had cheated me out of Carrie. I was almost glad to be by myself. I listened to the waves for a long while. They sounded way off in the distance. I got up and put my clothes back on, went out to take another look. The wind had died down, and it was warmer outside. I looked out to sea, and at first the waves were invisible. Then, when they broke, you could see the waves' silver tops, like long beautiful hair streaming down their shoulders. Lots and lots of stars. You could almost make out the yellow color of the sawgrass at the edge of the beach, though there was just this tiny little sword of moon.

It reminded me of the beach at Pawley's Island, in South Carolina. It was like being home. That's what I was thinking, it was like I was home. I went back to my room and lay down on the bed in my clothes, wiggling my toes and slapping myself, talking to myself. I was saying, "We did it. I think we did it." That sounded so good to me that I said it again. A bunch of times. "We did it. I think we did it."

Chapter

Toward the end of the summer I decided to do something about the itching. At first it was just a little one, an itch I couldn't manage to scratch, but then it got worse. I'd wake up in the middle of the night all sweaty, with this itch percolating all along the length of my tube. I bent myself double trying to scratch it. It was worst when I pissed. It was like pissing fire.

I lived with it for a while, but one day in Angela's Vault practically all I did was rub myself up, trying to get to that itch. When I came home I went right to the restroom. I knocked on the door and went in.

Evan had his head real near the toilet, examining it. "Say buddy," I said, "have you noticed anything funny lately?"

He just looked at me. Evan made sort of a point of not noticing funny things. He liked to just go on.

"An itch," I said.

"I've had an itch," he said. "Inside my penis. Is that what you mean?"

"You usually have itches there?"

"No."

"Yes," I said. "That's what I mean." I was being real sarcastic. "That's the itch I'm talking about," I said. "I have one like that myself."

He smiled. For a second I thought he was just going to go back to checking out the toilet again. "So what do you think it is?" I said.

"Venereal disease, I suppose," he said, very calm, and then he did go back to checking out his toilet.

I couldn't believe that Evan was going to start painting again. But that's what happened. After a while I said the obvious question.

"Well, what do y'all think we should do about this, buddy?"

Evan stopped painting. He put the end of his brush in his mouth, thinking. He liked to put something in his mouth when he was thinking.

"We're going to be able to answer that riddle, I think," Evan said.

"What riddle?"

"We're going to hear the sound of three hands clapping."

Carrie applauded when I told her what Evan said. Actually, she only did it twice, then put her hands down.

"That's the sound," she said. "Two hands clapping. I don't itch. I don't feel a thing."

"So?"

"So it's your problem, Sweets."

"That's real dumb," I said. "How the hell you think I caught this itch?"

"I do not know," she said.

"From you. And you got it from Evan."

"But I don't *have* it," she said. "How could I give it to you?"

"Maybe you didn't know you had it, but passed it along to me," I said, not feeling too sure of myself right there.

"You seem to be assuming Evan had it first. How could Evan get it?"

"I don't know," I said. "That's a real good question." I gave her one of those meaningful looks.

"Don't be ridiculous," she said. "Look. If one of you got it from something other than sex, then the other one could too. Maybe it's from the soap you both use to wash your underwear, or the nitrites in that braunschweiger you both love for whatever unsightly reason. But it can't be venereal disease. Because I don't have it. Maybe you got it from each other."

"How?" I said.

"You've been great friends lately, haven't you?"

"Not that great," I said. I was being sarcastic again there.

"Sweets," she said, "this is none of my fucking business. Literally."

So it was just me and Evan who went down to Outside/In Clinic, a free clinic on Taylor Street, downtown. There we were, surrounded by little signs telling how important preventative medicine is. I knew what the preventative medicine was for V.D., and I didn't want any truck with it.

I went in first. My last name begins with a C.

It was a woman doctor, a young little short Oriental one. "I'm Dr. Benson," she said. She wasn't wearing one of those white coats. "Elizabeth if you like," she said. "Now. How are you?"

"Fine," I said. "How are you?" I was just kind of looking at her. She was pretty good-looking, too.

"That's good," she said. "I don't hear that a lot. It's nice to talk to a healthy person for a change."

Then I remembered what was on. "Well, actually I have a problem," I said.

"Thought you might," she said, smiling. I liked her smile, though. It wasn't one of those doctor smiles.

I have a sort of big crush on women doctors. I don't know exactly why that is.

"I have venereal disease," I said.

"Why do you think so?"

"I itch in my penis. And my friend has the same problem."

"I see," she said. "Did your friend come down here today?" I nodded, and she said, "Do you mind if we all discuss it together? That way I can talk to you both. After all, the problem belongs to both of you."

I went out and got Evan. Dr. Elizabeth smiled at him. She shook his hand. "I see," she said. "You two are close friends?"

"Well, yeah," I said. I started to explain. I said, "Actually, I have a friend who is my friend's friend. His friend is my friend."

"So you're all good friends," Dr. Elizabeth said.

Evan was just laughing. He wasn't going to help me out. I said, "Well, yeah. We're all good friends. But I meant we both sleep with the same woman."

"Is she here today?"

"No."

"Why not?"

"She doesn't have the problem," I said. "I think it's because she doesn't have a penis."

"That's good," the doctor said. "That's as it should be. Now we're getting somewhere."

When Evan and I finally got out of there, I was feeling a little weird. Dr. Elizabeth had stuck this little glass tube up me, and I felt sort of faint. She'd stuck one up Evan too, but he was all smiles now. It was that tiny little smile of his.

"What are you so happy about?" I said.

"I like ridiculous situations," he said. "I liked our Dr. Benson. And it was good to hear you say that."

"Say what?"

"That we are all good friends. Because we are."

It turned out to be this little urinary infection. The reason it didn't bother Carrie is because women don't piss out of their vaginas, exactly. But Carrie did pass it from one of us to the other.

"But where did it come from?" I asked Dr. Elizabeth.

"Probably a toilet seat," she said. Then she said, "And don't forget to look both ways before you cross the street."

I didn't know what the hell she meant by that. She gave us some white pills to take, told us to abstain from sex for ten days, and our itch went right away. Most of the ten days fell during Evan's week, but he didn't care. He kept saying, "Chastity is good for you. It builds men. Sex gives you warts."

I knew he didn't care about sleeping with Carrie. I did. But I could wait. I knew I'd have my chance again soon enough.

Chapter

You find triangles all over the place. You find them in books and movies, and it's always messy. They're supposed to be like a form of torture. Somebody in the triangle always hates somebody else. Everybody always gets hurt. People are always skulking around like spies, lying to each other, somebody ends up shooting somebody else, and you're supposed to understand, because it's a crime of passion. You're supposed to think that it's actually okay to shoot your wife if she's been horsing around, because it's so passionate. You're supposed to like passion. Nobody ever tries to work through their feelings, they go ahead and shoot, and it's supposed to be tragic as hell. And it is, too. But it's also stupid.

Triangles don't have to work out that way. It's normal to care about more than one person. So in a way a triangle is more normal than a couple. But you have to treat it like it's normal. If you think you're doing something weird, pretty soon you'll want to go back to being normal. Or most people will, at least.

What you lose in security, you make up in intensity. You don't get bored like you do in a couple. You don't ever get bored with the sex. When you only have a shot at it every other week, you look forward to it, you don't want to miss out on your big chance. Never mind that in a couple you can accidentally go a week, maybe two, without sex. There's no thrill to it, because you can do it whenever you want, so you never do it at all. But in a triangle you don't miss a week. Because that's all you got.

Nothing is more exciting than Maybe. You get a lot of Maybe out of a triangle.

You're living with someone, but you don't lose your freedom. In our triangle there was plenty of quiet time. It was like being single half the time. I could do whatever I wanted.

Carrie was the one under pressure. She had both of us to keep up with. I don't guess Evan made all kinds of demands on her time, but just the double strain of loving is enough. Other people always thought she was the one who had it good, but after a while I got to thinking maybe Evan and I did.

Evan and I were on vacation half the time. It's good to get a little break from your honey. And then everybody knows how nice it is to come back from a vacation and be with your honey again. It was just like that. Except that Carrie didn't get much of a vacation.

I didn't even get too jealous. I knew Carrie didn't have time to get into trouble with the two of us always around. It was hard enough for her dealing with two men, I didn't think she'd go for three. And I didn't have to be jealous about Evan.

It took me a while to get comfortable with Evan. He doesn't talk that much. Which is kind of surprising, because he's real good with words. Words in books, at least. He's logical. I'm not too logical all the time. I like to figure things out, but I'm not real logical. I'm better with feelings. I'm not afraid to feel feelings, like some people. I'm really not. Sometimes I overdo it, I'm a little out of control. I do that on purpose somewhat. I'm just trying to be extra alive. Not totally sure it works.

I would go and talk to Evan a lot, and he would listen and paint. Sometimes I would go see Carrie, she'd put her writing aside. We'd drink a glass of wine together, talk. But mostly she'd give me a kiss and send me away, and I would go hang out in the restroom with Evan.

"How's it going, buddy?" I'd say.

He'd shrug.

"How was school?" I'd say.

"We don't talk about school," he'd say, real even, and start dabbing at his picture with a tiny little brush. The brush part of those things are made out of camel's hair. I wonder who got the idea to start using the hair of camels to paint with. Some maniac.

When I used to feel extra good, I'd stop off at the OLCC store by the Hawthorne Safeway and buy a fifth of Jim Beam. I'd take a couple of shot glasses from the cupboard and go up to see Evan. I always sat on the edge of the bathtub, drank it neat, and watched him drink and paint.

I was getting to like his pictures more. I liked the way the colors fitted together, like a jigsaw puzzle. His pictures were a little blurry, but I was getting to like them all right.

Evan didn't talk any more drunk than sober, but he smiled more and laughed a whole lot more.

I think the thing I liked best about Evan was how he would laugh at my stories. He always laughed. Sometimes he would laugh without making any noise. He thought I was a pretty funny guy. Sometimes I wouldn't even be kidding, and he'd still laugh.

We were up there drinking one day, and I was reading a letter from my mother, sitting on the edge of the tub. Evan said, "What does your mother write you about?"

"About my brothers, mostly. Not too much about her." I read a little more of Marge's letter. "She still thinks Donny Duckworth is stealing the mail."

"Donny Duckworth?"

"The mail guy. He's been delivering to our house for thirty years. My mother thinks he steals mail."

"Does he?"

"Maybe. I know he steams open the letters and reads them before he gives them to us. When he delivers them they're always real wrinkly."

Evan started wiping the canvas with a rag. That meant he hated what he had just painted. But you couldn't tell that from looking at his face. He always looked at his painting with the same expression, like a dentist looking into your mouth.

I was thinking about old Donny Duckworth, the mail guy, and his beat-up Chevy. I said, "Hey. Buddy. Could you tell me something? How long does a fly get to live for?"

"A fly? You mean like a housefly?"

"Housefly, or a bluebottle fly. How old could that fat old fly be?"

Evan looked over at the window. "I don't see any fly," he said. So I just dropped it.

I read my mother's letter some more. "My mother spends all day reading the newspaper," I told Evan. "She's got money enough. She got insurance money from my father. Plus she got money when my grandfather died. The mortgage on the house is all paid off. When she gets a little strapped she just sells off land. They're putting up another batch of condos by the river."

Evan laughed. I didn't know why he did, but I was glad. I always like people to laugh at me. Sometimes I think that's all I want.

I said, "So she spends all day reading the newspaper. She clips out the obituaries and sends them to me. She always tells me that her friends are dying. They are, too. It's weird, she's fifty-seven years old and all her friends are croaking. It's always cancer." I could see my mother at her kitchen table, clipping obituaries, smoothing her clear plastic apron, smoking cigarettes, thinking crazy thoughts. "She's terrified," I said to Evan. "She's afraid of dying. She's afraid of cancer."

Evan stopped painting. But he was still looking at his painting, not at me, when he said, "Aren't you?" Then he said, "I am. Not for long, though."

"Why not?" I said. "You planning on jumping out the bathroom window one day?" I gave this sort of nervous laugh.

"No," he said. "I plan on thinking about death as little as possible."

"So you think that's the right way to go about it?"

All of a sudden we were right in the middle of this discussion. Evan was a little uncomfortable to be there. Even I was. But he answered me anyway. "I don't know about right way," he said. "It's just *my* way."

I let his words hang around in the air for a while, seeing if they'd go back in his ears and sound bad to him. There's an echo in the restroom, so he probably heard himself a few times, anyway.

I said, "I guess once you've found out who you are, you just have to accept that, huh?"

I didn't actually think I believed that. I just said it because I thought Evan believed it, and I wanted to see how he would react. Evan shrugged. He didn't say anything.

I was just sitting there wondering if Evan really believed in the way he acted. If he thought you should just accept everything, the way you are and the way the world is. And if he didn't believe that, I wondered what the hell he did believe.

I started talking about Marge again. "My mother is one of those people who gets old and feels cheated," I said. "Like she didn't expect that it would ever happen to her. Plus she thinks she didn't get a shot at it while she had the chance. She doesn't know exactly what it was, but she thinks she missed it."

"Uh-huh," Evan said, looking at his picture.

"The funny part is that she's a real smart lady. She's not dumb or anything. But that doesn't stop her from acting dumb."

"Uh-huh," Evan said, painting.

Hell, I wasn't going to do all the talking. Let him do it for a while. So I said, "What does your mom write you?"

Evan smiled. He even put down his brush. "My mom," he said. "Mrs. Davis." He tapped his lips with his index finger, and then he started telling me. "Mrs. Davis writes often," he said. "Mrs. Davis documents her social itinerary. She lists the personages attending gatherings which she has had the honor to attend. Affairs, she calls them. Mrs. Davis discusses her recent escorts. One of them was a university president for over twenty years. Of course, he is at present confined to a wheelchair. Of course, he is rapidly going deaf, and Mrs. Davis has to shout to make herself heard. But she enjoys a good shout. She hopes that this man will ask her to be his blushing bride. She will be greatly pleased when he asks. It will be her great pleasure to refuse him." Evan smiled again. "Mrs. Davis usually contrasts the stagnant social position of her only son with that of his two older sisters. Their husbands rapidly scale ever more dizzying heights on the corporate ladder, and acquire ever more amazing and dubious toys, pleasure machines of fantastic hue. Then Mrs. Davis invariably devotes the final paragraph of her letter to critical remarks concerning her son. I always enjoy my mother's letters."

I'm not as good a listener as Evan. I was listening to him, but I was thinking about something else. When he finished, I said it. "Hey, Evan. Do you feel threatened by me?"

He looked at me for a second when I said that, like he wasn't sure he heard me right. Then he said, "No." He added on, "I like you, Rice."

I said, "You couldn't feel threatened by somebody you like?"

You could see him blinking behind his glasses. "Why do you ask?" he said. "Are you threatened by me?"

He was getting a little red in the cheeks, and he was blinking away back there. It wasn't like Evan to talk like this. I used to always want him to, but I was surprised when he did. I felt a little ashamed, like I made him do it or something. I picked up a bar of soap off its little shelf, just sort of held it in my hand and looked at it. "Guess so," I said. "Maybe. Hell, I don't know." It was true, too. I didn't know if I *was* threatened by him any more.

I put the soap back on the little shelf. Then I realized that here I was, having this talk with Evan like I never got to do, and I was just playing with soap and feeling all ashamed. I rubbed my fingers into my palms to get the soap off, and I said, "Don't you feel jealous sometimes?"

"I don't want to," Evan said. "I don't think I have to."

I wiped my hands on my pants, and I saw the soap on my pants now. I got a little mad at that, and I said to Evan, "So what are you afraid of?"

"Meaning what?" Evan said, and he was annoyed.

"You practically hide out up here in the restroom. You don't talk about stuff that bothers you." I was getting all hotted up. "What is going on with you, anyway? We live in the same house together, and you've never once said that I piss you off. That's crazy. I piss everybody off. Sometimes I get the feeling you don't care about anything. I don't even know if you care about Carrie."

I saw that his face was getting all red. He frowned, but it was at his painting, not me. Then he started talking real softly, so you had to know he wasn't too pleased.

It looked like he was going through a list while he talked, he started with one index finger on the other pinky, then went right up the hand. "One," he said, "I'm not threatened by you. Two, I come here because I like being here. This is where my work is. Three, my work is important to me." His hands were shaking as he ticked things off on his fingers. I never saw his hands shake before. "Four, most of the time you don't piss me off. Most of the time I think you're a funny guy. Five, Carolyn is important to me. But I don't think you have the right to tell anyone how to act. Particularly if you love them. I think that if you love someone, you have to have faith in them."

"To do what?" I said.

"Whatever they want." He stopped talking for a second. "Whatever *she* wants," he said. "We're talking about Carolyn."

I knew we were. We didn't usually, but we were. "So that means you don't care *what* the hell she does," I said. "That's just great."

"Listen," Evan said. "I just think that love has no strings."

"What good is it, then?"

"What do you mean?" he said.

"What good is it, without strings?"

Evan sort of stopped for a second. Then it was like he was listening to us all of a sudden, instead of being us, and I could see that he was regular Evan again, and I could see that a joke was coming out, probably. "It doesn't always have to be a stringed instrument," he said. "Love is various. It's the same melody, but everyone plays it on a different instrument. There's a whole orchestra. Woodwinds, strings, horns, percussion, you have a choice. I would play the bassoon. It's the hardest to hear. What would you play?"

"Drums," I said. "No. Violin. Something with lots of strings."

Evan laughed. "Of course, we would both have to take turns playing second fiddle," he said. "And I believe that Carolyn would play the triangle." He laughed again. He was real relieved, you could tell. He picked up a brush and dabbed it in blue paint. He held the brush up level, and then he began touching his canvas with it, smiling, and painting blue.

When I thought about blue, I had to think about the other day. I was sleeping with Carrie in her room, where you could look out windows to the east and south sides, it was late summer, and when I woke up dawn had just happened. A ton of birds were singing in the holly tree in the back yard, and another ton in the monkey-puzzle. Carrie was lying tucked tight around my butt, her arm thrown over me. She was asleep, but her fingers were moving in little circles on my stomach. These sweet little circles. Her room is all beautiful white, white sheets white bedcovers white walls white wall to wall, and the sky just then was this terrific shade of blue, pale and clear. It was spotless, the sky was. It was like this clean blue dome over us. It was like this blue dome that was protecting us. It was keeping us happy. It was keeping us from having to live the sad little lives that other people had to live. Tons of birds were singing, because it was dawn, and because the sky was a clean blue dome for us. For the three of us.

When I look up at that sky today—August 30, 1980—it's still pretty clear. But there must be traces of volcanic ash left in the air, or else smog, because I can't look at the sky without thinking of the smoke in there, and the carbon monoxides, all the different kinds of poisons. It's hard to believe that someone could look up, one dawn, and see in the sky everything he knew about happiness. And even harder to believe that the someone was me.

I turned over and looked down at her closed eyelids, when all of a sudden they opened, and I was looking into her swimming-pool-blue eyes, and they were looking into me.
She said, "Wide awake, Sweets?"
"No, baby. I'm dreaming."

Chapter

So finally I got to know them both, even Evan. I got to know their little habits—the way Carrie rolled up her toothpaste tube, perfectly even, or how she rubbed her feet in circles as she dropped off to sleep. Like the way Evan snuck downstairs for a little tipple from the bottle before bed, fooling nobody, or how he put mustard on his potatoes. Even mashed potatoes.

After a while I even began to see why they were still together. It was on account of all the time they had put in. They knew each other like a book. If Carrie was gone when Evan got home he usually knew where she went; if I was looking for something, even something like tacks or rubber bands, he always knew where she'd put them. If Evan went shopping Carrie knew what he would buy, and what he would forget to buy. She knew what kind of toilet paper he thought was the best and what section of the newspaper he wanted first, the weather, and she knew pretty much what all he was going to say. And she seemed to like to hear him say it, too.

Sometimes it got almost scary. That Christmas Carrie went off to see her mother again, so we had our own private Christmas a couple of days early. Carrie opened a present from Evan, looked at it and started laughing. It didn't seem exactly funny to me. It was a book called *A Home,* by a dead Swedish painter. It didn't seem too funny to me, particularly because the guy was dead.

Evan took one look at his first present. It was from Carrie. He didn't even have to open it up. "Let me guess," he said, and he did. "*A Home.*"

"That's right," she said.

"You two are psychic," I said.

"No," Evan said. "Just good friends, actually."

The winter, which in Portland means rain, was mild. The only catastrophe was a storm in early January that coated everything with about three inches of ice. A lot of trees broke, and the ones that didn't bent over like old men. People were killed in downtown Portland by branches falling in the Park Blocks. The huge horse-chestnut tree in our front yard came down in the middle of the night. It sounded like an explosion. The roots tore up the sidewalk and the branches knocked a whole tangle of wires down onto our front porch and all around the house. So we were prisoners in our home. The power and phone went out, and they stayed out for three days, like sixteen-year-olds with the keys to the car and first love brewing up a storm.

It wasn't bad, though. It was London during the blitzkrieg or something. The three of us sat around the fire, eating popcorn with brewer's yeast, or with butter, or plain, and drinking red wine. Maybe the blitzkrieg wasn't exactly like that. We slept on the floor in sleeping bags. Did they have sleeping bags in World War II? I guess not.

Actually, it wasn't bad. Carrie suffers from Food Anxiety, she shops like a lunatic, so the freezer was full. We roasted stuff over the fire. We tried to roast frozen pizza and frozen cauliflower and peas. But we also had a couple of steaks and some Dungeness crab in there. I don't think there was much crab floating around the London Underground during the blitzkrieg. Probably wasn't even any popcorn.

Finally the PGE truck came and rescued us. They told us that none of the wires had been hot. False alarm in London.

The ice cracked and melted, the rains stopped, the basement dried out, you could see cracks in the clouds at sunset. Our triangle entered its second spring, and it was blooming.

Maybe I should have thought about things a little bit when Mount St. Helens went off right around then. The first little eruption was a Thursday or so. The mountain sent a plume of steam and junk up to about 7,000 feet. It was just a tiny little eruption. Everybody in Portland started going crazy, but it was just this tiny little eruption. You couldn't see it from our house. We weren't about to pay attention to mountains going off, or broken mirrors, or black cats. Because we three were lucky thirteen just then.

Then one day maybe a week after that first little eruption I got back from work and Carolyn wasn't home.

I went up to the restroom. We traded hellos. I said, "Seen Carrie, buddy?"

"She wasn't here when I got home."

"How's the picture?"

He shrugged. "I took Lancelot to Laurelhurst, by the way," he said.

By what way? "Good," I said. "Thanks. How was school today?"

"We don't talk about school," he said, painting.

I made coffee, brought Evan up a cup, then sat down at my kitchen table. I didn't know what the hell to do next. Sometimes I just don't. You like to think you don't get bored, but sometimes you just do. I was nervous, because Carrie wasn't there. She was almost always there. I was too nervous to read, even the *Oregonian*, but I wasn't too nervous to get bored. I sat at my table twitching. I was waiting for Carrie to get home, that was all I was doing, I couldn't pretend I was doing something else.

I know people who play a lot of solitaire. I get the feeling that solitaire people are waiting for something. They know nothing's going to happen, and they're not on the edge of their chairs. But waiting can be habit forming. You begin to play solitaire over and over, like chain smoking. It's kind of comforting, because it doesn't matter how your games turn out, but it can drive you crazy too. Because it just doesn't matter.

Yeah, I played a little solitaire, sitting in the kitchen.

Then I tried to put Lance in my lap. I get kind of weird with Lance sometimes, and he knows it, but I had a funny feeling that day. Like I was sore in my chest, and I wanted to pet Lance so I could feel better. But he's a big dog, and he wasn't about to sit in my lap. He struggled, then fell on his face on the floor. Lance hopped away looking hurt, as if I'd been trying to hit him or something. But I wouldn't ever hit Lance. I wouldn't hit anybody, really.

Finally I heard the clunk of her clogs on the front step. She opened the front door and closed it behind her with a bang. Carrie clunks a lot. She's graceful, but she's also pretty clunky.

I realized that I was holding my breath, waiting for her. I wasn't going to move till I saw her again.

But she came right in to see me, smiling, shining. She kissed my mouth. She took my hand, pulled me to my feet, and led me to the bottom of the stairs.

Then she called up, "Vandy. Come down quick."

It didn't take too long for Evan's head to appear above the banister. "What's up?" he said.

"A news flash. Come on down."

When he got to the bottom of the stairs, she was still holding my hand. She reached out for one of his. She held them both in front of her face for a second, looking from one hand to the other, like they were strange. Then she raised her two hands, and our two hands, as high as she could, like a ref telling both boxers that they'd won the fight.

"We're all pregnant," she crowed.

The first thing I did was kiss her hand. I must have closed my eyes for a second, feeling the grooves between her knuckles, the bones moving right under her thin skin, the tiny hairs above the wrist. When I looked up I saw Evan kissing her other hand. I felt like I was looking into a mirror, and Evan was me. I was watching my double kiss my lover.

"How pregnant?" I said.

She didn't tell me. "I think one," she said. "One child."

"We'll call it Esmeralda," Evan said.

Evan could goof around at the weirdest times, considering that he was not essentially a goof.

"Who's the father?" I said.

She said, "We have two suspects. But their names will not cross my lips, officer."

"Do you know?" I said. "You know, but you're not telling?"

She put her hands on her hips. She looked like Jane Fonda, only with long hair, when she put her hands on her hips. "What's it to you?" she said to me.

"Esmeralda Pritikin. Esmeralda Pritikin the Aforementioned," Evan said, laughing. He always laughed at his own jokes. Actually, he always laughed at any jokes. He tended not to make any noise, even when he was laughing real hard.

I wanted to tell Carrie that I loved her, I loved her totally, I loved her right out of my senses, but I didn't manage that. I stood and watched Evan recover from his joke.

"Why don't you two just share?" Carrie said.

Evan was all finished laughing. "The biological paternity doesn't matter to me," he said. A little smile crept onto his face again, but he put it away.

I challenged him. "You telling me you're not even curious?"

"Not even close to curious," Evan said, with such a straight face that I knew it was true. But then he said, "Hungry, yes. Curious, no." He started laughing again. He was in a pretty damn good mood, I'm telling you.

Carrie's eyes were on me. Her steady eyes. I felt like I was being told to pledge allegiance to the flag or something.

"All right," I said. "I give up. We share. But that includes the damn diapers, buddy."

Carrie smiled now, and she said, "I really don't know whose it is, Sweets. And I'm glad."

"Was it an accident?" I said.

"No. I wanted it."

"Then I guess it's yours," I said.

"Ours, Sweets."

"All right. Ours."

"Esmeralda Baobab. Esmeralda Baobab the baby. Esmeralda, definitely," Evan said. He was laughing like mad. I sort of wasn't.

I went out and bought two bottles of champagne. Carrie said she wasn't supposed to take alcohol now, but she made the toast. "To the unborn," she said. Then she went ahead and drank. She was happy, but you could tell that there was something working on her mind. You could always tell with Carrie. It was somewhere right around the eyebrows.

"I think we ought to do something to make it official," Carrie said.

"What could be more official than champagne?" Evan said.

She said, "I think we ought to write a book together. If we can live together, we can write a book together."

"Sure," I said. This was me being sarcastic again. Evan didn't say anything.

"We should make a book in celebration," Carrie said. "In celebration of us. The improbable, implacable fact of us." She took a big drink of champagne. She was getting going, the way she could. "In celebration," she said, "of the blessed completing of the square."

"Go right on ahead," I said. "There you go. Go right on ahead. I'm not stopping you. But I'm not going to write no book. I'm not even too terrific at reading books."

"It's easier to write one than read one," Carrie said.

"The hell," I said. I didn't believe her for a second. But they went right on talking about their plans, or Carrie did, at least. We were supposed to write the life story of one of the others. About the person growing up. How that person got into our triangle. Blah blah woof woof. It was going to be the history of our triangle. Carrie even had a name for it already. Delicate Geometry. I tell you, Carrie was happier than a pig in shit.

"I can't do that," I kept saying. "I can't write no book. Believe it." I wasn't going to, either. Carrie got an old dusty glass bowl out of the top cupboard in the kitchen. She wrote down the three names on little pieces of paper, then dropped them in the bowl. I said, "I'll fetch up one of those papers, if you're fool enough to want me to. But I'm not about to write no book."

Carrie said to me, "You go first." She pointed at the bowl. I'm telling you, she was happier than a pig.

I reached in, grabbed a scrap, pulled it out. It said RICE.

"Autobiography," Evan said.

Carrie was holding her breath, and her face was twisting like she didn't have any air left. Then she let her breath out. "No," she said. "We don't want straight confessions. Put it back, Sweets."

"It's not like I'm going to write the damn thing," I said. But I put it back, picked out another one. This one said EVAN.

So it was Carrie's idea, natch. Everything was Carrie's idea.

Evan got CARRIE and Carrie got RICE. Both of them started right in the next night, sitting in their separate rooms, writing away. Evan just jumped at the idea. For a while he pretty much put away his paintbrush. I don't know why, but he jumped at it. I thought about it some, but I knew I would never do it. I'm not exactly the author type. I guess that's obvious.

It's funny that I'm doing it now, now that it doesn't matter any more. But it was Carrie's idea. I know that's got something to do with why I'm doing it now, or at all. I'm thinking that maybe she still wants it. It was Carrie's idea, and I'm doing it for her.

Chapter

Not too long after that I came home from Angela's Sub-Basement Vault early. It was my week. All day long I did absolutely nothing at work. I was thinking about Carrie, dreaming about her, wanting her. I wasn't half bad at coming up with fantasies, and the longer I spent with Carrie the better I got. I got in a lot of practice. That day while I was sitting on my butt in the Vault, Carrie and I engaged in some pretty erotic enterprises. I knocked off work an hour early.

I walked in and the house was real quiet. I don't know why, but instead of shouting, "I'm home!" I closed the door behind me real carefully, without making noise. I told myself that I was doing it so I could surprise Carrie in the back yard. But that wasn't why. It felt like the day my little brother told me to go to the attic, because my father was hanging up. I knew what I'd find.

I looked out the kitchen window, into the back yard. Carrie's Indian blanket was out there, and the plastic orange-juice pitcher with Donald Ducks on it, and her notebook and stack of paperback books. A pair of sunglasses was upside down on a tube of suntan lotion. It was all just as Carrie had left it.

I slipped off my shoes. I started getting all methodical. I checked in my bedroom. Nothing, didn't think so. The basement light off, not there. Upstairs, I tried her room. I tried looking through the keyhole, but I couldn't see anything except the keyhole. I opened the door real slow.

Nothing. Thank God.

I realized what a damn idiot I'd been. Did I actually think that Carrie would be fooling around in there? Evan would be home by now, I could hear his noises from the restroom. She wouldn't fool around, not with Evan painting right in the next room. Evan's tolerant, I thought, but nobody's *that* tolerant.

"Hey, buddy, how you doing?" I said as I opened the restroom door.

I hadn't guessed. There they were.

Carrie and Evan.

Evan was wearing the big floppy straw hat and a raggy old short-sleeved cotton shirt with little boats on it and a huge ridiculous pair of sunglasses I'd never seen before. Carrie had on a pair of sixties-style wire-rimmed glasses, though she usually wore contacts, and there was this wool ski hat on her head, though it was May. She was wearing a white blouse with great big ruffles at the shoulders, and a big long scarf.

They were both standing in the dry bathtub, close together, Carrie with her back to Evan. A floor-length skirt was wrapped around Carrie. When I looked closer, I saw that it was wrapped around Evan, too.

They were standing real close. Evan had his arms around Carrie's middle. She had her hands on her hips.

They turned their heads toward me. But Evan didn't exactly look at me.

Carrie did an amazing thing. She smiled at me. "Hello, Sweets," she said.

I didn't say anything. I closed the door.

I went downstairs, went out, taking Lance with me. I felt like I was all of a sudden crippled, just like Lance. Somebody had just sort of casually pulled off one of my legs. I went down to Belmont's Inn for a drink. It was fucking Happy Hour.

I remember saying to Carrie, later on, "So what the hell were you doing in there?" I was practically yelling.

And I remember her looking up at me, her swimming-pool eyes more beautiful than ever, and her saying, calm, not even close to apologizing, "It isn't any of your business, Sweets. It just isn't."

The only thing I could think of, to say back to her, was, "But it was my week, Carrie."

"Sweets," she said. "A large Southern man was seen with someone who looked like me in a VW parked in a cemetery last week. Last week was Evan's week. Careful. I have an eyewitness here."

"You were watching?" I said.

"No," she said. "*She* was."

It might have been the next day. It was practically the next day, it felt like the next day, Carrie and Evan and I were sitting at the table eating dinner, and then it was over, and I got up to take the dishes into the kitchen. But I had that feeling again, and at the kitchen door I gave a quick look back over my shoulder.

I saw Carrie's hand reach out. It landed gently on the back of Evan's neck, and her long thin fingers started stroking him there, softly and delicately curling the hair at the nape of his neck. Evan was sitting facing me. He looked up and saw me see. He grabbed his napkin out of his lap and right away started wiping his mouth, like he had just dribbled or drooled or something. I think his face was about to get red, but I just kept on going into the kitchen.

I'd caught them again, and I was sorry. But what the hell was I supposed to do?

Around then earthquakes were beginning to go off all the time up at St. Helens. The Goat Rocks were beginning to bulge, and one side of the mountain was moving up, as if somebody had strapped a corset around her down below. I was beginning to get nervous. Any afternoon Evan and Carrie might be fooling around with their restroom sex games, and I would never know. They might be doing it every day, after Evan came home and before I did. That's why I quit my job at Angela's Sub-Basement Vault. I quit so I could be home afternoons between three and five-thirty. It might not seem like such a good reason, but it was good enough for me. I felt like I had to quit. Of course I was glad to quit, too. I'm always glad to quit.

I started spending my spare time out in the back yard. The whole east end of the yard was a mess, and in Oregon that means a blackberry patch. There were dead remains of rosebushes, swarmed under by blackberries. I wanted to make a garden there, where the blackberry bushes crawled. I wanted it to be like a garden back there, with roses. That's all I wanted.

I hardly talked to Carrie at all. I just went out there and did my work, maybe every once in a while saying something to her, a little joke or something. She spent a lot of time out there on her old Indian blanket, but I didn't go out there to bother her. I wasn't trying to guard over her. I just wanted it to be like a garden out there.

She said she was writing about me, and my being there broke her concentration. I told her that didn't make any sense, it was dumb. I might have said one or two other things. She picked up her spiral-bound notebook and went in, in a huff, like girls you knew in high school or something. I worked for a while, then went in for a beer.

When I came in, Carrie went back out. She plunked herself back down on the blanket with a mug of hot tea. Hot tea, and it was practically summer. She started writing like mad in her spiral-bound. I drank a few beers in the kitchen, sitting at the table, watching her out the window. She sat there cross-legged, real still, nothing moving but her hand. Every once in a while she moved both her hands back through her hair. I just sat there watching her. I thought I could hear the sound of my own pulse, and it was going fast.

I started going out there wearing just my red gym shorts. No underwear, no jock strap, no T-shirt, no shoes, no nothing. Once Evan asked how come I didn't wear more clothes when I went into the briar patch. I told him I was trying to get an allover tan, but that wasn't why. I did it because I liked to watch what the thorns did to me.

It was something to see. The thorns would catch onto my skin and rip me every time I moved. I didn't pay any attention if one snagged me, I just went on snipping at the bastards, cutting down thornbushes and dragging them away. I was all streaked with this red blood. It kind of matched my shorts. But the red in the blood was different, because it was a real color, it wasn't just some dye that you put onto cotton. It was alive. It was me. When it first came out, it practically sparkled. But after it had been in the air a while, it seemed to die. It turned all boring brown, dead-looking.

I thought about that. I felt like I understood what was happening to the blood. The same thing was happening to everybody. You spend time alive, breathing air, and you don't even realize that every second you're losing it, bit by bit you're dying, turning old and brown and stale. Every minute you die a little more, and that's all you do, actually. I grabbed a thick one in my bare hands and tried to pull it up by its roots. But they hold on as hard as they can, those blackberry bushes. They don't give up that easy.

Every afternoon Carrie and Evan would write on their book. Evan started the minute he got home from school. He didn't exactly do a lot of housework. He didn't exactly do a ton of dishes.

I would go up and check on them, but not too often. Carrie knew what I was up to, and she would get pretty pissed at me for doing it. But I couldn't help it.

Then one day I was out in the patch, finished with the thorns, smoothing over the dirt I'd carted in with a wheelbarrow, raking every last little tiny stone out of my beautiful black dirt, I was just ready to put in the roses, when I heard a sound coming out of the kitchen. It was a steady sound, and at first I didn't hear it. It took a while to come up to the top of my mind, the thinking part, like a bubble squiggling to the surface of a beer. But then it did, and I stopped working and listened to it. It was the teakettle whistling, going full blast.

I knew Carrie would come down for it in a second. If I could hear it out in the yard, she could hear it upstairs for sure. I knew it would stop in a second, so I went back to raking.

It didn't stop. I leaned on my rake and wished it away. Maybe she's in the restroom, I thought, but right away I thought, So where's Evan, then? I took a couple steps toward the house. I walked real slow, the way you do when you're going to answer a telephone that's already rung ten times. You know it's going to stop ringing the second you pick it up, no matter how fast you go. Except that I knew no one was going to pick up the teakettle. No matter how slow I walked, it would still be whistling when I got there.

I came in the back door and went through the kitchen, past the kettle, to the bottom of the stairs. I didn't want to go up those stairs. I shouted up, "Water's boiling, Carrie!"

There was silence, except for the whistle. Then her voice came out of the restroom, all cheery. "Could you get it, Sweets? Be right out."

You talk about what happened on this day or that day, you say exactly what you want to say, and it still comes out wrong. Something's always missing. It sounds like a conversation you have every day. I say Water's boiling, and she says Could you get it, Sweets? But that leaves out the way normal words can get you. It's not so normal on the inside. Be right out, she said, and I felt like my damn heart was ripped right out. It's hard to write the way you feel about the dumb little things that happen. You can't get across pain that's inside you, that whistles and whistles and never stops.

I went back into the kitchen like a condemned man. The teakettle was whistling like crazy, going full blast, but I didn't take it off. I stood there and watched it spout steam, blowing its own brains out, and I didn't do a damn thing.

Chapter

The next day was a Sunday, a Sunday in Evan's week. I woke up with sort of a hangover. Not from drinking. From feeling bad. From feeling bad too long. I hadn't slept enough, my calves felt all tight, and there was an acid taste creeping up to my mouth from my stomach, like my insides were starting to go bad and smell up the place. I woke up, cranked myself up, went shuffling around the kitchen, tired and sore.

Every morning I have coffee. It's not a rule, or a habit, it's just what I do, and there isn't any question about it. It's good to have a little security in the morning. But that Sunday my nerves were already boiling, and I didn't even drink my coffee. I made the coffee, then just sat there with it, like the coffee was sick and I was taking care of it. I let it get cold. I knew then that there must be something wrong with me. I felt like I must have died or something, it wasn't me any more. In the end I tossed the coffee into the sink. While I watched the coffee drain I was thinking about Evan and Carrie. It was his Sunday, the two of them were upstairs in bed together, when they woke up they might start up with some kinky sex, I could see it starting, the coffee left a brown stain in the sink as if somebody real dirty had taken a bath in there and didn't clean it up.

I just wanted to get out of there.

It was a warm, sunny morning, May. I thought I might try a bike ride. Just ride around the neighborhood, and relax. Relax, and try to disappear.

It was a real Portland kind of thing to do. In Oregon you have to be outside on sunny spring mornings. It's a rule. Despite that I dragged Evan's old three-speed up from the basement, and wobbled around the neighborhood, with Lance hopping along beside me, his tongue hanging. While I was riding all I could think about was Carrie and Evan doing weird things to each other. I could see them standing in the bathtub with all their funny clothes on. That was worse than naked. I just couldn't get those two out of my brain. I couldn't even get them out of the bathtub.

One part of me was saying in a loud voice that it was funny, that's all it was. They were just clowning around. But that was like telling somebody who's just been hit with a pie in the eye that it's all a joke. He's not about to laugh, because funny is in the eye of the beholder. Then see if *he* laughs.

I was getting all worked up, and I'm not actually that terrific on bikes, and the bike was too small for me. I got real tired. I could hear my heart drumming in my chest, and I was breathing in gasps. It sounded like someone talking after their vocal cords had been cut out.

I stopped to give us a rest at an antique store, a junk-store antique store, and I plunked down in one of the chairs on display outside. The junk-store owner was sitting out there too, soaking up sun. He was friendly, like most junk-store owners. I was all sweaty, and getting his chair all sweaty, and not exactly on the edge of buying his chair, and he was still friendly. He must have been in the habit.

He was this huge fat guy. "Nice day for a bike ride," he said.

I started imagining what it would look like if I found *him* in the bathtub with Carrie. Him with the skirt around him, and the floppy straw hat, and the huge ridiculous sunglasses. I couldn't believe that things like that could cause me pain. It's even harder to believe now. But they did.

"Real nice," I said. "Hey, get off there. Get down, Lance."

"You hear about the mountain?"

I must have still been thinking about the skirt and hat and the sunglasses, because I didn't understand. I heard what he said, but I heard it wrong. "No," I told him. "I'm just out for a bike ride. You must be thinking of somebody else. Goddamn it. Lie down. A lot of people look just like me," I said.

The fat junk guy gave me a funny look. Then he gave Lance one. "What happened to your dog?" he said.

"Born that way," I said. I always say that, but it isn't true. He got hit by a cable car on Powell in San Francisco.

The junk-store guy pointed. "See those clouds over there?" he said.

I looked. The northern sky was filled up with huge black clouds, rolling up, building on top of each other. They were like South Carolina thunderheads, and they were like the clouds of steam in Marion's Oyster Roast in Murrell's Inlet. The clouds were rising in the sky north of Portland, tumbling together and then rolling away.

"Heard it on the radio," the junk guy whispered to me, like it was some kind of secret. "That's St. Helens going off."

I watched the clouds rolling up, mountains of clouds.

He said, "Major eruption, they say. Say stuff went up to 20,000 feet. That's big."

I didn't say anything.

"Real big," he said. "That's what you call a major eruption." I was still just watching it all. After a second I saw him sidling me this weird look. He gave his knee a little slap, and then he said, "Well, is there anything I can show you?"

I turned and looked right at him. I thought about what he would look like in a floppy straw hat, and it was only after staring at him for a long time that I realized he was talking about junk.

I wobbled home as fast as I could. Ten-thirty, but no one was downstairs yet. No sound of them. I threw Evan's bike back into the basement and went right out again, slamming the door to let them know I was gone, and furious.

I drove my truck up to where you can see the mountain, just off Stark near Mount Tabor. The street was jammed with cars, and the little grassy area full of people. The old people leaned against their cars, and the young ones sat on the grass. You could see everything. Northeast Portland was laid out in front of us. Beyond it was the Columbia River, with the new Highway 205 bridge arching over it, half-built. In the northern distance, the mountain on the horizon was pouring into the sky. It was still sunny in Portland, but the sky above St. Helens was black. You could see the smoke billowing from the mountain toward the northeast like a gigantic black river in the sky. Sometimes sideways bolts of lightning lit up the darkness above the volcano. Usually St. Helens looked like a vanilla ice cream cone. Now it had a flat top, and was as black as the sky.

I sat and watched with a river of my own going off in my mind, a black river of steam and gas and ash. The stone had finally turned to fire.

A family poured out of a Pontiac, whipped out their beach blanket, sat down next to me, and passed each other cheese and Triscuits. Then they were ready to watch the volcano go off. Most people had something in their mouths. Most people looked at the mountain through something, binocks or camera or spotting scopes. Like you couldn't see it with your plain eyes.

People were talking about exposure time and lava and lens settings and whether that vertical cloud on the left was another eruption, all in the same tone of voice. People were talking and talking, chattering, talking to strangers about where their kids went to school, about where the mountain began and the smoke ended. After a while kids started to get bored and ride their bikes around and get into fights. The grown men drank more beer and laid on their backs on the grass and closed their eyes. It was a Sunday afternoon, after all. The family next to me got their Doritos and dip out of the Pontiac. A new vent opened up on the side of the mountain, probably about where Spirit Lake was. This tremendous column of smoke shot up into the air, then headed east. A polyester guy in front of me ran out of film and had to go to black and white. His girlfriend wanted to leave, because she had to use the restroom. He said, "Just let me finish this roll," and she said, "Well, hurry up."

It was like a crowd watching fireworks on the Fourth of July. They had seen fireworks displays just like this one before, and they even knew what the Grand Finale was going to look like. They were going to save their oohs and ahs till then.

There was no sound during the explosions, just the Portland traffic going by below us. It didn't seem to cross anyone's mind that people might be getting killed on the mountain. Everybody watched the destruction on the horizon like it was a movie you figured would come out all right in the end.

They didn't seem to understand that we were watching the earth spit up its insides, groaning and puking. They didn't seem to understand that we were watching all hell break loose. The smoke kept going up in the sky, the evil kept coming out of the mountain, poisonous jealousy and unhappiness that had been held in for a hundred years. And nobody seemed to know that the volcano was releasing a billion tiny twisted little creatures, and that they were coming to Portland soon, coming to turn houses into stone and stone into ashes. The Portlanders kept eating Doritos and dip.

I didn't know what the hell I'd do when I got home. I walked in and Evan was wiping his brushes clean in the kitchen. When he turned toward me, I could see myself reflected in his glasses, and smoke and steam and ash was blowing out of me like a river. Evan looked at me without any expression on his face. He said, "Igneous a lavaly day?" He laughed without making a sound, he went right on wiping his brushes. And somehow he was unharmed by the poisons that kept on pouring out of me.

Vancouver, Vancouver, this is it.

Chapter

It was the chicken hearts that did it.

The chicken hearts started a couple months before. I was driving my truck one Saturday, doing this that and the other thing, and finally figured out, at about three, that I'd missed my lunch. I only had a buck and a half, but I stopped at a fried-chicken place on Woodstock Avenue. I was thinking french fries, but then the guy in front of me got a whole pint of something for ninety cents. They were tiny little deep-fried chicken organs. I thought they were hearts, but now I'm not sure. I was kind of watching the waitress, actually, she was dressed up in a brown and orange outfit that looked like it was made of napalm. I just asked for the same thing as the guy in front of me. I really thought they were chicken hearts, but now I'm not so sure.

If I had three wishes right now, I'd take one of them and go back and find out what kind of organs I ate that day.

They were real good. I was hungry, I admit that. But they were good. I'm telling you.

I got home that day and told Carrie about how good the chicken hearts were.

"Uck," she said.

"Listen, it was good. It was real good."

"I wouldn't like it," Carrie said.

"How do you know?"

"I don't know *how* I know. I just *do* know."

I gave up then, or at least I thought I did. But a couple of months later, in May, it was the first Saturday after Volcano Day. The three of us were driving across 39th Street, headed for the Rhododendron Gardens across from Reed College. We just had lunch, so I wasn't real hungry, but I suddenly got the urge to prove to old Carrie about the chicken hearts. I swung the truck left on Woodstock and pulled in to the chicken place.

Carrie said, "What are we doing here?"

"I want to show you something," I said. I went in and got a pint of deep-fried chicken hearts. They smelled terrific. I practically ran back out to the truck.

"Here you go," I said, handing them over.

"What are they?" Evan said.

Carried opened up the pint. "Chicken hearts," she said.

"That's right," I said.

"Look at them," she said. "They look like little birds' hearts. They look like the hearts that somebody cut out of little birds."

"What are you doing, going vegetarian all of a sudden?" I said.

"No. I'm not. But I'm not going to eat the organs of little birds."

"What the hell's the difference?" I said. "What does it matter if you eat its leg or its liver?"

"The difference is that I hate liver. I don't hate legs."

"You don't hate these," I said.

"Yes I do," she said.

"You can't. You never ate one. You can't hate something you never tried."

"Yes I can," she said. "You don't have to eat something to know you don't want to eat it. You don't like tires. You don't like tin cans. I don't like chicken hearts."

I was getting worked up. I was getting so worked up that I didn't *know* whether I liked tin cans or not, because I had never tried them. I probably would of eaten a tin can right then, just to prove my point. But I finally thought of something to say so I wouldn't end up having to eat a tin can.

"Tin cans aren't food," I said. "This is food."

"No," she said. "It isn't. It's the hearts of little chickens."

Evan was sitting between us. He was looking straight out of the windshield. There wasn't anything there to look at.

I said, "Come on, Carrie. What do you have against chicken hearts, anyway?"

"I don't *like* them," she said, and now she looked out the truck's *side* window. Evan's face was red, and so was Carrie's, and so was mine. Carrie had her teeth all clenched together, and her eyes were real small slits, and her forehead was all clenched together too, and her hands were little fists.

I drove down to the Rhododendron Gardens, not saying anything. When we got there, we all just sat in the truck. The chicken hearts were just sitting in Evan's lap. I wasn't going to let those things just sit there. I sort of identified with those chicken hearts. I don't care how it sounds, it was true.

After a while I snatched the chicken hearts out of Evan's lap.

I tried again. "Look, would you do me a favor, Carrie? Just try one. That's all I want you to do. *Try* one." I was practically yelling. I was pleading, practically. "Just one bite. If you don't like it, you can spit it out."

She looked at me in this hard, suspicious way, like a little kid who's been locked into her room.

"This is absurd," she said.

"You're right," I said. "It is. I know it is. I can't exactly explain it, Carrie, but it's real important to me that you try a chicken heart. My whole day will be ruined if you don't. My whole life will be ruined if you don't, practically. But I'm telling you, if you just try one of those old chicken hearts, you'll make me the happiest goddamn guy in all Southeast Portland."

"Ridiculous," she said. But she reached over Evan and took a chicken heart out of the carton, and I thought my heart was going to split, I was so happy.

Carrie held on to the chicken heart for a minute. Evan sat there looking down at the chicken heart in Carrie's hand. I said, "It'll get cold," although it was already pretty cold. Then, to demonstrate, I picked one up and popped it into my mouth.

I think that was where something started to go really wrong in my mind. The moment when I first started chewing on that chicken heart. I didn't recognize the trouble right away. But by the time Carrie put the chicken heart half into her mouth and took a tiny bite out of it with her little front teeth, I was already completely, totally furious.

"Oh," Carrie said, like she was surprised. She opened the truck door and spat the chicken heart out into the parking lot. "It's tough," she said. "It's like a little hard heart."

I was so mad that I couldn't talk for a second. My mouth opened up, but the only thing that came out was steam and ash and smoke.

Some part of my brain knew why I was so angry, and it was because the goddamn chicken hearts *were* tough, and I knew it. She was right, and I knew it. I knew it even before she put the heart in her mouth and spit it out again. But the part of my brain that knew she was right wasn't doing the talking.

I said, "You didn't even *taste* the thing."

"I did too. It was tough."

"You didn't *want* it to be good," I said. "It was tough because you *wanted* it to be tough."

"That just isn't true," Carrie said. "The stupid thing is tough all by itself. Can we stop now, please?"

"You had your mind all made up," I said. "You didn't even try it. You spit it out because you were afraid it was going to be good."

"You *said* I could spit it out. You said I'd make you glad if I just took one bite. I did. I think I've done my bit for the day."

Evan hadn't said anything. Now he put his hand down in the chicken hearts and picked one out. He timidly put it into his mouth and rolled it around, chewing, like he was working on a chaw of tobacco. Then he raised his eyebrows and opened his big fat mouth.

"Well, just for the record," he said, "it *is* tough."

"You're just taking her side," I said.

"No," Evan said. "I'm not." He was still chewing.

"This is none of your business," I said.

"I guess not," Evan said. He was still chewing hard on the chicken heart. In my anger it looked like he was trying to exaggerate the toughness of my chicken heart.

I shouldn't have been angry. What the hell did those chicken hearts mean to me, anyway? But Evan shouldn't have jumped into the middle, because it really *wasn't* any of his business. Then I shouldn't have *told* him it wasn't any of his business. But he shouldn't have exaggerated the chewing. But then I didn't stop making mistakes. I took the pint of chicken hearts and turned it upside down on Evan's head. I shouldn't have done that, either.

The chicken hearts bounced off of Evan's head and his shoulders and one bounced off his glasses. They rolled down into his lap and behind his back, and some of the chicken hearts stayed there, behind his back and in his lap, and some fell on the floor of the pick-up.

Little crumbs from the brown deep-fried batter stuck in his short hair, and some of the batter landed on his shoulders, but he didn't brush it off. He just looked at me, with his eyebrows raised, like he was going to ask me a question. His mouth went straight across his face.

One of the chicken hearts fell into Carrie's lap. She grabbed it and pushed the door all the way open. I thought she was going to heave the chicken heart out into the parking lot. She didn't. She jumped out of the truck and started running down the path into the Rhododendron Gardens, with the chicken heart still clutched in her hand.

I jumped out too, and started to run down the path after her. She had a pretty good head start. I was yelling after her, "Hey, Carrie. Hey, Sweets." I didn't usually call her Sweets. She called me Sweets. I felt all terrible, because I had been way out of control, and knew it, and because I was still way out of control, and I still knew it. I wanted to tell Carrie how goddamn sorry I was, what a complete and total asshole I was, and how much I loved her and hated me, so I ran after her on the path and yelled at her to stop, all the time thinking about how stupid I was and which names in particular I was going to call myself when I caught up with her. The other thing I wanted to tell her, in case she didn't know, was that I was only out of control because I loved her all the way, with everything, in my skin and my twisted bones and in the maze of my stupid, stupid mind, and I wanted her to have my baby. So I ran after her on the path. But she didn't stop running.

She ran pretty fast, too, for a pregnant woman who doesn't run too often. She turned before she got to the second bridge and ran through the azaleas and rhododendrons. It was real pretty in there. There was a lake off to the left, with ducks and things, and plants all over the place. A patch of grass was at the end there, where the path looped around, and we ran toward it, with me gaining on her. I knew she was going to run to that patch, and then stop. She was going to turn and face me, and I'd explain, tell her that I loved her, and we'd hug, have an electric kiss, and then stroll back to the truck with our fingers winding around each other. My fingers winding around hers, I mean. Hers around mine.

She didn't stop running. I got right up in back of her, and I could hear her gasping for breath, but she didn't stop. I tapped her on the shoulder, but she didn't stop. We got almost to the end of the grassy patch, and I got the weird feeling that Carrie was going to keep going, run right into that muddy old lake. I put my arms around her from behind to stop her, sort of hugging her. I expected her to stop then, but she gave another lunge forward, our feet tangled together, and we went down, with me on top.

"You all right?" I said, right away, because I'm not real light, and because she gave a little sort of cry when we fell.

"Bastard," she said. "What are you trying to do, kill everything?" Then she said, "Let go of me, please."

"What do you mean, kill everything?" I said. "I just wanted you to try a chicken heart," I said.

"I think you were trying to kill your child. I honestly do." I could tell then she was crying. She kind of coughed when she said child.

"It's mine?" I said.

She was sobbing away. "I was speaking *collectively,*" she said.

Carrie could say the weirdest things when she was crying. It was like Carrie was crying, but *she* was talking, right through Carrie's tears. "You're violating me," she said. "Let *go,* damn it."

I saw that I still had my arms around her. It was sort of a hug, but Carrie didn't know that. I let go, and then helped her up.

"I wasn't," I said to her. "You know I wasn't. I want that old baby."

She shook her head. "You don't. You don't even want me. You just want to wreck everything you possibly can. Everything you love, and yourself most of all. That's why you drink so damn much," she said.

"Don't say that," I said. She was upset, she didn't know what she was saying. I wanted to talk about how much I loved her instead. But just then a bike came whizzing around the corner. It ran right over Carrie's little foot. The bike bumped and went right on.

The kid on the bike might have been eighteen. He might have been a Reed College student or something. His face was all pasty, at least. He called "Sorry!" over his shoulder, but he didn't stop. He didn't even turn his head.

The bike path looped around the grassy patch. I raced right back across the grass and cut the guy off.

I didn't know what the hell I was doing, I really didn't. I was just sort of watching myself.

I stopped the guy. "Get off the fucking bike," I said to the kid.

He stood there, straddling the bike. "It was an accident," he said.

"Why the fuck didn't you stop?"

"I didn't hurt anybody," the kid said. "Why bother?" Then he said the wrong thing. "Stop playing he-man, would you?" I don't know why he wanted to say that.

I took a couple of steps and hit the kid in the mouth. It hurt the hell out of my hand. The kid went flying off his bike, the bike went over on its side, wheels spinning, the kid was laying on his side in the path. I wasn't thinking anything except about how much my hand hurt.

I looked at it. There were cuts on two knuckles, and blood all over it. I could hear Carrie shouting at me across the grass, but I couldn't hear what she was saying. The kid was laying there with his face turned away from me, not saying anything. He put his hand up against his mouth real slow, and when he took it away I could see blood all over that too. He did a sort of cough, and blood came out, and so did some other things. They landed on the bike path. They were teeth.

The kid was laying there looking at his bloody hand, like it was the hand that hurt. Finally the bike wheels stopped spinning. I took off back across the grass. I never hit anybody before, and I was in a state of sort of shock. Mostly I was thinking about how much my hand hurt. I guess I was wondering about Carrie too. She was standing there with her arms dangling. She wasn't crying any more. She just looked real sad.

When I got back to her I stopped, and we looked at each other. She said, real quietly, "I think I know what you were doing. You were hitting me, weren't you?"

"No," I said, real quick.

I was telling the truth then, and I knew it. Because it wasn't her I was hitting. It was me. I was hitting the whole world, but mostly it was me.

But I didn't tell Carrie that.

"Let's get out of here," I said, and grabbed her arm. I felt like I was yanking her, all the way back up to the truck. Evan was still sitting there, not doing anything, with crumbs of chicken heart batter still in his lap. He saw my hand when I jumped in. He asked me if I was all right, but I didn't say anything. I rammed the key in the ignition. I grabbed the empty chicken hearts box from the dashboard, threw it out into the parking lot. Get rid of the gun.

Then I drove on out of there.

Chapter

After that Carrie wasn't really talking to me much. It was Evan's week, so I don't know how I knew what was happening. But I guess I knew Carrie a little. She wasn't saying anything, but for a couple of days she was reading children's books, and she was eating mainly orange sherbet, up in her room. She didn't come down for supper and she didn't even bother to read the *Oregonian*.

After supper one night Evan was doodling on his napkin. It was just us two.

I said, "Well, do you hate me now, buddy?"

He tried to look surprised. Maybe he *was* surprised. "Because of the chicken hearts?" he said.

"Uh-huh."

"Not at all."

"Why not?"

"It was time for me to wash my hair," he said. "You've done humanity an infinite service."

I felt all grateful to him, and I wanted to tell him. But I couldn't think of how to put it. So I just jumped up and did the dishes, and Evan sat there doodling.

Carrie was up in her room reading children's books and thinking hard about something. It was me, I thought. I thought she was wondering what to do about me and my stupid, stupid mind and my crazy love for her. But I wasn't exactly right about that.

She went out one day during the day, and the next day, and the day after. I tried to talk to her, but she wouldn't let me. She walked around the house doing everything real slowly and carefully, like a mechanical man, like she had to think about each muscle she was moving. Evan didn't even try to talk to her, he knew better, but I kept doing it. I had this feeling about Carrie. It was like she was walking around in a dream, noticing all the tiny little details but not thinking about anything at all. I kept talking to her, trying to wake her up. I watched her flipping through the pages of a magazine, and I could tell she wasn't reading it. She wasn't even looking at the pictures, and I wondered what she *was* doing in there, and if she was in there at all. Just watching her made me sick to my stomach. So now I was the one with morning sickness, all day.

Evan came home one afternoon when Carrie was gone and I was there, sitting there at the kitchen table, sipping Scotch and feeling strange. Scotch is not my special favorite, but it's all right with ice. Evan likes Scotch. He's the one that buys it. It was all we had, anyway.

Evan came in, said Hello, started upstairs. I was feeling kind of reckless, mad and sad. I shouted up after him, "Hey, buddy. Carrie's not home."

"Okay," he said, not stopping.

"Where do you think she's at?" I said, louder.

"Don't know," not stopping.

"You think she's sleeping with somebody?" I shouted, real loud, and he stopped at the top of the stairs. I knew that wasn't the kind of thing you yell up to somebody on the stairs, but I just didn't care.

Evan came back down into the kitchen smiling. I was surprised to see him come down, and I was surprised to see him smiling. I shouldn't be real surprised at anything Evan does, but I was.

"I don't think so," he said. "Does it matter?"

"You don't think it matters?"

I'm never surprised when Evan shrugs his little shoulders. He said, "The fences are down. We don't have the right to pretend they're still up."

"What the hell you mean, buddy?"

"It would be ridiculous for us to say, 'You can sleep with four men, but not with five.' You know and I know that any given number is arbitrary. You can't start making rules now."

"Sure you can," I said. "*Two* is the limit. Me and you."

Evan smiled again, and then he did something that wasn't an Evan-type thing to do. He patted my shoulder with his hand.

"You want a whisky?" I said.

"Maybe later. I have to go upstairs now."

"Still writing about Carrie?"

"No, I finished that. Weeks ago. I'm back to painting the sink and toilet again."

"I'll let you know when Carrie comes home," I said.

"Don't worry," he said.

"Why not?"

"Bad for your digestion."

"Living is bad for your digestion," I said. Evan smiled, but I was serious.

"Don't worry," he said again. I think he just about patted my shoulder again, but instead of that he turned around and went straight on up to the restroom.

It wasn't long after that when I heard Carrie's heavy footsteps on the front steps. I jumped up and met her in the front hall.

She looked real, real tired. She looked like hell, as a matter of fact. Her eyes were all baggy and she walked like she was a ton of bricks.

I said Hello, and she gave me this weary Hello back. She walked right by. I said to her back, "You still punishing me for the chicken hearts, Carrie?"

"No," she said, but she didn't stop trudging. She got as far as the dining room, then sat down there. She sat down like she was collapsing. "Sweets," she said, her voice soft, and my ears pricked up like a hound's, because she hadn't called me Sweets in days and days. "Could you be coerced into making me a cup of tea?" she said.

I would have made her about a million cups of tea if she'd wanted them.

I made the tea, then sat down across the table from her. We were going to have this nice little normal conversation. She was going to call me Sweets, just like normal. I was real eager to have that nice little dumb conversation.

She took a tiny sip of hot tea. Hot tea in the summer. Carrie. She put the teacup back in the saucer. It made a little rattle when she sat it down. The cup and the saucer were both white. All white. Carrie.

She said, "I'm not pregnant any more, Rice."

There was this sudden little blaze in my head, like a burst of orange, like a flare going off. She took a second tiny sip.

"What in fuck are you talking about?"

"I'm not pregnant any more."

"Why not?" I said. I don't know what the hell I was thinking. I think I was thinking about the teacup and the saucer. I think I was trying not to have heard what she said.

Carrie was actually smiling a little. Her forehead was wrinkling with trouble at the same time. "I've had something of an abortion today," she said.

"What in fuck are you talking about?"

"An abortion. Today. At Lovejoy Clinic."

I think I was thinking about drinking hot tea in the summer. It didn't make much sense to me, I don't know why she did that. In the summer I like it with lemon and lots of ice.

"You okay?" I said.

She nodded. "Tops. I'm flying. First they give you tranks and then something like morphine. It's quite a ride."

I reached across the table and picked up her teacup and took a sip out of it. I don't actually drink much hot tea. I don't know what the hell I was thinking.

"How pregnant were you?" I said.

"Eleven weeks."

I started thinking about the damn baby. I shouldn't have done that. I should have kept thinking about the tea.

"What kind was it?" I said.

"What do you mean?"

"The baby. What kind was it?"

"The dead kind," Carrie said. "Very small and very dead."

I practically cried then, thinking about the damn baby. Maybe I even did cry.

Carrie could see it on my face, anyway. "I thought you were pro-choice," she said.

"I am," I said. "I didn't *have* any choice."

"You didn't have any baby, either," she said. She had that half-smile on again. "Thank your lucky fucking stars," she said.

She drank more of her tea. I was thinking about the dead baby, and whether I was the one who made the choice, in the Rhododendron Gardens, and in my blackberry patch, and in my stupid jealous mind.

"You all right?" I said again.

"No," she said. "Not." She cried and cried.

I went over and knelt beside her and tried to put my arms around her. You couldn't tell if she knew I was there. Because she definitely wasn't.

She went on for a long time, sometimes pretty loud. I don't know if Evan heard her or not, but he didn't come downstairs. Eventually Carrie went up to the restroom, still crying away. I just let her go up there. The restroom door closed behind her, and I didn't hear anything else. For a while I didn't think anything, and then, because I was me, dumb damn me, I got to wondering again if that dead baby was mine. I was thinking that it was. Then I stopped thinking again. I sat there, not hearing anything, not thinking anything. Finally I drank the rest of Carrie's cold, bitter tea.

Chapter

I asked her, the day after, why she'd done that. "I kept asking myself," she said, "whether it was fair to bring a child into an impossible circumstance." She was talking about us. We were the impossible circumstance. She said, "It was lunacy to think we could simply live happily ever after." She looked straight at me with her blue eyes. Swimming-pool blue. "No," she said. "You're wrong. It wasn't revenge. I just came to my senses, finally."

My mind doesn't run in real straight lines. I said, "You still writing about me, Carrie? I want to finish reading it." I think I sounded like a little kid when I said that.

"Almost finished."

"Good," I said. But I was wondering, Was that good?

"I think I'll finish very soon," Carrie said, and she looked real sort of dreamy.

Two days after the abortion I went out and got another job, working at the Volcano Control Center in Vancouver, just across the Columbia. I still work there. That's where I'm at right now, as a matter of fact.

The Volcano Control Center is in a trailer, across the street from the Federal Building. We don't actually control the volcano here. We just watch it. There's a huge Betamax TV, and a camera is always focused on the mountain. All day the people who work here sit in this room and look at St. Helens on TV. But I work graveyard shift, and there's no point to watching the volcano at night, because it's dark and you can't see anything. So we just watch regular TV. There's usually three of us here. We spend a lot of time arguing about which show to watch. Kate doesn't want to see anything that has violence in it, because she's a woman. But Rick and I outvote her, we get to watch what we want, and Kate just knits hats. We got a regular democracy going in here.

Every hour somebody has to get up and go check the instruments in the next room. There's three seismographs, and teletypes, and magnetometers, and Rangemasters. You have to go back there to see if the mountain is going off. Usually it isn't.

I don't much mind controlling the volcano. Sometimes I write on this thing, in the instrument room, while we're controlling. I don't actually do anything, but this isn't a bad job. I guess I'll be here until it erupts again.

I didn't have to worry about finding Carrie and Evan in the tub when I got home from work. I come home at six in the morning. But I knew they weren't in there at all. Because Carrie wasn't talking. Not to Evan, not to me. She was writing about me. It made me feel good to know she was writing about me, but when I read the beginning of what she wrote it didn't seem like me. They were my stories, but they weren't about me any more. I don't know what happened to my stories.

When Carrie came out from writing about me she wouldn't even talk to me. When I think about it now, I see her writing away, furious, exorcising me, like I was a demon. If I could have stopped her writing, maybe everything would have been all right.

When she did come out of her room she mostly cleaned house. She floated around with a sponge, dabbing at spots on the walls. She would just go around touching the walls every so often, leaving a little glistening wet spot that smelled of ammonia. When you heard a scratching sound, that meant she was sweeping. Once or twice I heard a scratching on the stairs in the middle of the night.

Sometimes Carrie would put down her sponge, put on this one record, listen to this one song. It was Otis Redding singing "I've Been Loving You a Little Too Long to Stop Now." She played that song over and over, loud as anything, and it was enough to drive you right up a tree. If you asked her to turn it down, she'd take it off without a word and go upstairs to read children's books and eat orange sherbet, or else just wander around with that ratty old sponge again. You got the feeling that you were being all cruel to her, because you didn't want to hear "I've Been Loving You a Little Too Long to Stop Now" for the ninetieth time in a row. You felt like you were a murderer or something. I did, at least.

I guess she finished her part of the book maybe a week after the abortion. That night, finally, she was her old talky self again, only more so. She drank a lot of red wine and talked a lot and gesticulated like crazy with her hands and arms. She was wearing a sleeveless top. I remember things like that, the sleeveless top, because of her bare freckly arms, but I don't remember much else. I had a lot to drink. It was just red wine, but there was a lot of it, and it went in there and swilled around and made a scene in my stomach, so I don't remember what Carrie was talking about. She went on and on. I remember the way she perched her arm over the back of her chair, so her hand was propped up as if there was a cigarette in it. But she didn't smoke. I remember her smooth, freckly arm, and her bright eyes, and the way her face got red, like the wine.

There's been a lot of times in my life when I didn't want a woman to look good to me, but she did anyway and it bothered hell out of me. That night was one of them, with Carrie's smooth arm held up like on display, bare right to the shoulder, and her breast poking toward me, naked underneath her clothing, and it crossed my mind that you can't tell yourself not to want a woman you love. Because the more you tell yourself not to, the more you do. If I could invent a button you push not to desire, I'd be a millionaire. A happy millionaire.

We went to bed pretty early that night. It was supposed to be my week, but Carrie hadn't been sleeping with anyone since her abortion. I laid down in my bed and actually went right to sleep. I dreamed about something that had happened. It was the three of us walking on Cannon Beach, the night when the sunset turned the sea and the sand and the windows of the houses all completely red. I knew it was Cannon Beach in my dream because Haystack Rock was there, and I knew it was the same night because everything was red, but this time as we walked along the three of us were talking about the volcano. Carrie said she'd seen it go off, and the blast had been very white and clean, and filled the sky with puffy white clouds like the ones you see on blowy spring days. Evan said he hadn't seen it go off, but he had dreamed it, and the volcano's smoke was all colors, like a soft watercolor, pale and shining. And even in my dream I knew they were wrong, they were both wrong. When it went off it was black, black as hell. But I didn't have the heart to tell them.

In my dream we walked along the beach until we came to a huge dead sea lion. Carrie screamed and turned back, and Evan turned right with her. But I was kind of interested in that sea lion. I wanted to have a closer look, see what had killed it. Carrie yelled to me that it was rotten, it stank, it was dead. I didn't smell anything, maybe because it was a dream, but Carrie kept yelling to me to leave it, it was dead, it was dead. So I took one more look at that sea lion, trying to learn what I could from ten feet away, and then I turned and followed Carrie back the way we came.

That hadn't happened the night in Cannon Beach, in real life. But when I woke up from the dream and my mind slowly came back to our house on Southeast 31st Street, I heard the sound of someone crying, and I knew they were crying for that dead sea lion.

When I woke all the way up I realized that it was Carrie crying. I heard her crying and spitting up sort of alternately in the kitchen.

I don't know why, but the first thing I thought was How come the kitchen? You don't go downstairs to spit up when there's a toilet in the next room. So I guessed that she came down to the kitchen because she was talking to me.

Carrie was bent over the sink, her mouth was dripping with stuff, she was coughing and crying at once, and a good-sized puddle swam in the sink.

I came out and she was sort of staring at me while she spit up. I hung around by her, hovering. I patted her back once or twice. Then I looked at myself, and I saw that I was acting like Evan, being kind and passive and stupid all at once, and I took my hand away.

"Don't stop," she said. What the hell, I thought, and I started patting her again.

"I don't want it to stop now," she said, and made a little groan.

I didn't know what she was talking about, even though I'd heard that damn Otis Redding record maybe a hundred times that week. "I won't stop," I said.

She gave up some more stuff. "Too much red wine," I said. I was looking at the stuff. It was mostly purple-red, like the wine. There was gray and green in it too, that was probably some of Carrie's insides. I was just kind of peering over her shoulder at the stuff, patting her on the back, and then I saw all this white stuff, and it hit me just what the hell was going on.

"So what the fuck is this white stuff, Carrie?" I said, pointing at the junk that had come out of her.

She rubbed her mouth with her wrist, getting puke on her arm, and she looked at me and said that it was aspirin.

"That is real cute," I said. I said, "What was the idea? Fuck over the guys, or what?"

I was furious, and I didn't know what the hell I was saying. But even if I did know what I was saying, I don't know what I would of said.

"No," Carrie said. "Everything has died. I couldn't stand what has happened to us. This was just a stupid way out."

"It looks like some kind of demonstration to me," I said. "Make the guys feel sorry for Carrie."

I was still patting her, if you can believe that. She was still bent over, holding on to the kitchen sink, and I was still patting away. Because I was furious, but I was sorry too.

Carrie straightened up. She looked like she wanted to hit me. I was wondering if she would, and I was looking at the drops of gray junk on her little lips. She didn't say anything for a minute, nothing at all.

"Why'd you come down to spit up?" I said. I think maybe I did want her to slug me one. I actually do. "Why didn't you just do it in the restroom?" I said.

I saw my hand, and I made it stop patting her now.

"Evan's in there," she said. "He's always in there. He's painting."

"Not now."

"Oh yes. Now."

"At night?" I said, but she didn't answer. I knew that somebody was way off, but I didn't know if it was Evan or her. And just then I had this feeling. I was thinking that there isn't any more reason to go right to sleep at eleven than there is to stay up all night painting or spitting up aspirin. The rules are just made up, I was thinking. But then I tried to stop thinking that, because I knew other people who had said the same thing, and they were all crazy.

Carrie wasn't totally through with puking. She bent over and let fly again. But when I watched this time it was different. It was like something snapped in me, all of a sudden everything just changed, all by itself. And just then I was looking at her like she was somebody I didn't even know. There was this real beautiful woman vomiting into the sink. She had a lot of blood in her face, so she looked like she'd been running around outside in cold weather, all apple-cheeked and healthy and beautiful. She was beautiful. But she was nobody I knew.

You can kick yourself later for not doing the right thing, for not feeling the right thing, but that doesn't change anything. You can't make repairs on the past. And that last time I watched Carrie spit up, I wasn't feeling anything at all. My bare feet were a little cold, but the rest of me was numb.

It was like I was watching her spit up on TV. Except that people don't spit up on TV.

If somebody had told me that the woman I loved would try to kill herself, and that I would watch her cough up the aspirin, I would never guess that at the end I'd go to bed because my feet were getting cold. But that's what happened. I wasn't frightened then, and not even upset. I was tired and mostly my feet were cold.

I was at the end. That's where I thought I was, at least.

"Goodnight," I said to Carrie, and then I patted her one more time. "Hang in there," I said, and I went right to bed.

Chapter

It didn't hit me, what had happened and everything, until the next day. And then it was too late.

I've always been a good sleeper, and since I've had this night job at the Volcano Control Center, I can sleep anytime, anywhere. Maybe I was just tired, and maybe I didn't want to wake up that morning, the morning after Carrie ate the aspirin and I got cold feet. Maybe I couldn't think of what I was going to say to Carrie first thing that morning. I heard a lot of banging around upstairs, but not much talking, and I didn't get up until the front door whammed shut.

Finally I stumbled out. Evan was pouring coffee.
"You got any more of that stuff, buddy?" I said.
"This is it, but you can have it," he said. "Feel all right today?"
"Fine."
"That's good," he said. "Because Carolyn left today."

He handed me the cup, I took it. I was thinking, He tells me she's gone, and the first thing I do is hold my hand out for my cup of coffee. But if I thought I didn't care, I was wrong. Because the world stopped right then. Or maybe it didn't stop, but it stopped being what it was. And everything that I did, I did the way a condemned man smokes his last cigarette. You wonder why you're bothering to smoke it, and then you wonder why you ever bothered to do anything, and why anybody ever bothers. At the same time, you know you've never had a cigarette that tasted as good as that one.

"Did she take her stuff?" I said to Evan.
"Some. Not much."
"She's got a lot of stuff," I said.
Evan smiled. "That's right," he said.
When he smiled I had to wonder about him, probably for the thousandth time or so. I'm telling you, I really wonder what goes on in that man's head.
I said, "Are you okay?"
He shrugged. "So-so."
I was going to ask him if he tried to stop her, to talk her out of it,

but I knew. So I said, "Did you help her carry her bags out, Evan?"

"She didn't want my help."

"What did she say?"

"Goodbye."

I had been going along fine, but I lost it right then. I saw myself in Evan's glasses, I didn't look too hot, and I could see Carrie when I closed my eyes. I opened them again and watched my jaw wobble as I talked. I said, "Did she leave a note?"

"No. But she left her part of Delicate Geometry on her desk."

I had completely lost it, I don't know why I kept on talking. "She left her desk?" I said, and he smiled again and said that she had.

"You drink it," I said, and gave him the coffee.

The first thing I had to do was to find that Otis Redding record, which wasn't hard, because it was on top of the stack, and the next thing was to take it upstairs and then out on the roof with me. It was early June, but it wasn't much of a day. It was cold and windy and ashy, and the sky was one color, and it wasn't blue. I sat up there on the roof, the way I do sometimes. I was holding on to that stupid record and remembering without wanting to the shape of her face and the exact perfect color of her eyes, trying to put my finger on the thing that made Carrie different from the other women I knew, and only being able to think of her crying, how her face looked when the couple of freckles got wet. I could feel another eruption coming on. The lava dome was on too tight, and it was going to blow. Then I could feel the brains in the back of my mind popping, and my forehead rising, lifting off of my face with the force of the explosion. I could feel everything breaking, like ice in rivers come springtime, I could feel the past smashing, I could feel Carrie leaving me, going out of my body and my mind. I could feel things people can't feel, and everything I felt was breaking.

I stood up on the roof with that Otis Redding record in my hand. I took the record out of the album cover, held it like a Frisbee, and I threw it as hard as I could. Everything was breaking, and I wanted it to break too. I couldn't tell you why. It bounced on the street a couple of times, but it didn't break. Then I knew I was wrong. Nothing breaks. Nothing ever breaks.

When I went downstairs again Evan was sitting at the table reading the *Willamette Week*. The classified ads. I sat down, and sat there for a while, not saying anything, just registering the things I could see. I could see everything. The table reflected in Evan's glasses. The little ragged edges on the newspaper. A dust fuzzball in the corner. That kind of thing, but everything.

Evan stood up, and he yawned. He folded the newspaper and laid it on the table. "I'm going upstairs," he said.

"To the restroom?"

"Uh-huh."

"To paint?"

"Uh-huh."

I had to say it. "Carrie left us today, and you're going to paint."

Evan said yes.

"Hey, will you tell me something, buddy?" I said, and then I thought about everything that had happened to me so far, more or less. "Evan," I said, "how come everything I touch turns to shit?"

Evan touched his lips with his index finger and thought about it. His eyebrows went up, and his finger left his lips. "I don't think the blame is yours," he said.

"I could never stop myself," I said. "I wish to hell I could have kept it under control. I always felt too damn much."

"That's probably what Carolyn liked most about you," Evan said.

I had to think about that. He was right, I thought. "So tell me," I said. "What in hell you going to paint today?"

"With luck, a good sink and a good toilet. Both. Together."

"I thought you were so devoted to her," I said.

"I am," Evan said. "That's why I'm going to paint."

I'm telling you. I can't understand that guy. Not now, not ever.

When I closed my eyes, I could still see Carrie there, with her face miserable as hell, her couple of freckles wet, her swimming-pool eyes looking at me the way they used to look while we made love. So I didn't close my eyes. I walked around the house, because it was my house now too, walked around with my nerves buzzing right at the edge of my skin. I already knew what I was going to do. I was going to stay right there. Keep on living with Evan. Keep on controlling the volcano. Nothing ever breaks. I was going to keep right on. I was going to go upstairs and read the last part of what Carrie had written about me. But I did that, and the last word she wrote was Goodbye.

Rice,

    I'm glad you got around to writing this.

    To be fair, I think you've exaggerated the absurdity of my painting, and also its significance to me. I realize that painting, because it is an art, smacks of a certain romantic lunacy. Painters are presumed to be permanently stationed at the brink; they fall into swooning raptures about the light, or else slash their wrists up to their elbows. I'm not that way. I don't *have* to paint; I do it because I'm interested in the various ways life appears. Some people do crossword puzzles as a pastime, I paint. The only reason I paint so often is because it takes me a long time: there are still so many blanks I've yet to fill in. At the same time, I don't expect to fill in all the blanks. I don't mind a few blank places in my puzzle.

    I wanted to tell you, tell everyone, that in a way I don't fully understand (I don't mind blank places), your writing this has provided a final verification, a validation, of our triangle. Despite our obvious difficulties, I don't think anyone can doubt our intentions, our seriousness, our strength—our love. We've even taken the trouble to write a book. That's no little trouble. The triangle has mattered to all of us.

    We haven't been wasting our time, Rice. We had something worthwhile. Samuel Johnson said of *Tristram Shandy:* "Nothing odd lasts." He was right; uselessly so. Nothing lasts. Life isn't fixed. But we can fix the past (though not repair it) in memory. We had something; we still have it; we'll always have it: this is the blithe conjugation of memory, our consolation for loss.

    And we have this book. Despite the ubiquity of time, it can't get in here; can't seep in and destroy us, here. This book is our sanctuary. Perhaps the writing of it hastened our triangle's dissipation; perhaps Carolyn exorcised us both. But I don't think so. I don't think she'll ever be thoroughly rid of us, Rice.

    I have the feeling, instead, that she'll come back to us. Clearly we both love her, however differently and however badly. I don't believe she'll find anyone who will love her as we do.

    Yes, I think she'll come back.

    The three of us, then, are walking together, alone, along a luminous red beach. The thrashing sea on our right is red, deep red, as are the drifting clouds that wander slowly toward the horizon. The white houses on our left are flushed with red, and their windows flash it, blazing. There is no sound of wind, only the crash of waves. The beach is flat and straight and extends in front of us a long way, possibly infinitely far. We walk along as night falls, and in this red darkness we do not stop walking.

This is our dream. We tried it, only to have it leave us when we woke. But there's a delicate geometry in dreams that get away. It can't be measured or reduced to axioms; it's a slippery, protean geometry. It deals not with points, lines, planes and solids, but with lives, with people, with the erratic rhythms beaten out by the heart.

But what am I saying? The three of us walk on the beach, and this is no dream. This is a memory, and a possibility.

In the meantime, we have each other, Rice. In difficult friendship. In common loss.